## Praise for Glass Barbie

Michael Botur portrays a seamier side of New Zealand life that some people don't want to admit exists. Yet his characters are hilarious and big-hearted and always ring true. I had great fun reading Glass Barbie – it's an entertaining caper and highly recommended.

- Dave Armstrong, Award-winning screenwriter

Glass Barbie is a great ride told from the unlikely POV of a common Kiwi crim who rates himself well above perception. It's a self-deprecating tale of a man with good intentions who struggles with selfish aspirations. In true form, Botur rips the scab of New Zealand's underbelly, reaching into those dark uncomfortable corners we try to avoid but need to see.

- Scott Butler, Writer, Shortland Street

Cheerfully amoral Karl Copley is an endearingly naive wannabe gangtsa and inept bounty hunter whose story -pacey, funny and frequently hair-raising - should win Botur plenty of new readers. Fans of his down and dirty, genre-busting writing will lap up this latest slice of Northland noir – part kidnap caper, part road movie, part farce, it moves at breakneck speed propelled by the author's hyper-vernacular prose, wound up to fever pitch.
- Paul Little, Publisher, Author, Canon media awards Reviewer of the Year 2020

Glass Barbie is a hell of a ride and Michael Botur's main character Cockroach Karl is the perfect guide for a road trip through Northland's dark underbelly of drugs and gangsters. Karl is a wonderful creation: shocking, funny, vulnerable despite his best bluster and, like all good cockroaches, unsquashable. His relationship with his old buddy Snitchie Richie who inexplicably went off the rails and became a cop is by turns hilarious, infuriating and touching. And when they join forces to find their missing schoolmate Barbie, buckle up because the ride is about to get very bumpy, just like their friendship.

- Angus Gillies, author, Far North

## Praise for 2023 horror collection Bloodalcohol: Ten Tales

A compelling set of stories that delivers powerful messages about the human – and particular Kiwi – condition. All the content warnings apply; this is a collection that doesn't shy from New Zealand's darker side.

- Nikky Lee, Award-winning spec fic author

This collection takes us into some dark places, which is what I'm here for. Botur

'delivers, in his consummate style which never relents, pushes past where you think he might take us which is part of the fun.'
>
> \- Scott Butler, writer, Shortland Street

'Bloodalcohol is muscular, brutal, dark, gritty and compelling. Botur sure knows how to write - all horror fans should get their bloody hands on this one.'
>
> \- Gary Davies, Award-winning horror film director

'Michael's writing sets out an easy flow, in a quintessential New Zealand tone, words and thoughts flow as though they are your own, sometimes with such a quick pace that they don't allow you to finish your own sentence. At times with such depth that you can almost feel sympathy (usually not for long) for the main character.'
>
> \- Andi Podesta, award-winning playwright

'This is a series of visual, wonderfully unsettling stories that fill the reader with dread and ill-ease. Settle in for some evocative, jump off the page writing and stories that do what all good horror should do - repulse and intrigue.'
>
> Kathryn Burnett - Award-winning Screenwriter/Playwright

## Praise for The Devil Took Her and other books

'One of the most original story writers of his generation in New Zealand.'
>
> \- Patricia Prime, Takahē 86, on Spitshine

'Michael Botur's work grabs you by the throat and won't let you go. His stories throb with what feel like real people, real conversations, real moments of pain and hope, misunderstanding and reconciliation, remorse and surprise.'
>
> \- Maggie Trapp, New Zealand Listener, on True?

'Written in unvarnished street language about the rougher side of life - drugs, jail and death, the book shows rare bravery and honesty [...] The thing about Michael Botur is his voice is very much a street voice. His language is street language: it's raw, it's coarse, it's obscene. It's tough and it's confronting [...] There are gems— some of them are absolutely great.'
>
> \- Ian Telfer, Radio New Zealand on True?

'I loved this book. Horror with a side of rare clinical detachment. Great prose and a wonderful sense of just where to end a story.'
>
> -Lauren Roche, Bestselling NZ novelist

# Glass Barbie

Published by Lasavia Publishing Ltd.
Auckland, New Zealand
www.lasaviapublishing.com



ISBN: 978-1-991083-23-4

# Glass Barbie

## Michael Botur

LASAVIA
PUBLISHING

# Cheers

Cheers to all my streetfighter, burglar, skinhead, pothead, bonehead, biker, brawler, burglar, bogan, druggie, deviant and dead friends for giving me a lifetime's worth of material to write about.

Cheers to the fellow authors and supporters of this book who are sick and tired of the literary establishment being so pompous and wanky and who welcome Cockroach Karl's fresh voice, 'cause they agree New Zealand literature needs some freshening-up.

Cheers to the diverse people I got to know while working as an alcohol and drug researcher at Whangārei Central Police Station – the guy who robbed the Dargaville dairy with a rifle and didn't feel any remorse, his sidekick who felt terrible about it, the thug with a reputation for putting his enemies in freezers (alive), the alcoholic Brethren who beat up his dad, and the friendly young meth cook woman who was eager to chat about her colourful life.

Cheers to the cheeky cop who asked if I was planning to drink the urine samples before sending them to the lab, the way-too-trusting cop who didn't mind me being in the room as he planned a raid on some criminal's house, the bully cop who was uncomfortable to eat dinner beside, the caring cop who shared her battle scars, the jolly fat cop who didn't remember pulling me over, the weary jailer who brought out an endless series of interesting arrestees for me to interview, the sergeant who said unfortunately I shouldn't donate a box of books because some arrestees would rip out the pages and block the toilet and flood their cell, just to be dicks...

And cheers to Lasavia, the only publisher with the balls to publish this book, unlike that other publisher who said they were going to publish it, then got cold feet and backed out because the book might offend the delicate sensibilities of upper-class Kiwis who don't want to be reminded what the world is really made of.

Mike B

# EX-CON TENTS

# 1

# "Tryina be a mate the only way I know how"

I strut into the cop shop just before 5am and hold the General Enquiries buzzer long enough to summon a piglet, walkin up to the counter all weary and groggy, picking a dried booger out of my eye. I'm here to speak to Snitchie Richie Littledick – except, I actually say I'm here to see "Richard McMullan," in case his pig-pals don't know his special name.

Dude haaaates being called names, if I remember correctly, and remembering is the name of the game: it's been eight years since I've seen the guy and considering the amount of substances I've smoked, my memory's not the most reliable. Chances are we've both got new bodies and now he'll be Senior Constable Richard McMullan, 75 kilos, flat torso, responsible haircut, no tatts. Still a Minja, as in half-ginger half-Māori, wide nose, cornflake freckles, hair the colour of rust. To be honest, it's way beyond midnight, Whangārei's boring as an amputee peepshow unless you've got a bellyful of crack and I've found myself drawn to the lamplight with nothing to do except wind my old mate up for shits and giggles. I might unload certain underworld goss about a certain kidnapping, see if I can get paid as a confidential informant. Get some of those sweet witness protection hookups. New house, new threads. Maybe even get a labradoodle.

This sleepy cop minding the counter, some Indian guy – amazing the colours of cops these days – tells me Senior Constable Richard McMullan's in his office and he'll be out shortly.

'They gave the prick an office?'

'I knooow,' he goes, rolling his eyes.

I'd sort-of heard through the grapevine they'd made him a senior piglet. Musta risen through the ranks with hard, steady work and dedicated professionalism.

Pfft. Fuckin tryhard.

Usually you only become a senior constable after 14 years, but it sounds like they made an exception for my ol' Richie Rich. I spotted the update on Facebook on my mobile. They gave him a big ceremony and shit, like it was the Carrot Top Awards and he got named Ginge of the Year. Richie ain't been in the police force for 14 years, but what he's done is condensed 14 years of squeaky clean goody-good suck-up nark holiness into his *eight* years till they gave him an early promotion, the fuckin overachiever. He did all the profesh development night classes he could, while I did all the periodic detention I could. PD for both our arses.

The Indian cop wanders off. Through a gap in the sliding doors behind me, a whisper of warm summer wind touches my legs and I can feel the sky begin to glow. December, baby: early summer. Can't enjoy the season without a mate though, can ya.

I don't appreciate being left standing in the darkest part of the night in a boring-arse foyer so I drop my pie wrapper on the floor and look around to see what I can steal. I can't reach a whole arm through the layer of bullet-deflecting, intruder-stopping plastic that hangs down over the counter but I can get my fingers through and snaffle whatever's on the counter, which turns out to be a HotB magazine. HotB's *Heat on the Beat*, a police association mag, by coppers, for coppers. There's gotta be some sensitive information in the magazine. Hundred bucks to hand this over to the Hells Angels, I'm thinking.

Finally a new cop drifts up to the counter, says, 'Thanks, Rohit,' to its pig-pal and looks at me and its mouth opens like a goldfish.

Ohhhhh shit. It's Richie, and Richie recognises.

That's right, you so-called senior motherfucker. You remember me helicoptering my schlong in the pool changing rooms, Year 10, how I taught all the boys that the trick was to jack it so it's hard first so you've got maximum cock-length to spin. I know that look on your surprised face, bro. We know each other inside-out, homie.

I take my beanie off and scratch the bugs outta my scalp. Guess I look a little different, scars all over my skull, ink on my neck, skinny arms, big shoulders from doing push-ups at 4am at the bus station 'cause I was too cranked to sleep.

'Sup, Chief,' I say to my oldest, bestest mate, secured behind two panels of plastic. Mister Senior Constable is protected with a stab-proof vest, walkie talkie, a taser tucked into his belt and fresh new pips on his light blue uniform. New threads, sure – but he's still a ginge, which means I still look down on the cunt. 'Up to?'

'Cockroach Karl,' he goes, sticking his thumbs in his belt. Our secret handshake's supposed to be two slaps, knuckle-bump, fist-dump, pssht blow it up, but he gives me no handshake or nothin.

'Look at you. All tattooed up. Nice earrings.'

'Cheers. I got piercings down south, too. That's a story for ya.'

'You picking up lost property, Karl, or… ?'

'Nah, bro. I just, I dunno, thought we could catch up or whatevs, listen to a little Limp Bizkit, play a little Limp Biscuit, what do ya say?'

I'm tryina be a mate the only way I know how, but I can tell I'm rubbin him the wrong way. Story of my life, bro, I seem to piss off 99 percent of people. Might be why they call me Cockroach Karl.

'I'd say you're wasting police time, which carries a maximum sentence of six months imprisonment or a thousand-dollar fine.' He takes a step back from the counter. Down the hall behind him, I can see a smidgen of the office he's come out of. Neatest fuckin office I've ever seen. He's even got a potted fern by his keyboard, the pindick.

'Listen, there's this thing I wanted to talk to you about,' I go. 'It's about Barbie. Barbara Konstantinou from school, from our year, 'member her fams were on the rich list 'n shit – she got abducted, like, last month, bruz. She's missing, anyway. I's thinkin we could, y'know, bounty hunt that shit.'

'This person's name is Barbie, you're telling me? As in the children's doll?'

'That's what we used to call her, remember, the Greek chick? Barbs, Barbwire, Barbarella, Conan the Barbarian. You know her, bruz, I'm tellin you, from school.'

'There's legitimate work I need to be prioritising right now,' Richie goes, peering past me, hoping there are people wanting to report lost cats. Anything better than my annoyingness. Too bad for him. I'm in shorts and a basketball singlet at 5 in the morning holding a pie, at the only 24 hour manned police station in 10,000 square miles. I need Richie. I don't got nothin else to limpet onto.

'Legitimate, eh Rich. How's that workin out for ya?'

'Policing's been good to me. How's being... whatever you are?'

'I'm a artist,' I go. 'You oughta follow my socials. I'm kind of a big deal. Done a bit of stand-up comedy down in the big smoke. Do a few welds, too; got my truck licence. You can do free courses in jail. It's pretty sweet. I'm mostly a influencer, though.'

'Of course you are.' Richie repositions a piece of paper to make it look like he's busy tidying things. He wipes his fruity little ginger moustache with a finger like I'm a bogie he's smearing off. 'Ah well, thanks for coming by, Karl. Have a good- '

'I wanna help yous out. This hot-as fugitive Barbie? Either she's on the run, or the run's on her. I wanna bring her in, know what I'm sayin? Collect me some a that reward money. 'Member how rich her folks were, them immigrant Greeky people? The pillars on their mansion and shit? They had two maids, bruz, *two!* And the dad ran for council, 'member dat?'

'You know about the reward?'

'I know shitloads more than it looks like I know.'

'We don't use the word "fugitive," Karl. Somebody's not a fugitive unless deemed so retroactively by the court when they fail to- '

'Bro, I'm getting cold, standin here. Let's grab a beer. I wanna talk cash cow. Make a plan.'

'You're suggesting a beer now? It's 5.40.'

I shrug. 'It's night time though, innit. Night's when you're sposda drink beer.'

'It'll be dawn in 20 minutes.'

'Peeps are sayin there's ten grand up for grabs if we bring her back. You could use ten grand, couldn't ya?'

'I get a ten grand bonus if my name's attached to charges leading to successful prosecution rates of 75 percent or greater. Round here we do things the honest way, Karl. I've no interest in dirty money.'

There's steam on the plastic divider now. I'm desperate. Meanwhile Rich the Snitch is slowly backing away, going back to his little fern.

'Listen, the money ain't dirty. It's her folks's money. And it's not about the money. It's about, like… '

'Impressing a female? Because your genes instruct you to pursue any faint hope of reproducing?'

'Exactamente.' I go to high-five him. My palm smacks the invisible plastic. ''Member how fine Barbie was?'

'Karl, okay, look: I'm aware of the case. Obviously I'm aware Barbara Konstantinou's been listed as missing. CIB's handling the reward. I suggest you liaise with them when you have something useful to share. Until then you'll have to turn your body 180 degrees, put one leg in front of the other and walk away, my friend, nice seeing you but I really do have to–

'I hooked up with her little sister. Shana, the flat one. Gave her some pity attention, y'know? Liked Barbie way better, though. Something was a little off with Barbs, know what I'm sayin? Like she'd gotten traumatised, but in a good way, made her all loco and wild like Amy Winehouse sorta thing.'

'Watch yourself,' Senior Constable Richie growls. 'What's the relevance, anyway?'

'Barbie's a homegirl. She's old school. Get the Konstantinou sisters 'n you and me together and we could have a mini Sacred Heart reunion.'

He takes a deep breath, almost says something, walks a few metres down the hall, puts a hand on the door of his office, hovers. Dude's kind-of shuddering, like when you get really pissed at a toddler but you're not allowed to dropkick it.

Guess I'm the annoying toddler.

'I finish my shift at 8. But that's still too early to be drinking alcohol.'

'Shit, watch *me* drink then, if you want. Jovial Jug Pub at eight then. It's over the ro- '

'I'm aware of where the Jug is located. *I* stuck around my neighbourhood after we graduated. *I* didn't leave my community to go be an influencer, as you claim.'

He shakes his head and retreats, pausing in the corridor to fold his arms and yarn to some lame-looking cops – the Indian one, plus a girl and a fat cop. Dorks United. I see Richie hands a book of Sudoku puzzles to a piglet and the piglet hands back a book of wordfinds and Richie shuts his office door real firm.

Me, I walk out the sliding door of the copshop. It's a month till Kiwi Christmas and summer dawn is making the air thick and warm like one of them carb farts when you've only been eating McDonald's for a month. There's a pub metres away, I've got a valuable magazine down my pants and I'm looking forward to wheelin and dealin and catching up with my favouritest bro.

I didn't really dig the dude's snobby straighto attitude just now, but I know he'll come right. Back in school, I took all the risks while he followed like some kinda half-lamb half-pussy hybrid, and he always appreciated the risks I took for us.

I hope some of the old Richie's left.

# 2

# "Do I look like I need backup?"

The Jovial Jug is a pub that never closes. Good place to go if you've just been paroled and the government haven't sorted out a motel for you to doss down in. I reckon cleaners never come through. Stinks of ciggies from the smokers' section and hot chips, and the floor's sticky. Smells like home, yo.

Half the place is towers of slot machines crammed together tight as changing room lockers. Waiting for Rich the Snitch, I sink a couple of beers and get a little glow goin on. The, uh, 'dietary supplement' I took while I was at the bus station is wearing off and I guess my hungry tummy's making me a lightweight. I get dizzy and lose ten bucks on a pokie machine and sit on my stool with a grumpy face and blame my drunkenness on Rich McMullan. Snitchie Richie Littledick. It's his fault I'm stuck in stanky-ass Whangārei with $19.30, not even enough for the five hour ride to the Big Smoke even on the discounted-est, shittiest bus you could ask for. His fault I have to come up with some pretty desperate scheme. His fault they've let me pay for my beers with a Paywave credit card that ain't technically mine, a card with some Pakistani kinda name on it I won't be able to pronounce if they ask me. Old Rich might find himself buying the next round. If they even serve him, that is - there's a Peppa Pig sign on the wall with a red Ghostbusters slash goin through Peppa. A lotta the rougher pubs in Northland got them signs. Means Pigs Not Welcome.

There's harness racing and greyhounds on the TV, but either I've got ADHD or that shit gets real boring, real quick. I have a ciggy out in the smoking section, which is just a partly-walled-off square of the main pub floor, and watch a little UFC on a TV fixed to the ceiling. I don't want a second ciggy, so I'm twiddling my thumbs. Us party people, we get jittery if we haven't had a proper actual smoke – a little pick-me-up, y'know. Meth-am-fuckin-phetamine, bro, if you need it spelled out for ya.

During the ad break, I read the posters on the walls. Reggae band played five months ago, male strippers coming up. Posters for Jim Beam, bingo, some craft beer club. Adverts for a tattoo show comin up in the Bay of Islands. When I run out of posters to eyeball, I check out the four or five people in little dark corners of the pub, drinking their breakfast. I size up what ones I can roll. In my life I've aggravated-robbed guys built like statues, I've aggrobbed women, I've aggrobbed pussy-arse little exchange students outside of private schools, but there's this one fella in here wearing red white and black numbers and letters on his hoodie and I ain't about to aggrob that fella, hell no. Them's dangerous colours, son, like you'd see on a lionfish or a rattlesnake.

Gangsta colours.

Mister Gangbanger, he's missin' hair on the crown of his head, and the hair's settled on his top lip and chin and throat – not to mention a tattoo of a fuckin' scorpion. He's wearing hi-vis safety gear and thick boots with concrete on the toes like dried up porridge, but it's unlikely he's been labouring. Dudes that measure their income by thickness of wad instead of numbers don't do manual labour. He's probly a headhunter, probly rolls drug dealers. The cuff of a long-sleeved cotton shirt sticks out from under the devil-coloured hoodie. I can see a patch sayin 1% Support Crew; I can also see a rectangle patch with strips of the five main club colours: yellow, black, red, blue and white. There's only one type of person that can claim they support many different colours. Fuck me sideways.

I spin my stool the other way. Best quit eyeballin him if I wanna keep my eyes.

Senior Constable Richie eventually walks into the pub. It's 8.08am, according to my phone, and I think to myself, yup, same old square bastard as always: the eights in his show-up time are symmetrical. Everything in that cunt's life is symmetrical – cept for me, the one crooked part.

His distrust of the place is obvious, because he struts halfway across the floor, decides the bar and its drinks are unworthy of him, and slots into the booth opposite me, sitting stiff as a dick on Dole Day. He's so upright that he won't let his back touch the leather of the booth. His arse barely even touches the seat.

'Now then,' he goes, lacing these short fingers with nicely clipped fingernails. I'd forgotten how neat his face is, perfect jaw. Clean skin, freckles laid out all symmetrical, plus those neat pink ginger-Māori lips. 'We have a missing individual. And I understand you're wanting me to clean up the mess.'

'It's *me* that's gonna help *you*.'

'That a fact?'

'Have a beer, bruzza, fuck's sake.'

'I don't drink much, let alone when it's the start of the work day.'

'But you just clocked off.'

'But it's 8.11 a.m., Karl.' He wafts smoke out of his face.

I take a big slurp and a big suck on my ciggy. 'I know what's going on with your career, Little Dic– '

'Don't you bloody say– '

'OKAYokayokay, *Richard*. I know where you're up to with your policing career, Snitchie Richie.'

He actually laughs, tipping his head away for a moment, I guess to avoid catching some feelings for his old mate. What's that nitrous oxide glowy thing you get when you feel dope about the past? NOS algebra or whatever? 'You *think* you know, Karl. That's always been your thing. You go through life taking stabs and guesses and risks, seizing things, grabbing them, pulling them towards you without really pausing to think if you're doing the decent thing or not. The *decent thing*, just so you know, is to actually *ask* people if you can take something instead of shoplifting.'

'You're sayin I shoplift, now?'

'You think I haven't kept an eye on your arrests? There was January 2nd 2015, December 8th 2016, December 6 2017, October 31st... need I continue?'

'Admit it, you missed my entertaining arse, didn't you, ya fag.' I push my beer glass forward, not that he has a glass to clink with. 'Not sure about this spying-on-the-working class thing though.'

'You're working class, now?'

'You don't have to *work* to be working class.'

'As for spying, that's not the word I'd use, but I keep abreast of active offenders, yes.'

'Shouldn't you focus on real crims?'

'I *am* focused on a real crim.'

I lol at that and get up, go to the bar, grab two beers – a fruity one for my fruity friend and a real man beer for me. The floor tilts a bit; maybe we're at sea and I've forgotten. I'm tipsy enough about having my old buddy here with me to hiss as I walk past Mr One Percenter Red White 'n Black Scorpionthroat in his corner booth, for no particular reason. He's old and ugly, grizzled, hair all stubbly-silver, lookin like if Santa Claus did twenty years on death row. Dude's rolled the sleeves of his hoodie up to let his thick old bacon-coloured arms stick out and show off his tattoos of wheels with a median strip going between the wheels. It looks like %, which means he's a nomad. Takes a certain type of dude to go 1% nomad. Dangerous as it is to be a hangaround or a gopher or a prospect for any club, nomads are a different breed. Nomad status is for ancient veteran blokes that've dipped a toe in so many rival clubs that rules say they're not allowed to call for backup when shit gets heavy. This means nomads have to be Seriously. Fuckin. *Hard.*

I bring back the beers across the floor of the ship and Richie says he doesn't want one.

'You think they have spirulina?' he goes, straining his neck to try read the chalkboard menu, and I'm just about to answer when he winks at me. Not a smile, just the wink. The man's got amazing teeth, they're a shade of white I only see on women's in fashion mags. Old Firecrotch here doesn't smoke, doesn't drink coffee, and flosses instead of brushing. I should know. We were flatmates. He started preparing for Police College while we were still sharing a toilet when we were, like, 18. Then he started getting good grades, passing fitness challenges in record time and pretty soon, his new mates were elbowing him, like *Hey aintcha flatmate got a criminal record? You went to school with him, eh, and he turned out a crim? You can't flat with someone like that.*

Not that Carefree Karl dwells on that stuff.

'I can give you five minutes on Barbara Konstantinou,' says my cop friend as my eyes try to get a good picture of him. Damn beer's got me all sleepy.

'Better known as Barbie.'

'You're the only one who calls her that, Karl. She– '

'Fuck off it was just me. Sacred Heart yearbook 2010, that was the name they printed, 'member? Cause she'd dyed her hair lightbulb-blonde to look less Greekular? We had some big belly laughs about that, 'member?

We switched her photo with a piccie of a Barbie doll cut out of a K-mart catalogue, 'member? 'Member when you had a sensa humour, Rich?'

'Shut up for a second. So she's not been heard from in 19 days. That's established. Family's concerns were first brought to our department's attention five days ago. The CIB is aware. Are you listening?'

'23 days missing if you count the days people thought they saw her in that cruise-casino, up in the Bay.'

'It's 19– and don't go contradicting me again – *19* days. Now, this is all public information. If you've come here in the hope I'll give you something we haven't given the larger media, forget about it. I may as well hand in my hat today.'

'Hand it to me,' I go, winkin' at the man. 'D'you know how much police hats fetch in the fuckin' black market?'

'I know how much a Police Association magazine might be worth to someone dumb enough to steal it in the belief it contains classified intel – which it doesn't. Slide it over. Attaboy.'

'I don't know... ah, fuck it.' I reach inside my pants, pull the mag out, try to uncrinkle it and shake the smell of my nutsack off it. 'Sorry it's a bit... you might wanna pull that pube off, just there. Got snagged. You saw, uh... you saw that homeless guy stick it down my pants?'

'Police see everything.'

I do a big nod and swallow some beer and light my seventh-to-last smoke – one of the special smokes I keep in the pack. 'Security camera spotted me?'

'*I* spotted you.' He smacks at my illegal cigarette smoke as it curls through the air. 'I'm extremely observant.'

'Observe this.' I stick my middle finger up at his perfect face. 'How many fingers?'

He reaches across, grabs the finger, puts a knee on the tabletop, uses the leverage from my strong middle finger to pull himself across the tabletop and ends up kneeling on my lap, his forehead pressed against mine. I can smell the Listerine on his tongue, and then all I smell is arse as he presses my face into a cushion. My arm is twisted into a pringle-shape and I'm about to wet myself. Shouldna had all them beers just now.

'Stop, stop, fuck's sakes, bruzza.'

With that, he lets go of my finger and arm. *Bruzza.* We used to call each other bruz 24/7 when we were ten. We thought organised crime was cool-as, and all our fantasising and role-playing was about defeating cops or sticking evidence up our butts where they'd never find it.

'Fuck are yous two bum-chums up to?'

It's the big ugly scorpion-throated Nomad, arriving at our table to step us out. Up close, I can see the patches of what I'd thought was receding hair have been deliberately shaven. There's a silver mullet like a dead possum crawling down the back of his neck, as if that makes up for the white fuzz on his actual skull. His temples have had the hair stripped back and on the shiny pink skin he's had red devil horns inked. My dick shrivels and I drop all resistance to Richie as I feel his grip lighten. Richie's in cop mode, watching our new friend.

I'd thought Mr Nomad was a dark boy at first; now it's obvious he's a woodskin White man. Blue eyes covered in lines like cracked windscreens.

'Want me to sort this cunt for ya?'

'We're fine,' Richie goes. 'You're drunk, mate. You think you want trouble, but you don't. I'm in charge.'

'You ain't in charge,' I go, putting the sole of my shoe against Little Richie's arse. It's a shitty tennis shoe I've been meaning to chuck for – how many years? I'm pretty sure I owned these shoes when I flatted with Richie.

'Pigs ain't welcome in here,' Nomad goes. 'You saw the sign.'

'Cheers for letting us know, *Womad*.'

Fuck me and my mouth… Richie arches his drowning eyebrows like *You don't actually think you can say that without Reaper Cushins?* and I see his fingers tickling his hips. He must be looking for his walkie-talkie, but all the guy's got is his cellphone.

Callin' the cunt Womad's a pretty sick diss, cause Womad's like a softcock festival for Peruvian panpipes and reading poems about your period 'n shit.

Gambling addicts and alkies in the corners turn on their stools to watch the ruckus begin to boil.

Nomad's beer glass is down around his waist, and sinking lower, and there's only a trickle left, and he's tipping the dregs of his beer out and positioning his body to hit someone with it. It's obvious Richie doesn't lurk in dodgy pubs too much and can't see a glassing coming – but I see it, and Nomad's aimed his glass at yours truly. I watch it slow-mo. The beer glass – empty of liquid, pure weaponry – is suddenly up in the air and it doesn't matter if it dents Richie's skull or not because the tea-skinned, pink-eyed silverback is grabbing Richie's collar as the fight kicks off, and considering the guy's gut, and the muscle around his man-boobs, he's got to weigh twice as much as Rich. He's bent Richie backwards over the table and his thumbs are pressing into Richie's eyes. Too bad for this guy, he's let his beer glass go. I'm being squished into the booth by 200kgs of fighting men, biting their own lips and tongue, blood mixing with their spit. A stench-cloud rises up off the Nomad's body, reeking of rotting socks, and my legs are bent up into my stomach because I've barely moved Richie away, but I've got a vantage. I pick up Nomad's beer glass with the thick, solid bottom and bang Nomad as hard as I can above his left ear, aimin' for the guy's crown.

Oh shit. There's now a hunk of skin with a devil horn stuck to the base of the glass.

He gives Richie a final shove, then touches his head. There's white shit exposed. Skull and that mashed white fat you get when you rip someone's skin off.

Two splotches of blood land on my beer mat. All pretty heavy for first thing on a weekday when I just wanted some breakfast brewskis with the homie.

Richie stands up, and while Nomad's touching himself, amazed that one collision could've torn off a whole postage stamp of skin, Richie reaches between the guy's legs and tips him upside down. Richie works like a busy little ant, hopping over Nomad's pants and boots and avoiding the guy's fists and knees and folding Nomad's arms like he's trying to cram one last sweater inside a stuffed suitcase.

There are three people standing in front of the bar, drinks slanted. Shocked. Watching us.

'Where's your cuffs?!' I yell, while Richie works out the optimal way to get his arms around the guy he's folded up.

'Police - *ngh* - property must remain within - *ngh* - withinpolicepremises.... urng.'

'What about your vest?'

'Just help me, Karl, would you? Sir: I am arresting you for - *ngh* - for common - *ngh* - assault. Needyourname.'

Richie manhandles him like shearing a sheep. The Great White Nomad is wincing each time his forehead touches the dirty, dented wooden floor, weeping blood. He can't free his arms and his legs are no good – Richie keeps sweeping them away to keep the guy off balance. Already a chip is mashed in his eye and there are hairs sticking to his snotty nose, hairs which don't belong to him.

Richie tells me all I have to do is hold his fingers against his shoulderblades by kneeling on his bent arms and pinching the palms of his hands. I test the pressure. The big guy squeals.

This shit's amazing. How many fights have I been in when I could've used some Israel Adesanya shit like this?

'You will be escorted to Whangārei Police Station, where I will remand you in police custody until your, *ngrghh*, appearance in a, *nngh*, court of law on a charge of assaulting an officer. Get up. Karl: you can get off him now.'

I don't want to let the bucking bronco go, but I inch away. Richie can take him down if he attacks us again.

In ten seconds I've exerted my arse more than I usually would in a month – with four beers on top of the exercise.

'Don't you wanna phone for backup?'

*'Do I look like I need backup?'*

We haul him out and across the road, one arm under each of the Nomad's arms, and take the side door into the police station, one I've come out of a few times after nights in the drunk tank but never entered. I feel like a detective after a bust. I feel important. We got the perp.

As we're handing the heavy gangsta over to the Indian cop and the girl-cop, Richie asks his staff for handcuffs, turns to me and says, 'Hands in front, please.'

'Ha. Nice one, bruz.'

'Just put your hands out, like this.'

'The fuck, bruz?'

'Karlos Copley, I am arresting you for theft.'

One of the constables holds a door open and swings me into a holding cell of concrete which has only 20 percent of its white paint remaining between 100 years of scratched tags – weed leaves, swazzies, lighting bolts, black power fists. Kilroy's there, too, and he's sayin Welcome back, Cockroach. Each tag's got to have been scratched with someone's Prince Albert, cause they take everything from your body and leave you in t-shirt and undies with a blanket thin as a tortilla. A cock piercing's about the only thing you can sneak into these cells.

'The hell, dude, you're arresting me over that stupid-ass police mag? What's that worth, three bucks? How the hell you gonna get Barbie back without me? C'mon, man – who's your bruz?'

'There are 418 staff serving in this region who I call brother,' Richie goes, closing the heavy door on me. 'You're not one of them.'

# 3

# "We're gonna find this girl."

I'm bummed out to have fallen asleep in a pig sty – surprised, too, since the concrete walls are freezing and look like they've been through World War Two and no heat comes out of the one naked light bulb and the toilet is stainless steel and reeks of piss. Falling asleep is bad in a place like this. You're sposda be on your guard in a police holding cell, alert, fists firm, left foot forward, boxer-posture. I've always prided myself on having a few attributes giving me a fighting chance if gangstas get chucked in the cell with me. I'm not sayin' I'm some superhero like The Great Gatsby or Moby Dick or nothin. I'm 5'8", I'm wiry and I've got me one of those noses that's been broken so many times it can't be broken anymore. The point is, cockroaches are survivors. Karl can outlast any challenge.

I don't have a watch or a phone and I can't see daylight. I try work out the time. I think it's morning. You always lose time in the cells. Even worse when you've had six beers for brekky.

I think about who I am to try and pull my head back onto my shoulders and make the most of this mess. Because I've got no idea when the boredom's gonna end, I spit on my index finger and thumb, reach down my pants, bend my wrist ninety degrees, massage my bumhole till it lets me in then pull out this pill stashed so far up my arse the cops were never gonna find it. I peel the Glad Wrap off, give it a wipe on my shirt so it's clean, then gulp it down dry. It's Fentanyl - Fetty, Chill Pillz, Backdoor Morphine, whatever you wanna call it. Melts my muscles. Cools down the Cockroach. Gets me 'laxin.

*Rap, man, rap,* I think. *Art saves lives. Make poetry from your poverty.* You're a emcee. That's one of your things. Expert in the oral arts. Stage name's Cockmaster Karl, the cock with all the roaches.

I start rappin some Cypress and imagine a whole stage show till a tiny speaker in the corner of the ceiling clicks and makes a sound like wind. 'Be quiet,' says a voice from above, and then whistling wind, then a final click.

'You can't oppress me,' I go. 'D'you even lock up that nomad guy? Fuckin hypoxia, man.'

'If you want to get out of here today, I suggest you stop acting up,' the speaker responds. 'And the word is Hypocrisy.'

Damn. Richie's listening.

'Let us ouuuut, Snitch.'

No response this time, pfft. Selective hearing.

'Cause of the time I got locked up, I've missed the court van and I won't be appearing in court today. I still get breakfast, so that's alright – a little box of milk and a packet of cornflakes with no sharp edges, in a plastic bowl and spoon with Buzzy Bee patterns. Guess it cheers me up a teeny bit. I like Buzzy Bees. Or maybe I'm just blitzed on Ass Morphine and I like everything for the next couple hours.

The way the cells are quiet tells me they've just cleared out all the crims apart from Nomad and there won't be fresh people for a couple hours. The only way I know the time hits 10.30 is when a wrapped salad sandwich with buttery grated carrot sticking out of it gets slid through the slot. There's no glass in the door, and forget about windows in the cell, but I can tell it's Richie's hand sliding the tray by his silver watch and his nice fingernails.

'Don't close that flap! You can't just leave me here, bruz, c'mon. This is lame. Let's catch up, shoot the shit. Maybe get a little Limp Biscuit goin.'

'No music in the cell.'

'Nah, g, not Limp Bizkit – Limp *Biscuit*, bruz. You get a pack of wine biscuits, you take your pants off, last one to cum on the biscuit's gotta eat– '

'This conversation is finished.'

'Gemme one of those suicide blankets at least, them things is cosy-as'

'I'll get you a blanket if there's no work of higher priority,' he goes. 'And presently, you are not a priority.'

He disappears and I'm left there counting Mister Sippy one, Mister Sippy Two for a bit of variety. I stand in different corners of my cell. Check out the view. Cinderblock horizon. Find a cockroach. Pick the gorgeous golden fella up, let him run over my fingernails, twitching those beautiful antlers or whatever you call that shit sticking out of roaches' heads. He wants to stay, but I guide him back to the crack under the door he came through. Nudge him on his way. Tell him to spread those wings nobody thinks he has and *fly, little roachbro, fly.*

After ten thousand bazillion years the panel rattles and he slides a scuzzy blanket through. Doesn't even have any cool Transformers on it.

'Come through for questioning.'

Once I'm wrapped up like a taco, Richie lets me walk ahead of him through a corridor that's all painted concrete and stainless steel and metal grille. I picture him taking down the silverback this morning and I get this little ripple of fear passing through my body, like when you're skinny dipping and a stingray floats past. There's not been many times in this life I've feared Little Dick. We grew up wrestling. Whenever I got a concussion or part of my brain died if I was in a chokehold too long, I always felt it toughened my bones and flesh, like how when Richie studied exotic fight techniques and was always creative with weapons and he'd always have an interesting way to win a fight. He wasted me with a vacuum cleaner, one time, when Mum had gone outside for a smoke and left us in the hallway with the Hoover. It wasn't the hard metal pipe he got me with – it was the plastic hose, which he wrapped around my wrists until I couldn't move my arms, then he switched it on and the pressure in the hosepipe squeezed my arms till they turned purple.

The bruz is a genius at fighting if you think about it. Baby-faced Assassin. The ginger ninja.

I do my pimp strut past some empty cells, shoulders back, then I plop into a seat in a tiny-ass room with – I count them – three, no, four cameras. One's mounted on a tripod, one's a tablet fixed to some sort of dock on a filing cabinet, and there are cameras on the ceiling and door.

Just 'cause I was too busy to go to actual university, doesn't mean I didn't go to the University of the Streets. There's psychology attached to where a person sits in a room. I've watched enough *To Catch a Predator* to know this shit. I take the dominant seat, to let Richie know he hasn't completely erased me. I sit on the far side of the room, with my back to the wall, and this subliminally tells Little Dicky Snitchie Richie he must take an inferior position, making him a weak little bitch.

'This ain't about me stealing some shitty magazine, is it?'

Senior Constable Richard McMullan clears his throat. Congratulations to ya, bro, you're a lean, mean, cleanly efficient cop. You've got shitloads of control over me. Still a ginge, though. Sucks to be you.

'I want to make something clear,' Rich goes. 'You will not breach the Crimes Act 2018 in my presence. You will not fight in public. You will pay for what you consume. And you will not embarrass me by stealing police property while you're visiting my place of work under the pretence of walking down memory lane.'

I fold my arms and smear my chin against my neck, frowning. It's hard to make a double-chin when most of your diet is smoke and fat won't stick to your body. It's important to let the prick know this is a negotiation. My side of the table needs to carefully consider before responding to any offer. Cause, y'know, I'm as important as any pig, when it comes down to it.

'Don't I get a cigarette and a coffee?'

'Don't I get the right to have my work protected from theft while I support my staff to investigate a kidnapping?'

'It wasn't a pretence, Rich, the memory lane thing. I wanted to see the ol' bruz.'

'That's– .' Richie's about to say something smart and stern that'll shut me up and assert him as the crisper, better-organised, more responsible and more powerful of the two of us, but he just snorts instead.

'Rich. What happened with that one percenter, that Nomad?'

'He was spoken to; held on a minor outstanding warrant. He won't be charged. I believe he's being released today.'

'So you gonna let me go, same as that dude?'

'I booked this room for an hour.'

'I'm not gonna talk about a shitty magazine for sixty fucking minutes.'

He looks around at the cameras then back to me. After ten long silent seconds staring in his eyes, he goes, 'Barbara Konstantinou. Tell me everything you know.'

'Barbie? Finally. Thank fuck.'

I put my feet up on the desk. Maybe a little bold of me, but hey: you do crazy things when Fentanyl melts ya. It's obvious by the way he's staring at my shoes that he wants my disgusting smelly feet off the desk, but I figure he's the bad guy for taking my shoe laces so I can't hang myself. If he don't treat my feet with dignity, I'm not gonna treat his desk with dignity, so the stinky shoes stay on.

'Karl, the so-called Barbie so-called disappearance is a CIB matter. Me, I'm not a detective. Detectives are the only branch of Police with the authority to disburse reward money on an investigation– and we both know you're sniffing around for the reward money. Family's wealthy, that's no secret. Now, if I were to receive information that led to the recovery of Ms Barbara Konstantinou, I wouldn't be appreciated firstly by CIB for taking their work away from them, nor would I be appreciated by my team for– '

'For being an overachieving nerd who forgets his mates?'

He looks away. Truth hurts, bruz. 'You're clearly in need of money, and most thefts you've committed have been when you've been desperate for money. I don't want any more drapery stores broken into in my city.'

'You're still giving me shit for that?'

'Who steals curtains, anyway? Lace, weren't they, if I recall correctly.'

'Lace is expensive, G. I scored me, like, three hundred bucks' worth that night. There's a market for that shit.'

'As well as vouchers. Five hundred dollars in vouchers. For a drapery store.'

'*Don* Drapery, motherfucker. That's me.'

Richie does the tiniest little laugh, squinting like there's a bee up his nose.

I haven't noticed the file he had on the table. Barbie's mugshot's printed on the front, with the words KONSTANTINOU, Barbara Anna. God, man. Thanks to the drugs – or whatever trauma she's packing – she lost her old sexy blonde Jessica Simpson thing. She looks bad. Reeeal bad. Skinny, dry, bony, all the moisture sucked out, like when you squish a lizard in a school library book and get it out again next semester.

I see he's got papers tucked inside a white cardboard folder, too. He doesn't open it, just touches it, and the words flow up his fingers and arm like electricity and spill out of his mouth.

'Barbara was last seen November First this year, Saxon's Ale House, Lower Dent Street. Now, Ms Konstantinou's family have traditionally been about franchising their landscaping business, which I understand is fairly successful. What they do for a living may or may not have a bearing on the movements of Barbara. Might interest you to know, Karl, they're one of the more helpful advertisers in *Heat On The Beat*. You follow me?'

'Hurry up and bail me so we can bounty-hunt his arse. The kidnapper, I mean.'

'Are you familiar with the street slang fishhooked?'

'Bro, I invented street slang. Fishhooked's when a hot little number has a hot little pipe, and that pussy-pipe combo can haul even the biggest fish onto the wharf, and once he's on the wharf, that's him done forever. Dried-out, thirsty. Usually girls tricking boys. Pussy and a pipe. That'll make a slave out of any man.'

'Your language is, just appal... Anyway, I've been told CIB are exploring the avenue that Barbie's trading sex for drugs, and of course drugs could've taken her to all sorts of places her parents will have trouble coming to terms with. Such as into the company of organised crime.'

Richie drums his fingers on the table. I see he's got no wedding ring on.

'You didn't get married, Rich? No girlfriend? No bit on the side?'

'We're not discussing me today.'

'Maybe we oughta. Cause I've been holding back. Boys here at the station don't like you. You're too fuckin' anal. Everyone knows you're a nark. They want you to get promoted out of the station, though, so they'll be keen-as if you Bring Back Barb. Three Bees. That's why you gotta work with me.'

He takes a long deep breath, gets up, ushers me towards the door. 'Last chance. Nothing concrete you want to share that'll help us both?'

'Not exactly right this minute, but, bro, I'm psychic. I bin tellin you since we were like thirteen. And my psychic senses tell me we're gonna find this girl. If she's been kidnapped, we'll hogtie the cunts, bring the kidnapper back and charge him and get a payout from Barbie's fam 'cause her dad's rich as shit. And you'll get all the credit, Police Academy.'

He leads me back near my cell, hesitates, frowning at the concrete floor. I can tell he's sitting on the fence. Picturing strapping me into his car, letting me show him what I know up north, and that I'll probably get immunity from prosecution after this for any dirt I do in future.

Richie goes over to the jailer, whispers in the jailer's ears. Stares at the keys in the jailer's palm.

I don't know where Barbara Konstantinou is exactly, but I can bullshit and string Richie along till we get to a certain place where there's certain peeps that do.

# 4

# "Lost ya Barbie doll, kid?"

Doin a cringey five kays an hour less than the speed limit, we pass through these bend-in-the-road towns as Whangārei becomes the mid-north. Shacks, sheep, swamps, hay bales, cows, silos, logging trucks, tree ferns, brown streams. Tufts of tropical forest on the hilly bits of farms, like God's glued buds of weed on the land. Beautiful.

At Kauri Flat, Richie finally makes a noise other than humming to classical music. He grizzles something about how he'd rather be out surfing right now with "the boys," mentions he's got four months' worth of leave queued up 'cause he hasn't taken a holiday in nearly five years. He's driving the candy-arse electric Kia – orange, urgh – and I'm sitting in the back with a pile of self-help books beside me, and I shit you not, he keeps reminding me that I'm on PMB, which means Police Bail (Monitored) – so Richie gets to babysit me, pretty much.

God knows who "the boys" are that he wants to surf with. Buncha Cambodian bum-chums, I imagine, five for a hundred bucks.

Richie's got one of those little bags of dried flowers pinned to his heater vents. I take a deep breath of popery or whatever it's called and think about garrotting Richie from behind his seat, KGB-style. I'm about to do it when I realise the prick never gave me my shoelaces back, so I just slump back and watch the cornrows and cows pass by. Nice place, Northland just before Christmas. Hot, stinky and rainy. Decent place to be homeless, the temperature's real nice for sleeping outside all night.

The world's greatest philosopher Christopher Wallace, AKA the Notorious

BIG, once said 'Spit up some prayers for the shit you got / Cause you might get run over or you might get shot.' Them gratitude-words is playin in my head as I manipulate myself into not minding the journey so much.

I'm *grateful* I'm not cuffed, I'm *grateful* Richie's car doesn't have a screen separating the back seats from the front, but this is bullshit on so many levels. He treats me far more like a crook than a bruz. He's got the child lock on, meaning I can't open the rear doors or wind down the window, and he covers his phone with his hand whenever he's taking a phone call, pullin over on the side of the road 'cause there's no drivin 'n dialin with this guy. Every call's something to do with rosters or policing tactics, not footy, not social soccer, not poker. It's obvious Richie doesn't have any mates. How much of a cunt do you have to be to hit 30 with no friends?! Shit, I've still got mates in about 12 cities up and down the country even though I don't reside anywhere for longer than three months at a time. Dealers, hookers, gangsters, prospects, alcohol and drug counsellors, hell, I can't keep friends off me.

I'm about to get some pity going for him when I check myself and think Nah, actually, y'know how come Richie can't find people to chill with? Cause arrestin someone for borrowing a magazine ain't fuckin' chilling. Rich needs to learn to relax. Good thing his best bruz is here to school him.

We pass this buzzy billboard for a kumara farm. It's got a talking kumara on it with eyes looking right into my soul. I blink and wonder if I'm still trippin from the acid I dropped before I rocked up at the cop shop.

'Yo, Snitch.'

'What is it, Cockroach?' His voice is flat as a doormat, but I banter with the prick anyway.

'Y'all got any free police shit? Like a key ring or something? You guys get tasers, right? Gimme a taser to play with. I'm bored back here.'

'Weapons are for the weak,' he goes.

'See, that's a ignorant-ass attitude right there,' I say towards the front of the car. 'Bro, if you gave your staff guns, maybe they'd actually respect you.'

'I'm more than happy to return you to the cells if you're going to carry on complaining. Bear in mind it's Saturday and you won't appear in court until Tuesday.'

'What about Monday?'

'Monday appearances are only for people charged with category 1 offences. Rape, murder, et cetera.'

'Well let me outta the car and I'll murder somebody. I ain't waiting till Tuesday.'

'I suggest you use your time up north to shake the tree, see what these contacts you claim to have say about Barbara Konstantinou going awol. I'll pass on to the police prosecutor whatever intel you bring for us, should it prove reliable. Category 3 information or higher might mitigate your sentence.'

'Sentence?! For stealing a mag people use to line their cat's fuckin litter tray?'

'And about twenty burglaries in the West Auckland area, Karl.'

'Lemme ride up front, mall cop.'

I kick the back of his seat and Richie swallows and continues driving. I kick for a solid five minutes, watching the clock on his dashboard.

At 11.46, Richie eases the car into the forecourt of a dusty Mobil service station in some little mouldy town that looks like a Wild West film set. Place with one road and a concrete quarry and creaking stockyards straight out of The Texas Chainsaw Massacre. Place called Hikurangi.

The Tavern's on the main street, beside the kindergarten. Biker pub, couple of bigass choppers outside, chrome and black. Picture of Peppa pig on the outside with pellet-holes where someone's blown the face out with a shotgun. Pigs unwelcome; chicks drink free.

'You finished with your little tantrum, Karl?'

I boot his seat one last time. 'What do I have to do to earn a seat up front?'

'Become a category 3 informant or higher. As discussed.'

He opens up the file in his head where he stores nerd-words. 'Category 4 informants provide information generally already known to Police. Category 3 informants provide concrete details which go into a case file. Category 2 informants give information which contributes to a successful prosecution. Category 1 informants can personally testify in court. Because they have integrity.'

'Category 3 sounds like me. I'll go yarn to some locals. Lemme out. I'll get you intel on Barbie. Shake them trees you were talkin about.'

'Nope,' he goes, 'Let a professional handle this.'

Professional tryhard, more like. Richie hops out of the car, presses his fob firmly until the car doors lock, waits for a cyclist to grind past, then waits a little more until the only thing likely to run him over is a tumbleweed. I watch him go over towards the motorcycles shining blackly outside the pub. There are bikers on the deck and I recognise their waspy black and yellow-striped patch – Defiant MC. It's priceless. The two dudes in leather vests and black jeans shuffle their stools and turn their backs to the officer of the law, and the barmaid curls her hair with her middle finger. The Fuck You sign.

Senior Constable Richie tries to start a conversation over the noise of an 18-wheeler going past with big logs and a digger on its two trailers. I can see two bikies, a solid one and a fat one, tossing cigarette butts and ice cubes at him and dissing him and taking pictures on their phones. They'll be sending a pxt to HQ. I guarantee it. They'll get Richie's face printed on those Pig Hunt playing cards they hand out at Poker Runs with the faces of wanted cops on them with bounties printed on the cards. You get thirty grand if you Wishbone someone on an ace card, that's what I heard. Wishboning – as in, what you do with a wishbone after a Christmas turkey - is when a pair of bikers chain someone between two motorcycles, and they hoon off in different directions and they–

It's hard for me to even say, even for Karlos the Jackal, legendary lawbreaker. They split a man like a wishbone.

Over on the pub deck, Richie thinks he's about to elicit some information when I watch one of the black 'n yellow bikers grab his crotch, unzip his big tattooed cock and piss as close as he can to Richie's boots.

Richie turns his back on the bikers, defeated. They're laughing at him and clinking glasses. He waits patiently for a safe time to cross the road, looking left and right, mindful of his safety, then comes back to me and leans in the driver side window.

Luckily we're a little way down the street and the bikers can't see that Rich is with me, cause I'm embarrassed to be associated with the prick right now.

'No information to be had,' he concludes. 'We'll ask around elsewhere.'

'Are you literally kidding me? Let me outta the car. I need a smoke.'

'You *want* to smoke. No one *needs* to smoke.'

'You don't understand how good smokes taste, bruz.'

Richie fucks around as much as he can. He shuffles, he moves into the centre of the road, he comes back to me, he pretends he has to check with his seniors about whether I'm allowed out of the car, starts dialling, stops dialling and chews his tongue, frowning. He checks for any special new warnings on his phone that might've come through, as if something's suddenly been discovered about me.

Finally he opens the back door. Guess he's acknowledging he needs some help from his bruz.

I'm out into the air that's hay-y and grassy and so much more refreshing than the perfect 18 degrees Celsius of Richie's ride. I strut across the highway, fuck it, gimme a twenty-tonne logging truck, I don't care. Freedom feels good.

'Wait!' Richie's shouting, trying to dodge a tour bus. 'Karl, I am required to escort you at all times as directed under Section– '

'Section shit!' I wait for a Kawasaki Ninja to pass. 'Fuck off or they'll know I'm friends with a cop! Least, I used to be.'

I'm lucky I'm not a pancake already. Kawasaki Ginger watches me go to work.

I walk up the wooden steps of the Hikurangi Tavern bar-pub-hotel-hellhole known as the Hika to most. A sign claims it's also a café and I can see a teenager going around the tables taking orders. One of the bikers turns and spits toward my feet but I see it coming. So many peeps've spat at ol' Karl over the years, I've become a pro at spit-dodging.

I strut towards the source of the spit with confident legs, pretending I don't have invisible shackles on and wishing my smokes weren't locked in the safe box in Richie's car's trunk. I stand so I'm evenly placed between the two big biker boys. Both crackers, which isn't good. It's these whites you've gotta watch out for. Dutch, Viking, Afrikaner, big angry Scottish genes, I don't know what the formula is but some of these guys get reeeeal tall and reeeeal dangerous. This guy right in fronta me is like Stonehenge. All the fat he has to carry seems to have made strange parts of his body like blocks. His neck is big as my thigh. His arms look like they don't bend.

'Got some intel yous might want,' I go to him.

'Who the fuck are you?'

'Aw, I'm like, y'know. Pretty notorious. Pretty inn-famous. Just got out of Ngawha. Done a lag for, y'know. Five murders, couple frauds, 20 assaults, old peeps, young peeps, pssh, anyone.'

His slightly-less-fat friend presses his nose against me, his body touching my crotch, stinky breath wetting my eyes. It's horrible and kinda sexy in a gay way, cept he'll do somethin pretty unsexy in a couple seconds if I don't make it clear I'm a big boy.

'Assaults on young people? What kinda assaults? Sick fuckin paedo.'

'Nah, nah, um… .' Think, Karl, think.

My brain suggests two comebacks to show them I'm equal-tough, it thinks up a retort about the paedo thing, but I also wanna say 'Your Mama' – except both comebacks kind-of get jumbled up.

'My mum's a paedo,' I go. Wince. My mouth moves along real quick. 'Listen, uhhhh, one of your boys has been waylaid and he needs ya. Just thought yous'd wanna know.'

'Dunno what you're talking about,' says the bigger biker. Someone – probably the waitress – has put on his table a flyer for that tattoo convention that's comin up, Bay Blue Tattoo. Some Black Power/Crips-sponsored thing to make their brand look good.

The fat one bumps me with his belly again. 'Tryina drink here. Get in my face again, you won't be seein your family at fuckin' Christmas this month.'

'I wouldn't mind that, to be honest, my old man thinks I'm a waste of space… Listen, oi: mate of yours, devil-horned dude with a mullet, he was in the Jug pub and he's in the cells right now and I know where he is. Someone's gotta bail him.'

I don't tell the Defiant I hit their brother with a glass and that my best friend – a cop – folded him like origami and locked his arse up.

'You tellin tall tales, boy? Want a fuckin slap?'

'He had on this faggy, I mean, *colourful* patch with five colours. He's got a scorpion tat on his neck? Decent bod, not that I'm into dude's bods, I only root pussy and… Anyway, Nomad, I think is his name? That's your bro, right?'

'Red-and-blues get him?' asks the quieter biker, the not-as-fat one, scrolling through some text messages on his phone. He's referring to the Rebels, not the baddest or meanest bikers in Northland, but they *are* the biggest. Three chapters in a region with only one city: that's overpopulation. And that's just Rebels, not to mention Heads, Defiant, Angels, Highway 61s, Tribesmen, Filth.

'The Peppas picked him up. Bit of a scrap in the Jug pub down in Whangaz. Arrested him. Needs a mate to bail him out.'

'How the fuck d'you know that?'

'I's in the cells with him.' *Seriously, Karl: do not slip and tell them that you and*

'He ain't goin to court on Monday, it'll be Tues. Just thought you should know, guess he'll slip you a few bucks for bailing him, eh.'

'They take his colours off him?'

'Peppas always take ya patch, bruz.'

'Motherfuckers,' the two guys mumble together. The fat one turns to the Stonehenge-shaped one. 'You got Nome's old lady's deets? Give her a bell now. Use my phone.'

I'm not expecting gratitude, but there is something I've gotta get out of these guys. 'Just thought yous oughta know,' I go, pretending to turn and leave. 'Oh by the way, y'all seen this chick named Barbie around?'

'Hur-hur. Lost ya Barbie doll, kid?'

'You'd know she's Barbie if you saw her. Pretty decent rack, bit saggy. She's like platinum blonde, big red lips cause her skin's so pale, ummmmm, thought she mighta been at one of ya poker runs. Barbara's her court name. Konstantinou.'

'Aw, that skank,' goes the bigger Defiant. 'Arks Kenny.'

'Kenny, right. I totally know Kenny.'

'Kenny D'Souza. Indian dog with the dreadlocks. DJ, plays beats. Sells puss to the club cause he hopes it'll get him a patch and protection. Kenny's her pimp. Assumin you want a piece of arse.'

'Iiii am after a piece,' I say truthfully. 'But the cops want her badder so I'm just, y'know. Tryina make a buck.'

'So you're a informant?'

I gulp, take three, steps away, four, and I'm almost gone from their lives. 'They're up at, um, Cape Reinga, right?' I go, stabbing in the dark. 'Barbie and Kenny?'

*Barbie and Ken,* I think. Huh. Buzzy. Destiny or something. Or maybe my brain's kicked into Detective Mode and I'm seeing patterns and I've got some kind of gift like Rain Man or something.

'You're about a hundred kays off, boy,' Stonehenge goes.

Hundred kays from Cape Reinga there's only one settlement where this DJ Kenny person could pimp his ho, get some snatch, cash, a patch and probly a rash: Kaitaia. So that's a hell of a clue. And it's the only clue I'm going to get today, unless I want to get my face flattened.

I cross the highway again and stand not far along from the empty

Hikurangi Gasoline Alley service station, by the roadside, sticking out my thumb. Cars start pulling over, so I have to stick out my middle finger to get them to move along. I see the bikers takin' a look at me and laughing. They raise their glasses, but they're half-hidden behind unpainted wood with a sign advertising some local concrete layer. Dumbarses seem to think they live in a world where people come up to them and give them useful information about their brothers just because the public respects them so much, or some shit. They don't know I've stuck a secret needle into them and extracted intelligence. 100 kays from the Cape? It has to be Kaitaia, Gateway to the Fuckin North.

Richie glides up and tries to coax me into his back seat like a paedo.

'Nuh-uh,' I go. 'I founded out where Barbie is, so you're letting me in the front.'

'You *know* where she is, or you *think* you know?'

I can't talk for thirty seconds as a reeking truck comes past, leaving a moist brown funk in the air that tastes like sheep shit. 'Richie, seriously, I got the goods. I'm your partner, yo, your second-in-charge, your THC. Don't chuck me in the back again.'

'If you promise to go straight, I might consider it. Then again, a promise from you's not worth much.'

'Kaitaia, there, fuck it, I've said it. An hour up from Kaikohe. Guarantee that's where she is. And this pimp of hers is with her, apparently, Kenny? Some pimp she met workin the avocado orchards I think? Let me in. I don't wanna eat sheep farts again.'

Richie snorts and rolls his eyes and looks at traffic. He's close to driving off and leaving me here.

'You know it's true, bruz. You know the code. Tell the truth in the underworld, get to stay in the underworld, right? He who lies dies. You musta heard that little nursery rhyme. Lemme in.'

'If we get to Kaitaia, and fail to locate her within reasonable time, I can promise you you will be riding in the rear of my vehicle all the way back. Because I don't want you in my region.'

'Unless I'm useful to investigations. Which is the dealio we got right here.'

He chews on this.

'Oi, what about this Kenny fuck? We can track him down, take Barbs off him, arrest his arse for pimping.'

'Facilitating sexual services is not an offence under the Prostitution Act. Unless it's coerced.'

'Which we can only find out by nabbing the cunt.'

That stumps the cunt. A door unlatches, and not just any door. It's the front passenger door. Shotgun seat. Where partners ride.

# 5

# "You're not seriously goin in there?"

We hoon north up State Highway One, headed for the last town in the country before the land tilts into the Pacific Ocean. Three hours to go. Should be fun.

It's nice, this thing we're doing. Two bruzzes, one mission, not that Richie acknowledges our mission has begun. Richie's totally in denial. He still reckons the CIB are gonna retrieve Barbs, as if crims will just hand her over because they respect the Peppas so much. Pfft. Nah, dawg. You need a double agent. A silent, stealthy animal that can slide in and out without people noticing.

You need a cockroach.

There's not much to eat in Richie's car apart from breath mints, and I don't want the dried apricots Richie nibbles from a bag between his legs, 'cause the apricots are ginger-coloured and they resemble Richie's nuts.

I finger a cigarette to get my appetite down and out the window I watch hawks and tractors and logs and pine trees and fairly slow drivers overtaking us. Rich switches to jazz on the stereo, and I think about grabbing the steering wheel and swerving us into an oncoming truck, the music's so lame.

Richie drives with right hand and does these Callous Thenix exercises, holding his left wrist steady on the wheel and flexing his fist. He doesn't start one single conversation, so I throw out some bait.

'I need to stop for a smoke pretty soon,' I go.

'Perhaps,' Richie goes.

'Sure you don't want me to drive?'

'I do not want a remand prisoner driving a vehicle belonging to a police officer, no thank you. Just sleep.'

'Can't sleep without a smoke first.'

'Seriously? With how much money to your name?'

'Spend less on food when ya smoke. Makes hunger pangs not pang so much.' Methamphetamine – crack, we call it round these parts – is the ultimate hunger-killer. Makes your smoke reeeally smoke. I always keep a few ciggies that've been dipped in liquid crack in my packet.

Richie stares down the barrel of the highway.

'So tell me how you've been making money the last coupla years, then.'

'Nah G – *you* tell *me* how much money *you* have.'

Richie shrugs. 'Depends which account we're talking about.'

'How many accounts you got?'

'Five.'

'Fuck you need five bank accounts for?'

'Recreation, necessities, house, investments, kids.'

'You don't got kids. Guarantee you haven't even popped your cherry.'

'By kids I mean my youth group. They need a bit of a financial leg-up. Few bucks here and there.'

'Sounds about right, you've gotta borrow kids cause no one's gonna marry your skinny nark ass.'

We pass an endless dark green forest that rolls over the hills. Real Lord of the Rings shit. I'm pretty sure I see a couple orcs frolicking between the tree trunks.

'Sorry about the marriage thing. Just a joke.'

'I don't see why you consider yourself a major catch.'

'Yeah, but at least I *know* I'm not a catch. Maybe it hasn't sunk in with you yet. Sounds like you're married to promotions.'

'I have been seeing someone, on and off.'

'Oh really? She in a wheelchair?'

'No.'

'Blind?'

'Shut up.'

'She's overseas, isn't she. C'mon, tell us. She's a ladyboy, right? From fuckin Thailand?'

Staring down his steering wheel, Richie says, 'I'm not interested in judgement from the likes of you.'

'So she's from a loser country,' I chuckle, 'You sifty motherfucker. What, couldn't get a normal Kiwi chick?'

'How'd we get stuck on this anyway?' Richie goes.

'Reminiscing, bruz. Old friends reunited.'

Richie just glares as we zip past a pyramid of hay bales with a rusting boat on top, miles from the ocean.

"Member how your dad had that real quiet vacuum cleaner he brought back from Dubai that had real gentle suction? Member you put your cock in it when we were, like, nine?'

'Stop, already.'

' - And I was like "I want a turn" and you were like "My house, my vacuum" and I was like well I'm not sharing my lubricant and you were like "You don't got any lube" and I was like "Shows what you know, toothpaste's the best lube there is" and you got all jealous and –'

'Enough.'

' –And you squirted like three inches on your schlong except you grabbed the wrong tube from the drawer, it wasn't toothpaste, it was Deep Heat, and stuck your lil dingaling in the vacuum and the paramedics had to treat you for chemical burns and– '

'Enough, Karl.'

I'm crying with laughter, thumping the seat, so happy I don't even need drugs right now. 'That medic was putting jelly on your cock to treat the burn! And you had this massive stiffy and it wouldn't go away and I was like, Bruz, you're lovin it!'

Richie's car slows, someone zips past, hooting at him, and he glides onto the edge of the road outside the Towai Tavern where a goat looks at him like, 'What up?'

Richie takes a breath, checks his missed calls, checks his texts, checks his email. He refuses to look at me. Finally, he eases back into the traffic. We're still being overtaken by grannies.

'I got dirt on you, Rich Boy.'

'Well I've got dirt on *you*.'

'Maybe the dirt's so sticky it's pulled us back together like when you bust a real sticky nut. Bonded 'n stuff.' We pass some fields with wild turkeys and peacocks strutting in the shade of red-flowering pohutakawas. The Kiwi Christmas tree, people call them things. Beautiful, but I want to get to our destination so we can collect Barbs and get on the piss and talk about the Glory Days that passed us by in the wink of a young girl's eye.

'How many kays we done?'

Richie looks at the odometer. '42 kilometres, thereabouts.'

'Sall good if you drive like a noob. Oi, 'member Matilda, that German chick? Bruz, she was wiiiiild. 'Member that party she put on, with the balloons with NOS in em? You'd grab a balloon, take the peg off it and suck the NOS, feel ya brain tinglin...'

'I never sucked NOS.'

'It's a legal high, bruz. You're not gonna get in trouble.'

'Would've been a bad look.'

'You weren't a cop then, though.'

'I was born a cop.'

'Ho-hooo! I love, I love it. That's gangsta.'

'Do not call me a gangster .'

We pass some billboards, the turn-offs for a couple of boat repair places, a church, a mountain of oyster shells, and fields with sagging barns, the outsides tagged up with massive-arse bombs in orange and cyan. Rolling pine forest. Splashes of native bush, probably stuffed with weed plantations.

Out Richie's window, you can see the ocean over the lip of some of the fields.

'Can I roll a window down to smoke?'

'Tell me why you went off the rails, Karl, and... perhaps I can stop so you can have a single cigarette. Just one.'

A minute later, I'm standing beside the car suckin a spliff while Rich reads his FitBit, measuring his resting heart rate. I think we're near Ngawha. Aside from hot pools and a jail, it's the middle of nowhere.

'Wouldn't mind some Mickey Ds,' I tell him. 'Can we veer over to Kaikohe?'

'That's a forty minute detour.'

'Pleeeeeease, bruz.'

We get the wheels rolling silently for ten mins. Highway One continues north, but I notice Rich take the Kaikohe detour where the road forks at the Ohaeawai pub.

Yusss. Victor-eee for Karly C.

'So,' he goes as we get close to Kaikohe. 'You promised you'd tell me what's landed you in court for, amongst other things, soliciting a male prostitute. A male prostitute who was in fact an undercover police officer.'

'It wasn't like … a'ight, so we're nineteen, right? First night after you were gone. I remember 'cause it was the last night the flat was clean. Obviously when you moved out you did a full-on clean, scrubbed the poo-barnacles off the rim of the toilet, washed the curtains, bleached the basin, all that.'

'It's required by the Tenancies Act, 2005.'

'Well it ain't required by your average punter, I can tell you that. No one'll clean a toilet if they don't hafta. Where was I? Anyway so yeah, you had your leaving shindig, then this guy, Rake, moves in the next day. You could tell something was crooked about him just 'cause of his name, short for Raycon apparently. Anyway, Rake's got me smoking crack that very night. You're there, I never smoked crack; soon as you leave, boom, I'm smoking, so it's kind of your fault. Anyway we smoked in the bathroom and I remember these little bits of burnt crystal that smell like burning hair falling onto the sinktop and me going to Rake, 'Richie's not gonna be chuffed when he sees that,' and Rake was like, 'Snitchie Richie don't live here,' and I was like, 'Truuuue.' And that was us, day labouring for a bit, wheeling barrows of broken paving stones up wooden ramps and tipping the shit into giant bins on them building sites down West Auckland ways. Had a nice routine for, what, one week before my stuff starts goin missing, like my flatscreen and iPod and that, so obviously Rake's stealing from me. Good thing I could still fight, I put Rake's head in the fuckin' oven and switched it on, but it took ages to heat up and it got kinda awkward kneelin' there so I let him go and he moved out and left me having to pay two rents, hooked on crank and havin to do twice as much work out on site.'

Richie stares dead ahead at the road.

'Such a struggle,' he goes, finally. 'Amazing you survived.'

'I didn't survive, Snitch. I died. Straight up, bruz, I used to laugh back when you were living with me before you went to police college. Going to the movies, chucking popcorn at girls then saying sorry and getting their numbers, fuck, the worst fights we'd have was, like, in the boxing gym or at league or something. No bad behaviour off the field, none whatsoever. Then within about a month I'm loose as a goose.'

'Do I really want to hear this?'

'You said you wanted to know. May as well tell you. I assaulted a girl-cop. I wasn't even getting arrested. I was just in this bar, saw this random dude havin a altercation with two girl-pigs, and I just went in, bruz. I figured I'd make it even but I went in a bit too hard and, you know, thinkin about it now, no one was swingin' till *I* started swingin. I grabbed a lemon from behind the bar and squeezed it so my fist was all acidy. Got some in her eye when I was punching so yeah, nah, yeah. That's on my record. As you know.'

Neither of us says anything for ages. I did so much unclean shit, it's amazing I remember. Mostly what sticks out in my memory is the first time I broke some moral. Borrowing Lion Mints donation boxes full of coins. Getting in a scrap with some hobo in a wheelchair. 4am on K Road shagging a big-boned hooker with hairy legs. Breaking into the Salvation Army to score tins of baked beans from the food bank.

I suppose my thoughts are floating about in the air and Richie's absorbing my thoughts because he eventually goes, 'God has plans for us all, Karl. Do you know what your plan is? For improving your life?'

'Can't improve nothin while I'm on police bail, can I?'

He finds that funny and something reminds him he's hungry. We pass fruit stands and siloes and – hollaaa! – we arrive on Broadway, main street of Kaikohe, a town that kinda looks like the entire place was bought for five bucks at a garage sale. There's a pigdog in the middle of the road, sniffing a dropped pie.

Richie cruises slowly, looking for a place to park. I see a ten-year-old Crip on the corner of a shitty street and I wave the Bloods sign at him, just to rile the kid up.

Over by the skate bowl we find McDonalds and I'm thinking, score. But he doesn't go through drive-thru.

'You bought cigarettes at that Mobil. How much does that leave you? You can't have a lot of money.'

'I got nothin,' I tell him. 'I actually had to borrow six bucks from your parking coins. I'll pay ya back. Pay day's next week.' I elbow the door. 'Can you let me out? Gotta smoke again.'

'What exactly do you do for income, if you don't me asking?'

'Government pays me.'

'So my taxes subsidise your lifestyle. Terrific.'

'Just let me out, G.'

Kaikohe's a dried-up old crossroads. The main street is all these faded shops with dusty windows. Every sign for every sad shop has got stickers on it or tag or lichen growin over.

There's a dude sleeping on a traffic island. He's wearing high-vis and camouflage, but it's pretty obvious he ain't been at work.

I light a Dipper - a premium Marlboro, dipped in something special. Dippers are the best thing since sliced crack. You heat up the crystals as you inhale; you step on board an elevator of happiness up at your head which slowly descends to your toes and goes into the ground.

I'm Puff the Magic Dragon, feeling magical outside a McDonald's that's kinda sorta not-that-bad if you've got some smoke in you. Mattera fact, I'm starting to love this place. The graffiti on the skate bowl is coming alive. A Chinese dragon winks at me; some letters spell WAT UP, KARL. I get to staring at the bird life of Kaikohe. I never thought about how graceful the sparrows are, how angel-y white the seagulls. Even this chicken eating noodles out of the garbage looks dope, its feathers a real nice shade of chocolatey brown.

Richie has parked a picnic basket and thermos on top of his car and he's walking in circles while he dips crackers in something that looks like hummus. Sounds like he's humming Moat's Art to himself.

After another quick smoke and a few texts, I announce we oughta roll. 'Get in to Kai-Tai; find Barbs; cruise back to Whangaz; maybe get Domino's for dinner. They've got five buck pizzas. My shout.'

'What about the McDonald's you so desperately craved?'

'Lost my appetite.'

'You sure those cigarettes haven't expired?' Richie goes, sniffing. 'They smell... *off*.'

I stub out my smoke and tell him we seriously need to chase the sun.


We go back the route we came, past a big round muddy lake called Omapere and connect with Highway One again. The crack high wears off as Richie begins climbing this endless steaming rainforested mountain called the Mangamukas, slow switchback after slow switchback, and sleep pulls a dark sack over my head.

I'm dreaming of high school, dreaming of giving Barbara her first tattoo by scraping out her skin and breaking open a Bic and rubbing the blue ink in, carving my initials into her. God I hope she hasn't tattooed over the tat. If I had a time machine, man, I'd definitely go back to age 15.

Everything in my dreamworld feels marshmallowy and safe and then suddenly we're slowing down and I'm rolling forward and I open my eyes and we've arrived in another dimension where they speak some kind of alien language, according to the big sign at the front of town.

*Dobro došli,* the sign reads. What the fuck? What planet is – *Welcome to Kaitaia.*

Ohhhhhh. Our destination. Choice.

We veer off the main road and rumble east – least I think it's east – into the shitty fringe of an already shitty town. Wrecked rusty cars on people's berms, graffiti on broken fences, a wandering dog with about fifty nipples. And barbed wire. And stacked shipping containers. And a dude in black and yellow, patrolling.

*DMC* painted in huge yellow letters with black outline on the corrugated fence. Clubhouse of Northland's hardest biker gang.

'Rich! Did we – are we in Kaitaia, man? That's the Defiants's pad, bruz – you're not seriously goin in there?'

Without taking his eyes off the gang compound, Richie puts his edible ginger testicles away in the glovebox.

'Dude...'

Richie pulls the handbrake up hard. From some corner of the Kia, he pulls a stab proof vest and shrugs it on. 'Stay in the car.'

# 6

# "You don't wanna be busting into my house."

The pile of shipping containers looms over us, stacked like castle towers, blocking out the hopeful sun. There's only one little curl of barbed wire you can see the sky through. To call it intimidating doesn't do it justice. Former sawmill. Blades everywhere. The place is like Mordor meets the junkyard from my favourite movie Wall-E.

I've jogged up beside Richie, who stands on the grass berm outside the Defiant fortress in Kai-Tai. I'm panting. Fuck me, I'm unfit. Those bus stop push-ups I used to do, to be honest, I only did them once. And I was cranked-up to the gills.

What we're looking at's gotta be the only three storey apartment building in this little town. The Defiant have painted the concrete black and taped Jim Beam and UFC and *Bay Blue Tattoo December* posters on the windows and covered entire doors with the numerals 4-13-3 – meaning the fourth, thirteenth and third letters of the alphabet, DMC, for Defiant Motorcycle Club, get it? It's painted on the fence in Wild West-style lettering. Outlaw motorcycle clubs like this are always mostly truckies and tradies and angry apprentices, including signwriters, so when they paint their numbers and letters and colours, it looks profesh. Little 4133s everywhere you look – the edge of the gutter, the mailbox of course (although I heard the postal service tried to tell them their location was number 219 and they weren't allowed to just choose their own address number, and then a postie went missing and NZ Post kinda backed down and let them pick whatever number they wanted).

We're about to irritate the shit out of a major gang, but Richie doesn't seem worried. He's like a dog obsessed with a scent. He's peering between a gap in the black-painted corrugated iron. It's not as if Littledick could see over the wall. Each panel of corrugated iron is ten feet high.

'I see eight units in two blocks of four,' he mutters to himself, or me, or some secret radio, half-crouched on the grass berm. I'm surprised security cameras haven't picked him up. 'Seeing… three males within the premises. Two garages, eleven Triumph motorcycles parked outside.'

Richie looks at his watch, goes back over to the trunk of his car. This dude is seriously on the verge of getting spotted. If these people don't take kindly to postmen, imagine what they'll do to a piglet.

I follow, yapping like Lassie.

'You sure we shouldn't get a motel and a feed? Richie, what are ya dooo – wow. You're really doin this.'

Richie has slipped off his top and is tucking in a police polo shirt instead. He slides his stab-proof vest down over it. Not bullet-proof, just stab-proof. He slides an ID card into the plastic sleeve of his vest. He has no radio and he hasn't actually taken the taser, fuckin weirdo, but his belt is large, his pants are pleated and his boots are shiny and black so he looks pretty cop-ish. I don't think Richie really finished work when he left the station and said he was taking two days' leave. This workaholic motherfucker, he has gradients: on duty, slightly less on duty, prepping till he's on duty again. Never quite *off-duty*.

Richie hits the big hard tall gate and begins toeing the gravel at its base. I'm wondering why you would bother kicking a puddle of pebbles then Rich is down on his knees, scraping like a dog burying a bone, flinging pebbles everywhere, then the Mission Impossible motherfucker squirms on his back and rolls under the gap he's created beneath the gate.

The hell's this prick doing? Fuck, Rich, slow down, I wanna shout. I don't want him to say 'Cover me' or 'Back me up.' As in, me having any kind of responsibility.

Not sure where Richie's been keeping the hero sauce, it's impressive and I'm stunned, for a wee bit. Dude's impatient, fired-up. Keen to get a stronger result before the end of the day. I need to keep up, need to show him my balls, and not like back in Year 7 when I used to draw eyes on them and aim them at people in the changing room.

He's disappearing into a closed area where there's a tower of pallets, ladders and rails too, which get you onto the top of the shipping container stack – painted black with yellow slashes, of course. Wasp-coloured. Like a bug that can kill you.

There are vests bolted into a wide wooden panel. It's a trophy wall of all the enemies they've beaten in fights. Flapping in the breeze I can just spot a Stormtroopers vest, a Rebels, and there's the red-on-black of Filthy Few. The Defiant skin your hide after they take your patch, that's what I heard. They take off the leather, then they take the skin off your back.

There's still no one on sentry duty on top of the containers, lucky for Richie.

I gulp a little bit of bravery, trembling like a wet puppy, wishing I had time to smoke something courageous, and lie down in the puddle of pebbles against the gate. My back seizes and I need to piss. I squelch under the gate, emerge inside the compound. God, it looks like Mad Max in here. A wasteland of drums and wire, tyres and weapons and rusted hulks of cars with a gravel pit in the middle.

The path narrows between the shipping containers. It's a deliberate strategy. They make prospects keep kettles of water boiling at all times, that's what I heard, and if someone unwelcome comes into the pincer between the containers, the prospects can get on top of the containers and pour–

'Rich! Bruz! Where are you?'

'Did I say you could raise your fuckin voice in here?'

It's a Defiant, tall and burnt-honky crimson, with pointy cheekbones, looking like a surfer and a Nazi had a baby. He's appeared out of nowhere, standing in my way, arms out as if ready to make a rugby tackle. He's not got his patch on, just black tank top and black jeans – and jandals. *Yellow* jandals.

Black and yellow. Wasp colours that sting.

Where's Richie gone?

I think about flashing the FTP tattoo that's on my chest, like I *'m one of yous, for real*, but exposing myself is unthinkable right now. 'I'm looking for my f-f, um. My mate.'

'That why you come in uninvited?'

Some brown teenagers appear behind him, Māoris or Samoans. They have shaved heads with skanky little mullets and dreadlocks hanging off the backs of their skulls like sheep dags. You can see on their heads all the scars from every bottle they've had smashed on their skulls. They come out in front of their master, eyes and teeth yellow with excitement, like little rockpool fish that've got something new to eat. These are prospects – prospective gang members. No glamorous lifestyle for these little mafia wannabes. Behind them there's Slayer pumping from two different units and about ten recycling bins overflowing with bourbon 'n coke cans. Broken windows patched with duct tape and cardboard. A pile of coal, some welding gear. Stack of steel crayfish pots and orange net.

'Sorry to, like, burst into your pad –'

'This here's my house, ain't no pad,' Burnt Honky Crimson goes. His head is clean as a shaved nutsack except for some scraggly grey shit on the back of his skull. Boy's got a goatee, and he's skinny. Muscle wrapped around his ribs and arms like vines. 'You don't wanna be busting into my house. Fuck's ya name?'

'Karl, Karlos.'

'You a Jehovah's Witness or a dead cunt? Make up your mind, Karl Karlos.'

'Snitch! Richie!'

B.H.C. tries to grab my hair and I twist my head and the twist makes him feel he's experiencing resistance, so he goes for my throat and I have to shove him against a wall but not so hard he feels I'm overpowering him and he gets desperate, and it's just half a second before the prospects with the shaven heads begin clawing. One of them whams my head with the butt-end of a Monster Energy bottle and my head rings like the doorbell in a little country store and I want to puke and I sink to one knee, exhausted, and see Richie between two fat dark Defiants with his arms folded, nodding carefully as they talk to him and chew on ciggies.

'R-Rich,' I stammer, afraid to vomit. 'Help.'

'Now now, boys, quit the horseplay,' he hollers, cheerful, as if I'm playfighting instead of getting abused. 'I'll give you each six months for affray if you're not careful.'

So fuckin casual, like this is all easy if you're a bigshot hero with the power to get people locked up. God damn it – need to show the straighto that cockroaches have uses, too.

I struggle through the guys and get to the safety of the two senior gang members talking to Rich. Why the actual fuck is Rich doing anything other than shooting and tasering?! Can't believe I've brought my only friend with me here, and he's pal-ing up with the bad guys. I catch my breath and pick glass out of my sore head and the gangsters snort at me. Richie shakes his head and goes, 'Sorry about this.' Can't believe I came in here to save his ass and I've ended up embarrassed and broken begging feral fuckin' teenagers not to smack me over.

Richie winds up his man-to-man conversation, says 'Thanks, I'd appreciate that a lot' to the gangsters for some reason, and they shadow him as he approaches a set of stairs leading up to an apartment unit on the third floor of the compound and jogs briskly up it. 'You'd better come up,' he calls down to me, 'Can't have you getting into trouble down there.'

Honestly, man, we live in an unfair world. Why Richie hasn't been nailed to the Trophy Wall I do not know.

Richie is about to knock on a door, but a senior Defiant guy with a silver ponytail and black shades taps on Richie's fist and Richie unwraps his fingers and the senior gangster does a special knock, two sets of three knuckles, then waits ten seconds. They push on in, and I'm running up the stairs, thinking, this is it. This is fucking *it*. She must be in here. We got her, bounty time, goldmine, baby, and it took less than a day to get up here and achieve what we've achieved. Usually God shits on me, but today he's pissing gold all over my face. Barbie could be dead, she could have a needle sticking out of her arm right now, but nothing's gonna stop me hogtieing her and putting her in Richie's boot and trading her in for some large notes back in Whangārei.

Except here's what we see: two mattresses in the centre of a dusky room where light doesn't get in. Wild Grouse whiskey posters plastered over the windows. Bedsheets used as curtains. Chips of glass in the thin carpet.

No Barbie.

No humans of any kind.

'We're thinking Barbs was holed up here?'

'So I've been told,' Richie goes, tutting, peering, craning his neck. 'She turned a few tricks from these, er, premises. If you can call it that. I understand the reason they let this Kenny hang around without getting his patch was he'd procure ladies for the boys.' He pauses, for a mo. 'Procure one lady in particular.' Awkward, now. 'Let's see what we can find, shall we.'

*Yeah, bruz*, I think, *We. Partners. Bounty-huntin boyz.*

A cigar's been stubbed out on one curtain-sheet. Wrappers spill out of shopping bags and a beer box they've been putting their rubbish in. There are wrappers for condoms, ciggies, little Glad resealable plastic bags for packing your weed or crack in, cheap White Owl cigars, NOS canisters, bags of potato chips, more Glad bags, beetroot dip, Dove moisturising soap, more cigarettes, light bulbs with scorch marks on them and little twists of tinfoil, several broken crack pipes, another box of White Owl cigars, a box of fifty Glad bags – plus more broken pipes. Maybe Barbie is clumsy; maybe her man is. Pipes only cost four bucks a piece if you buy a box of 300 in bulk, like I once did. The glass goes dirty brown after just one smoke. Makes you feel like you're not classy. Disposable pipes are the solution. So, a rubbish tip, empty bags of various shit, and overall, a room with the imprint of Barbs and Kenny but no Barbs and no Kenny.

'What do you reckon went wrong with her life, Rich? That made her, y'know. Lose self-respect.'

'Indeed, how exactly does a person with all the opportunities in the world end up a lowlife? You tell me, Karl.'

'I – I ain't – .' Dude's left me shellshocked. Like as if he's saying I'm the male equivalent of a dirty crack ho.

As he's disappearing, I get a second thought. *Take it as a compliment, Karlos. He means you're like a criminal profiler. Only you can see the world from the eyes of the illest lawbreakers.*

Richie heads back down the stairs, pausing to say to one of the gangsters, 'I'll bet this Ken fellow's racked up a debt. If you wouldn't mind pointing us in the right direction, perhaps whatever he owes you will be recoverable.'

The gangsta smears his scarred brow with his fingers, squints, does some mathematics in his head. ''Bout eighty grand, Kenny owes. And you're not fuckin' with Barbara? The bitch? Cause I's gonna make her *my* bitch, y'unnerstand. When she comes back.'

'We're going to, you know, enjoy a few beverages, Kenny and I, when I find the guy,' Richie goes, scratching an itch under the stab-proof vest. 'Where's the best place to pick up a box of cigars to go with them?'

'Vicar Of Liquor,' says the gangsta, pointing. 'Get back up on Commerce Street. Take the first left by the bait shop.'

Damn, dawg. Richie actually knows how to milk information.

Cringing as I squeeze through the narrow neck between the shipping containers, hoping nobody pours a kettle on me, I scurry after Richie, who gets the gate opened for him by a prospie with hungry eyes and a mouthful of smashed teeth. The prospect – who can't be much beyond 12 – looks me up and down and makes a slurping, chewing kinda motion with his mouth. He wants to eat me. For once I'm glad to be in Richie's shadow.

The gate clangs behind us. It's only when we get to Richie's car that I catch up and grab his stab-proof vest and rattle him, irritated that he's so laid-back, so calm. So fuckin professional.

'Cigars?! What the fuck? You gonna tell me what that was all about?'

'I thought you were street, Karl?' He smirks. 'While we were inside, I reminded Mr Johns and Mr Ikilei that they have mandatory appearances coming up in Whangārei District Court a month from now. Gave them advice about how best to prepare to impress the judge. They seemed to appreciate the reminder. Softened them up a bit. "Finesse" is the word.'

'Sounds kinda gay. And, what, they promised they wouldn't hurt you since you were just here to look for Kenny the pimp?'

'Nope.'

'What, you told them you had backup waiting round the corner?'

'Nope.'

'You musta seen how run-down that compound is? Looked like a refugee camp, bruz. They're outta money. They're broke, bet you a million bucks, if they're talking about eighty grand debts and shit. Bro, they fuckin… .' I pinch the bridge of my nose. 'You know them scumbags set fire to this halfway house I was stayin in down Ruakaka ways. I dunno if they were after me personally… think they had some beef with these two crackheads that'd been in the basement for a month. They cocktailed it one day – not even nighttime. Didn't even disguise themselves or nothin, five or six of the yellow bastards rolled down the driveway like four in the afternoon when it was daytime, lit up a cocktail, dropped it down the basement stairs, set this washing line on fire, and the washing line fire spreads up this, like, dead ivy vine upside of the house, lights the fuckin' roof up. Crazy, crazy shit – and we all had to sleep in the place after the fuckin fire crew had squirted the blaze out. We didn't have nowhere else to go. So that's my experience with the 4-13. One star review from me.'

Richie unlocks the car, guides me into my seat.

By now, a whole bunch of prospects are clamouring around the gate.

Two are on top of the container watchtowers. They both have crossbows and they've draped camouflage colours around their necks, like as if they're going hunting.

'Drive, already, dude, fuck!'

Richie doesn't respond. I calm down a little. Guess deep-down, I feel a teeny tiny bit safe with Rich around, now that I've seen his gutsy side.

'So they got a Vicar of Liquor in Kaitaia?'

'Five minutes from here,' he concedes. 'One-twelve Commerce Street.'

'That's where we'll find them, grab 'em, nab em. Then we part ways and, hell. Then I guess our story's over.'

# 7

# "Boost, Richie, boost."

We slow down to forty kays an hour as we roll into Kai-Tai Central. Where the main street intersects with the STD clinic, which is expanding with a second storey and a big new car park, there's a filthy piss shop with unpainted concrete floors so the staff can hose puke off every morning. The whole street is smoky. Someone's burning their garbage in the field behind the shop. This town doesn't have suburbs. Commerce Street presses hard against the oyster factories and farms.

Richie drives right through the Vicar of Liquor forecourt, out the other side, goes up the street 50 metres, and stops. I'm thinking maybe I've eaten something bad because my stomach's crumpled up like a used condom.

'Enter separately. You first. Get moving.'

I flop my feet out and onto the pavement, hovering with my door open.

'Stay cool, and don't come close enough to attract attention.'

'I'm just nervous, is all. 'Member when Toby stapled the back of Barbie's skirt to the flag then started hoisting the flag up the pole? And everyone saw her pussy?'

'Karl. Find the target and remain close. I'll follow soon after. *Do not engage.*'

I drag my feet, getting out of the car and moving along the street. A giant buzzing neon sign resembling a whiskey bottle blots out the sun.

Being outside the safety of Richie's car makes my dick retreat up into my belly. I'm stalling, okay, I admit it – see, if Barbie's a crackhead with an uzi, she might start firing. I rummage up some memories of her. Memory-Barbie is the one I wanna bring back, the one with *Barbara* written on her locker in glitter pen.

I'm getting pictures in my head of Barbie at school swimming sports, trying to pull a swimming cap down over that epic blonde hair of hers while she argued with her way-less-hotter sister Shana, who was judging and timing everyone, because she was a nerd with short legs and a haircut like that nerd on Scooby Doo; pictures of Barbs standing beside overturned hurdles on athletics day, crying. I think we were maybe in a mixed soccer team, when girls could play with boys, and there'd be girl-boy punch-ups all the time. So much gets eroded in your head. Every time I drop acid, that's another five or ten memories lost.

There's a familiar-looking poster pasted on a pillar for the Bay Blue tat show on December 19 that the blue gang are putting on. I read it, note the date, fantasise about going, hitting someone up for an apprenticeship, learn the ropes, new career. Except right now my career's supposed to be Private Detective.

I light a dipper as I walk into the bottle shop. Vicar of Liquor is a big warehouse with roller doors and a strong breeze. No one gives a fuck about smoking rules. It's two seconds before superheated particles of meth are floating through my throat and telling my body to stop taking life seriously, and I'm looping a pyramid of vodka bottles and sucking special smoke and between the monuments of grog, I'm spotting a woman in a leopard print tank top slurping an energy drink whose hair is held up with black stockings tied tightly, holding that hair up like a bunch of glowing hay from a rabbit's cage, and I'm giggling, I'm excited an–

Bingo. It's her. Bony and lightbulb-blonde, like Cinderella from that Disney movie, if Cinderella was a crackhead.

So this woman with skin like trim milk, sort-of greeny-white, that you can tell is junky-thin and damaged and has spots on it, she looks tonnes like the Barbie we knew back at Sacred Heart. Just mummified, is all. Dried-out, held together by hair spray and tats. It's definitely her, wanderin round like she has no idea people are worried about her. Not sure what she'll think of havin two people coax her butt into a car to drive down to Whangārei. She's presumably pouring all the family money she can get her hands on into this short-arse dark brown skinny rasta guy with dreads hovering nearby, real grubby-lookin cunt, and that's coming from *me*. They have an invisible cord that tugs them back together whenever they separate a few metres in the

Mixers aisle and they're babbling some conversation about what juice they need. Getting fucked up tonight and sessions with Barb to pay off Kenny's debt to the DMC, I imagine.

Woulda been nice if one of the locals had told the cops she was marching around in daylight, but then again, Northland locals don't like to stick their neck out and pry into each others' business. Few years back, five hundred million bucks of crack got brought in by boat and only two goody-goods out of two hundred thousand raised the alarm, so there ya go.

I'm trying to sneak around these guys like a cat so I can get a good vantage. When I get upwind of the stinky, wet-dog-smelling motherfucker I see that Kenny – it must be him – is even more disgusting than I realised, with a bundle of dreadlocks in a pile on top of his head, a couple of loose limbs of filthy sticky hair bapping the back of his neck, and a portable speaker in his pocket rattling with reggae. Dude's got no shirt on and his pants are some billowy fabric that looks like the sails of an Arabian junk ship. Like Bob Marley mixed with Aladdin.

Just as bad as the no-shirt is the lack of shoes. Presumably the Defiants've been taxing him the money he gets from his girlfriend 'cause of his massive drugs bill and I'd imagine he's taken a few kicks to the head if he doesn't care about how hobo he looks.

While I pretend to choose between vodkas, Barbie comes up behind Kenny and drapes herself on his shoulders, resting her head as if she's going to sleep. I notice the baggy fuck's got five boxes of White Owl cigars in his right hand and a bottle of hooch in the left. Barbie's got a bottle in each hand too.

I ain't a medical expert, the only doctor I know is Doctor Dre, but one thing that's good about being on crank is it speeds up your reflexes, so time slows down.

Right now Karl the Kamera is seeing slow-motion taking place. Richie – moving like a street mime – emerges from inside a metal shelving unit and places a hand on Kenny's bare chest and I hear some words about police and I'd-like-to-ask-you-a-few-questions. That's a score for us, but Richie doesn't seem to have a plan for apprehending Bounty Barbara, who spreads her stance like a cornered chicken lookin to run through our legs.

Those chunky glass bottles in the crackheads' hands? They can't be good news.

Mattera fact, Richie's pretty much pressed the on button, 'cause suddenly it's *on*.

'Duck, Rich.'

Kenny swings a big clear bottle at Richie's head. Richie steps backwards, seizes Kenny's arm and raises his knee into Kenny's elbow. He almost snaps the arm, but I can see he's more intent on Barbie, and he tosses Kenny off, not, like, tossing him off as in making him cum or nothin, he tosses him like you'd toss a kid out of the way at a lolly scramble and he sprints three steps, moves his head to avoid Barbie's bottle, grabs Barbie's wrists, spinning around behind, forcing her down, kneeling on her spine, tying her hands like shoelaces behind her back and saying loudly, 'Police.' There are a lot of truck drivers in budgie smugglers in this store, and if they decide they don't approve of police tactics, they won't wait till next week to express themselves with a letter to the editor. In fact, considering most crusty Northlanders' opinion of the cops or vaccines or any kind government, they'll probably join the ruckus against us.

We need to take our captive and go.

Since Richie's trying to cuff Barbs, it's over to me to grab Kenny, who's about the same size as me, but twice as filthy and desperate. I'm not sure how to place a hold on a man. I grab the dirty gronk's dreadlocks and try to bop the cunt's head on the naked concrete floor until the cunt's unconscious.

I hiss and pull my hands back instantly as I see the gleaming tip of a needle sticking out of a dreadlock.

'Motherfucker's booby-trapped!' I screech. 'Bruz, we gotta take Barbs and jet. Hurry! He's getting up!'

Richie stands up, one arm curled like a python around Barbie's shoulders, squashing her arms and pinning her in place. To hold grubby Kenny as well, he simply steps on the guy's wrist. The heels on Richie's police boots are an inch of solid rubber. I think I hear wristbones crack.

Richie's holding both of them; I'm picking up beer cans and apologising to the store manager. Confused, high, I think I accidentally say we're the Fashion Police.

When we hit daylight and wince and squint and fumble for our car, I notice Richie has no gun and no taser and realise he hasn't given Barbie any reason why he's squashed her boyfriend and he's arresting her.

'Let me go let me gooooo,' she bleats. 'I'm being kidnapped. Faaaaaaark.'

To say it's awkward marchin her over the road is an understatement. She sticks her foot in an uncovered sewer, drags her toes on the asphalt, tries to hold onto the aerial of a car. She's been wearing these slutty pumps with high heels and her uncovered toes start bleeding. Unemployed, perma-pissed, hostile people are peering out from storefronts.

Richie unlocks his orange Kia, opens the boot, finds a siren and light and places it on the roof, givin' his girl-car a bit more balls.

'I'll pop the boot, yo.'

'She's not going in any boot.'

Richie forces Barbie into the front seat, forcibly puts the seatbelt over Barbie, who sobs and complains and fiddles with the child safety lock. Richie hasn't handcuffed her. He reciting her rights and telling her why he's detaining her, something about Section 15-b of the Apprehension of Victims of Trafficking Act 1999, detain, reclaim, necessary force, UN Convention on the Trafficking of Women, blah blah blah.

Kenny, behind us, is trying to cobble together a posse on the forecourt of Vicar of Liquor, tugging and urging some bystanders who just want to collect their bourbon 'n cokes and go fishing. Kenny's dancing and waving and flapping like an angry tribesman. For now, it's okay, 'cause I sense Kenny's too skinny to fight us. What makes my cock really shrivel up, though, is Kenny's got the power to say any damn thing he wants, and in a desperate-ass, lawless town like Kaitaia, if he bleats to any gangstas, we could have a problem on our hands.

Rich revs the engine, turns the wheel – and waits politely for an old lady's car to pass at 35 kays an hour.

'Boost, Richie, boost.'

We got her. We have secured the target, the prize, the bounty. The story, the saga, the fable, the legend of the cash cow. It's almost over. I can phone Mr and Mrs Konstantinou and ten thousand bucks can be in my account overnight.

Everything is peachy, for the first ten minutes.

For the 600 seconds, yessiree, we're following the fifty kay zone down south outta town till it becomes a hundred kay zone. Kaitaia waves 'Goodbye and good luck' with palm trees, a playground, a holiday park, a summer sky blue as a swimming pool, fluffy clouds, and a sign that says *Haere ra* and *Dovidenja* and *Farewell for now, come back!*

It occurs to us halfway out of town, though, that if we came this way into Kai-Tai to grab Barbie, we're going to have to drive out the same route. Back past the Defiants' clubhouse, where they were lookin at us real hungry half an hour ago.

It ain't good that Richie has – thoughtfully – left Barbie's car window open, and that Barbie's screaming something very dangerous as we pass outside #4133 State Highway One.

The Defiants' compound. Where the number of agitated people in the black and yellow bee swarm has increased to about thirty.

Mingling, swarming, amped and angry, waiting for a reason to attack, the bees come out of their hive and stand on the kerb when our car zips past – not nearly fast enough – and Barbie screams, 'They're gonna nark on all you fuckin guys, follow this caAAAAAAr.'

# 8

# "You ever wondered why I'm fucked up now?"

Letterboxes zip past. Up front in the passenger seat where we've strapped her, Barbie gnashes her teeth and froths and complains like an Insinkerator and the wind blows the spit back and I feel it spraying on my ears. I offer her one of Richie's apricot-testicles and she swats the bag out of my hand. While she huffs and puffs and knots her elbows, hunched up like a crayfish, I study her body. Needle dots on the inners of her arms. Fine yellow hairs on crusty skin. There's a tattoo fading on her ankle, a not-very good tattoo. Real erratic thickness of the lines. I'd heard Barb trained up as a tattooist at one point when she owed some thugs some skrilla. She'll do a lot for drug money, this girl. I reckon I can straighten her out, though. Straighten us both out, maybe.

It was good to leave behind that dropkick man of hers in the rear-view mirror, running out onto the Vicar Of Liquor forecourt, dreadlocks flapping on his shoulders like a cape, dropping cigars everywhere, ranting and swinging his arms.

We pass an avocado orchard with a bunch of Samoans in it. They lean on their spades and stare at me as I pass. I remember, I promised I'd sell the King Cobras a bunch of hot credit card numbers down in Auckland, then I went over to Otara and sold them to the Tribesmen instead. Maybe word's got around. KCs, Tribies… something's making me fidgety. Sore stomach. Needles under my butt.

Going past the Defiants' place felt like walking over hot coals. Something ain't right.

'I think we should swap, Rich. Get her in the back. Can you pull over?'

'Your thoughts?' Richie mumbles to Barbie, sitting stiff as an old person, barely even turning his head.

Barbie's been preening in the pull-down mirror, checking her camel teeth, scraping shit out of her gums. I finally hear her speak for real after, God, what, a decade of imaginging her voice?

'Probly best if you rearrange your bums,' she goes. 'Your arses is gonna get sniped, I reckon.'

Far out – dunno why I'd thought she'd speak like Princess Di. Reality hits. Westie accent. Sounds like she has to clear out a garbage dump from her throat every time she speaks.

Richie eases to the side of the road, so slowly that a passing ute with beehives in the back honks at him as it overtakes. 'It's not entirely safe for you, ma'am.'

'I'm all good, G,' she snorts. 'Yous might want a bulletproof vest though.'

Oooookay? Farkin hell, that's a crude-spoken woman. Spastic of me to've thought she'd be polished like her rich fam. Can't wash the black out of a black sheep.

Richie gets out of his Nanamobile, comes around the front, lets Barbie out as a little sunshower sprinkles us. For a moment, she's standing over me, a little sunlight between the soggy clouds shining nicely through her bun of straw-coloured hair. I can see her braless nips, I can see a little tattoo of a butterfly around her belly button. It's a weird, poetically beautiful detail for a grumpy bleached woman with period-face.

Meth takes 25 years off your life, they say. That's like a third, meaning for each year you live you've only got eight months enjoyment before you go way too soon onto the next year. Your birthdays come more regular, bam-bam-bam, then you die of a heart attack. To me, she looks like one more smoke and she'll lose the last smidgen of hotness she was born with. I swear that when this is all over, I'm gonna deliver her into the hands of people that can grow her beauty again.

Barbie gets into the back with zero resistance, wobbling with a little drunk-high crack-high, sporting a cheeky little smirk, like as if she knows something we don't. I pretend, for a second, that we're a couple getting escorted to prom, then Barbie pulls down the seat divider and puts her tattoo-spangled arm on it and goes, 'Go sit up front. You're creeping me out.'

'Sorry, I's just, um. Just admiring.'

Her eyes go cold. 'Hundred bucks for thirty minutes if you want a piece of this. Talk to Kenny. Sure he'd be real happy to take a call from you.'

*You don't have to sell your ass*, I wanna tell her. *You're beautiful, Barb. Treat yourself better, know what I'm sayin?*

God knows what's been goin on in her head. I'm startin to think she hasn't minded bein pimped out by Kennyboy much. Probly gave up hope some knight in shining armour would later come for her, after her parents proved themselves useless.

Richie nods towards the front seat and I shift up there, proud to be riding shotgun, but a little deflated, like a penis that's gotten scared. Guess I can understand why she might not be stoked to have the lifestyle she was dependent on ripped out like an IV drip.

I'm left sneaking glances of Barbie's rack in the rearview as we slowly trickle out into traffic. Slow enough to let anyone catch us up – which I've got a baaad feeling about.

I fiddle with the car stereo volume as we build up speed and enter the foothills of the Mangamuka mountains. Richie slaps my hand but his resistance fades as Hootie and the Blowfish comes on the radio.

I put on a nice deep barrytone and pinch my ear, simulating Hootie's legendary diamond earring. They're singing our favourite song.

'You're only mad at me until I get myyyyy way,' I croon. 'Somethingsomething million bucks and when she died, it came to me, there's nothin I can dooo, I only wanna be with youuuuu. Hootie, bro, Hootie, 'member?! C'mon, sing along! I know there's a little Hootie in you!'

'You're cognisant that the singer wasn't actually called Hootie?'

'Ooh! I like this part! C'mon bruz – don't get mad at me just 'cause I'm lookin at other girls.'

'I'm "mad" because you live for the moment without thinking about the consequences of anything and it's people like me who have to clean up after you,' he complains to the steering wheel.

'*You're* not arrested,' Barbie sneers at me, 'So why the fuck you back here? Who the fuck are you guys, anyway? You're an informant? You're undercover with Detective Dick?'

I need a smoke if I'm gonna tell my story. I pull the box out of my pocket. Most of my smokes have broken in half from all the twisting and crumpling. There are two ciggies left, dipped in delicious crack to keep my hunger away. I light a dipper and I'm thinking: at least one's left.

'Don't even dream of smoking back there,' Richie goes, slowing down at the last BP service station before the Mangamukas.

'Stop the car then,' I go, and snort. 'Stop the car and let the Defiants catch up.'

Richie doesn't say shit. He flicks an indicator on, thinking about pulling back out into traffic.

'One for me,' Barbie goes.

'Er... Can't really go giving these things away. These're worth like twenty bucks each, they got something special in 'em, Barbie, if you catch my drift.'

'*Barbie?*'

'What, people don't call you Barbie anymore?'

'I recognise this arsehole driving, but you? I supposed to know you?'

'Shyuh. We went to school together.'

'And we were friends?'

The answer is no, in truth, but we saw each other like a hundred times a week. I have a memory of pashing her at this party after we won the dodgeball tournament, whupping Bream Bay College in a best-of-three, though I'm not entirely sure the memory wasn't just a fantasy dreamed up on shrooms. And she was dabbling at the time. Well, more than dabbling. Losing whole weekends to drink and drugs and dudes. Dropping out of sport. Embarrassing her parents. Hate to admit it, but she might not remember.

I give her a taste of my spicy smoke. She's taken two puffs before Richie opens the door goin 'Oh no no no, not in my car.'

'Just let us smoke outside, bruz, c'mon. I'll call you Officer Whateverthefuck in front of her if that's what you want.'

'This is so irregular,' he's going, 'Get over there – over! I have petrol to pump.'

Barbie's arms and legs are free, and so are mine, though we don't leave the forecourt of the BP gas station. Many people would run in a situation like this. Others would choose to smoke instead of run. We blow about 300 seconds' worth of escape opportunities while Richie finishes pumping the gas, uses a fucking napkin to wipe a dimple of spilled petrol from the rim of the tank, carefully puts the pump back, pays, exchanges how-do-ya-do's with the forecourt attendant, and comes back to fetch us, stopping only to use a second napkin to dab his shoe.

Earthquake behind us. The growly rumble of bikes from somewhere in the hills.

'Now we run,' I joke to Barbie, elbowing her in the side, and I can see she's thinking about it.

'Just drive me back to the clubhouse,' she goes. 'Look, you fuckwits are in trouble and you know it. That arrest was wayyyy illegal. And Kenny's gonna beat the shit out of me when he catches up with us, so congratulations. You can own that.'

She's right. I try talk Rich around.

'Bruz, just park up here for a bit. We'll hide the car, let the bikers go past. Maybe go down one of these unsealed boat roads to the river, hide out with Barbie overnigh–'

'Quit callin me *Barbie*! God I hate it!' Barbie reaches across and tries to headbutt me, or bite me. 'And watch your mouth round me, Karl. You're gonna getcha self hurt.'

'You remember me!'

'She's right,' Richie chimes in. Green hills, forest reaching over the clifftop road. He's going past all sorts of good hiding places uphill at his steady 89kmh, and nobody knows it but I'm sweating like a paedo. Every grumble of Richie's engine's got me thinking there's a swarm of Defiant wasps coming up behind us. They'll buzz loud, they'll move as a unit, they'll sting us from fifty different angles. 'I wouldn't wind her up too much.'

'A'ight, look, spose I remember you a little,' Barbie goes. 'Failed to wipe it out of my memory, more like. You used to pull my frickin ponytail. I was going out with Tony Hauraki, and he got kicked out of school, but he comes marching back into cooking class, d'you remember that? We had that Martha Stewart sorta lady as our teacher. I can't fucking remember– '

'Ms Moko,' I go. 'Loco Moko, we used to call her, Ms Kokomo and Coconut and shit. Fuck was that country she was from? Zimbabwe or something?'

'Anyway, Tony Hauraki hadn't been at school for a week, just smoking weed and playing Grand Theft Auto, but he comes in and you were literally over at my table, prodding my pizza dough, and he grabs your shoulders like he's about to hug you– '

' –and he knocked me the fuck out with a headbutt. You'll have to say hi to him for me. Tell him No Hard Feelings.'

'He hung himself bout four years ago.'

We look out the windows for a while. It was always amusing that the Konstantinou girls went to Sacred Heart. They seemed so airheaded, well, Barbara did, not so much her sister, Shana, who used to go around correcting people on their English. We treated them like they were less human, as if they *chose* to be the kids of rich immigrant success-story Thai Coons.

'Guess it's sort-of alright to catch up with you motherfuckers. Oi, d'you remember you had that wang-hole in your school shorts, Karl? You used to stick your hand in your pocket and poke your finger out of the hole, pretending it was your finger, and chase us girls and we'd all scream and shit?'

'That was my athletics, Barbie. Only reason I'd run.'

'Gah! Stop calling me that!' There are unmistakable happy twinkles in her eyes though, like part of her deep-down enjoys the banter. Her bangles spin as she talks with her hands. 'You ever wondered why I'm fucked up now? Maybe it's coz I got, like abused by creeps like you?'

'But you were rich. You shouldn'a had problems.'

'My *parents* were rich. My *sister* ran the Young Business Club at school. Me, I was just a little girl with a whole bunch of responsibility on me cause we were, like, the only Greeks up north. Gimme a break.'

I stare out at a chicken and egg factory in some shithole bend-in-the-road called Rangitihi. Feathers and dust stick to Richie's windshield. It stinks, and we all hold our breath. Richie's car veers to the far side of the road as he comes around a corner, and he suddenly pulls over, squirting soil.

'I think a bit of a conversation needs to happen,' Richie goes, cricking his neck. 'Better to get these things out of the way.'

We're against an electric fence. Cows back away from us.

I feel like crying. The low rumble has turned to a buzzing. That'll be the lighter bikes, the nifty 250cc dirt bikes they make apprentices ride. Motorcycle clubs put apprentices on little, humiliating bikes –the type they can ride into a store, grab a hoodie-ful of vapes, squeal a 180 and ride out of there.

In a convoy, ten apprentices ride at the front, followed by ten prospects, with their rockers and jackets, not a full patch. Skull-masks, thick shades, black scarves, thick gloves, and after the prospects are another ten fully patched gangsters on 1200CCs. Bikes built like tanks. War bikes. You can hear 'em from the other side of a mountain.

'Guess we might have to catch up some other time,' Barbie goes. 'Cheers for the trip down memory lane. I've gotta get back to work.'

'Back to being kidnapped, more like.'

'I wasn't *kidnapped*, shithead. I don't wanna be with my friggin parents. And I don't wanna be with you two homos.'

I grab her wrist but she wriggles out.

'My ride's here,' she goes. 'Laters.'

We are surrounded by loud, black wheels. Big men in thick black armour with yellow accents the colour of biohazards and wasps and danger. One of them, the only one with a completely yellow helmet, dismounts his bike – and takes a photo with his smartphone? What the fuck?

His knock, on Richie's window, is surprisingly polite.

Richie is not polite, though. His lips go tight, his eyes squinty. He tightens his stab-proof vest, flips the central locking, extracts his keys and unlocks a square box under the steering wheel. I've been in enough cop cars to know that's the place cops keep their handguns.

# 9

# "Fuck him up good, Dad."

*'Drive, bruz, drivedrivedrive.'*

I am fiddling with the child lock on the door, trapped in a wussy car on top of the Mangamuka mountains with big rumbly smog-spewing wasps swarming us.

'Nothing to be frightened of, team,' Richie mutters. Fear has found its way into the car like a gas. He's hoping it'll evaporate if he acts calm. He shifts the gear stick into two, though. Second gear's hardly used on automatics. Second's reserved for squealing around in a circle as fast as you can when you're cornered.

It's the hangarounds and prospects that've got me shitting myself. They approach, hungry-eyed, nipping and sniffing at the car. They've only got the most basic helmets on, plastic helmets more suitable for BMXing, angry kids with no parents to tell em to chill. They have scary patches and metal on their jackets plus thick, weightlifter belts made of meaty brown leather. They wear black hoodies with yellow hi vis vests, the type road workers would wear – as close to the club's yellows as possible. The pups take off their helmets, exposing raw scalps. Pimples and scratches. They have beards, goatees, little moustaches. They probe the car for a weakness.

'Well, Dumb and Dumber, time to say bye-bye,' Barbie goes, holding her hands up, as if she has handcuffs to get off. She isn't cuffed, never has been. 'You won't be seeing me again.'

'We'll come back for you,' Richie goes, low and mumbly. Richie's concentration is on his gun.

'Fuck you mean come back?!' I gasp. 'Put your foot down! Don't let her get out!'

I can see Richie's eyebrows wriggle as he does calculations.

'You have to drive, bruz, off the edge of the cliff, into the bush, man, *somewhere*. They're gonna rip the doors off.'

'That would be unwise of them.'

'Then they're unwise, fuck. Barbie!'

'We're also surrounded, Karl. I don't intend to hurt anybody.'

'Tell em to clear out of the way, use your horn, fuck!'

Barbie shakes her head. She gets wholesale prices on crack from this gang. They've been generous, taking her in, and she doesn't wanna disappoint them any more. Plus her pimp needs his finest ho to come home.

A barrel-of-a-man with military medals fixed to his jacket waddles over, putting the kickstand of his bike down. His bike has to be 2200cc, more powerful than our car. His motorcycle is so chunky that he's got a pitbull dog and two kids on the backseat.

The man's big as a water tank wrapped in leather. His skin is pink and shiny and covered in sweaty stubble-hairs. We're looking at the president. I've seen him on Police Ten-7, Crimewatch, on the news, on Facebook. Heard his name uttered with dread at parties. Pork is his name, or 'One Percent Pork' to use the whole title – means he's like a one percenter and a cop. Yeah – a former cop. How fucked-up is that. Dude's an urban legend. He's spent his life twisting out of trouble like a crocodile. He puts on these charity boxing tournaments all the time, reckons his little lackey 18-year-old thug hangarounds need him like a mentor, tries to get the public thinkin the DMC is a boxing and motorcycle club instead of a firm, and he boxes hard – loves to challenge the CIB to a scrap for charity, smash detectives' heads in. Know why? Got kicked off the force for doing a home invasion on some dealers, taxing their merch. God, have I heard some stories about Pork... Pork taxes everyone who wants to get into the club bad enough. The tax is you have to hand your missus over to him for a night. Prima noctre, apparently it's called, some old creepy medieval shit, cause he's basically the king around here. Pork's taken bullets and blades over the years but no one's ever knocked him off his perch. There's muscle under his scaly, 63-year old crocodile hide.

'Bout to break ya glass in a minute,' he goes, knocking on Richie's driver's side window. 'Open the fuck up.' His medals tinkle and shake. *Please be smashproof glass*, I pray. Pork hasn't explained why 50 wasps surrounded us and forced us off the road, but this whole intimidation thing must be about taking Barbs back with force. Must mean Barbie's a valuable revenue source to 'im, like some kind of cash cow.

His fat fingers tickle Barbie's door on the outside, fat gold rings chinking.

Pork thumps the window again. The zips and buckles on his jacket make little noises as the old pink crocodile leans in front of Richie's face.

'Three seconds.'

Richie is squeezing the steering wheel. He's never made a mistake in his life. If he opens Barbie's door, that's a mistake. If he touches a single biker with his car, that's a mistake. If he negotiates or compromises with a criminal, that's a mistake.

Richie chooses to do nothing. He sits facing forward, still as stone, waiting for the swarm to clear.

Pork buckles his yellow helmet, gritting his teeth so I can see his old-man gums and white stubble, checks the kid on the back of his bike is safe then does something wild.

He headbutts Barbie's window like that goddamn bald-headed headbutting dinosaur. For most people, headbutting reinforced glass would knock them the fuck out, but not for this tank-of-a-man with his helmet on like a demented Spitfire pilot. He reels back only a tiny fraction. Pork has to weigh 140 kilos, maybe even 150, the fat fuck. His body absorbs the shock and he gets ready to ram again.

A small chink appears in Barbie's not-so-smashproof glass.

Up front, Richie has his little gun box open. He's even fingering the handgun a little bit. Dude can't bring himself to use a weapon, though. Not Richie's style. Shooting someone, to Rich, is impolite. Even if they're tryina kill you.

All on its own, the crack spreads. The window begins to fail with a root-system of cracks. Crinch-crunch.

The end begins.

With two headbutts, a crack that looks like a spiderweb appears in the window, then Pork winds back his fist and punches the glass into fragments. Barbie covers her eyeliner-black panda-eyes, but she doesn't cry. Cubes of safety glass decorate her. Pork reaches in and grabs her hair. He'd haul her through the window-square if he could, but it's not working out. Barbie's complaining, 'Ow-ow-ow.'

'Fuck him up good, Dad,' squeals Pork's child – or his grandchild. Some bastard feral spawn Pork is training to grow up gangster.

The pitbull growls like a chainsaw. The bikers rumble and spit and fold and clamour, folding and unfolding their arms, preparing for a feed. We are wasting their time. They want us to roll over and give up and let ourselves be devoured.

Richie, staring straight ahead, waiting until this annoyance leaves his life, speaks through his teeth. 'I am not opening that door. She is in my custody.'

'Warned you, fuckin pigshit,' Pork roars. He walks around to where Richie is and headbutts the driver-side window and leaves a fat star-shaped crack. Immediately after, he punches the window with a fat fistful of rings. The window disintegrates. Another punch. This time, with no glass protecting Richie's skull, Pork's fist reaches all the way to Richie's ear. Rich absorbs the punch and falls forward on the steering wheel, restrained by his seatbelt, the hard plastic mushing his cheek up so his teeth and gums show. His sleeping fingers touch the gun he was too polite to raise.

Pork reaches his thick arm through the smashed drivers window, flips a switch, undoing all four door locks. I've given up hoping there's any option to protect Barbie anymore. She steps out by herself, closes the door neatly, picks glass out of her cleavage and gives Pork a kiss on his sunburned, scarred old cheek.

'Thanks for comin to get me.'

# 10

## "A friend doesn't ask why."

A Peppa Pig opens the hatch on my cell.

'Copley! They want a talk with you.'

It's a Papua New Guinean cop – and she's a she. I'll be damned. I collect exotic cops, and this one's a new variety, like a rare Pokémon. What'll it be next, I wonder – a wheelchair cop?

'Who's they?'

'Seniors. Put your hands behind your back and walk out gradually, please.'

'They want me for like a little debrief or full questioning?'

'Boss didn't say. Just come out, please. We need this cell for serious crims.'

'I *am* a serious crim, lady. I almost got a kidnap-person back from, like, being held hostage.'

What happened was the Defiant spun around on their bikes and Barbie went with them. I was left on the lonely Mangamuka mountain pass with nothing but birdcalls, broken windows and a comatose cop – a cop who groggily woke up after I poured mouthwash into his ears and chucked me back in the cells after we'd limped back to Whangārei, wind smashing us through the missing window. Apparently I was on police bail the whole time and if he let me go, there'd be a warrant out for me.

The cop's nose squiggles and squishes. 'Smells like piss in here.'

She looks at my undies. Still black, still damp, still reeking. Finds me a boiler suit to step into.

Around a couple grey hard angular corners I encounter Richie McMullan in Senior Constable Mode. There's something different about Richie's face –

a bulge, a hump of medical tape holding down some cotton wool and gauze against the side of his head where his ear got busted by Pork. Seems strange, to have your wounds treated. Me, ever since I was, like, 13, when I've had an injury, I've always just walked it off, you know, let the air cure it. Like, I got a head injury from taking on this bet that I couldn't dive into the shallow end of the school pool in winter and my skateboarding helmet not crack, so I strapped the helmet on and dove in and okay, yeah, it cracked, but I was fine, apart from the blurriness and throbbing skull and a patch of my hair turned white. If there was water in the pool, people woulda been mega-impressed. Anyway the point is people reckon head injuries is supposed to make you dumber and more impulsive, but look at me. I totally walked it off, and today I'm a success story.

For years, actually, there's been no one to patch me up. No mum, no sisters, no lover, just Richie. Hate to say it, but Richie's the closest thing I ever had to, well. To a partner.

Speak of the devil, Richard McMullan – former best friend – is right here in the interview room, Whangarei Police HQ, three hours drive south from where we lost Barbs. Snitch Rich doesn't give me any special recognition when I enter. Beside him's this Asian chick with fussy horn-rimmed glasses in a suit with letters sewn into her buttoned-up blazer saying *Integrity Inspector*. She could still be sorta hot 'cause of her skinniness, like Barbie. I get a stiffy as I'm thinking about that skanky leopard-print singlet of Barbie's and I have to cover my crotchal region with my hands.

The Integrity Inspector woman's notes are on a tablet or iPad or something and she flicks through them with neat, fussy shiny fingertips.

'Comfortable, Karl?' Richie goes, 'Good. This is my reporting manager, Integrity Inspector Nantakarn.'

'What's a integgidy inspector?'

'You've heard of Internal Affairs?' the uppity stiff Asian woman goes. 'Think of us as the people who keep Internal Affairs clean.'

My eyebrows nearly shoot to the roof. So she's a nark that narks on narks. And she has power over Richie, who's so clean he makes bleach look dirty.

'What's integgerty though?' I ask them.

They roll their eyes at me. They think I'm joking.

This is such bullshit, all these interrogations and rule-followers leaning on other rule-followers leaning on honest heroes like Yours Truly. There's top shelf hand sanitiser on the table, 20% alcohol, and they're not even drinkin it. Pompous, yo. These people need to cut loose a little.

'I'm about to hit the Record button, and you're about to make a statement describing your involvement in the translocation of Barbara Konstantinou.'

'Bro, I'll bet *you* know a few trannies' locations, ya queer cunt.'

I elbow Richie, try to get the prick to have some lolz.

No one laughs.

'Can I smoke?'

'No.'

'Vape?'

'You don't have a vape.'

'I was gonna borrow one.'

'I don't have any vaporisers to loan you, and I doubt Senior Constable McMullan does either,' Nantakarn goes, adjusting some pins holding her hair back. 'So I'm going to begin– '

'What happened to your hand? Zit broken?'

'My hand was injured while arresting a man on drugs who was assaulting his wife and children while I was off-duty. He grabbed my thumb and pulled it so that the tendon was extended until it snapped. I was a top three regional grade water skier; now I'm restricted from entering competitions for two to three years, subject to review by the Waterskiers' Board. Anything else I can help you with?'

'Nah nah, cheers for sharing.' *You're into water sports, come see Karl sometime*, I feel like saying with a wink. Then I get the impulse to apologise for whatever crim assaulted her. 'Sorry he fucked up your hand, that guy... Guess I can make you feel better. Tell yous how I got onto Barbie's thing.'

'Barbie's "thing" is a matter we were gently negotiating before you got yourself involved, Karl,' Richie goes. Richie is on a maaaaassive period. Bet there's blood dripping from his pussy down his pants right now, spattering on the floor. 'I think you owe us an explanation.'

Without a smoke, I put two fingers to my lips and take an imaginary puff.

'A'ight. So Facebook's where I first heard about Barbie droppin off the face of the earth, it wasn't just Shana posting the Missing message, it was a couple of her gal pals, peeps from school and shit. Everyone was posting this piccie of Barbie looking happy at some party, and the words on it were like– '

Integrity Inspector Stickupherass begins hassling me. 'Give us a date, Copley. When you first became aware Barbara Konstantinou was being sought by her family. A precise date.'

'Date, ahhhm, musta been a week ago, just. Yeah, I remember. I seen that new *Avengers* movie that day...'

'D'you have a receipt for your visit there? A ticket stub?'

'Stub schmub, you just walk on into the movies when the peeps at the counter aren't looking. Fuck kind of a sucker gets out their wallet when you can see movies for free?'

Nantakarn makes a note on her iPad.

'Look, forget I said that, I's just joking,' I tell her. 'I'm more a DC dude than a Marvel dude, anyway. Cause how Batman solves crimes, I can relate, y'know?'

Nope. Cold faces. They cannot relate.

'Like, okay, so I'm on Facebook, on my phone – well, okay, if you want a receipt for that it wasn't my phone, per se... '

The corner of Richie's mouth curls upward.

'...Look so I'm hangin out at, y'know, basically the normal set of places you go if you're in town and you've got nowhere to snooze. Museum's good, there's that spot behind the big giant fig tree where there's a pile of blankets, you can lie down and sleep. Botanic Gardens are not bad, either, if you're ever needing somewhere to kip, there's that greenhouse with the room full of those foam pads they use around the gardens? Get a mean sleep on them. Nanta-whatever-your-name-is, you should write that down. Anyway... where was I? Oh, yeah, Barbie missing on Facebook.'

'Can you refer to her as Barbara?' Integrity Inspector Stick-up-her-ass interrupts me. 'This is not contributing well to the case I have to submit to the prosecutor. Bar-bar-uh. Three easy syllables.'

'Shana wroted on Facebook that Barbs was last seen about five weeks ago in the company of that lil cocksucker with the dreadlocks.'

'Kannaya D'Souza,' Richie goes. 'Barbara's... *handler.*'

'Kenny the pimp, on the streets,' I tell 'em.

Nantakarn's fingers bang a little information onto her pad.

'Mr Copley, what made you think you could act as an unlicensed bounty hunter to seize this woman?'

'Eh? You can get a licence? Where do I get me one?'

'The information's easily found on the ministerial website. Please go over how it was you began your pursuit of Ms Konstantinou.'

'Guess I asked around, first. These two patchmembers at the Hika Tavern I yarned to said they'd given Kennyboy a hiding a few times, honestly, about three separate people all reckoned they'd smashed his nose up at some point. Dude must have a smashproof face if he's still walkin and sniffin. Oh, yeah, speaking of sniffin: I figured Barbie would have some top notch gear. Find the babe, find her pimp, find the fix, that's what I figured. So Facebook's the first place I went, and her tweets. Two months ago she TikTok'd that Ken cunt, whole video about how she's hashtag #Inlove#sohappy. Then on Facebook, bout six weeks ago, she put up that meme sayin, like, *'The difference between friends and acquaintances is when you need help and it's life or death, a friend doesn't ask why.'* So that said a fair bit about what she was up to, I'd say, and I was following her at the time, y'know, I'm always interested in what my school bruzzas are up to. Anyway, she's turned out a whoooooore, man, she took dick like you wouldn't believe. I mean Pork the biker prez, for example? I heard he rooted her on the dance floor at Saxon one night, trippiest, ugliest, wildest shit you ever seen. That's what I heard. These underworld peeps, man, they're all connected. Anyway, I always wanted to sorta whisk her away from the thug life, get her to pay off my debt collectors and court fines, maybe even introduce me to some manager so I could put on gigs again –

'Gigs?'

Richie clears his throat. Most people I know would hoik their green snot into the ashtray, but not Little Dick. He swallows his and goes, 'Karl believes he's a performer.'

'Don't say it like that.'

'I have a shortlist of the charges I'll be preparing to lay against you, Mr Copley,' Nantakarn interrupts, leaning towards Richie. '1, theft, that's not been denied; 2, Fail to report threat to kidnap, 3, Interfering with a police investigation –

'Whoa! Time out!' I look at Richie. He's supposed to step in and help right now. 'She ain't charging me with this shit, seriously?'

Richie folds his arms and leans back. He ain't my bruz. He's just another pigshit. 'I cannot understate how disappointed Northern Police are with the absconding of Barbara Konstantinou. We're under a lot of pressure– '

'Well don't take it out on me! Fuck's wrong with you? Do I look like a gangster?!'

Nantakarn takes a print-out from a Hello Kitty folder and slides it across the table at me. It's my LinkedIn profile. I'm at a party with Filthy Fews and we're hanging a dummy dressed in a police hat and setting it on fire.

'LinkedIn profile of one Karlos Copley,' Nantakarn goes. 'Occupation, "Gangster," it says here.'

I shake my head. Fuck this humiliating shit.

'I put it to you you had early warning that Ms Konstantinou was going to go missing, whether or not she was cooperative. So you know more than you're telling us. Untrue? What made you convinced Barbara Konstantinou was near Kaitaia?'

'The-the-the intel from them bikers at Hikurangi? Right, Rich? Step in here, bruz, help us out.'

'Yes, actually Senior Constable McMullan, I've been looking forward to your input here – certainly, I'm baffled by your motivation. You removed Copley from the cells and escorted him quite a distance - can you speak to this? Your last shift was on the Friday, and then? Can you explain your decision to escort Mr Copley upon his release from in custody?' Nantakarn opens a file on her iPad. 'I'm struggling to find any rationale for signing Copley into your custody on a charge likely to result only in a fine, and then failing to notify prosecutorial services. Were you planning to bring his theft charge to prosecutorial services or not?'

'Yes.'

'You took this man on your little road trip for what reason, then?'

'I'd rather not say right here and now.'

Ho ho ho! The Perfect Prefect's in trouble for the first time ever! This is gold. Wish I had popcorn while I watch this.

'I'd encourage you to, lest I commence a motion to have you investigated for mismanagement of your investigative boundary. You're one of eight third-tiers covering Northland policing district. You drove through the jurisdiction of at least five other managerial constables in the weekend's incident. Now I'm to understand you drew your weapon on motorcycle enthusiasts? Or you were close to? I hope you know they've laid a complaint with the Independent Police Conduct Authority. I'm told one of them took photographs of you drawing your weapon?'

'This is fucked,' I interrupt. 'Don't be harsh on old Rich. The bruz made a mistake. Thought he'd get a little overtime or some shit, it didn't work, not that big a deal. Plus Barbie's in the same place as where we first picked her up, I think–'

'Tell me under what grounds you entered the clubhouse of the Defiant Motorcycle Club.'

'Who says I did?'

Richie almost stands up. Half-yells, 'Quit the poor-me stuff, Karl. Integrity Inspector Nantakarn has every reason to think you arranged for Barbara to be handed over to your underworld friends and now you're looking to cash in on it somehow. Considering Barbara was taken from us following an effort which you, my friend, led us to, I do have my suspicions. Settle this once and for all. Did you set us up?'

Fuck this. I'm sick of my best bruz talkin to me this way.

I slap his tat-free, piercing-free, cold-sore-free perfect ginger fuckin' face. We're both stunned, for a sec. He's knocked back. His seat's teetering. He's trying to stand. I'm up. I'm anticipating some knuckles in my eyes, so I attack the cunt, pushing him right up against the wall, but he's slippery, ole Littledick, boy is he slippery. He gets heaps of leverage and throws me against the one window – all with his hip bone, surprisingly. It's impressive, actually, that Bruce Lee shit of his. I'm agitated, needing a drug fix, and I'm throwing out punches quick and sloppy, muscles contracted and sleepy from being in the cell. One decent punch catches the nark-pig-piece of shit in the throat and he withdraws the hold he was trying to put on me then changes his plan and does something worse, kneeling on the ground, pulling me down and catching my forearms, tucking them under his knees and pressing down. My arms are being crushed by his body weight. My face smacks uselessly against his thigh. I go to take a nice bite of piggy bacon but he pinches some artery in my neck. Off button.

I let my head flop, let the exhaustion-sweat dribble off me. I'm seriously out of shape. My face must've flushed the colour of beetroot. Richie hasn't sweated whatsoever and his shirt's still tucked in.

'You're…cug… sposda say something…. guh-gangsta when you waste someone.'

'Well I'm not a gangsta,' Richie goes, brushing himself off. 'We have a visitor arriving, and I suggest you tidy yourself up.'

Fuck me sideways. Holy embarrassment, it's it's-

'...aaand this would be Senior Constable Richard McMullan,' Nancy Drew says. While we've been scrapping, she's been showing somebody into the room.

Unlatching the door, Nantakarn leads this new chick in.

Like a cleaned-up, crack-free, fleshier, happier, cleaner version of Barbie, with hair that doesn't have chopsticks in it.

'Shana,' I say, pulling my head out of Richie's guts, smoothing my singlet out. 'Yo.'

# 11

# "I got her away from the bad guys."

'Coffee, Shana?' goes Sergeant Stickupherass, I mean Nancy Drew, I mean Nantakarn the Integrity Inspector. Mean to crims; nice to civilians.

'I'll take a coffee,' I go.

'You can have some fresh fruit,' Nancy Drew goes, sliding a bowl of bananas at me.

'No coffee for me, thanks,' Shana goes, squeezing into the table. Short, boyish brown pageboy hair; neat suit jacket. Like a little kid playing Grown-ups.

'I said I want a coffee, Miss Piggy,' I remind the copper. 'I pay my taxes. Well, I don't pay tax, on principle, but I would if I wanted. Milk and two sugars. Cheers.'

Nantakarn takes a deep breath, raises her hands, flips them and places them flat on the table. A relaxation exercise. Like as if she's trying to restrain herself from killing me.

Richie gives me a look and I hear his voice in my head: *Don't piss her off.*

I take a good eyeful of Shana. She still gives off annoying Goody-good vibes. Richie can have her. Shana's two years younger. I guess her responsible lifestyle is 'cause she's witnessed her sister mess up so often. I fingered Shana when I was 13, in the handicap toilets at this school disco we had, not that she probly remembers. My finger'd gotten bit by this guinea pig I was trying to glue to another guinea pig to make this kind-of guinea-hydra monster and my wound was all infected and leaking pus and glue and it had a Bart Simpson Band-Aid on it, well it did before I fingered her, then I lost the Band-Aid, probly up inside her. We'd never even exchanged words, really, before I tugged her off the dancefloor and we got points off each other. I got a nice stinky finger to stick under the nose of my bros, and she got points for getting with an older, cooler guy, 'cause she was never in my year, Barbie was peers with my ass, and Shana was just the nerdy little sister on the school council.

Did I jab my finger up Barbie's nose and go "This is what your lil sis smells like!" while Barbie was in the corner sitting on Mike Mercer's lap making out, though? You betcha.

Anyway, sitting here in this cold, unfriendly, sterile-ass interview room, I wonder if Shana's thinking about Bart Simpson Band-aids right now. She seems to be looking across at Richie Rich, not me. In fact, if you think about it, she's avoiding looking at me on purpose. I kick Richie's shin under the table and he flinches and cradles his bandaged ear. There's a wee strawberry spot on the white bandage. Must've started bleeding when we were fighting just now.

Integrity Inspector Stickupherass pops a single breath mint into her mouth and begins talking. 'I'd like to thank everybody for attending this meeting,' she goes. There's something a little bit perkier to her words, and she's making an effort to smile between sentences. What's goin on? Why put on a show for Shana? Nancy Drew turns her iPad upside down and drums her fingers on the top of it. 'I'd like to tell you all a story about my administration. My administration has never had an editorial written against it by the Northern Advocate news, nor has coverage been interpreted as critical of my administration. As I've emphasised on today's blog, which I'd encourage you all to subscribe to, my administration has not been criticised by Council. My administration has had its funding increased by the allotted two percent allowed in two budgets in the six years I've been in my position as Integrity Inspector. Kay? My administration is *per-fect*. I do not use that word sparingly. My administration is *faultless*. Free of corruption, free of incompetence – that's why we're known as The Best Administration. TBA, we call ourselves. And this review we're conducting here? This is routine TBA to me. The outcome of this meeting has limited variables. None of the variables allows for harm to my administration. Just to clarify.'

'Yes, ma'am,' says my bitch of a snitch of a bruz, taking orders from a little girl who's probly too short to ride half the rollercoasters at the fun park. Pretty sure she was a prefect at Whangarei Girls High School, Rhodes Scholar after that. Three overachievers at the table.

'Shana,' Nancy Drew continues, clearing her throat, picking up an apple and biting some vitamins and minerals, 'Thanks again for attending – it's so important to the culture of my administration to have whānau with us every step of the way.'

'Translation: Please don't sue me,' I go, and kick Richie again.

'How would you like it if I sued *you*, Karl?' Shana goes.

'I'm bankrupt so joke's on you, Barbie Two.'

'Let me finish' Nancy Drew snaps. Pretty harsh words from a delicate little Geisha mouth. 'I'd like to hear your ideas on what outcome you might desire, regarding the return of Barbara. We're about keeping families together, here, Shana.'

I wanna say something Mafia to Nancy Drew, something staunch like Tony Soprano would say, but I don't have the guts right now. Instead, I listen, and as Shana talks, her voice is soothing, like them honey and lemon lozenges you nick from the pharmacy when you've got oral thrush or whatever.

'Well, I mean, guess it's no secret my sister has addiction challenges. Iiii had concerns about her that Odyssey Outcomes was just washing its hands of,' Shana goes. 'I mean, I was the only one looking after Barbara, except for the drug dealers of course, I mean, ummmm, let's see, gawd, I mean, for years now Barbara's been increasingly involved with, you know, hangarounds, prospects.' She looks around to check that we're keeping up. 'Ah, patched gang members, coming home at 9am, sleeping till 6, getting up and eating Special K and Red Bull while the family's sitting round the dinner table, I mean, hel-lo?' Shana looks at all of us for confirmation that we're unimpressed with her sister. 'Barb's lifestyle was the defi*nition* of unhealthy. And this guy working in the avocados she had at the time? Gave us all devices – I mean, his entire *trunk* was full of phones and pads and computers and– '

'Cool story,' I go. 'Look, I've really gotta be going. I got shit to do. Can yous bail me or what?'

I stand up, turn and stand in front of the door. I face it for ten seconds, twenty, thirty... this shit's getting embarrassing. I turn back around. They're all seated at the table glaring at me.

'I'd like to provide my perspective,' goes Richie, lacing his fingers, adjusting his buttons, licking his ginger moustache in Full Snitchie Mode. 'Shana, look, you know I'm dissatisfied with the outcome of the action I instigated as a result of a tip-off from an informant who proved be unreliable.'

'Registered informant?' goes Nantakarn, looking at Richie real cold.

'No, but he is *an* informant.'

'Did you begin the registration process?'

'I did not, Integrity Inspector.'

'Did you notify any of your superiors you were pursuing Ms Konstantinou based on a tip-off from an unregistered informant?'

'Intuition was the main – ah. No.'

'Say that again so the recorder can pick it up.'

Richie actually puts his mouth closer to the recorder. Sellout. 'I had intuition guide me toward what I thought would be quality information sourced from Karlos Copley here. I wasn't completely mistaken. As far as I'm concerned, we got Barbara Konstantinou into police custody, albeit briefly. I'll concede she was not exactly secured for as long as, uh, desired. That's something I'm trying to remedy.'

'You lost her.'

'We misplaced her.'

Shana reaches across the table and brushes Richie's hand, a little bit flirt-a-liciously if you ask me. 'We're all on the same page. Don't sweat it too much. I'm mad as hell at Mr Copley, here. Karl, she could be dead. Are you even listening? You're standing in front of the door for some reason.'

'I was tryina storm out.'

'Well it's inch-thick steel and it's locked, dude, so storm back in and sit your butt down. There's no remedy for what you've done. My sister's with the bad guys cause of you.'

'I got her away from the bad guys, for cryin out loud. Want her back? Give Pork a ring. Make a trade-off. That's my two cents.'

'And how d'you expect us to do that?'

'I got his number on my phone.'

'You've got our main suspect's *cellphone* number?'

'Course. Everyone's got Pork's number. Where else ya gonna score drugs from?'

They all frown. Like I've stepped in dogshit.

'I'm surprised yous haven't phoned him already.'

Nancy Drew splutters, 'That's probably not going to– '

'Best idea I've heard all morning,' Richie goes, standing up. 'I'll get your phone for you, Karl. Unless you have any objections, Integrity Inspector?'

# 12

## "Group Awesome, roll out."

What Rich calls church is more like a five-star hotel. For a dude on police bail – ie. babysat by an anal cop – this is pretty sweet. Plus we get a show on some sort on stage – there's a drum kit and microphones and speakers and projector screens. I can pretend we're at a strip club, 'cause some of these Christian honeys are immaculate.

We're inside the giant new Salvation Army church behind the KFC in Whangārei. They seem to have built it while I was coma'd out. Thick, fluffy cream carpet, details of marble, pews made of wood the colour of maple syrup. Scented candles, soft air coming out of heat pumps, and the place smells as nice as real good urinal cakes, like when you spend the night in a sleeping bag in a public toilet and you luck out and score a freshly cleaned one. Flatscreen TVs on every wall, an iPad on the end of every row of seating. The place has a high ceiling, fancy lights hanging off the beams, which reminds me of the one that the bruzza Jimi hanged himself from after his comedy shows didn't work out in Hamilton. Happened when we were like twenty. We had a funeral for that one at a church, actually. I remember searching the rows of people in black suits for Richie and not seeing him 'cause he was away at police college. Never to be seen again.

Least, until I busted back into his world.

Barbara was at that funeral too, come to think of it. Barbie the departed. God, she could be dead now, too. Getting to second base with Jimi up in heaven.

Here, now, in the Salvo Fortress, I shuffle behind Richie, feeling like I've got the invisible shackles on again. I take off my beanie. My scalp's so greasy, I can smell it. Heads turn. I feel conspicuous as fuck, specially 'cause my hoodie's got *FTP* written on it and this is presumably a church of nark-lovers. These people in church bunching near the front, chirpy and happy to be out of bed, teenage girls with slim necks wearing t-shirts tucked into hot little skirts, boys with shirts as white as tablecloths, old fogies with their hair petrified with gel, women with new haircuts dyed real good, smellin of expensive shampoo. Everyone skux, and handsome, and their attitudes are even warmer. It's me that's cold and stinky and trashy. Me that needs to scurry outta here. I am determined to get Barbie back, don't get me wrong – it's just a little hard to do today, with no resources, no money, no ride, not many people who trust me, barely bailed with a shitload of police attention, led by Shana who represents some seriously rich people who want their seriously irreplaceable daughter back.

'Psst – bruz – that's her.'

Nancy Drew Stickass is taking a seat in a pew and I'm trying to tell Rich he's been followed into church by his so-called integrity inspector, which should terrify a normal person. But it's as if he actually enjoys it.

'I invited her, Karl.'

Makes me wonder why he invited me – cause I'm stickin' out like a cold sore squirtin' juicy herpes over everyone.

Richie goes to greet Nantakarn, shakes her hand. She has a coating of foundation across her face, wet black lashes, lipstick. She looks straight-up bangable. She doesn't browbeat the bruz or say any harsh shit to him. They make each other laugh, then Richie comes back to me, and I shake my head.

This is Wonderland, G, and I'm Alice.

Sitting in the pews as the music changes, I put my lips near my man's ear.

'What are these? iPads?'

'Kindle Fire. They're tablets – e-readers. So parishioners can read the holy book. We don't do paper, here. Clean and green.'

'Can I keep one?'

'No, you cannot keep a three hundred dollar device.'

I drum my fingers on the back of the pew in front of me. In movies, mafiosos meet in cathedrals so they can discuss business without getting snooped on. The religious thing's supposed to be just an act. Just a cover. Except I think Richie's serious about all this God garbage.

'Bruz.'

'What now?'

'What do I, y'know, *do?*'

'Just take it all in.'

'And the holy spirit'll wash over me? Said on the poster in the lobby. I could go for some spirits right now, tell ya what.'

Richie does a 359-degree lookaround. Trying to find some eyes that share his annoyance with me.

I pull my head away and drum my fingers. I'm wondering which side of my jacket to stash a Kindle Bible tablet in. In my life, I've stashed plenty of tablets up my ass but never one this big. Then I'm like, of course. Stupid me – the answer's obviously the pants. That's the golden rule, man. People that get picked up for shoplifting are dumbasses. Me, I learned the hard way, security guards, pigshits, hell, even the president of New Zealand, none of them are allowed to touch you downstairs. The Undie Zone's out of bounds – and that's the beauty of it. You can stash anything inside your crotch and ass and no one can search you there. So that's where I'll stash my stolen Kindle-Bibles. Just as soon as I can clear the witnesses out.

Richie stands up and goes and gets his shoulder slapped and squeezed by some young men. The way they're grinning at him with their shiny teeth and big Adam's apples, he either pays them to do sexual favours or he's like some kind of father figure, like a youth group leader maybe. I follow him, hovering close like I'm a little kid and he's my dad. Everyone's singing Jehovah this, Nazareth that, Lift me up, I wanna be close to you, all that shit, and Richie says loudly over the music, 'I wouldn't, if I were you.'

'Wouldn't what?'

'Wouldn't risk doing serious prison time for a stolen bible.'

Richie gives me these cold eyes. I adjust a couple of things, move my dick out of the way, and the Kindle-bible falls through and thuds onto the carpet by my ankle. Shit.

He begins singing. Serious, bro: *singing*. Like a girl.

Halfway through the bit in the anthem where they're going Praise his naaaaame in that weepy Black American style, a PayWave eftpos terminal comes round and Richie waves his cash card and I look over and see how much he's gifted and there's a disturbing amount of zeros on his donation, woo-whee. It's annoying, too, cause I was gonna grab me a few coins if there was a collection plate.

After the song ends it's something called 'What's Up time' where apparently they're tryina be street and you're supposed to turn to the people around you and ask them Wassup? and everybody shares their problems. It's disturbing, man. Rich shakes the hands of all these family people and a couple of big units slap his back and – I swear I'm not making this up – this 10-out-of-10 redhead honey kisses Rich on the cheek and her husband doesn't even knock Richie out, I can't believe it. Like their whole community's built on love and trust and all that fluffy fabric softener shit.

Me, I've got no one to wassup with and I step over some annoying shiny church shoes and hang out in the shadow behind this pillar against the wall. I don't belong here, yo. My clothes stink, my fingernails are dark green, I've worn my undies forward and backwards and turned them inside out. Even if I had a wash and a new set of threads, chances are I'd still feel dirty. I was born dirty, 'cause my mum poured pints at the Working Men's Club and got Salvation Army food packages full of white bread once a week. All I can do with my dirty life, I guess, is try help get Barbie home, then maybe I'll take the Jimi way out and top myself. No one'll miss me, least of all Richie.

They do another unending praise song and dance with three guitars and ten singers and two drummers, and I keep asking him the time and it's 19 minutes long, the fuckin thing is, in the end, but eventually church wraps up.

We must be three years into the future after that neverending shit.

'Where to now?'

'Beach,' he goes.

'Nice!' I squeal. 'We'll get some brewskies, get a little something to smoke, bucket of K-fry, coupla surfcasting rods, we'll– '

'Youth Group,' he says, 'Come this way. A few friends to pick up.'

Mothers flock around him, asking what happened, stroking his busted ear. 'Work stuff, that's all,' Richie tries to go. Far, man. Rich could have any of these chicks. It's like he's laid a foundation by being, like, polite and a good listener and supportive.

There's free food out in the wharekai, which means *Kitchen/Dining Room*, according to the label. Everything here's got a Māori subtitle label and I notice about half the people here are posh Māoris, real stunning Māori princesses with immaculate black hair and good-looking men in tight black t-shirts with thick shaven pythons coming out of their shirt sleeves. Jeez, man. Yet another reason why Kaucasian Kracker Karl don't belong. It's like I'm getting shoved down the ladder of importance. Maybe I should emphasise that I'm homeless so they get me on stage and treat me like a king, take my brown socks off and cure my toe-fungus.

Cruising the white trestle tables in the wharekai, I pull my FTP hoodie away from my belly and stack the little hammock with cookies with fudge on top, bagels with Swiss cheese spilling out the sides, kranskys and salamis. Then I cram my mouth with cookies so no one can try make conversation with me – not that anyone tries.

A Christian woman placing a fresh cheesecake out on the one remaining spot on a table asks if I need anything else and I'm like, "Where's the smoking area?" and her face crinkles up.

Meanwhile, across the room, unreachable thanks to a huddle of 20 clean Christians, there's Richie, being mobbed by fans, including fucking Nantakarn the Nark. They squeeze his arm and drizzle their fingertips down his chest and I notice they're all nudging their sons over to him, the clean high school athletic boys with long basketball limbs and thin necks and veins bulging in their forearms.

The mob begins moving and the honeys wave their fingers as Richie leads the boys off to war, or something. I quickly swallow a hunk of quiche and try to get in the pack.

'Group Awesome?' Richie's calling, making sure he's got three, four – seven boys. 'Let's roll out.'

*Group Awesome?! Fuck kinda inspirational shit is that?*

Through the lobby, past the Pastor, through about ten high-fives from clean-cut Māori dudes who really oughta act less joyful, Richie leads his little flock. Out in the carpark he switches vehicles. The mob of teen boys and their 28-year-old leader pile into a van and it rocks as everyone buckles their seatbelts in.

Carefully packing my pocket with a salmon and cream cheese bagel so it doesn't squish, I'm the last to hop in the van and just as I'm about to do so, I see written on the side in flawless, expensive airbrushed letters, YOUTH GROUP AWESOME.

Surfing?! Can't believe he's taken us surfing. G – taking a person away from shops, away from pubs, away from dealers and cellphone towers and places you can catch a ride… it's just not right.

The water's fuckin wet, that's the first annoyance, and the sand is all sandy. The irritations keep piling up. I curse Richie for springing this on me, and it sucks I don't have anything to drink or smoke to convert this into a party.

Put me in a bank, in a clinic, in a choir, put me in a school, hell, put me in a hackathon with 13-year-old geeks and I'll find a way to get a good time and get high or low or whatever state I need to get in to counteract the heavy shit I've had that day. But realising I'm stuck at Ocean Beach an hour from Whangārei with a youth group leader who I know for certain's never even smoked a ciggie, listening to Christian rap booming out from our van in the carpark, bruz, you may as well put me in Siberia.

Ringleader Richie parks on this flattened sand. He's out of the front seat lickedy-split, bouncing with joy, and that leaves me strapped into a seatbelt by myself with these six or seven rent boys in expensive singlets hopping over me and getting their surfboards out of the back of the van like the Monkees or some shit.

As I'm filling my pockets with any police-issue items I can find – bumper stickers, mints, business cards, and condom packets with Christian crosses on them – wind and sand comes into the van and pesters me, nibbling my shins. It's not even a sunny day, bro, sky lookin all bruised like it got a hiding from the Mongrel Mob. It's nippy. I can feel icy sea-spray pricking my skin. Eventually I get out and scurry a few metres, then turn back and stare at the van: it's just me, the wind, four wheels – and a set of keys sitting in the ignition of a vehicle that's good to go.

*Boost it, Karl. The world owes you.*

How could Richie trust me, how could he leave me with temptation like this? He's put me in shame. That's what he's done. I'd be shamed-out amongst this group if I stole the van. What that manipulative prick has done has made me feel like it's wrong to steal something. And I resent the cunt for that.

I've been to Ocean Beach, I remember as I drag my feet through the sand. I was with, like, six ladies and this pimp, Kirilan from Turkey or Kenturkey or Turkmenistan or somewhere. He was a fuckin' party animal, I tell ya. He got with two of the ladies personally, and I had one, and he got the others suckin his toes in the water. It was wild. We popped a few tabs and smoked two packs of dippers and even though the water felt like being whipped with a cold wet towel, and it rained, we still splashed about and poured petrol on a tyre and built a bonfire and the girls kept calling themselves mermaids and there was, like, a girl of every race and colour and I saw so many damn United Nations titties that night.

Richie's brought my backpack, interestingly, as if maybe he's gonna release me from custody and say See-ya. My backpack is on the passenger seat and I reach inside, past the supermarket shaved ham I had been keeping for sustenance, the classy top-quality stuff they call Champagne Ham that the cops put in my box of possessions when I first got locked up that they've finally given back to me. I pull my Sacred Heart yearbook out and underneath is my puffy jacket and I think about hauling it on so I don't get touched by wind or droplets or laughter.

There's one other thing in my backpack. It's pressing on my brain. Gotta deal with it sometime – though munching my stinky Champagne ham is the first priority right now.  Spose I could leave the ham a couple more days, cause champagne's supposed to get better with age, but I've got the munchies real bad, in spite of the religious feast.

Where Team Overachiever and Richie enter the water, there's these two boulders similar-sized, evenly-spaced. I remember sitting on one rock with my track pants around my ankles getting some brain and Kirilan standing on the other rock with his hands on his hips, performin YMCA with his cock n balls. I laughed so fuckin' hard that night.

Kirilan drowned at the end of that summer, bro. Pinoy Cripz did it – fuckin Filipino gangsters, ordered to give Kirilan a scare to earn their patch. They held his head underwater. Real serious fright, it turned out to be. Kirilan had this bach at a sleepy corner of Whangārei Harbour called Parua Bay. They invaded, one night, people told me. Ten of the little Filipino toerags, two on his arms, one on his head. Forced his face underwater. Kirilan drowned in his own damn spa, dawg. What message is a brother sposda take from that? Live a good life, make ladies happy and you get murked. Whole world's unfair. That's why you can't take nothing seriously. Why you should expect disappointment.

Richie blows a whistle tethered around his neck and the li'l God Squad pile into the unpainted wooden changing shack. 60 seconds later, he blows his whistle again and Richie's junior snitches come out with their shirts off and with wetsuits around their waists, standing on the hard black wet sand where the foam fizzes. Richie holds a stick about a metre off the ground and they each have to do 20 kicks above stick-level, else he gives them a playful tap on the flesh behind their knees. With their wetsuits flapping around their waists and their hard grape nipples pointing north, Richie walks a line of them with his open palm out and they practice throwing boxing jabs. Mostly he shouts out 'Excellent' and 'Again.' He doesn't call them whiny little maggots or anything motivational to toughen them. 'Pair off!' he yells, and blows his whistle, and while their rubber and foam and zips swing around, brushing their knees, and sea-spray makes sand stick to their chests, they throw each other and grapple and wriggle in the sticks and seaweed, putting their heels in each others' armpits, twisting each others' elbows, pressing their faces down, saying 'I'm placing you under arrest!'

Police cadet training. As in, preparing to apprehend criminals. Shit, man. I bet Richie wishes he could go back in time and train himself.

The golden Christian youths, cleanskin, hairless, ripped, tattoo-less, they're all acting in these simulated pairs, crim and copper. Kinda like me and Rich. Cept me and Rich aren't pretending.

Richie's putting his hands on their shoulders and spines as he pulls their zippers up, stroking their lower backs and – I shit you not – patting their butts, sending them into the waves now that they're trained up as junior SS. They surf and laugh and paddle and ride with determination. Young and skilled. Amazing mentor. Full of promise.

God, man. I've never really had a dad near me. This is that father-son shit you see on movies, but, y'know. For real.

I don't know exactly how long the little overachievers are out. It feels like four sessions of one hour. They come back to the van and scoff apples and protein bars. I study their muscles and their abs. I sit there wanting a smoke so bad that I put a bit of driftwood in my mouth and light it and it tickles the back of my throat and I wanna puke.

Sun pours through this notch in the clouds and I shelter in the van and think about motorcycle clubs and church and Nancy Drew. I try and work out why I'm always in recovery mode, why I'm always partying hard to get over the upset of being locked up, or picking fights to get my mind off the deaths of friends, or banging freaky witches in the Portaloos at glowstick festivals then wondering the next day why mums at parks urge their kids not to play too close to me as I wake up on the park bench.

Thank God it gets too cold and rough for the boys. Richie inspects their surfing injuries as they come back in with fistfuls of plastic and cans which they stuff in a rubbish bin. A youth sits on a rock and Richie picks up one of the boy's legs and tries to find where the blood is coming from, tracing the crimson stain with his fingers. Richie loves kids – not like a paedo or nothin – he could be someone's old man. I can see that. Dude's got all the wholesome vanilla man-loving qualities. He's fit, caring, active, hard-working, disciplined. He's smart, he's popular, and good things are attracted to him. Our friendship was like one of them curled-up things butterflies sleep in, a crispylips, and now he's a butterfly that's out and its beauty is showing and – not that I'm queer for saying this – the discarded crispylips has no right to try and suffocate the beautiful butterfly.

The troop finish their swim and get back in the van and strap in. Rich and his boys compare the cuts on their legs and in the rear-view mirror and I realise this is the first time in a week I've seen Richie smiling and bantering, his eyes creasing with laughter. He gave his whole day to these little hardouts. He didn't surf himself, didn't swim, just stood out there waist-deep getting cold and sandy. I wanna tell him he's a beautiful butterfly, but it sounds weird, so I go back to being predictable Cynical Criminále Karl.

Until Richie's mobile phone goes off, that is, and I snatch it off him while he's driving and read his message, just to stir the pot, just to drum up some excitement, and low and behold, a certain female is reaching out to a certain law enforcement officer.

Shana bloody Konstantinou.

Fuck this to-and-fro teenybopper messaging shit. I tell her to come over to Richie's house with a quick message before Richie's God-gang bend my fingers and prise the phone out and give it back to Richie.

Too late, though. I've invited Shana over on Richie's behalf, cause little does she know that if you want Richie, you get a Komplimentary Karl, too. I'm going to help it up or fuck it up.

Probably both.

# 13

# "You've got some growing up to do."

Fairway Drive. Posh side of Whangarei. Broad tree-lined boulevard with gorgeous 1960s Art Deckle mansions and Teslas in every driveway. Flashest street in Whangaz. Richie's pad is number 202. The number probably represents the number of times he corrects people on their English every day.

Shana's SUV is a whole lot of car for a woman that doesn't have a wedding ring on her finger. Maybe that's half the reason she's emerged out of the night, parking right outside Richie's bachelor pad, hopping out and taking a deep breath as she faces his house.

Shana Konstantinou has parked under one of the big, protective oak trees on Richie's street. I can see she's got one of them personalised plates. It says KNSTN2. Konstantinou 2, eh? Interesting she thinks of herself as second fiddle. I don't have a sense of what this lady is all about, yet. All I remember is back in school, Shana was a real softie, always raising money for starving Somalians and finding furniture for crims on parole 'n stuff. She was also desperate and jealous and eager to do anything to get ahead, like so frustrated that she didn't come out first that she spent her whole life chasing Number One. Being a little sister means you're always the one left behind the fence when the big kids have jumped it to go play.

Senior Constable Under Review – yup, SCUR, that's his latest title, as if he's a scourge on the squeaky-clean system – SCUR Richard McMullan comes out with me onto his porch with one of those long-ass police torches they use to smash poor people. He's been letting me crash on his couch so I don't make a nuisance of myself downtown and we've been playing Grand Theft Auto on his Playstation and I've been running over hookers and smashing bystanders with a baseball bat. I've been winding Richie up cause he tries to only apprehend crims in the game but his avatar accidentally whacked a little girl in the face, which was epic lols. Maybe Shana will join us for a three player game.

Richie's searchlight paints colour on our short-haired female friend on his lawn, wearing a pant-suit that's swirling coffee-caramel colours, dynamic shades of dark and light brown. She wears a cardigan on top, that's red, and red shoes that match the top. Hmm. Dressed to impress. Earrings, too, hanging low enough to scrape her shoulders. She'll probably tell us she's stopped by on her way from somewhere important, but y'know what? I reckon Shana's scrubbed up especially for some Littledick, if you know what I mean.

'Kia ora, kei te pēhea koe?' she goes, stepping up onto the porch. It's not Māori Language Week – Shana's just trying to be a perfect citizen. 'Cheers for inviting me over.'

'I actually didn't invite you over,' Rich responds, ants in his pants. 'You need to know my phone's been... Well, our friend texted you from my phone. I never invited you here, for the record.'

'Ha ha. Seriously, you guys... same two clowns from school. I'll take a coffee.'

'Sup, Shana.' I move to the front of the porch. 'Rich, gonna tell her the freaky shit you get up to on your little Playstation late at night? This guy's a stone-cold killer, Shayn. Twacked a little girl right in the head.'

Richie's face goes dark. 'Least I don't punch women in real life, Karl.'

'What, that one thing on my record? Pfft, she was a pigshit. Doesn't count.'

'Women aren't "bitches" and police aren't... that horrible word, Karl.' Shana's a foot shorter than me, but she's looking down on me right now. 'You've got some growing up to do.'

She trots up the stairs and we follow Rich back inside the house, Shana's fancy shoes clopping. He stands sentry by the door then pushes it firmly closed behind us and snibs one, two – a total of three locks.

That clacking, tocking sound coming from the bottom of Shana's suit makes us focus on her. Her expensive shoes have got thick wooden heels. The lady's really gone all-out. I wouldn't fuck Rich myself but I guess there must be some appeal. Rich is like a clean square new G.I. Joe action figure out of the packet, if you bought a ginger action figure (which no one ever would, yuck) and he comes with skin with wiry orange-haired brown-freckled muscle on a short body. 5'6", plain hair with no imagination, nearly crew-cut. Cross between a baby and a grown-up, if you ask me. Not like me, I'm pure youth, and youth's the coolest age a motherfucker can be. Peeps call me immature on a daily basis and I always blush, like, Cheers, guys.

'I'm gonna go ahead and sit,' Shana goes, taking a place on Richie's fresh-out-of-the-packet furniture, drumming her fingers. He has two two-seater couches. No idea where I'm supposed to sit. This could get awkward.

'Smoke if you want,' I go, offering her something smokeable from my packet.

'Not in here,' Rich snaps as Shana reaches for one of my ciggies.

'Calm the farm. Better head back outside to smoke.'

'You gonna offer me a coffee?' Shana goes.

'Beer for me.'

'I don't stock beer and I don't have many caffeinated beverages unfortunately,' Richie goes. He hasn't sat down. 'I don't get a lot of –'

'You don't get a lot of visitors 'cause you're a loser who for some reason doesn't have no wife and no kids. We get it. You're a bumboy. No one's blamin ya if you're born that way.'

He shoots death-lasers from his eyes. 'Rooibos, I've got. Ms Konstantinou, I'll make you one of those.'

'Don't ever call me that again. It's Shana, honey.' She smiles sexily as she says this.

Holy moly. These two are gettin' it on just with their words.

We smoke on the deck as we wait for our drinks. I'm surprised to find she's got that little bit of badness to her and I wonder how deep the badness goes. As I light her smoke, conversation gets going immediately and Shana won't shut up.

'KarlKarlKarl,' she goes, battling me to talk more. We've just come off some banter about the wacky, violent start to getting Barbie back. We're in good spirits considering a woman might be dead now. 'Listen, darl, I've seen you run through the girls' changing room at school with your little dingaling out, mmkay, I know a lot of your embarrassing secrets.'

Her eyes are wild and she's talking real quick. Hang on, could I have accidentally given her a dipper instead of a normal ciggy? I check the number of meth-dipped smokes in my pack and there's one less dipper than there should be, which means ohhhh shiiii – 'Somysisterlikeliterallyhoggedallthebestboysbecauseshewasliketotallyeasy,' Shana rants, talkin fast. 'Honest, we were all perverted little monsters together. I don't pretend to be the Pope and nor should you. Actually – no, shut up, Karl, d'you know tonight I was actually literally at our community law centre blessing with the mayor. The may-or. I am a curator of art. I am a director of two trusts which direct funding towards young artists. Do I act all High Society? Like, literally, should I be pure and holy for the rest of my life just because I took risks to get attention so people don't write me off as just someone's little sister?'

I'm blinking, man. Not sure if she's asking questions or just likes to hear her words reverbliate off the porch like bat sonar.

I pat her on the back. 'This is good banter, Shayn. Oi, sure you only want a Rooibos? Want something stronger? You got a little party underway.'

'I want my sister back. That's what I want.'

Richie calls us through. He's put steaming mugs of South African tea on his coffee table.

Shana can't sit. She inspects all the stuff on his walls – the MMA trophies, the framed certificates, the photo of Richie with Elon Musk.

She's pointing to a bottle of liquid shaped a like a statuette. Because Richie doesn't have many lights on in the house. I can't tell if the liquor's red or dark yellow or brown.

'That's Unicum. From Hungary.'

'So crack it open,' I tell the stiff prick.

'I won that at the jiu jitsu internationals in Singapore. I got silver. There was this visiting team from Budapest... '

'So crack it the fuck open! What do you think it's for, decoration? This has gotta be the first time you've had friends round in, like, a million years.'

'But it's never been... ' he begins, but doesn't finish the sentence. Guess he's realising how Assburgers Syndrome he sounds.

Richie gives in and brings us a glass of the liquor each. It's a pathetic little amount he's poured into the glass – only one shot – but I'll humour him. I inhale parsley and mouthwash, and that ticklish, irritating, burning sensation of alcohol. I toss the drink back in one.

I give Shana a second smoke. Shana supplies the lighter. The night is purple 'cause there are fancy street lamps in iron cases painted green. Through the window blinds, a dog trots along the far side of the street. I'm about to make a joke about Richie arresting the dog for not having any ID, but I don't. It's getting tiring, hassling these guys instead of enjoying them. Plus I've decided, after being left out of the Hitler Youth at the beach, that I'm gonna try get more respect in the world. I'm gonna get Barbie back to her family and when they offer me a Royal Humane Society medal, I'm not even gonna be there to accept it, 'cause I'll be a volunteer firefighter, and I'll be saving a milf from a burning building.

Shana ditches her smoke-butt and goes to the toilet and we hear a flush. Richie's fingers tense into claws. This is gold.

The conversation has cooled and I'm just talking with winks and eyebrows, like, C'mon, lovers. Get it on, already.

'How was the drink?' Richie goes. 'What'd it taste like?'

'You seriously didn't have a sip of your own drink? How many Hungarians' arses did you kick to win that bottle? And you won't even reward yourself?'

'When are we bringing her back?' Shana interrupts. Oh man. 'There's no one else to ask, it's, it's, it's – it's like, it's my sister, you know? She's difficult, God she's difficult, but you have to. You have to.' Her eyes melt. Shana must be hurting real bad.

'I guarantee we'll get her back,' I go.

'We cannot guarantee,' Richie goes. His fingers are laced on his stomach. His feet are evenly spaced on the ground, as if he's been studying a manual on how to fucking sit down like a normal person. '*I* can't guarantee, at least. The restrictions on my duties were formally outlined by letter this afternoon. I'm on professional probation. Not supposed to leave my office.'

'Let's go, let's go, now, c'mon, please,' Shana's saying. Her knees are trembling. Her fists are shaking. That'll be the dipper, cranking her anxiousness.

Damn, dog. First-timer, she's sensitive. What's that Chinese proverb? Give a man a fish, feed him for a day; give a straighto some crack, make 'em jumpy for a night.

'CHAOS have become... involved.'

'Chaos?'

'Criminally Hostile Armed Offenders Squad. Like SWAT. You'll hear about it when the compound's raided. I'm sure the media will fill in the details. Not our job. I'm... I've been ordered to keep to the side. Under review and all that.'

'Shana, man, sorry to break it to you, but you can get six figures for someone that's got rich fams. Not to mention she wants to be kidnapped for some reason I can't wait to figure out.' I cough. 'Reckon she's been sold.'

She looks at me like I've just told her she's got a penis on her forehead.

'Sold? Sold?!'

'Gotta lower that volume, please Ms Konst– Shana. Shana, listen – Karl here is not police. Nantakarn's told me our friend here has a 65% certainty of being charged as an accessory to Barbara's kidnapping.'

I toss the drink back, pour another. 'I can handle another lag. Just put it on my tab, bruz.'

Shana's playing with the blinds, now, twirling them, making them ripple and move, stroking them. 'I brought cash.'

'You brought cash, for... ?'

'To speed justice up, Richie.' Her eyes are hard and straight. 'There's ten thousand dollars in my handbag. Mamá and Baba, they'll give anything.'

I don't stop to ask for details. I cross the room and open up a handbag made of red leather with gold clasps. I take out cash, in twenties. Hundreds would've been better, slimmer, but I thumb through the twenties. I lose count after 70. If there's a hundred 20s, that's two grand, and five stacks of those make–

'Shayn: Forget Richie. I'm your man. I'm goin back out there.'

'Whenwhenwhen? Whencan you get her? Nantakarn and your bosses, they haven't authorised, it's not, they're not– '

'Shana,' Richie goes. 'You're amped up.' He looks like an unimpressed principal. 'There something in that drink?'

The room is light blue now – Shana fiddling with the blinds has let the dawn come in. Damn, dawg: we've been up all night. That's crack for ya. Time melts.

'We're bounty hunters, baby!' Shana goes, and I clink glasses with her. We're drinking and dancing, and it's only just breakfast time.

'Let's go for another ciggie,' I go, tugging Shana's elbow. 'Hey, Rich, we're back on, yeah? With a little cash to splash? Put out a bounty? I'm off police bail, right?'

He's not saying no. That's good enough for me.

The bounty hunting begins.

# 14

# "Know what a finder's fee is?"

Our location is Downtown Whangarei, under five looming storeys of police station with a giant badge big as a billboard. Reminding people who's in charge. Corner of Cameron Street and the paved one that I got my face stomped on that time by those Bangladeshian guys when I sold them fake tickets to the cricket. Walton Street, that's it. I always remember cause when I was getting my skull pounded by these guys' sneakers, I read the detail on the metal plate above the sewer and it said *Walton Street Repairs* and I thought 'How the fuck much are dental repairs gonna cost me?'

Never got 'em done. Life got too busy. Spent the $900 I could've spent on new teeth on prozzies and pokies.

I've ended up working with Shana. Hovering in her SUV and everything. The vehicle's so massive and new and shiny it barely quakes. Just the tiniest little rumble behind the dashboard lights. There's a pharmacy bottle of Quetiapine in the drinks holder that I can't stop staring at until Shana reaches over and pops one.

Shana's pretty much come in as an umbrella, letting the world know that it's not just cops that've got an interest in Missing Barbs and that the Konstantinou family should really be in charge. Guess she's sort-of a bridge between family and cops and crims. Apparently some of the bikers held this, like, charity fundraiser thing in her community law centre two or three years ago. I even saw a photo of her with her arm around Pork on Facebook which made me go, WTF?

'I feel weird, this morning,' she goes from the driver seat, the drugs wearing off.

'You're excited, thas all. Big day ahead of us, yo.'

It's 7 in the morning. Rich The Snitch was with us a moment ago. We've just dropped him at the pigsty, where he has to brief his bosses on the Konstantinou family's bounty and how Shana Konstantinou – who's the spokesperson for her fams – has said she doesn't mind me helping get Barbie back.

The final words Rich said as he was hopping his tight little buttcheeks out of the door of Shana's car was that he needed to video conference with his little TBA police admin dorks, some of who work from home, doin flexitime, whatever that is. Makes me wonder if he's gonna make an effort to relate with the other cops now that he's been pushed to the edge by The Best Administration. Now that he has to be holier than he already was.

We stare at the lights of the police station. You can see detectives in long sleeved work shirts at their computers.

'So,' Shana goes. 'Today we're going to increase the bounty? And put word out on the street? Does that sound helpful?'

'Guess so. Do I get a cut? For helping you?'

'Nobody gets any cut. We're volunteers until we get her back.'

'What, you ain't tempted to take the bounty to Sky City Casino? Could double it, y'know.'

'Do you want me to slap you?'

I say sorry. After an awkward silence, watching a homeless rasta in jandals playing his ukulele for coins on the corner, I go, 'So you need to take time off work or something? What do you do again for, like, work and shit?'

'I'm self-employed. Ministry of Justice contacts me if defendants need a public service lawyer. Vulnerable people just use my gallery to get away from the stress of legal action. It's a whānau-friendly space, judgement-free.'

Hmm. Judgement-free enough that Pork and them Defiants have been known to hang out there. Photos on Facebook. Kinda looks like Shana's more than just a defender of people against police excess. Almost looks like she's bros with them.

I squeeze her shoulder. Kinda chubby. I wish little Shana was as bony as her big sister. 'Can't get your sis up without a pissup,' I tell her. 'Let's go do some planning at the Jug pub, over the road. Sound good?'. Step into my office.'

By the time we've settled into the Jovial Jug, Shana has gone from sulkily dawdling to overtaking me. She's through the saloon doors and past the sports betting desk and across the pub floor, hitting the wooden floorboards hard. I can tell Shana's disoriented, though. This pub's like the inside of an old galleon, dark wood, low ceilings, and wooden beams smacking against your hips.

Main problem, though, is I spot a big bulky unit of a grizzly-scalped white man with a bunch of colourful patches on his leather vest. Shit. Nomad is here. The man who's probably gonna kick my arse so hard my rectum will squirt out my nose.

'See that dude?' I put a hand on Shana's shoulder and try to get her to glance at that big bully motherfucker, the horn-head Nomad. He's behind the bar, interestingly, doing something on the till. Nomad's got a laptop computer plugged into the till. Guess he's such a resident at the bar, they've gotten him to programme their point of sale system. Done a course in jail to make him employable, I'm guessin.

'Stay the hell away from that guy,' I shout-whisper.

Shana's like, 'Why did I agree to come in here with you?'

'Exposure to crims. Down this end of the bar, c'mon.'

The Jovial Jug has the last cigarette machine in the country. Shana buys Benson & Hedges from it. Classy smokes for a classy woman, although she looks like a little girl playing dress-ups, and her haircut doesn't sit perfectly on her head. The hair's almost a little heavy, or her body can't take much weight. Like she has to work double-hard to represent the family. Barbie contracted Fuck-up-itis from the age of 14, and I wonder what kind of complexes Shana's olds have given her. Some people get that schism thing where they get so much pressure to perform when they're teens that they have a psychotic break when they hit their 20s and start being all devious and shit. I saw it on *True Crime Files* on National Geographic channel one time. I like to imagine Shana's hiding some sort of dark side. Truth be told, it ain't fuckin likely though.

Crazy and psychotic is what you have to be to let your guard down in the Jug, and that's what Shana's doing right now. Not only is she dressed-to-rob, Shana's casually scraping her handbag across the floor, totally unafraid of getting rolled. 'Why the fuss over the barman?' she goes.

'Met him about a week ago. Not the most approachable of people. We kinda got in a bit of a scrap.'

'Presumably you were the problem, Karl. Stop me if I'm wrong.'

I squint at her, send her away to get me a beer and order us up some wedges for breakfast. I'm fuckin thirsty, and I'm fuckin scared of the Nomad barman spotting me.

Shana brings a jug back with one glass.

'Yo, hope you weren't wanting me to pay for this. What with your trust fund 'n all… .'

'Ha! Trust fund sounds liberating, but it's the opposite.'

'So how do you get your folks' money?'

'God you're impolite. I don't get anything from my parents, for your information.'

'Yeah right, if you say so,' I go, pouring beer in the glass and sliding it to her. It's fizzy and sloppy and leaves the tabletop wet. I take a slurp from the jug and say Ahhhh. Cold as milk. Breakfast of champions.

She fiddles with some Dolce & Gabbana logo on a scrap of leather on her blouse, hunched in the dark pub, insecure, looking like she's wet her pants but doesn't know how to solve the problem.

'They do coffee here?'

'You don't want Nomad makin your coffee. Dude's got hepatitis. On that note, look, reason I invited you here is that sasquatch behind the bar is the man you want to hit up for gossip. You're Barbie's sister. You're famous, kinda, in the underworld. And these people, man, they'll love you if you've got your parents' chequebook.'

She's pondering, watching Nomad slap down drinks for some Comancheros wearing black vests over their muddy orange overalls.

I knock back my beer. 'Question: that integrity inspector dyke, the Nantakarn one, are yous two licking each other's pussies out? That lady sure was eager to please you.'

'I'm taken.'

'To another dyke, or…?'

'To a *man*, Jesus! My partner is a surveyor. Works primarily in the Pacific, West Papua. Engineering flash flood mitigation.'

'So where's he at now?'

'We're… experimenting with a …remote arrangement.'

'So you're available. That's cool.' I drink up, shielding my face from

Nomad, feel a glow come on and settle in for a speech. 'Pretty sure Little Richie's got some lovin' for ya, just hit him up if you're horny. He's not been laid ever, as far as I know. I flatted with him for almost a whole year and there was no proof he ever cracked a crack. Girls High School was like, 200 metres away, and they used to come round to buy dippers off me, all the little party girls, one time we put this seventeen-year-old in his bed and got her to strip off and wait there for him, and we had to wait til he got home from the bank, 'cause of course he was workin in a bank, you know our Snitchie.' I toss my glass down my throat, refill it, offer Shana a sip. 'So anyway he gets home and we've got this li'l honey ready to go, and Rich carefully takes off his tie and name tag, and he's wondering how come me and my other flatmate and these girls are stalking him up the stairs, yo, and he takes a shower and rubs talcum powder on his body and we're like, Come oooooon, and he's getting real 'spicious, and eventually he places his shoes on the shoe tree and enters his room, goes over to his bed, peels the covers back, and there's this hot chick just lyin there and– '

'And the point of this story is?'

'In the end he didn't root this girl. I was getting to that.'

'What's wrong with that?'

'So he's either gay or he's never been laid. Doesn't that blow your mind?'

She shrugs, pulls her handbag on. 'Some people put progress first, hedonism second. And you know what?' she goes, pushing back from her barstool and, putting her feet on the ground and getting ready to confront a monster. 'Time to make some progress.'

'Wait – don't – Shayn– ?!'

Shana Konstantinou goes over to the bar. Nomad pushes down the lid of the laptop. I point an ear in his direction. The grizzly man is chewing, and when he leans in to ask Shana what the fuck she wants with a blast of breath, I'm certain I can smell rotten socks in an ashtray.

'I've been encouraged to ask you if you've seen my sister. Barbie's what certain people call her, well – one person calls her. Idiots, mostly – like my friend over there.' They both look over at me, and Nomad's face flushes red. Nomad comes around the bar and marches across the pub floor.

'There's witnesses!' I squeal, falling off my barstool. 'Over in that corner! They'll see if you kill me! Don't do anything stupid!'

'Sir, slow, slow, nnng, I juswannatalktoyou,' Shana grunts, restraining him by tugging Nomad's long sleeved shirt, like a guinea pig tryina pull down a rhino.

Dragging Shana behind him, he arrives at my corner, where I've holed up behind some pub furniture. The giant leans onto my table. I smell the cunt's stench, glimpse his fiery pink eyes. I briefly consider standing up and showing him I'm not afraid, but I reckon he'll want revenge and punch me across the table, then put a table leg on my stomach, then put all his weight on the table and push the table leg through, nailing me into the floor.

'Stand up.'

I rise, put my hands in front of me.

'Nomadnomadnomad, bro, I'm-I'm-I'm not here to fight, honest man, th-that lady that hit you up just now, she's rich as fuck and, dude, juslisten, you know how the Defiant've got a special guest with them at the moment? This here's her li'l sis. The bitch hangin off your sleeve.' Pause. Breath. Moisten tongue. 'She's your cash cow, bro. Worth shitloads.'

Nomad doesn't look away. I can smell him. His armpits smell like old newspapers crawling with worms, rotting in a compost pile, wet and earthy. He smokes too much, too, and I can smell it radiating from his scary yellow smoke-soaked Fu Manchu moustache.

'Shitloads?' he goes.

'Shitloads.'

We hunker deep in our corner booth. There's a Band-aid on Nomad's temple with a horn drawn on it.

'Any idea what it cost me, *shithead*, getting locked up the other day?' he goes. 'Bout a grand, you owe me. We're gonna get President Pork on the phone. Your arse owes him too.'

'You're talking about Glenn,' Shana goes, squeezing in this gap beside Nomad's elbow. So there's a wee corner conspiracy going on, a'ight. Kinda cool, like we're having a clandestine CIA meeting. 'Glenn Hamm. I suppose you're aware I represented him three years ago when police brought fairly hefty charges against him.'

'Whole town's aware you two got close,' Nomad goes.

Shana hates this. She gives him a devil face. Oughta see my face, though. Feel like I've just been slapped with information.

'He was a client, briefly. Community law services for disadvantaged members of our community. All clients get close attention.'

Nomad gives her a hard, tunnelling stare so that I don't have to. 'You don't have some ongoing bloody arrangement?'

'No we do not have a so-called "arrangement." I haven't seen him in, like, twenty months.'

Nomad pulls his cellphone out of his arse pocket and dials. 'We'll see if you're tellin fibs, little girly.'

'Gimme that,' Shana goes, sudden, insane, seizing Nomad's phone without thinking twice. Stupid crazy impulsive bloody –

'Hello? Hello? Glenn, is that you? Pork? From the Defiant?' *No no no no no, lady, what's wrong with you...*

She presses the speakerphone button. The other people in the margins of the pub pretend not to eavesdrop. I wish I could wriggle out of the corner and run. I don't wanna be around when Pork orders Nomad to flatten Shana's face.

'Tell him who you are,' I'm whispering. 'He'll offer you a deal, you pay up and your sister could be back at your parents' place pronto.'

She takes a bottle from her handbag, swallows. There are Valiums in my pocket. I push a few into her hand.

'Sposda be the phone of ol' Nomad,' Pork's voice goes. It sounds like he's got a grin that goes all the way from one eye to the other. 'Buuuuut this is not the voice of Mr Nomad. This is the sister. Of the troublemaker. Correct?'

'Her name is Barbara,' Shana says. I watch a tear roll down her nose. 'We just want her back.'

'Know what a finder's fee is, sister?'

Shana sniffs and bites her knuckle and nods.

'I've, I've, I've only got ten– '

'Twenty grand, you want her. But keep it out of the fuckin' news, oi.'

'Put her on the phone....' Damn. Tough Little Mrs Responsible is dissolving. Both eyes are watering now. 'I'm gonna, gonna tell the media, everyone, you give my sissy *BACK*,' Shana snaps. After a beat, her voice switches to moaning. 'How do I, how do I know she's not dead?'

There's a pause, and a little snicker. 'I'm sure we can get a finger sent to ya. Maybe it'll twitch.'

# 15

# "If they're about to pull Barbs out for good then this whole story's over."

On the Friday I try to set up in the Tote n Poke pub in Cameron Street Mall but I get half a day of work completed before there's a fuckin Santa Parade goin past, glitter blowing in my face, kids squealing, dads smiling and all that fruity shit, so I move over to the Whangarei Central Public Library as my office, not that it's much better, stinky-arse pine tree covered in baubles and fake-snow spraypaint in the middle of the damn building that my taxes pay for, in theory.

I'll hundred percent rent an office when I'm full-on pro, no doubt about it, but for now everything's borrowed. I'm on a borrowed library card, on a borrowed laptop, on borrowed wi-fi, and when I say borrowed, I mean the person I borrowed these things off doesn't know I've borrowed them.

We didn't get far talking to Pork – his message on the phone was basically that there's a wall up, and you've gotta give him money to share intel on Barbie – so the operation right now is I'm gonna break into Kenny Boy's Facebook account. Cause this is the new Karl. The up-and-at-'em problem-solvin' Karl. I spent a few years actin feral, true, but now I'm professional bounty huntin styles. Gonna get me some business cards printed. Maybe some of those pens that have a lady in some goo and her clothes come off in a little bubble when you tilt the pen.

It's cool and safe in here when everything's hot and mean outside. Cops criticising me, crims calling me mean names. Library's my safe place. My humble Northland peeps are in here, all the vagabonds that make me feel at home. There's a guy with his ankle bracelet wrapped in tinfoil havin a nap on some bean bags in the kids' section. There are two pregnant teenagers stuffing their hoodies with free fruit. One guy washes his dog with hand soap in the disabled toilet and blow-dries its paws.

On the borrowed computer, I concentrate on trying to crack the password of Kenny D'Souza. Cunt's email address is kenny69@facebook.com, that wasn't hard. His password's probly Pu$$y, same as the letters I noticed on his charm necklace when we ambushed him in Vicar of Liquor, but the Pu$$y password doesn't work and his settings are surprisingly private and I just search his friend list for anyone named Barbie and I scratch my head for a moment when I can't find anyone by that name. Then I realise I'm after *Barbara* and I put my face in my palm 'cause I'm the only dawg that calls her that. Those dippers I smoke? They leave some sort of residue inside my skull. Shana's lucky she hasn't had her brain damaged like me. Maybe I shouldn't keep tryina get her to party. Cept that means I'll be Lonesome Karl, and tryin not to be lonesome was the whole original reason I reached out to Richie in the first place.

The parts of Kenny's Facebook profile I can see say he's apparently single and unhappy. Location? His timeline doesn't mention, which makes me scratch my head (also I scratch 'cause I have nits). His location would explain a lot of shit. Why ain't he reunited with Barbie? We only took her away for an hour.

Needing a break, I search for images of some celebrity titties. Sadly, the photos don't scratch my itch. I push back from the plain library table, sigh, drum my fingers, studying an alphabet poster on the wall.

I want Shana, but she's gone to work. I want Richie, but he's not answering his phone. I want someone with the skin of a rhino to charge into the Defiant clubhouse and do my dirty work for me.

I want it so damn bad that the gods make my phone go off. A Library Cop glares at me with a 'Turn-your-phone-off-you-homeless-animal' look, and I give her my cold face. Book-stackin phone-banning bloody–

'Karl? Nomad here.'

'Nomad?'

'Don't make me repeat it, son. I've figured out a use for you.'

I stand up and my balls crash down to my ankles and roll out of the cuff of my pants as I put the phone into my ear.

'So for this cash cow thing, how much money's her sister got? I've been told to ask.'

Nomad's in control of this conversation from the get-go.

'Told by who, um, if you don't mind me asking... you're working for, like... you're helping the DMC?'

'Nomad works for Nomad.'

There's a Grand Canyon of silence on the phone.

'How much budget they got, the family?'

'Two hundred grand, or more. Shana can probably go higher.'

'I'll do it for half that.'

'So you're, like, a middleman?'

'Correct.'

'Wouldn't she need some sorta guarantee you're gonna get the job done?'

I go over to a section where the librarian can't death-stare me.

'Cause Shana's been shitting herself. She doesn't wanna go near the clubhouse. Happy to let a CHAOS team do their thing. If she's told Richie that Pork's holding Barbs at the clubhouse then, shit. They're probably on their way.'

'Listen, dumb-dumb. Everyone believes Barbie's being held at the clubhouse. But that's a little too obvious, innit.'

'Well fuckin where, then?!'

'Meet me outside the copshop. You'll need some wheels.'

Shana has wheels. Better take her car. It's an emergency. I'll tell her later, if I got time.


Shana's office is located in that Hunterwussy, however you pernounce it, that Australian fruity dead artist who draws like a five-year-old with all the tiles and spirals and trees and shit.

Within her office-gallery is a mini-gallery sponsoring and supporting paintings and carvings made by crims from the jail up at Ngawha. Jeez, lady, if you're gonna try be a patron, go all the way, why don'tcha... anyway, Anal Shanal still deals the odd painting, gives the proceeds to one of them Books

For Prisoners programmes, feels good about herself. She doesn't get a trust fund. Shana just gets funding to represent crims in court. Doesn't pay that well, from what I've heard. She does it for passion, I understand. Bleeding heart defence lawyer and all that. Loves crims as much as the good guys. Well, crims except me.

Her office is at the end of a cramped stairwell, low ceiling with a water pipe scraping my head, bricks and pipes and wrought iron around the entrance. You go in a few metres, then descend some stairs, and it becomes these corridors. Fuckin' claustrophobic, but the paintings and couple of sculptures are alright. One drawing of the inside of a prison cell signed by Glenn Hamm, actually. Made by the Porkster. Hmm. Shana's got a soft spot for the big beastly bastard.

Whangārei's not very big, maybe a hundred thousand peeps. It's only half a kay from her Hunterwussy office to the cop shop. I can hear Shana talking on her phone with someone with a fat, loud, staunch voice, who says one word for every twenty that Shana says. I have to dart through the shadows, glimpse Shana, glimpse the little kitchen, glimpse her handbag hanging on a hook beside a Rheem water boiler and a slim Apple laptop, one of those Macbook Air things. Footsteps coming towards me. I pull some clothes off the coathook down and lie on the ground, coats draped over my head and body, then I reach out and pull the laptop in with me. I feel like a loser, but it's not as bad as the dumpster full of nappies I hid in that one time I burg'd a daycare centre and the K-9 came and the dogs were snuffling the outside of the dumpster and I could just about feel their wet noses through the metal bin.

With a slow gentle dusk settling on the city, stretching shadows, I take Shana's keys and her laptop and a bottle of meds that look fun then scamper away, bumping a painting done by one of her underworld adoptees.

Night is oozing down the sides of Whangarei's big green Mt Parihaka and I'm out. I'm behind her building. I've got a laptop worth a quick hundred bucks buried under two layers of clothes. I'm beeping the key fob to open Shana's car then I'm behind the wheel, laptop open, find some wifi, no worries about passwords and a minute later - because she's saved the access code and because the security question obviously has 'B@rb1e' as the answer (I'm a private dick-slash bounty hunter, remember), I'm in her internet banking. I'm checking her transactions to see who she's recently paid, how much she forks out. There are quite a few five figure payouts going back and forth. Cheaparse should'a bought me extra beers yesterday.

I pause on the street for a moment. Walk up to a post shop, buy a courier bag big enough to fit a laptop in, put the courier bag in my backpack for later. Gonna need it. A real bounty hunter always thinks three moves ahead.

Then I take Shana's SUV, move it into a car park to think. Who should rip the door open and hop in? Lo and behold it's frickin Nomad. Damn he's a hefty cunt. Even if this is a two-tonne vehicle, it still shakes as his body settles into the passenger seat.

'I owe you an ashtray in the face,' he goes.

'Nice to see you too.'

Nomad takes a box out of a backpack. He switches it on, chucks it on the dashboard, and we hear people talking Cop. What Nomad has is a police scanner, a decent one too, Tait T2010, handles 66-88MHz. Respect. The 5-0 keep mentioning something approaching, T-minus three minutes, T-minutes two minutes thirty.

'Gimme the computer.'

'What computer?'

'Nomad sees everything, boy. Hurry up.'

No point fucking around. I slide Shana's laptop out and hand it over. Almost night now and the electronics are glowing.

Nomad continues using the wi-fi of the shop we're parked outside of. With his big thick fingers, which look like they could unscrew the lug nuts on a car wheel, he types in an alphanumeric version of the shop's name, and booyah: that's the password. 'Dumbarse monkeys,' he mutters. Damn. Dude's a blackhat. Kinda impressive. Makes me excited to go to jail again so I can study computers like this guy. He's online, descending beneath WWW, pure Dark Web, some site called CopWatch that doesn't even have banners or ads or anything, just police surveillance feeds and – whoa! The fuck is this? And why is he showing little old me?

Playing out in the green and black of night vision, I'm seeing video feed of motorcycles, shipping containers, gravel. Helmets. Body armour. Guns like you'd see on a Arnold Schwarzenegger film. What we're watching is views of the perimeter of the Defiants' pad up in Kaitaia. Torches dip and dart. Whoever's streaming this night vision footage is trying not to be seen.

I'm hearing 'Raid Operative, aaaaand commence.' Somethin epic's about to crack off.

'Holy shit – this is happening now? That's – that's a feed of the Defiants' bloody... clubhouse?'

'CHAOS are about to raid the place. They've all got GoPros on their helmets.'

Damn, I'm thinking - if they're about to pull Barbs out for good then this whole story's over.

Silence for a second, while the other shoe drops. 'SWAT team's just gonna pull out Barbs and boost?'

'Apparently.'

'What if there's a shootout?'

'Supposed to be gentle-as. No shooting unless Pork shoots first, and they phoned him in advance and he said he wasn't planning to go Waco on the cops, so nah, they won't shoot first. They'll have the safeties on on their weapons. Don't wanna risk the little birdie gettin hurt. She's worth a lotta money, remember.'

*She's worth a lotta money. Worth a lotta money...*

Words echo in my ears.

Cramped in the vehicle, watching through a safe screen, I kinda like this hanging-out-with-a-stinky-ogre-that-wants-to-kill-me thing. Like I'm safe between his legs or, like, if I keep him talking, keep him passionate about his police scanner and our mission to break off a piece of the cash cow cash, he'll forget that he owes me a hiding.

Meanwhile CHAOS gets paid, and Police get paid if they can rescue the princess.

'So the parents of this lil chickadee that's got herself kidnapped. They'll be handing out tips if they get her back?'

'What makes you say *if*?' I go.

'CHAOS are incompetent motherfuckers. Shit, Pork probly rang CHAOS himself and invited them to raid him, just for something to sue them over.'

I give Nomad a look.

'He a friend of yours, ol' Pork?'

Nomad shushes me and turns up the volume on the police scanner, so we get narration to describe what's happening in the video. 'Just watch and keep ya mouth shut.'

Live feed. Cops creeping up like leopards in the night in one of them

David Attenborough videos. Bout to drag a gazelle up a tree.

Whoever's camera I'm looking through opens the lid of the Defiants' rubbish bins and has a peek inside, then rummages through their recycling. Then two of them drop onto their backs and wriggle under the gate just like me and Snitchie Richie did.

I worry about Richie. Frustrating as the prick is, I don't want Rich being part of this. I'm getting a forward-vision that shit'll turn out bad, like those *Final Destination* movies. What do you call those visions, when you see something in advance? Premenstrual, menstruation... promotion?

'See this camera here, how he's pacing the fence? Called a spotter. SWAT teams is so heavy with bulletproof gears and them helmets on their heads, they find it hard to look up. So they need a spotter to keep an eye on the roof.'

'How d'you know all this shit?'

'Brother, I been raided more times than I can remember.'

Can't believe he's calling me Brother.

Nomad shakes his head. 'If the swatties make the place messy, Pork's gonna start swingin. They got a arsenal in that cellar underneath the barbecue. Look at this piglet right here.' Nomad presses the tablet against my eyes. 'Mr Chaos here doesn't know his way around. Look at him, peering into that mirror. He'll be tuggin books out of the bookcase next, see if it activates a hidden door or some shit.'

We watch the Kaitaia raid from the safe cab of the ute in the Whangarei parking lot, me inhaling Nomad's beery ashtray stench. Through the camera feed on Shana's stolen device, our CHAOS guy with the GoPro totes a semi-automatic carbine rifle. Occasionally he tinkers with something on it, checks the safety lock, rattles it to see how far down the chamber the bullets are, or looks to see if there's room in the magazine. It's only a ten-per-clip gun. He's obviously nervous. So would I be, if I was invading the personal space of a gang that rode their friggin bikes into the debating chamber two years ago to try stop that bill being passed that makes it illegal to belong to a gang – and it bloody worked, too, cause the politicians had to adjourn the fuckin place. Bill didn't even get signed.

I get a glimpse of four Defiant gangsters lined up against a wall, smoking and stomping the ground. A CHAOS ninja comes into the scope of the camera, makes secret ninja signals with his fingers. The guy whose GoPro we're looking through doesn't seem to understand the signals. He inches along a wall, under a big scary black and yellow mural listing all the Defiants that've died over the years, their dates, their ranks, their nicknames, Shank and Marley and Big Midget and Pikachu, and the camera operator glances round the corner. Finds himself indoors, in a kitchen, inspecting boxes of cereal in the darkness (yeah, 'cause Barbie could totally be inside a box of cornflakes, genius).

CHAOS gives the all-clear to a room full of paint tins and goes back out into the driveway. Even though the colours through the GoPro are quite dim, mostly greens and greys, I can see darkness around the moon. If the Defiant wanna chuck some Molotov cocktails at the invaders now's the time. Light up the darkness a little.

But they're not chuckin anything. Me and Nomad get a glimpse of forty soldiers being herded into groups of five, two CHAOS herding each group, black boots, black jeans, yellow hoodies, black helmets, and a patched jacket that's plain black with lots of yellow wasp stripes. These guys want you to know they're vicious, they sting.

'Our boy's getting on a container. Check it out.'

We can hear the CHAOS ninjas talking to their bosses in crisp codewords as they lift tyres and rattle door handles and stroke walls and give orders to pissed-off looking guys with helmets and lasers who nip at them, blurting 'Stay the fuck out' when the Swatties stick their heads into shipping containers and portable cabins.

'All clear,' the ninjas go to each other, or 'Progressing' or 'Eliminated.' Seems CHAOS has control of the place and they're pointing their automatic weapons at various Defiant meatheads they catch skulking between the shipping containers. A bunch of them aren't arrested, though, and they mob together like piranhas then from out of nowhere, the Defiant snap to attention, straight up and down like toy soldiers, and a wide waddling water balloon shape appears between them.

It's Pork, the President, walking between his troops like Napoleon. He straddles his bike, guns it and the noise crackles our speaker, deafening me. I cover my ears. We watch through the CHAOS ninja's GoPro camera as Pork rides figure-eights in the parted ranks of men. He then uses his bike to pin a CHAOS guy against a wall, and some Swatties run over to confront him, and there's a scuffle, and a good fifteen bikers do their best to pin the guns of the CHAOS guys or wrestle their helmets off, and then a fist nears the GoPro camera, and the signal goes all spazzy, and we hear 'Getcha hands off, cunt' and 'Stop resisting' and 'Rohit, Rohit' as Rohit turns out to be our man, our eyes, our vision.

Seems he's been caught in a washing machine then it's - Man down! We've got a man down, lower your weapon, I repeat–

*POP! POP! POP-OP-OP.*

*Puh-puh.*

Then silence.

Everything is dark green.

'The fuck… You seein this?'

This Rohit dude's GoPro flickers back to life. We're deep inside the Clubhouse, now. There are stacks of cheap chairs, a bar with Triumph Motorcycle shapes carved into wooden panels. There are framed patches, photos of generations and generations of Defiant.

And there's Pork's face.

He's holding what looks like a bazooka.

'This thing on?' Pork wheezes into the GoPro, biting a cigarette. Fat in his lungs.

Through the camera, he's looking directly into my eyes. I need to piss.

'Should be,' says the Sarge, a hillbilly-lookin cunt with a long red beard, long goatee and overalls and a cap with the vest strangely on top of it all. He's chewing a cigarette like it's a hayseed.

'Now you listen to me, Poh-leece.' Like he's taking a selfie, Pork is holding the camera in front of his nose and he's talking directly to Richie and his colleagues. I picture the cops in their station, donuts suspended, mid-dunk, captivated, hypnotised by a giant TV screen. 'I've got fuckin' kindergarten to take my grandkids to tomorra. I don't have time for your shit. I'm gonna keep this souvenir I'm holding, and you're gonna beg forgiveness for stickin your head in where it ain't welcome.' White spit has painted the corners of his lips. Huge pink-skinned guy, shiny bald head, grey streaks above his ears. Old and full of testosterone. 'Raid my fuckin' house? Dirty my old lady's rug? I've got haemorroids, you wankers, Pork don't need this stress.'

No one responds. I'm still not sure how he's talking directly into our swat-boy's GoPro. It's sposda be attached to his dome.

'Know how I'm holdin this camera so far in the fuckin air, do ya?!'

Pork detaches the GoPro from whatever it's been sitting on and discards it near his feet. Then he drops the thing the GoPro had been attached to, a black Kevlar helmet, with something inside that's heavy and hairy and wearing goggles. Whatever's been in the helmet is cut messily at the neck, dripping, held by the straps and stuck inside the helmet.

It's the head of our SWAT boy. Rohit.

Bob-op-op.

Pop-pop.

More shots fired outside, briefly. Pork just glares to the right, like gunshots only piss him off as much as mozzie bites.

Shouting, swearing. Single scream of a siren. Squirt of gravel as emergency services get to the scene.

'Tried to tell you Blondie ain't here,' Pork goes, holding the GoPro to his face, aiming down at the ground so we can see him toe Rohit's head with his boot. 'Anyway, rubbish collection's on Monday. I'll be chuckin the head out then.'

Pork positions the GoPro under his boot. 'By the way, it's half a mil if you want her body.'

Pork brings his boot down on the live stream.

Everything is lost.

# 16

# "Do Whangarei Police always send one person against a whole gang?"

Settler's Discovery is a shithole of a hotel, but it's also the best in the city, which says a lot about Whangārei. Perfect place for a press conference, cause headlines've got people askin some haaaard questions.

Headline in the Herald: *Raid ends in horror police death; biker shot; Heiress still missing.*

Northern Advocate: *Police "failed" kidnap victim – Outraged family schedule conference.*

And in the wise words of the Whangārei Leader, one of the best papers for lighting a fire in winter: *Bikers "unfairly targeted," lawyers claim; kidnap unsolved.*

What. The fuck. *Happened* last night?

Scraping all the news and chatter together, sounds like CHAOS shot an unarmed male at the Defiants' pad and a brawl broke out during which a Armed Offenders Squad member "suffered a casualty."

Yeah right, frickin' nerd-words: That SWAT boy got his head ripped off by some angry angry wasps. I've dipped into the socials this morning and heaps of gangsta-opinionators are giving it their two cents on TikTok, saying the DMC slammed Mister Swat-man's head in a container door *AND* they're not even gonna get in trouble about it, cause the cops' warrant only gave the right to search buildings and not containers or something, Jeez Louise, man... plenty of times over the years I've felt like slamming Richie's head in a door when he corrects my grammar but you don't actually DO it, do ya.

It wasn't just the police that cocked up the recovery. There was Shana negotiating the ransom shittily, the parents maybe not releasing the purse strings like they should've. And yeah, to be fair, I was kinda in the centre of the cockup, though I was only there to un-cock the situation, not that I succeeded. We've gone from me and the bruz on a road trip, like old times, rescuing the princess, to having recovered a abductee and gotten her secure in a cop car, then next thing you know there's a headless piglet. The stress is costing me a lot of cigarettes. And I'm, like, partly to blame. 50 per cent. Well, 99 percent. Okay – I'm 100 percent to blame, but at least I asked nicely, to try and get Barbs back. This SWAT team basically shat in the swimming pool and the rest of us all have to swim through the turds.

Four coppers from the CHAOS team got bashed, one in the spinal unit, half of them taking sick days – and one with his friggin head ripped off in a steel door. The legal team representing Defiant Motorcycle Club president Glenn Hamm - acting all hard-done-by cause one of his boys got shot, claiming he's some kinda spokesperson for harmless motorcycle enthusiasts - cites some sorta Stand Your Ground laws and he's got these civilian-somethin lawyers backin him up, civil union, civil libraries, libertine, civil lesbian, whatever you call 'em.

Anyway, it makes sense that the old Konstantinou parents get some sunlight on the situation with a media conference.

Thirty reporters and just as many camera operators and sound guys are packing the hotel's conference room. Their coffee is poured by – lo and behold – Richie's little vanilla army, Group Awesome. The youths help unfold tripods and carry bags and spread the legs of folding tables. Some of them are even standing by the doors like they think they're security.

I spot Georgios and Anna, the parents. The dad is a small, dark, foreign-lookin guy in a suit, little bowtie, like a James Bond supervillain, but nice and friendly. The mum has real tall hair, all stacked on her head, and she wears heels and big dangly earrings. They're Greek Author Docs, some kind of church thing, and the mum's from like the Byzantine empire or whatever, in case you couldn't tell by their names, though they had to settle for Catholic school for their daughter. I tell ya, there are days it seems like everyone on earth's churchy 'cept me.

Shana's gonna lose the plot when she sees me at this conference, I betcha 20 bucks. Hell, there's most likely a warrant out for my arrest, for taking her car unauthorised then returning it to her place in the middle of the night and jamming a knife in the ignition to set the alarm off to let her know I was giving it back and waking up everyone on her street which, I acknowledge, was not the most sensible thing to do. As for Richie, shit, I got him in trouble with the most up-themselves branch in the whole police force. Piglets died based on intelligence recommendations that he was behind, and his whole department'll probly be ordered to say sorry to the DMC, cause Nantakarn's all about moving up the career ladder by selling out her squad, wringin' her hands.

Oof. To say Rich is distancing himself from me is a understatement.

Barbie's parents? They'll get on the hate train, too.

Stoned from the trippy old carpet, plus some old Kronic I bought from these kids in the abandoned mall in the centre of town, I watch the conference room fill up with everybody who wants to bring Barbie back – TV news, fat nerdy cameramen in t-shirts with bumbags around their bellies, concerned-looking mums creasing little flyers with Barbie's picture on them... and coppers. Pleeenty of cops. Detectives, too – I can tell by their nice pants and shirts and cause they're mostly white, mostly 41 years old.

Centre of the damn room, though, are Mr and Mrs Konstantinou. They're escorted by police up on to the stage and positioned in front of name-cards. No projector screen in broke-ass Whangārei – this hotel just provides four portable whiteboards on wheels with some phone numbers and rules for the media which the little Christian security snitches can't stop adjusting. Them boys need a real job, I swear to God. I should teach them how to press ecstasy pills. Training for the future.

About ten reporters take places in the front row of the audience, logos on their jackets and microphones, reporters from Newshub, Radio NZ, Vice, TVNZ, the Herald, shit even the Māori media's here – Te Kaea, Te Hiku, Māori TV. I recognise that weather chick off One News, the one who's got that OnlyFans account. There are swank chairs to park their bums on, but the good-looking young microphone-clutchers clamour at the stage, trying to get Barbara's parents to say something exclusive.

Reporters have even arrived from somewhere called NHK Network that's got a little Japan flag logo. It'd be nice if one of the foreign reporters spotted me and went 'Wow, it's you, Karl Copley, you're on your way to becoming a legendary bounty hunter, I'd like to consult you and broadcast your name around the world, tap your expertise.' Pretty rude how they ignore me, actually, the fuckin snobs. How come they're here in this hall, anyway? Is it 'cause of the Ken and Barbie angle, or cause the Konstantinou family are worth eight mil?

Integrity Inspector Nantakarn, a slim Mac Airbook under her arm, stops as she's moving through the centre of the media horde, steps through the trench of legs between the seats. How the fuck she's noticed me amid all the reporters, I'm not sure. Eagle-eyed frickin Babysitters Club mystery-solving bloody–

'Copley,' Nantakarn says, 'How was court?'

'What court?'

'Last I heard, you were due in court for theft of police property.'

My blood freezes. My heart has stopped beating. Court. I'd been so busy with my bounty hunting career, I'd fully forgotten. I think I was supposed to appear for that Grand Theft Magazine bullshit.

'Listen, you and I, we're going to have word sometime soon. There's also a laptop computer Shana Konstantinou says is missing.'

'Spose you wanna talk about Shana's car, too.'

'Why, what did you do to Shana's car?'

She's interrupted and called up to the stage, walking up with straight up-and-down posture and one of those dykey pants-suits like Agent Scully wears on *The X-Files*. Nantakarn's suit is dark blue, surprise surprise. And she's got a matching navy blue Covid mask on her dumb face, even though that whole pandemic thing blew over years ago, plus it was a hoax anyways.

She's brought one of those clapboard slates that they use on movie sets to get everyone to shut up and she clacks it twice.

First person to speak is the dad. 'I don't want this to take a lot of time out of your day,' old Mr Konstantinou mumbles into his microphone with a voice so weak and girly you'd think his throat's got its period.

'Louder,' someone yells.

'I'm sure you've all got important things to do, you don't need to help us with this whole silly mess.'

A Group Awesome gopher scuttles over and adjusts the man's lapel microphone.

The Konstantinou dad looks at his old crinkled wife. Hard to imagine these two making love and producing someone like Barb. They're so tame and vanilla and wrinkly it makes me wonder what in God's name happened to Barbie to make her such a bad bitch.

These parents, they've always seemed ancient to me. The mum's been dyeing the silver out of her hair as long as I can remember. The dad, Georgios, he's got zero muscle and no manliness in his voice. Little dark shrivelled motherfucker looks like a shrunken head. Fuck knows how he toughed it out digging trenches and hauling wheelbarrows before he franchised out all his landscaping, calling it Greek Gardens. He's written this memoir hardback book called *The Konstantinou Gardener* that's meant to inspire other immigrants, talks about him getting off a squid boat and busting his back digging trenches till he could buy his own backhoe to run his own landscaping side-hustle on weekends, then his sidehustle became his main hustle as work flowed in and boom, next thing you know he buys the business off his boss, buys a second business, replicates the model and Greek Gardens becomes the number one landscaping franchise in the North Island. His whole story's in the book, I guess, not that the prick even actually wrote it. His English is still shit and whichever reporter ghostwrote it is probably in this room.

'What's happening here today?' a reporter calls out to the stage from the third row. 'Are you releasing new information?'

'Mrs Konstantinou, police have failed to bring your daughter home, yet you're sitting side by side with them here today. Does this mean you support the current police methodology?'

'Georgios, sir, you're upping the reward, correct?'

'Is there still a ransom? Why haven't you paid, sir?'

'What's your daughter's life worth to you?'

'We actually have an order of business,' Nantakarn goes, taking over the microphone. The old man shuffles aside, looks lost for a moment, then sits back down. 'I can tell you that following question time and public comments from the parents of Ms Konstantinou, and review of Senior Constable Richard McMullan's handling of the case, our next step in the investigation will be a second approach to organised crime groups possibly connected to

Barbara's kidnapping.'

'Filipinos, I'd check them shifty cunts out if I were you,' someone yells, and by someone, I mean me. A couple heads turn but it's as if I'm just some local loudmouth they oughta ignore. Filipinos, yo. The crime world's favourite middlemen. I guarantee they know something.

Up on stage, Richie hasn't moved, shuffled, risen or said anything. Nantakarn may be five years younger but she acts like she's his mother. She looks harshly through her glasses at the audience.

'Our order of business commences with a review of Senior Constable Richard McMullan's, how shall I say "lone" investigation into the disappearance of Barbara Konstantinou. Senior Constable McMullan, can you speak to this, please?'

Richie catches a microphone tossed to him by a reporter. He looks like a idiot, fumbling with the mic cable, legs awkward, getting out of his chair, tallest person in a row of midgelets sitting on cheap seats in a cheap hotel at a cheap press conference.

'I heard Barbara was missing for a month before police opened a case, comment please?'

'Ms Nantakarn, do Whangārei police always send one person against a whole gang of kidnappers?'

'McMullan, you were seen in the company of a known offender and drifter, comment please?'

Richie puts a hand up. Everyone shuts up for a bit. He turns to Nancy Drew, points the microphone away from his mouth, but it picks up what he's trying to whisper. *Do I have to do this?*

'We appreciate your efforts, honey.' The low-muttered words of Anna, Barbie's mum, picked up by her microphone. She reaches across Shana's lap and rubs Richie's knee as if he's become some kind of son-in-law.

'Ms Konstantinou's whānau, who have been extremely useful in assisting – they've thanked me for sending a *scout*,' Nantakarn goes, 'It's just that the *scout* didn't achieve what was expected of someone sent in such– '

'I heard Whangārei police were clueless McMullan had gone after her. Comment, please.'

'That can't be confirmed at this stage, thank you. As you may well imagine, orders are given and received often in secret, with extremely discrete records of such orders. That's something I'll work out in time, thank you.'

A woman wearing a manly baseball cap stands up from her chair. A black tear streaks her cheek with mascara. 'This was his favourite cap,' she goes.

'Let her speak,' I yell. I get some death stares.

'Mrs Sabharwal, hi, hi,' Nantakarn coos. 'Listen up everybody. We're blessed to have in our presence Nina Sabharwal. Nina's the sister of Rohit Sabharwal. Ms Sabharwal is understandably devastated by the death of her husband in the line of duty,' Nantakarn goes. 'She's incredibly brave, just being here today.'

That turns a few heads.

'Do you feel your husband received adequate support, going into a bottleneck compound with no exits?'

'The fatal injuries sustained by Officer Sabharwal, accidental or otherwise, are something that'll form the basis of an Independent Police Conduct Authority review– '

'His head detached from his body. Are you really suggesting it could have been accidental?'

'Our staff are liaising with the eyewitnesses, some of who are alleged affiliates of a motorcycle enthusiast organis– '

'Why won't you charge Glenn Hamm with the injuries sustained by your armed offenders squad? Is that an admission of a wrongful raid on his property?'

'I won't be answering that question today.'

'How could you fuck it up so bad?'

My voice; my mouth. There's a collective gasp.

While the world is frozen, my phone buzzes, deep in my pocket against my dick. I'm enjoying the sexy vibration for a moment when a second text comes through.

Both messages from Nomad.

*We gt a software tracking option.*

*Meat me urgent.*

'Force is not the solution. We've worked that out,' Nantakarn continues. Her hands are placed in front of her, palms down, and she's pushing her palms towards her knees. The squeakiest, cleanest piglet in the country is subliminally telling everyone to calm down, 'cause she's smarter than everyone, see. This isn't about a communal discussion over how to retrieve a missing white girl anymore. It's a publicity stunt to let everyone know The

Best Administration is in control, and it has a brand, and must never have its budget cut, not when there's fuck-ups to un-fuck. 'Things get damaged when too much force is applied. Now, tomorrow I've scheduled a friendly meeting with a group of motorcycle enthusiasts who've kindly offered to– '

'Why you saying motorcycle enthusiasts, integrity inspector? Why can't the Defiant MC be publicly identified? Why no charges?'

'A Glenn Hamm, 62, has been charged with damaging police property, namely a mounted camera to the value of three hundred and thirty dollars,' she goes from her platform. 'That's a charge.'

'So you're conceding the raid on the clubhouse was unlawful? That you didn't have a warrant to search any shipping containers? That the club was allowed to stand its ground?'

She turns and slices through Richie with her laser-eyes. 'Like I say, we'll hold accountable those who gave our squadron bad advice.'

There are gasps. The clack and rattle of frantic typing. Reporters bang out words on their wafer-thin computers. Some of them pinch earpieces close to their mouths, whispering updates to their newsrooms.

'Ms Nantakarn, did you actually notify Mr and Mrs Konstantinou to state you thought you were closing in on their daughter?'

'Close liaison with family, uh, family spokesperson Shana Konstantinou meant our messages were being passed directly to the whānau members concerned.'

'I've been told the raid was an excuse to seize precursor ingredients to the manufacture of methamphetamine and there was never any expectation Ms Konstantinou was to be found there.'

Damn, dog. Big ups to whichever reporter yelled that one out. They've silenced the room.

'Your response, integrity inspector?'

Fuck this. Karl's taking charge. Time to turn some heads my way.

I step over several legs, massively uncomfortable, but glad I'll be outta here in a few moments. 'Guys, guys, hang on, I'm a bounty hunter,' I tell the media. 'Lemme tell you we're seriously close to getting her back.'

Four cops with Covid masks appear around my shoulders. I sprint nearer the stage and Richie rears up out of his seat. Half-afraid, half-disgusted.

Barbie's parents look at me like they're watching a gross sex scene on TV they can't wait to finish. They're moderately interested, though.

'No no no, absolutely not, you are not hijacking,' Nantakarn says into the mic, 'I can assure you Mr and Mrs Konstantinou have no interest in private bounty hunters. This man doesn't speak for us.'

Every camera has pointed its shiny snout-lens at me. Sniffing to see if I've got anything good to say.

'We got a plan to track her down, yo. Me and my friend. Don't trust what the pigs feed ya. Mr Konstantinou, sir! I'ma get her back for you, straight up.'

It's not that much bullshit. Well, it's a hundred-percent bullshit. But I'll try to make it real.

# 17

## "I think we need to plan or something."

McDonald's Bank Street, Whangārei. I'm actually trespassed from this place cause of that time I was in the playground havin a real good time and I got stuck in a plastic tunnel and the Fire Service had to cut me out, so I keep my hood up around my ears as I enter. The trespass was pretty unfair. They should've taken into consideration how young I was. That shit happened when I was, like, 25.

We've borrowed Shana's car again. She hasn't had time to get her insurer to swap it out for a new one, so it's easy to take it out of her driveway now that we've fucked the ignition and you can't lock it.

Dunno what to do. Pork's lawyers told media Barbie is not at their compound so… raid unnecessary? Cop killed for nothing? Distractions, all of it. Takin me away from getting Barbs back home.

We park in a McHandicap spot and I follow the big red Nomad, buried in the shadow his wide shoulders make. We settle into these metal picnic tables beside the play area. They've upgraded the slide and the climbing wall and I lick my lips, wishing I could have a play. But we've gotta stick to business. Nomad opens up his laptop and says he reckons he'll explain how his computer tracking plan works, but only after he's got a raspberry swirl McFlurry with Oreos and M&Ms.

'What if they tell us they can't mix Oreos and M&Ms?' I say across the holey metal picnic table, testing the loudness of my voice.

'Tell them to come outside and talk with me. Tell 'em I want a One Percent discount. They'll know what it means.'

Nomad gets onto the McDonalds free wi-fi and we each get our phones out. I stare at his gnarly arms as he types. They're thick arms, especially for a guy pushing 60. The hairy skin looks leathery and slippery and difficult to slice through. He's sipping bourbon straight from a bottle of Jim Beam and he's pouring bourb into my thickshake cup for me to slurp. Strawberry thickshakes are alright, but they don't make my problems melt like a nice bourbon does. When there's bourbon in your blood, you feel like you can smash anyone, root any woman, steal anything and get away with it. Big rugby-farmer dads look at me as I drink and curse near their kids, and I give them this look as if to say, Open your mouth to criticise me and you'll lose your tongue. Then my colourful friend here'll finish you off. Not that I'm sure if he's a *friend*-friend. He thinks I'm a piece of shit same way as my "friend" Richie does. A piece of shit with useful ideas, though.

He's got his McFlurry now. Licks ice cream off his spoon with a surprisingly delicate tongue.

'You do blokes. I do bitches,' Nomad goes.

'Eh? What've you heard? That was like once, twice at the most, I just needed a few bucks for– '

'On Tinder. Set up a new account. Turn your settings to sheila so you can search blokes to find that Kenny cunt.'

'How do we know he's on Tinder?'

'Every youngun's on that God damn app.'

'Can't we split the chicks, 50/50? You search half, I'll search half?'

Nomad takes a glug of bourbon and belches and rolls a smoke. A McSlave watches Nomad light up his ciggy but doesn't say nothing. Some kids pop out of the slide, stop and stare at him, then go back in the playground and clutch their mum's legs. 'Nahp.'

'60/50 spilt, then. Fuck, 75/35?'

'That makes 110, ya dumb fuck. Hurry up and get searching.'

I sigh and open up the Google Play store on my phone. I download Tinder, take a sip of harsh, sugary brown firewater with traces of milkshake in it, set Tinder to only show me guys in Northland. I've had fake profiles in the past – one of my favourites is called Karly-Rae Jepsen and it says

I'm a 28 year old blonde who loves to get wild, I used to run a few TradeMe scams with that profile and used it on Tinder to meet up with old blokes and take video of them begging me not to tell their wives. I've done that a couple times. Anyway I get Karly-Rae's sexy little profile logged in and start scrolling for horny men. It pains me to be doing this gaymo stuff when there's so many lady-opportunities out there, but it's important. I care about getting Barbie back.

I'd say I've never seen dudes posing like this on Tinder, but that wouldn't be 100% true – back in the day, I did a quick blue movie when I needed some skrilla, and that required some stuff in a hot tub with a whole soccer team that I'd rather not talk about (though the scrilla was decent.)

It's tempting to swipe left on all these dudes wearing tank tops, holding up freshly-caught snapper out in the Gulf, with their skater caps and their abs and the towels around their waists, it's tempting to flick through the forty thousand men, but Nomad could smack me over at any moment if he decides I'm not useful. You should hear the stories this guy tells.

Apparently he was a boxing rep in Lower Hutt where he grew up till he was 25. He hadn't done any dirt till he reached a quarter century, then his mum died and he didn't give a shit anymore. Smashed this cop that tried to arrest him for breaking windows at the public library. Done a one-year stretch, met some bad boys that influenced him. His blood was pissed off and his feet itched unless he was kicking someone in the skull. Electroshock in there too. Lake Alice.

Nomad scrapes the last blob of raspberry syrup from his cup and pours more bourbon in. 'You better be searching, boy.'

'Yeah, yeah I'm working,' I tell Nomad. 'I promise I won't go past that Kenny scumbag when I see him. What about you? Any girls look like Barbie?'

'Shitloads. She's average-looking as fuck.'

*You take that back*, I wanna go. *She's stunningly beautiful. Like a statue made of daffodils or something.*

*Was* beautiful or *is*? God, I dunno if she's alive, to be honest. Might've got her head ripped off like that police ninja.

'No offence, Nomad, but are you positive you'll recognise Barbie when you see her? I can describe what she– '

'You talk like I never seen her in person.'

'I presumed you hadn't, uh– '

'Shut up and listen. Got any more special smokes?'

I give him a meth-dipped smoke. He plucks stray tobacco hairs out of one end, pinches it, bites it, it lights it, sucks in, puffs out. 'I'm gonna tell ya a story about recognising cunts. Now, there was a Japanese fellow came into this whorehouse I was workin at. My own operation, technically, but you wouldn't catch my name on the books, taxman'd hunt me down and violate me if they knew the turnover I was turnin over. Now, our Japanese fella was attached to the consulate they've got there. Diplomatically protected. How'd I ascertain that?' He sucks in and puffs smoke right at me. I blink and light my own ciggie, and slurp a little more bourbonshake.

'How?'

'He had himself a Romeo complex. Liked to treat his women extra-special. He was the opposite of your woman-hatin psycho. Now, Mr Tetsuo, in a session I wish I'd known about, he'd proposed to one of my girls, name of Lydia. Lydia was impressed. Hadn't had roses before, hadn't had fancy lingerie. She'd been goin down in phone booths for most of her life before I took her in. Not classy phone booths, neither – we're talkin them new ones that don't have a door on 'em. Lydia thought a knuckle sandwich was one of the main meals of the day, she did. So of course she was gonna leap at the first man to treat her right. Now, our Tetsuo, that's the typa girl he was all about: beautiful, damaged goods. Mine wasn't the only parlour he'd been frequenting. As a consulate man, he worked hard, boy did he work hard, 5am to 5pm, but after 5? Piece of shit had a different whorehouse for every night of the week. Different fiancée at each place, too.'

'He was putting rings on the girls?'

Nomad smashes out his cigarette, flicks it into the McPlayArea and gulps Jim Beam. Two big builder-looking daddies, whose children pull them by their fingers, almost approach Nomad for a confrontation about the ciggy butt, sack it, then quietly put the butt in the bin and head towards the exit and leave.

'We had a gathering, me and the madams runnin the other girls. We worked out it was the same Tetsuo playing several girls, worked out he'd not contacted the girls for the same lengtha time. The emotional torture he'd done on the girls was worse than any sparkler I've lit and stuck down any man's dick-hole. Tetsuo fled the country. Know how I tracked him to his place in Japan?'

I want to come back to this thing about shoving sparklers down men's dickholes. 'How?'

'Gave the Japanese ambassador a hiding. Well, his driver. The ambassador watched, couldn't pop off any shots. They're not allowed to walk around strapped. Driver didn't have no karate skills or nothing.'

Nomad adjusts his legs and blaaaarps out this massive burp. A mum covers her little daughter's ears, shakes on her handbag and scuttles out. Nomad's basically clearing out Macca's.

'I only knew one word of Japanese, and I used it, boy: Tetsuo. Screamed it right in his fuckin face. Shook the driver till the handkerchief fell out of his breast pocket. Got Tetsuo's address within a couple of minutes. People are always helpful when ya smash 'em.'

'But where was the dude you were after?'

'Copley, if you're street, you'll know you could walk into any Japanese fuckin' karaoke club and find your man. Know how?'

'"Cause it's not about you lookin for them. It's about them lookin for you?'

'Attaboy. Innocent folks got no fear. Guilty man'll scuttle sideways out of a room like a crab. And that's all it took. Got me a flight to Tokyo, then Tokyo to Fukuoka, found the nearest titty bar to his pad, walked in there, sat by the entrance, watched cunts to see how much of a hurry they were in to leave.'

'What'd you, er… .' My mouth's gone dry. I suck more McBourbon. 'What'd you do to him?'

'Reckon I'd done enough at that point. Tetsuo was cryin in public. Jap cops came by, askin me what was up. I told 'em the situation, straight-up, with a interpreter obviously. They weren't impressed with our boy Tetsuo. Called him dishonorable. I took a photo on the typa cameras they had at the time, film camera, got the photos developed back here at home, gave them to Lydia, said There ya go. Man who cries in fronta other men, that the sorta man you wanna marry? That made her feel better.'

'Damn. How come you're telling me this story, Nome?'

'You need to know I'll track anyone, anywhere if they don't do the right thing.' My legs run cold and tingly. 'So just carry on fishing for blokes on your little app there, boy.'

I go back to my phone and catch up on guy-swiping.

Tinder offers me a selection of Northland blokes. Amongst these blokes, I look for a man with homemade sticky dreadlocks down to his hips, calling himself Ken – if I'm lucky. He could've had a haircut but retained his name; coulda kept the filthy clumps his scalp shits out and changed his name. He hasn't updated his Facebook since I last looked at it, when the status read 'Selling the missus lol. Owe sum nigga$ some $$$.' Jeez, what a trashy cunt. Hell, he could not even *be* on Tinder – but that's unusual. Ken is young, 28 I think. That's something Little Richie Richard told me – well, he didn't say 28, he gave me Ken's date of birth, typical cop, and I had to do the math myself. I've got a strong recollection of Kenny Boy's burnt brown druggy eyes, and I'm gonna do my best to hold that image in fronta me while I sift through pictures of men dressed like Magic Mike strangling their dicks with their left hands and holding a cellphone cam in front of a mirror with their right.

Swipe swipe swipe, bourb bourb bourb, smoke smoke smoke... I can only estimate the number of men I look through. Must be 1200. Another 39,000 to go, farkin 'ell. Nomad's not fucking around, either, he sucks his firewater and sips his ciggies and clicks his fingers at the McWorkers and gets them to bring him 40 more chicken McNuggets. My head drifts. I think about primmers. Everything in my world comes back to primary school eventually. Bloody monocultural-arse New Zealand. Same recycled dozen-odd names which keep coming up – Jonno, Timmo, Dave, Brad, Pete, Hemi, Shane, Mike, Michael, Mikey, Mickey, Kenny, Sam –

Hang on: Kenny.

From out of nowhere appears Kenny on my phone with dreadlocks. Profile says his hobbies and interests include DJing, Bob Marley, Bathurst, pimping and pu$$y, spelled with the dollar signs. That's gotta be him.

I swipe right, sending a message through the app that I wanna suck his dick, well, that Karly-Rae Jepsen, the woman in my catfish profile, wants to suck his dick. I pretend to scroll through and swipe a few more blokes, but honest: I've got a feeling this is the only Kenny I need.

The sun has appeared behind Nomad and his shoulders are so wide it turns him into a big black block of stone like them monkeys were dancing around on Space Odyssey. Nomad's busy doing his swiping, that's cool, respect, and I'm beginning to wonder if there's a way I can speed up this whole process without getting bullied again when my phone rumbles.

A little flame icon appears.

*You've got a match!* Tinder tells me.

I open him up and thar he blows: Kenny D'Souza. 28. Looking for, ahem, pu$$y.

The sun's going down, I've got some bourbon in me, and I've got a catfish on the hook… or I'm the catfish. Yeah, I'm the catfish, and my mouth is on Kenny's rod.

Sounds weird.

Irregardless, I begin seducing the dude.

*Cheers 4 match baby wotz ur idea of a gd time?*

A lull. A family of English people coming into Mickey D's mutter something about the "stench like a dying animal." The father of the group realises the stench belongs to stinky old granddaddy Nomad, hunched over his phone and nugget crumbs and booze with a ciggy in his fingers.

My phone gets the fire symbol. New message.

*Karly,* the words simply say.

My heart stops.

*Cut 2 the chase. Do u want 2 meet.*

I want to meet so badly. I want to shake him by his dreadlocks and ask where he put the woman I love.

*Defo. Letz meet wherever u want. I have party supplies ;0)*

*Canopy Bridge Whangaz,* Kenny responds ten seconds later. *Can u meet at 8.30 bring ur party suppliez. I got gear.*

This part's all good. I'll do anything. Hell, I'll dress up in drag and let him root me from behind if it gets information out of the guy. All my mind cares about, though, is where my perfect woman is. The woman with the wicked sense of humour, the leather soul, the sharp tongue, the gallery on her skin, the cheeky eyes.

*U sure u single?* I ask.

*Itz complicated,* Kenny goes.

Far out.

Long lull before he comes back.

*OK Ive got a blond who luvs 2 party hard.*

*Whatz her name? Tell her Karly sez hi.*

*Fucks that sposd 2 mean?*

Damn. I've been sprung. Cover, man, cover.

*Nuthing cu at 8.30.*

Night is about to fall. I'm so nervous I fill my milkshake with hooch and glug it back. It bubbles up in my throat like a smoothie made of puke.

I'm thinking Kenny must be still squeezing some profit out of Barbs, renting her out for an hour at a time to… who knows. Other clubs?

Suddenly, one final message from Kenny.

*We r kinda trying 2 avoid sum peeps wna kill me can we find somewhr quiet?*

I promise him we can find a quiet spot, hell yeah, definitely. So long as he brings his bottle blond.

Nomad downs another bellyful of Beam and when he wobbles over to the parking lots to piss into the drain, he nearly trips over his own boots in the after-dusk darkness.

He's sparked up a cone by the time he comes back and I smoke a session with him, trying not to make eye contact with the Hamburglar painted on the wall.

Finally my phone responds.

*I got a certain blond yeh but dunno if she iz alive or dead.*

That stops my heart.

'Nome.'

He's drunk and high and busy with his phone.

'Nomad! Bro – fuckin, I think I've, like… I've got a lead. Found that Kenny guy. I think we need to plan or something.'

Nomad gives me the type of hard look he's probly given bank robbers and screws and detectives and streetfighters over the years, sussing me out, weighing my words. Finally he nods, and almost mutters something which vaguely sounds like he's congratulating me on doing a good job. It's the biggest compliment I can expect from the stingy old ogre.

Me and Nomad, we pack up, go over to Shana's SUV, settle in the front, after one last piss into the parking lot sewer grate. A McWorker cleans up behind us, blasting our table with a hose.

We settle into the vehicle, spread a couple of jackets over our waists to keep us warm. Nomad places his police scanner on the dashboard and switches it on. Soft burbling murmur. Chit-chat about the rugby. The scent of rotting shoejam from decaying soles wafts off Nomad.

Just as I'm about to explain that I've lured Kenny to Whangārei's Canopy Bridge at 8.30 tonight with the promise of pussy and product, the bourbon and weed overtakes us as we both collapse into comas.

# 18

# "You will never be a hero."

I'm swimming through the clouds over The Great North-land. Floating back to discoes and surf days and signing yearbooks and second base and shenanigans in cars, high school, oak trees and bees and leaves and the tuck shop and skipping rope and tagging and chasing girls with dogshit on a stick.

Barbie, bro, *Barbie…* She brought her beagle to school on Pet Day and I swung it by its tail and it bit me. I biffed a poo at her car when I was like 8 'cause she narked on me for writing *Limp Bizkit 4 Life* on a tombstone in our school's memory garden. She was my first kiss, bro. We were 11 and there was this junkie living in this house that bordered right on our school, and he'd have his morning coffee and tell us to come round all the time and one day we dared each other all morning. Come lunch, we just went for it, and the cops picked us up like 15 minutes after this old lady seen us walking into the house, and I'll never forget how the house had everything stripped out of it, naked floorboards in the kitchen cause all the lino had been ripped out, no fridge, no food, no lounge suite, no rug, no TV, just a bedroom at the end of a long wooden hallway, huge superking bed, cerulean blue silk sheets, massive white fluffy pillows, and a couple of pot plants – and there was the junkie, asleep on his back with a *My Little Pony* Band-Aid on his arm.

We kissed right in front of him while he snoozed. My legs went fizzy with excitement, stomach full of bees.

Karl's first kiss, yessir. Only meaningful kiss I've ever had, if you must know.

Truancy services and the principal made us get tested for diseases, got in trouble with our olds. It was a whole week of drama, but if I could see Barbie just one last time, I'd say four words, My Little Pony Band-Aid, and time-travel her back to when life felt giddy and exciting.

I'd ask her about her tattoo, too.

See, we were 13, this was in cooking class, when all the boys had to wear these wussy aprons. I was havin a real aggro day. Something to do with Richie, I think it was 'cause he got that award 'cause he went to the Orienteering Olympiad, you get a hard-out medal just 'cause you can find your way around a patch of bush, whoop-dee-doo, and I was mad 'cause I had no one to cling to, after school. It was just me, the old man, and his oxygen machine, and I think Barbie was giving me shit about how I'd try to hitchhike. All the kids on the bus would see me and point at me, so I'd try all these tricks to hide my hitchhiking thumb, like put a umbrella over it, or my jersey over my outstretched arm. Of course no one picked me up 'cause they couldn't see my thumb, so I didn't hardly get any lifts, so I'd've hardly even got away from the school by 5pm. Eventually I'd go along to a bus stop, see what happens, get in a fight with the bus driver 'cause I'd try to squirrel onto the bus with like twenty cents, and the bus would pull up outside Burger King and Shana would have her pager that she sold Girl Guide biscuits to save up for, messaging away organising school fundraisers, always networking, organising, always socialising, always putting on events so the rugby boys like Richie got celebrated. God, I had a lot of reasons to hate Barbie and the Mercedes she'd get picked up in. I think I picked the cooking class fight 'cause she turned on the cold tap in the sink too hard and a little bit splashed my apron and turned the flour into glue, but I just went berserk, started throwing flour and syrup and raisins and food colouring at Barbie's face, and her girlfriends tried to turn their backs and raise their shoulders over their faces and shield her, and she had blue food colouring blooming out across her shoulder and a white face 'cause I biffed flour at her, and a fuckin' raisin stuck to her back, and I reached over her friends and lined up the two prongs of this carving fork over her shoulder and BAM: pricked her, right in the shoulder. Bro, I'd never heard a scream like it. Sounded like a fire alarm goin off. The whole classroom backed away from me like I was radioactive.

I only seen the damage years later at our flatwarming, the imprint, the mark I left on Barbs. Me and Richie had scored this granny flat together in Kamo at the arse-end of Whangarei, tiny little bungalow, one toilet, box hedges, pergola, trellis with ivy growin on it and a little path made of paving stones. At the flatwarming, people were liftin up the paving stones and smashing them on the driveway, makin big dents, and when the kegs were empty, someone switched a grinder on and grinded a hole in the top of a keg to get the dregs out, sparks and beer-gas goin everywhere, and people were drumming and playing bass guitar and singin Six60 and there was so much weed in the air, Richie'd wrapped a scarf around his mouth and put shades on his eyes 'cause he said the eyes are made of mucous membranes and he couldn't permit cannabinoids to be absorbed ocularly, whatever the hell that meant. When the party was at its peak, I remember trying to drag any old girl into the bathroom with me for a bit of a poke 'n grope, and I grabbed some chick with angel wings on her back and halo above her head, plus a blunt stickin out of her mouth, and we were about to have a pash when we look at each other and it was Barbie and we had a laugh, but she still looked down on me, right, she was like, 'Oh, I suppose you live here, don't you.'

'Yeah, babe. How bout we lock the door, have a lil private party?'

She started to move outta the bathroom, but there was no one in the hallway to observe whether she was snobby to me or nice, so she turned around and grabbed my throat and growled, 'D'you know what you did to me?'

I was getting a boner, partly cause she was squishing the blood down my body so it pooled in my cock, partly cause I just love feisty women.

'You gave me my first tattoo, dickhead,' she went. Barbs stood still while I peeled back the lacy garment she had on under her angel wings, and low and behold: two blue marks on her shoulder. If you squinted, they almost looked like a swastika and a love heart.

Or a K and a B together.

'Guess I tattooed you,' I chuckled. 'Holy fuck.... Did it hurt?'

'You stabbed me with a carving fork. What do you think?'

'Didn't get you that bad, did I?'

'Just the points on the end went in,' she went, 'Cause you've got skinny little arms and you don't know how to stab like a man.' Then she threw her arms around the next person comin down the hall, this Juggalo, and let the Juggalo carry her awayyyyyykkkkkuuuuppppp-

Awakeup.

Awake. Up.

*Wake up*, a stinky mean giant is whispering. Wake up, Copley.

A glove is over my mouth. It reeks of smoke. The fingernails are yellow. It's strong and thick, crusty. There are green tattoos creeping down his fingers, numbers and letters, stars and crescent moons.

'They got her. Get to work. C'mon.'

I rub my eyes, lean forward, rest my head on the dashboard. God, it's cramped in here. Why are we sleeping in a car?

'Whuh – what did you – '

'They got her. Or him. Fucked if I know. Bitsa some cunt's body.'

'Nahhhhh, nah nah n– '

'Shut the fuck up. They found human remains bout an hour ago.'

He's got the scanner locked on a private police conversation.

'Wh-where? How?'

'Cops, radio. Listen.'

*Needing an update on that body at the Canopy Bridge, 92.*

*Copy. Stand by. Detectives are telling me... elbows, at this stage. Two elbows. Forearms severed, ulna and radius cut through with... with whatever the divers are pulling up just now.*

*92. You know I've got supervisors breathing down my neck on this. What am I supposed to tell McMullan? Nantakarn? Over.*

*Tell 'em my diver's waving like a black metal shoelace out of the water... Chain blade.*

*From a chainsaw?*

*And my diver's also bringing up, uh... I don't know how to say this...*

*I'm listening, brother. Whatever you can give me.*

*My diver has three hands.*

*[...]*

*[...]*

*Three hands and an elbow?*

*Appears that way.*

*Male or female?*

*We've yet to determine.*

*Any other parts? Of the body?*

*Just a whole mess of blood. We're running DNA urgent.*

*How long will that take? The usual twelve hours?*

*Copy. Unless we find a chunk of skin with one of her identifying markers on it, know what I'm saying?*

I'm stunned. 'We oughta give Shana's car back....'

'Jam a sock in it.' Nomad's jabbing me with his finger. 'Ride's your problem. C'mon out with ya phone. See if Kenny messages back. If he does, then they musta found your bitch. If he don't message back, well. Ken's the bitch.'

Good thing I didn't meet Kenny at the bridge, then.

The scanner has a little microphone mouthpiece on it. I can't resist. I snatch it, and even though Nomad's giving me demon-ass hell-eyes with flames dancing behind them, I get a couple words out.

'Check if she's got my KB tattooed on her shoulder, yo! That's how you tell it's her!'

There's no response, for a moment. Nomad punches me in the head and I feel knuckles squish my brain. He's wrestling for the mic, but I have to spit a few more words.

'Divers, man, juslisten, it can't be her – nng.' Nomad pulls my fist into his mouth and starts biting my knuckles. 'NyaaaAAAArgh— '

*Sir, interfering with a private police communication channel is an offence.*

*92, requesting we switch to Channel Delta. Code Yellow. Over.*

Nomad gives my bitten-open fist back. He adjusts the scanner delicately, like we haven't had a scrap just now.

While I suck my cut-open hand and count the teeth marks, wondering about rabies and AIDS and whatever gross diseases I'll catch off the cunt, the diver-detectives start yapping again, thinking they're on a private channel.

'Keep ya mouth shut on this one,' Nomad rumbles, licking my blood off his lip. 'Moment of truth.'

*We safe, talking here? Over.*

*Copy. Little kids messing with the channels. I've told head office.*

*Just had word back estimating length of bone fragments as a proportion of total body height. Body's going to turn out approximately five feet.*

*What height is Little Girl Lost?*

*Five-seven.*

*Is it her?*

*Not known.*

*Identifying features, markings, piercings, tattoos?*

'Fuck, man.' I thump the window. I want to smash everything Shana owns. What have we achieved? Nomad's attached only as far as the money goes. I could use a catch-up with Richie, but does he give a shit? I need someone's shoulder to cry into – preferably not a shoulder that smells like wet dog and has little spiky bits of concrete on it. 'I've gotta talk to my bruz... .'

'Well you ain't goin nowhere till I get paid, so sit tight.'

'You can't keep me in here.'

'That a fact?' Nomad presses the child lock and my door latches itself.

'Look, bro, I don't wanna fight about it –'

'Good, cause you'd lose.' Nomad yawns.

'I just need a wee cry about Barbie, that's all – '

'This is billable hours, cunt. Getcha phone out and get swiping.'

'Now is not the time!'

'You're on my time, boy. Remember that slap I owe ya? Now lemme sleep.'

I can feel wet stuff inside my nose, and my eyelashes are fat and sticky.

One final look at the girls on Tinder couldn't hurt. I tug his phone out of his hands, turn a shoulder away. Let him donkey punch me, I don't care. I'm traumatised over this body they're talkin bout on the radio.

I swipe through a Ginger, a Shady, a Sabrina, two Mistys and a Dynasty, each name skankier than the last. Some lady called Barbara appears on the screen, 101km away, then I swipe left and she's gone.

She's gone.

'I found Barbie, it has to be her!'

Nomad's eyes half-open, but his sleepy body doesn't move. I josh his shoulder. 'I saw her, bro, she's a hundred kays from here, she's selling her shit like normal, or or or– '

Or someone's taken her phone. After they've dumped her in the ocean. After they've–

I reach across the patches on his belly, his fists and his pipe and his crotch-nuggets. I undo the child lock.

I pull the courier bag out of my backpack. I slide Shana's laptop into it. I'm impressed there's room for the power cord. These Apple MacBooks, bro, they're thin as an anorexic. I push the laptop into the bag, exit Shana's jeep, creep up Bank Street, slide the slim package into a postbox, and find myself walking back to Nomad. I guess good luck is associated with the old ogre.

I'm itchy. Barb, man, Barbara, Barbara's been seen! I have to run in circles. I have to do jumping jacks. I have to kiss the ground outside McDonald's with a petrified pickle stuck to it. I let myself out and my feet are about to hit the tarmac when everything turns to shit.

The arms of a slim, muscular man wrap around me. There's enough strength in the man I don't even touch the ground. My arms are restrained. I start kneeing the guy straight away, but he's got a perfect grip on me.

'Fuggoff me, rapey cunt,' I screech, 'Help!'

Looking around, I see Nancy Drew, four other police, and the guy holding me? Senior Constable Richard McMullan.

'The hell you hugging me for?!'

'That package you've just slipped into the post there,' he goes. 'What was in it?'

'I was sending you some evidence, ya ungrateful prick.' I try to suck breath back into my body. It comes in ugly chunks of hot air that don't fit into my lungs. 'Oh, and by the way, I found her.' Another few breaths. God, I need a ciggy. 'She's alive, man, doing prostitutey stuff over Tinder –probly – and she's... .'

'I don't think I want your imaginary evidence,' Richie says, ushering me into the rear door of a cop car. 'We saved your favourite cell for ya.'

'Fuck you and fuck jail.'

'Oh, it's a step beyond jail, my friend.'

'What, prison? For what?'

'Unlawful use of a private emergency services communications channel. Oh, and breaching bail conditions. We did tell you to stay away, Karl.'

They press me into the back of Richie's car, which is a real patrol car this time and not a pathetic Kia.

Nomad ain't coming to save me.

'Rich!' I squawk as the car door closes, 'I have to tell you something.'

I catch my breath. Rich looks like he can't wait for his pizza to come out of the microwave.

'Spit it out, bruz.'

'Just wanted to say, chuck me in prison all you want. But we ain't brothers.'

It rumbles him, for a moment, like a shockwave going through him. But Richie claps right back.

'You're right. You're right.' he decides. 'My brothers are heroes.' He slams the door, gets in the front, 'You, Karl? You will never be a hero.'

# 19

# "The whole thing's fishy as a mermaid's undies."

Being on remand in jail up at Ngawha Prison sucks, mostly, but it's not 100 percent bad. Like, since Christmas is comin up in a week or two, the kitchen's put on Santa-shaped meatloaf, with a triangliar red squirt of tomato sauce for Santa's hat, and mashed potato for his beard and peppercorns for his buttons and orange cubes of carrot for Santa's presents, so that's a'ight. And all us crims get together for carols once a day. That's pretty chill.

What's not chill is being crammed into a holding cell with a bunch of other dudes as summer heats up and the air con's not working. That's no way to relax.

Jail gives you time to think stuff over, and there's two things I simply cannot stop pondering while I spend the week at Ngawha, waiting to go back to court for interfering and breach of bail and unlawful use of blah di blah.

Number one thing I can't stop thinkin bout: How come the more money Shana gets given to pay ransoms, the less Barbie we get back?

Two: what the hell happened that made Barbie turn into a fuck-up in the first place?

I pace my concrete box pondering this stuff, stepping around the knees of the other dudes crammed in here with me, wondering what I could've done different this afternoon to find out who's benefiting from Barbs being dangled at the end of a money-rope.

What's happened is around 1pm, after I've finished my apple and sandwich and played with myself for a bit, there's been a visit from The Goody-Goods and they've invited me into something called the Whānaungatanga Room with pictures of the Wiggles on the walls and posters of tough guys cradling babies. Our little family conference has started off sorta okay. Richie's asked Nancy Drew and the Konstantinou parents if they want a prayer, and I've said I can do, like, a prayer, and they've told me to go ahead, Karl, and I've been all like "Life is a mystery / everyone must stand alone / I hear you call my name / and it feels like home," and they've asked me what the heck that is, and I've said "It's *Like A Prayer*, by Madonna, as promised," and they've stood up and told me off and it's sorta descended into bickering. Well when I say bickering, I mean me stirring shit up.

We're stuck in a vicious circle, except it's got five points, so it's a vicious starfish, I guess.

Here's the five points:

One, Richie's told me that after today, we won't be seeing each other, and I'll be driven down to court on Friday to enter a plea over these charges I'm rackin' up.

Two, Nantakaran's told me that I'm inches away from being charged for operating as a bounty hunter without a licence.

Three, the parents've told me they've paid the Defiant Motorcycle Club Incorporated two hundred god damn thousand bucks and it hasn't resulted in their daughter coming back.

Four, Shana reckons they have assurance that if they pay five hundred grand in total, the Four-13s personally guarantee Barbie will be picked up and handed back from "whoever has her."

Five, all Richie and the detectives need to do's check the shoulder on them dead body-bits and if they don't find a little tattoo with two letter-shaped dots on that dead body's fuckin shoulder, they'll know it ain't the body of Barbara Konstantinou (assuming the shoulder ain't been eaten by some octopus.)

None of these things are progressing. Like a bunch of nerdy virgins playing chess, everyone's afraid to move.

Meanwhile Shana's acting suspiciously sweet, not even hassling me for taking her car and stinking it out with Nomad. It's almost like Shana *wants* me to sponge up all these guys' frustrations to take attention off the fact that for a middleman broker, she's moved around a whole lot of cash and brought back not very much abductee to show for it. Most disturbing part today is seeing Shana rubbing Richie's arm and tilting her forehead into him, like a swan or something. She's buttering up a cop that can shield her, that's what I reckon. The whole thing's fishy as a mermaid's undies.

Know what I reckon? I reckon Karl Copley's the only one purely thinking of Barbara's welfare, and they can't handle it, which is why they get petty revenge after the whānaungatanga conference disintegrates, hauling me back to the holding cell – as in, a hard sterile unfriendly pen where they park short-termers and everybody can see you taking a dump.

In my holding cell we've got four Filipino Cripz, two TruBlues, a low ceiling and a concrete bench. There's no space on the concrete bench, the four Pinoys are hunkered on it, chattering in whatever Star Wars kinda language they speak, so I sit on the toilet, moving aside whenever peeps wanna piss in it.

There's a TV in the cell right now, cept the Pinoy Cripz are in control of the channels. Wish I was in control of something. Being a whiteboy on my own, I guess I have to be a one-man Aryan Brotherhood. Cell's a tight box of tension with buzzing fluorescent lights, a gladiator pit with no dark places to hide in. I'm so outnumbered, it's not even funny.

Breaking news interrupts a music video. The 4-13 are putting on a press conference, outside the hotel where Nantakarn put her own conference on. Pork is in the middle of what's gotta be the world's widest panel – about 40 Defiants, all wearing muscle t-shirts so black you can see 'em from space. They have yellow bandanas. Some wear eye patches.

'Ehhhh!' yelp the TruBlues in the cell with me, barging me out of the way, 'Watchthiswatchthis, crank it!'

Some screw somewhere turns the volume up remotely. The TV news people are eating up the Defiants' sloppy-arse, trashy-arse press conference. Pork is holding a deck of Poker Run playing cards up to the camera. He's sliding out a card, twisting his fingers skilfully and Nancy Drew's face is in the camera. '...Nantakarn's made the cut in this year's deck, proud t'announce, and her Senior Constable Richard McMullan, who I've heard she's rooting around with incidentally, he's got a card t'imself as well.' The cards Pork is holding have an in-joke on them. I get it. The reporters gasp as they relay the news.

Nantakarn and Richie are Jokers.

The camera moves up the line of bikers and down. Pork has no microphone, just that booming, crusty, husky voice from fat lungs and a smoky throat. He rants about The Best Administration endangering the life of the missing girl, harassing his club members, invading his property without a warrant. He spots a reporter with a boom microphone, grabs the damn boom mike out of the air, pulls it into his mouth and bellows that he's hereby announcing a charity fight night challenge against Richie's Group Awesome.

'Thas right, thas right, ladies and gents, let's find out who's really got the backbone round here,' he goes. His droogs clamour at his side like a bunch of sniffling rats.

Reading between the lines, what's happening is El Porko is publicly threatening to kick the shit out of Richie and his choirboys. Makes me nervous. Richie may be a snobby scum-sucking sellout, but he's *my* snobby scum-sucking sellout. If anyone's gonna kick the shit out of Rich, it's gonna be me.

I thumb the emergency buzzer. The one you're only supposed to use if your cellmate's raping you. 'Turn it off, screws. I don't wanna see this.'

'Shut up, G,' a TruBlue growls at me. Some sort of feeder gang for Black Power. They're only about one percent less dangerous than the Filipinos.

On the telly, fat old shaven-headed thick-bellied Pork's telling the public that he's some kind of a youth leader, holding up his framed youth worker qualification (probably printed off the internet) and he's name-dropping Barbie's parents' names, and lo and behold, the news camera pans around and locates the parents, and a mob of 16-year-old hangarounds in yellow t-shirts with concentration camp haircuts move aside and let Barbie's parents through. Anna clutches her elbows; Georgios holds onto his wife's shoulder. They approach the forty-odd biker conference and hoooooly Jesus, what's this, Anna is busting out her chequebook and Jabba the Hutt is wrapping his thick arm around her shoulder and–

And the TV goes black. The green power light on the TV turns red. The Pinoy Boys start babbling in Tag-a-long or whatever their language is called. It's obvious they're talkin about what to do with me. Three of them could hold my arms and legs while the fourth takes his time stomping me like a tub of grapes.

I try to stand near the Blues and strike up a chat about the league but I'm doubting it'll last long. Firstly I haven't watched an NRL game in yonks, second, I'm white, which for them guys makes me one degree closer to being a cop.

My corner conversation is drowning. I can't help watch the Pinoys strip their pants and shirts off, and it isn't because I'm queer. I watch them drop and do push-ups to harden their bodies, getting ready for some kind of war.

Surprising the Blues, who tell me to get the fuck away, I take my own pants off, stand on the crotch and pull my pants leg until the fabric rips. I begin wrapping the pant legs around my knuckles.

'Blues,' I go, trying to make conversation, sliding along the wall before the Pinoys begin attacking me, 'You blue boys've got that, um, that-that, uh, tattoo show you're puttin on, up at the Bay eh?'

'Yeah,' goes one of the Blues, trying to perch on top of the toilet like a chicken so he can stay out of the fight and keep his clothes on, not that it's even gonna be a fight, just a straightforward stomping. 'So?'

Think, Karl, think. Words spurt out of my mouth like jizz. 'Lookinforagirl,' I blurt, 'Like a, um, like a platinum blonde type thing? Like if Marilyn Monroe was on crack?'

'New chickie's doin tats at the tat show, Bay Blue,' the other Blue tells me, edging along the wall so the Pinoys don't attack him. 'Might be her. White chick. Does mean dragons.'

'She skinny? Makes her ears and head look all big cause she's so bony?'

'Looks like the one on the news,' the other Blue goes.

'*Bad* news, bro,' says the first Blue. 'Not worth goin after. Just worry about yourself right now.'

I'm about to carry on bantering when the Pinoys begin hassling me.

'Puñeta, you wanna suck me?' a Pinoy goes, grinning ravenous as a wolf. A wolf wearing tighty whitey underpants.

'How that two hundred thousand doll-ah?' Second Pinoy goes. 'You take up north?'

'Where'd you hear that?'

'Jus answer you question,' third Pinoy tells me.

The final Pinoy is a big fucker – as tall as me, and with a pack of boys to make him feel invincible.

I look over at the Blues. They're interested in seeing a 75kg white boy getting stomped by some little fifty-KG fuckers in their undies. The spectacle is obviously worth more to them than profiting off helping me.

'Why you friends with cop?'

'I'm not,' I go. 'Fuck that pig. He ain't my friend.'

'We heard you go to his house. You ride his car. Why you friend?'

'H-how do you even know that shit? Leave me alone, man. I just wanna sleep.'

Pinoy Four – the big one – slaps me. I soak it up, dizzy, feeling pukey, and move along the wall. They press me into a corner, their underwear looming close now.

I won't put my fists up yet. Lash out first and give them a reason to waste me? No thanks.

He reaches out and slaps me again. 'Cut me in!'

'Barbie money doesn't go through me. I swear to god, bro! It's her sister that handles it! Gimme a break!'

'You gonna take that shit, homie?' a Blue calls out.

'Four-13 don't like you,' says Big Boy Pinoy. 'Mister Pork, he tell me send message.'

I knew it. They wanna silence my ass cause I'm the only one piecing the puzzle together.

A truck collides with the right side of my skull. My ear is hot and the ceiling yo-yos towards me and back. A smack on the other side of my head comes next, then a dude's hair is scratching my cheek as he headbutts me, missing my nose and bending my teeth, which scream up into my face. The back of my head whacks the wall and as I dribble down it like a hunk of snotty spit and pool on the concrete, I see the undersides of their jandals as the Pinoys stomp me.

The all-seeing light on the ceiling that reaches into every corner of the room is crowded out by the jostling shrieking Filipinos, all teeth and boots and fingers on each other's shoulders so they can get more leverage to stomp, jump, boot, and I'm saying bye to the world, lights out, sudden insult thump farewell goodb–

*Clank.*

The stomping stops.

The rectangle in the cell door slides open. A pair of eyes look in. They can see the Pinoys standing over me, detaching fingers from each other's tightly-squeezed shoulders, panting, out of breath.

'Van time, nuff playfighting,' says the jailer, 'Gotta drive you boys down to court.' He unlocks the door, looks at the piles of clothes, the tighty whitey Filipinos and the Māoris huddled in the corner. 'How come yous are all in your undies?'

# 20

## "You're a free man, for now."

These vans that drive you the hour and a half from prison down to the courts in Whangārei, they got no way of letting you contact the driver if you're getting shanked. I'm still inches away from getting murked.

They have to take all four Pinoys with me, it seems. We've been made to put on boiler suits and we're tied with plastic straps, facing the front – cept the guards seem to have forgotten that a man can turn his head. When I turn I'm confronted with four murderous midgets eyeballing me. It's got me shitting myself. The van's rattling. *I'm* rattling – man, if my feet weren't strapped to the ground, they'd rattle too. Strap over my toes, strap around my ankles, strap holding my thighs together, strap holding my hands to my thighs.

'Hey, Cock-a-roch, Pork, he say we can do what we want to you,' Pinoy 3 calls to me, in a accent thick as paint. 'He say you fuck with his money, you out to tender.'

'It's pointless tendering,' I go, 'I ain't got any money for anyone.'

'We know you got a little something from the girl family,' Pinoy 2 goes.

'No I did not. Leave me alone.'

'I gonna break your eyes, white boy.'

'Puñeta ka. Hey, bibingka pussy. Look a'me when I talk to you.'

It'll take an hour and a half with this granny driving to get down to Whangas and to the safety of court. Ninety long slow minutes, urgh. I count every second and every metre. I'm piecing together slivers of vision I get through the side window, little glimpses of the outside. We pass the hot springs, the junction, the pie factory, the oyster place, the old train yard, the dump, the tourist toilets. All the places Northland is renownded for.

'You gonna pay me, white boy,' says Pinoy 4, the big fucker. 'Blue boys, they want pay, too.'

'You don't speak for them.'

'Money talks, honky,' says one of the TruBlues. 'Listen, uh, zit true what they say? You sitting on two hundred kay? You got some of that rich family money, G?'

'No. Straight up.' Desperate. Almost crying, like a pussy.

'How much them Konstantinous give you to hand over, anyways?'

'Nothing, like I said.'

'Where you live? Maybe I come over and see you.'

'This is where I live. In a van full of you guys. I got no place else.'

It goes on like this for ages, as we wiggle and wobble through the little swamp towns of Moerewa and Titoki and Hikurangi and I count the minutes. 54 million Mister Zippys and I'll be safe.

Finally I hear the wheeze of truck brakes and honking and seagulls bitching and work out we're slowing down for the big city. After twenty minutes of stops and starts, the panel slides open, and the guard looks in at me like I'm a suitcase or a gas bottle, just some cargo.

'Let me out last,' I yell. You're not sposda show people you're scared, and I have no control over what order I'll be called into the dock, but I do not wanna be kicked from behind and jumped on by dudes who have to shuffle like seals. They'll bite, if they're on top of me.

We've gone down into the underground parking lot beneath the Whangārei District Court. We seem to be stopped for good, now. The escort guards untie me with skilful fingers and pull me out first – despite my requests. They're Samoans and South Africans with creased faces and coffee breath. They start hauling dudes out of the truck. In front of us is a dark passage with a concrete ceiling and moist tarmac under our toes. A couple court staff appear. One's an admin-type stickboy with a tablet, checking off names and scanning the barcoded stickers on our chests. The other person's a little suited female jailer or lawyer or clerk or something. I'm barely looking at her, barely listening. Just counting the minutes till I get shoved into a cell with the Pinoys and murked.

'Can we talk for a second?' says the suited little woman to one of our van guards. I mostly tune out as they chat. I'm scoping the other dudes as they're brought off the truck, waiting for one of them to kinghit me.

The van guard digs his hands into the straps of his stab-proof vest, 'What's goin on?'

This little woman with her black cap and ponytail, she's all hair and heels. Hard to see her face, dark down here in the underground carpark with the light behind her, metal pipes fixed to the concrete ceiling. The little woman has hopped out of a car which looks sorta haphazardly parked, like she's gonna do a u-turn and burn outta here in a moment.

'....delayed proceedings,' I hear. 'They're not gonna try one of these guys till next week, it's been decided, so I'll need to grab one of your boys and send him back.'

'So we drove 'im down for nothing,' the guard goes, snorting. 'Typical Tuesday. How many crims ya after?'

'Just one: Copley, Karl.'

My name pricks up my ears and I straighten up and wobble like a praying mantis. Instantly, though, the predators seize the distraction as a chance to fuck me up before I can leave. A Pinoy headbutts me and I stumble across the petrol-stained, gritty underground car park and hit the concrete bunker housing the elevator. My skull cracks against the wall. I lash out and manage to kick the Pinoy's knee which bothers him and he lunges at me, but the female lawyery-terrible-car-parker-woman wrenches me into a boxy interview room beside the elevator to protect me or something and I wrestle out of her grip and spit.

'Got some more for you fucks!'

'Not wrapped up like a mummy you're not,' says a voice I know. Her arm brushes my shoulder as she locks the door to the little office. The anger flushes out of me like a bladder full of morning piss.

'I'm done,' I pant, putting my weight on a coffee table, 'I can't be fucked fight– Shana!'

She takes her cap off and shakes her dark dykey hair out. She stands in front of me, doing that thing where she grins at you like she's being photographed for a school council election poster.

'What the literal fuck are you doing here?'

'Happy to see me, for a change?'

'They're-they're-they're-gonna carve me up, man! There's gonna be a fuckin' tool in the next holding cell and they're gonna do it, you gotta think of something, Shayn.'

'You're my client. Of course my duty is to protect you.'

I squint, for a second, searching the Karl Kranium. Client means… she's a hooker? And I'm buying some pussy off her? No – wait – client can mean legal shit, too.

I collapse against the wall, slide down it, sit on the ground. This moment right here, with a plastic pot plant and two chairs and a little table and a person who may be a comrade again, this is perfection. This is paradise, relief, even if it might get interrupted in 40 seconds.

'I don't really have a plan, Shayn. For after this. Those guys out there… I got a price on my head or something.'

'Plan, okay, yeah firstly, we're getting you away from a serious beating. They're gang members, I take it? And they've, what, got some kind of a grudge against you?'

'Defiant sent them to fuck me up. There's a hit out on me, man.'

'Why would that be?' Shana goes.

'Cause I'm valuable, obvs.'

Shana folds her arms, looks at the ceiling real patient, tapping her toes.

'A'ight, I'm not valuable, but I know too much.'

She gives me this look like she wants to say, 'You don't know shit, dumbass. Again, she's polite. Bites her tongue.

'Just get me to the lab so I can tell 'em what to look out for in the autopsy. I'm tellin ya, if there's a shoulder – rest in peace and all that shit, obviously – if there's a chunk of torso from this body the divers found, you wanna look on the back of the *right* shoulder. Got it? The back of the right shoulder. A swastika-kay-looking mark and a loveheart, sorta K and B-ish you're lookin out for. Member when I stabbed your sis and put that mark on her? It's come in handy. Cause if the body doesn't have the tat, then it can't be her. You should be thanking me, oi.'

Shana's eyes squiggle up into little black flies and she's about to say something like 'What on earth goes on in that head of yours?' when there's a thud on the door.

'Copley! Get your arse out here.'

I hear swearing and screaming.

Shana looks me up and down. I am one dirty, disrespectful animal. I deserve to be in a cage. I'm lucky this lady is taking a chance on me, like when you're at the SPCA and out of pity you take home the retardedest puppy.

She shakes out a bag.

'Here. Your phone.'

'How the fuck'd you get this off the screws?'

'Richie never gave it to them. Show me. What you told Richie. Something about 101 kilometres away, you used some tracking system?'

'Way simpler: you just put out some skank bait and the skanks come runnin.' I unlock my phone, open Tinder. Thar she blows. The Holy Grail.

Shana stares at the phone, stares at the picture a long time, then locks it, shutting the picture down.

*Whump-whump-whump.*

Our nuts drop; I need to piss. A little bald screw is pressing his nose and his spectacles against the door window, trying to see inside the meeting room. Shana tells me to get out of sight, rips the door open, tells the screw to give the client and the lawyer another five minutes. The screw says he's going on his break, handing over to new guards as soon as he's put the last of the crims into the court holding room. A fresh set of guards will look after me from then. The screw says he's been on his shift since 11 the night before. Shana says she'll press the buzzer down the corridor to summon a guard to open the holding cell once she's done interviewing me.

Shana hauls a little light suitcase onto the table, pulls three zips down and opens it.

'I have a suit, I have a tie, I have a white shirt *which I ironed*. It'll be enough to get the judge to excuse you, move your date back.'

She pushes a tie against my collarbone and nods. 'You're a free man, for now— so dress like one.'

# 21

# "Self-aggrandising narcissistic delusion."

Hooooleeeee shitballs. I cannot believe Stuck-up Pig-pleasing Highly-Suspect-Shana got me out of court today. We drive up the ramp of the underground car park toward daylight.

'So this lead of yours,' she goes to me, 'This 101 kilometres thing... You got that from where? Tinder of all places?'

'Mmm-hmmm. Your boy's a computer whiz.'

'So my sister's phone, someone's switching it on? Because Police can't work out its location. It's operative?'

'How the fuck would I know?'

'By phoning her, dickhead. God knows me and the police and mum and dad and everyone haven't managed to reach her on the phone for a month, now. This Tinder information of yours, it could be months old, God, we'd have to get Police to apply for a warrant... Unless you have some news you're not telling me? Yes? No?'

I calm down a little, then. Bubble burst. Adrenaline evaporating. I hadn't really thought that the Tinder lead could be old. Plus she hasn't actually matched me on Tinder, so it's like a one-side handshake. Guess my plan kinda sucks. Maybe I shouldn't've skipped court. If seven of us convicts were due to appear in the dock – one white, two browns and four yellow guys – there's only a one in seven chance my name will be called first.

'Shayn. D'you excuse me from appearing in court?'

'Didn't have time.'

'So when they call my name and I don't step up, there gonna be a warrant out for my arse?'

'I'll reschedule.'

Shana turns through the Whangārei streets, past that buzzy trippy Hunterwussy chequerboard ugly-ass building that gets you stoned when you look at it. She hits Hatea Drive, the cruisy stretch that goes up the river valley and joins the motorway. We're facing north.

'Look, the Tinder thing... I don't wanna get your hopes up. I've just got that special psychic... what do you call that crime-solving thing you do with your brain?'

'Self-aggrandising narcissistic delusion?'

'Yeah, that shit. Oi, I cannot believe you busted me outta court like that! Gotta remember that for next time.'

'There won't be a next time. You're going 'straight' or whatever you hoodlums call it, after you've brought me back my sister.'

I turn away, slump my face against the passenger window, trying to appreciate the view. All this could be gone any minute. I could be locked up, could get stomped, could get chopped up into unmatchable Lego pieces by the Four-Thirteen, so today I notice and appreciate romantic stuff about crusty old Whangārei. The city's like a pair of undies you've had for ten years with holes and frayed elastic and cum stains but it's always there for you, no matter what's happening in life. The long-arse KFC drive-thru lines, the crazy bargains at the Kmart, the PakNSave chicken 'n chips combos for $4.99, the once-a-day buses, the 14-year-old homies with little black moustaches. I love how this city's got a forest-covered mountain in the middle of it, how the university is in a ghetto, the way every cunt robs a dairy when they turn 21 as a rite of passage. Even the worst bits of it, the wagon circles of shitty tourist campervans and the brown sludgy river and the neighbourhoods where the only place for kids to play is in the middle of the street. This here's my home, yo, and I love her.

God, I'm feeling, what's that word for them soft girly emotions dudes sometimes get – sentientmental? Feeling a tiny bit sniffly, tell you the truth. Might have a wee cry, bleed all the toxins out.

We go up Kiripaka Road where someone's lit a bin on fire and the green plastic has trickled down the hill like an alien blob. At the top of the hill, we weave through Tikipunga and find Vinegar Hill Road, then Shana speeds up and we arrive in some new developments called Totara Grove. Finally there's an oak-lined boulevard and there are these humps keeping the speed down to ten kays, decorated with rose bushes in flower boxes.

I stare at the hands driving the SUV, wondering how she got her car back. Nomad was in a bourbon'd-out coma when we got jumped by the pigs at McDonald's. I wonder if he put up a fight over the car. Broke some pigs' jaws for em.

I notice the space on Shana's left hand where there should be an engagement ring.

'Not engaged any more? So is Rich gonna propose to ya?'

She smirks with power, like she's caught me taking a dump halfway through and she knows I can't get up and leave for another minute. 'He'd have to ask me on another date first.'

'You a hussy, girl. Tell uncle Karly.'

'We've had two dates. Two and a half.'

'What, he stuck half a knuckle up ya? What's a half?'

Shana pulls over outside a marae with cows watching from a farm-fence. Goes to open her door.

Shana's phone rings. She's got a Samsung Galaxy with no scratches on it, the Version 8, the one that'll get you four hundred bucks if you snatch the right coloured one with the right charger. Pink's popular. I can see on the wide-ass phone it says someone named MUM is calling.

Shana presses her hand against the air in front of me, like she's telling me to go into another room. I open the door, and hop out. The posh end of Whangārei where the north part builds over old farms in the hills is like god damn Moneyland, every house a cookie cut-out. Concrete driveways, wrought iron, fake lawns. Piles of dirt and diggers.

I lean against her ride, open her door again, slide a Benson out of its gold box, take her nail polish too, dip the smoke in stinky nail polish chemicals and light that bad boy up. The first hit makes me cough till I think I'm gonna puke, but I force myself to keep sucking and get a buzz on from the burning chemicals. I feel classy cause it's expensive-lookin nail polish.

Shana's reaching over and locking the passenger door and it's like, Yo, I read you loud and clear, you don't want me to hear you and your mum talking about champagne and flower arranging, okay, but lady? Nomad hacked into your Bluetooth through your car synchroniser. All I need to do is click three times on my smartphone and I can listen in on your call.

'It's not enough,' I hear Shana telling the person on the phone, lifting her bottle of anti-anxiety meds, biting it open and shaking a pill into her mouth, 'Oh my God, Mamá, you want her to die out there? It's not enough to bring her back, you *have* to release more of the fund.'

Damn, man. I've never heard her talk like this. Always total composure with this chick.

'Don't yell at me,' goes old Mrs Konstantinou's voice, loud enough for me to hear it outside Shana's SUV. I switch my phone on, log in, use the little app Nomad installed and join Shana's conversation. I hold my phone a fraction away from my head – there's something sad and pathetic about her begging her daughter to treat her nicer. Mrs Barbie's got some guts, okay. And she hasn't melted. Me? I'd melt, if my daughter got turned into bacon bits. 'I'm only asking you to consider Italy,' the mum goes.

'Italy?' Shana goes, 'Italy? You've been to Italy 17 times. I can name every trip and every year, either because you dragged Barb and I along or because we had to stay here with some nanny from bloody Africa.'

'We've not been to Sardinia, is all I'm trying to say to you.'

'Your daughter – my *sister* – is worth five hundred thousand dollars. D'you not believe me or something? D'you think I'd just make this whole thing up? D'you think Barbs is stashed in the present cupboard with all the old Christmas decorations or something, Mum?'

Five hundred? Five hundred? Jeez, man, scarcity is value, too fuckin' right. So Shana's been negotiating Barbie's return for five hundy? Shit, I'll sell her my sister for a grand.

Shana thumps her steering wheel and the horn bleeps.

'So you'll have to go to six banks six times. So what, Mamá? You're the one who's responsible if we've got a chance to get Barbs back and you muck it up. Children are priceless, haven't you ever heard that expression? Invaluable, Mamá. You don't make one more pricier than the other. I've, I've, I've got to go. I've got someone with me,' Shana goes. 'Just tell me one thing, Mum, why do I always have to be the responsible one? Why do I have to always clean her messes up? I mean literally, when we were kids, Barbs would spill her cornflakes on the carpet, and I'd sponge it up so you and Dad wouldn't lose the plot when you saw it.'

In the car, there's a bit of silence before Mrs Anna Konstantinou pipes up. Guess she thinks all of her utterances are worth a thousand bucks. 'In the name of God, I, I, I apologise if that's the way you've felt all these years, I'd, I'd I'd ask you to bear in mind that your grandmother was *terribly* favouritist when I was growing up, why I've always set out to prevent any of my children feeling like they weren't– '

'Mamá, get the cash and get it before midday tomorrow.' Shana stabs the End button on her phone and biffs it so hard into her handbag I think it's gonna burst out the bottom.

Damn. Shana's sounding like a junkie who hasn't got her fix. Like as if she's addicted to money.

Shana's sucking in air and spitting it out, and pressing her eyelids down real hard.

Then she guns the engine.

'Cops know about the Tinder thing. They're following it.'

'So we got a little competition.'

She nods, squirts out into traffic, almost getting flattened by a milk tanker.

'101 kays in which direction, then?'

'Straight ahead, Shayn. Straight ahead.'

# 22

# "If he tels police hes playin everyone the whole thing wil fall thru"

Think islands like Froot Loops floating in a bowl of milk, palm trees, warm water, boats doing burnouts, backpacker babes in bikinis sheltering under pohutakawas, families posing for photos in front of the Christmas tree on the Paihia wharf and that's the Bay of Islands, baby.

I've burged a few of them luxury apartments but ol' Konservative Karl's chosen a humbler place to stay today. I'm peeling vegetables at the YHA hostel and, bro, that's how to get close to Tens. YHA hostels are where hot desperate 10-out-of-10 European chicks try to stretch a dollar to stay in the country a little longer. They'll do anything to share a meal, chuck their laundry in with your load or split some freshly-caught fish. You cook supper with 'em, their sticky hands reaching around your waist, your elbows brushing their hips. Karismatic Karl at his finest.

Anyway, Shana's sent me away, dropped me outside the YHA backpacker hostel in Paihia and wished me good luck, shut the door and droven off to work on the search through squeaky-clean channels. Thought she was untrustworthy for a minute there but she's proven herself solid. Now I'm on my own following the thinnest of threads, checking Tinder every 30 minutes to see if the kilometres are closing in – which, for now, they are.

Barbie is apparently just 29 kays away and I reckon I know precisely where.

I'm not in a hurry to move on from this hostel, though, watching boats and parachute-skiers and whatever you call them round red floaty things in the water. Salt in my nose, sand on the fungus between my toes. Dropped ice creams melting on the pavement. There are sleek, posh buses parked under palm trees, beach with sand the colour of a white girl's tummy. I'm only sixty minutes above Whangārei but I'm feelin like a new man. I guess it's 'cause Shana's been supportive. There's no Nomad to tell me I'm a pussy, no Richie to remind me how much better than me he is, no Nantakarn to tell me I'm frustrating the whole police force.

Brunhilde (she spells it for me) is from Dutchmark – no, what's that country in front of, I mean west of… I get confused where she's from. The point is, she's imprinted on me like a puppy, cause Kiwi Karl's the real deal, that's why. I'm the e-pityme, I think that's the right word - the best example of manhood in this country.

Reggae and barbecue smoke are lilting from over by the washing lines. The owner of the place is hosing a couple of Jucy Rental vans. Bliss, here. The Kiwi dream.

'Babe, what's the difference between Dutchmark and Denland?' I go to Brunhilde as we chase dishes on the stovetop in the communal kitchen. I brush Brunhilde's brown sugar hair away from her face. 'I always get them two countries confused.'

Bruni laughs and strokes my arm, then reaches around me and shakes a pan of frying jackfruit, whatever that is. She thinks all the dumb crud that comes out of my mouth is some ironic genius statement and I don't intend to correct her. Blue eyes, hair like tea, skin the colour of Russian fudge– bro, this woman's got me in another universe, plus she's got a friend she picked up, so it's like two Tens for the price of one, not that I've even had to get my wallet out. The friend's from Finland and she's called Dötti. Dötti and Bruni, man. They make me feel like an emperor.

As I'm boiling the peas, I do a couple raps for them and they're impressed. Nomad, if he were here, bro, Nomad would just throw one of the sheilas over his shoulder and walk off into the handicapped toilet to get his fuck on. But me, I've gotta rely on my, uh… whatever they call that sexy shit you secrete from your pores. Feralmoans or something.

'Karly, honey? You can pour the vegetable stock into the carrots, yes?'

Bruni and Dötti are vegetarians and I'm happy to become one if it'll get me laid. They're here in the Bay of Islands for the dolphins. They don't know anything about shoulder-surfing or getting lacerations on your arms from punching windows and they've never tasted pepper spray. Most of their tales are about smoking Tibetan weed in Lhasa, wriggling their toes in the sands of Kho Samui. I wonder about the parents of these globetrotting 19-year-olds with their passports stuffed with visas and permits. Their parents have no idea how many babies I could be putting up their daughters.

Course, there's only one woman I'd actually love to put a baby up. I'm workin towards that.

I'm just starting to feel at home in the kitchen, even wearing an apron, when they ask me to sit down with them. I've been enjoying cooking food. God, I haven't eaten anything that doesn't come wrapped in cardboard in 14 years, but I suppose when there's no more preparation to do, it's time to enjoy our work, get cultured. I haven't smelled coriander and chili in so long. I get enthusiastic about fancy flavouring and find a packet of these rare exotic little clear crystals in the spice rack, bite the packet open, delicately shake the sachet in. Something called Silica Gel. Looks expensive.

I take a seat between my intercontinental companions. I start picking up this curry-smelling thing called an angora or pagoda or pakora or something, and it crumbles through my fingers and it's obvious I need a fork and I bump the communal table as I reach for one and this 6'8" Ivan Drago-lookin motherfucker makes eye contact with me and I'm about to leap across the table and fight him but I realise all he's doing is glancing.

I'm just jumpy. Got tonnes of bullies on my back, making me view the world all darkly. Richie dissing my lifestyle, Pork sending Pinoys to hit me, Nomad telling me I'm useless... damn, dawg. Not much Konfident Karl left.

Anywho, there's a tiny perk to being gangsta-wired in this peace-lovin United Nations. I'm the staunchest guy in the whole backpacker compound, which makes Karlos a king.

'So deep in thought you look, Kar-ol,' goes Dötti, stroking the sides of my face with her soft hands as I wipe curry off my plate and suck my finger. 'A penny for what you are think.'

'Thought it was Euros,' I go, and the girls crack up laughing. Centre of attention for a day. This is sweet. If this King of The Backpackers gig works out for me, I don't know if I'll actually go fetch Barbie. I mean realistically,

I'm not gonna be able to just ride up on a horse and throw a net over her like on *Planet of the Apes*. My throne's pretty comfy and this place only costs thirty bucks a night. I'm tempted to just stay here and impress backpacker babes for a couple months.

Apparently in their country, bread and soup comes after what looks like a main. Dötti didn't even buy this shit from a store, she's made her own dough and chopped fresh garlic – bro, I've never even seen where garlic comes from before, let alone chopped it up. It comes in these little individual one-packs and it's all glossy, like oystershell – yeah so Dötti pushes the garlic into the bread with these sticks of expensive cheese she's carried with her all the way from Queenstown. We butter the motza (that's a type of disabled bread that Europeans eat), dip it in the soup, suck it down. I crack a can of bourbon 'n coke and the girls think it's nasty shit and the more I eat this wholesome food, the more I think, Y'know, these Dutch lusties are right. There's too much sugar in Kiwi kai.

I slide my bourbon 'n coke away and take a sip of this wine they've brought from Hawke's Bay, it's a – let me get the pernounciation right – it's a *Suave Anon Blanks* – and it's got the hooch in it, that part's sorted, but what I like is I find myself swishing and swirling it in my cup as I tell my story.

That's right, there are people out there in the universe – *important* people – and they've come all the way from the far side of the world to hear my bullshit. Cept it's not bullshit, what I'm spittin.

It's true I got caught up in a kidnap.

It's true people died.

It's true I was the one person in the underworld with enough of a conscience to chase after a woman who'd been wronged. You can compare me to Gandhi and Martin Loofah King if you want – your words, not mine. I'm too humble for that. I just wanna get Barbie back.

The sun goes down the toilet and blue and purple colour the bay. There's a bonfire smoking out on the lawn, glowing coals. Bruni and Dötti are near me; there's couple of Mongols, I dunno if that's the right word, Chinamen from Korea anyway, that are on stools in front of the breakfast bar. They're turned my way. There's these real nice Israelians too and they're sitting on bean bags with their legs crossed, thick novels resting their laps. Open fire is burning nice and low behind them. Stuffed stockings, candy canes. Moths bumping the windows. Night-heat.

'So yous wanna know how I became a bounty hunter.' I knock back a slurp of Suave Anon and make sure my girls are staring deep into the eyes of the Master of Oral. 'It all started when I trained this guy I knew to go deep deep undercover inside the cops. Richie was his name; some people call him Snitchie Bitchie Richie, 'cause he's a tattletale nark and he told on me for sticking a potato down this priest's tailpipe of his car – but when he's not snitching, he's a solid bruz, too. You ever seen *The Departed*? I think that movie's based on me and Richie, not that we got paid for it. I'm Leo DiCaprio, the hero undercover as a scumbag mafioso crook with the real good looks...'

I yarn and yarn and yarn. These exotic people can't get enough of my yarns. I tell 'em the story of how I faced down a whole biker crew and rescued Barbie, how I put Barbie back with the bikers cause it was in her best interest, how I fended off 40 of these eight-foot-tall Sudanese dudes that were kicking my arse in a prison cell plus I tell em how the police trusted me as the nation's greatest confidential informant, straddling the line between mafia and law enforcement. Most of all, though, I stress that I'm not asking to be called a hero. I do this shit out of the goodness of my heart.

Bruni asks for more war stories after 10pm, when most of the backpackers have gone off to bed; Dötti's shakin her head, mumbling little prayers and Tweeting lots on her phone. She tells me to save my stories for tomorrow. I tell these two to kiss each other goodnight, and they do it so delicately I can see their little tongues extend from inside their teeth like pink snails comin outta their shells. Their tongues meet and wrestle and they stroke each other's hair. I've got my black track pants on, the Adidas ones, and it's a good thing the fabric is black, else these girls'd be able to see my rager.

Fuck it, they're gonna see it in a few seconds anyway. The girls turn to me and say, from heads furred with the fire's orange glow behind them, 'We cannot stay for more than one night, we are sorry.'

'Sall good, sall good,' I go. We don't have any mistletoe so I hold up a big chunky handful of sticky green buds above their heads and pull both of their faces towards me and give the girls the best ten minutes of their life.

Usually busting a nut is all it takes to make my body sleepy, but as the girls get close to sleeping on my chest, one under each arm, I keep them talking about their adventures on the road, the seals they've seen flapping across steamy highways on the coast, the birds they've had land on logs in front of them in the rainforest, the 30 kilometre Te Araroa walks they've trodden through the big cities with backpacks taller than they are, just to avoid paying ten bucks for a taxi, so they can get the privilege of getting to some roundabout where two highways intersect.

There's been danger along the way – Bruni got dragged to a "party" at the Defiants' clubhouse last week, apparently. She ran out of there with nothing but bruises on her wrists. And Dötti had a teenage girl lead her into an alleyway to sell her a "bus ticket," least that's what the little ratgirl told Dötti. Dötti found out the hard way they were pizza coupons. My girls don't whimper though. Their lips don't go fat. Their eyes don't leak tears.

With some smoke and some vodka and plenty of Suave inside us, I begin singing to them. Well, rapping, mainly. Singing sucks.

I don't have a gat, but there's a ukulele.

I strum it and sing the ballad of Karl-King and his Missing Darling.

'What is this you sing?' Bruni goes, raising her head in front of the fire's darting orange tongues. 'You are a hip hop rapper?'

I take a deep drag on the cigarette I'm not supposed to be smoking inside. I toss the smoke in the fire and sit up. 'Nah. I'll never be anything spesh. Big dreams is all.'

'Who is telling you this to my Karl? Which terrible person is say this? Karlos, please, you are *un artiste*. A maestro. You won your country's highest award for bravery in the Land Wars, you were telling us? With Mister Willie Apiata?'

'Yeah, totes. For real.'

The fire turns from a glowing orange star to a few red eyes watching us in the black lounge. I carry them to their beds, cover them with their sleeping bags and jackets. Night-night, ladies.

When I was about 16, I worked out how to walk on the front of my feet, the ball that's under your big toe. It was the perfect step for sneaking into student flats and stealing all the meat out of their freezers, since I had to cook for myself. I lived off steaks and bacon taken from fridges at 4 in the morning.

I go to reception, luckily open 24/7. I ask if there's any mail for me and what do ya know: a laptop-shaped, laptop-weight, laptop-solid package arrived for me yesterday. Feels good to hold the Macbook again.

I use this springy step now to move down the hallway softly into my room. Why I've got a whole room to myself, I'm not sure. I haven't even paid for it, just told the Canadian chick on reception I'd sort her out for some dough in the morning and gave her a wink.

There's a magazine in my backpack I've been carryin with me. Our school yearbook. One photo of Barbie and Shana running a three-legged race together. Barbie's so happy that her teeth are pointing out ahead of her. Shana looks fucked-off about something. Beneath their feet is red rubber with white strips painted on it. Race track, athletics stadium, Sports Day. Big mat behind them with some dude leaping over the high jump bar. I pull the mag against my face, try and stare inside Shana's skull.

What's behind them eyes, Konstantinou Number Two?

Fuck that. I slide the yearbook away and pull out the hard, wide, flat special somethin' that's been making my backpack heavy. I slide it out, lick my finger, wipe a little bit of dirt off the juicy sweet Apple logo. Shana's laptop – that's right, bitches, Kunning Karl posted the slim little fucker right here in a courier bag knowing it'd be waiting for me if I checked in here. Little bit of dust, but no missing keys, no scratches on the screen – and the original software stickers is on there. Bro, when I offload these things, I get 40 more bucks for the sale if the original stickers is on. Stickers make shit look new, nah'm sayin?

Got a whole dorm to myself. I think I'll call it my office. Bounty hunting professionals need an office.

Shana's laptop's got no password to get onto the hard drive. Nice. Actually – this a decoy or what? I thought Shana was sophisticated. Her desktop background is a picture of her with two arms and shoulders on either side of her. You can tell one of the people cut out of the picture is Barbie 'cause the arm's got these tattoos of lovehearts that are supposed to be mistaken for butterflies – and another tattoo of the 1% symbol on the diamond background. Silly girl didn't know she was playing with fire...

Shana's left her Zoom password saved, which is sweet, 'cause I haven't been on Zoom since this little honeytrap swindle I tried to pull on the police commissioner that didn't work out.

I log into Shana's Zoom and the list of contacts is ridiculous. Sure I'd known Shana was a upstanding citizen, mates with people in the city council and the lawyers association, I've seen her pictured shaking hands with Rubin the Hurricane Carter at some conference about injustice, and

I'd seen her name on advertising at the stadium saying her art gallery was a sponsor. But yeah, people she's been having yarns with on Zoom are hard-out high achievers. We're talkin the deputy mayor, the coach of the rugby, the netball, the soccer, the hockey, heaps of famous business leaders that've ended up in court for smashing their wives or for fraud, and lots of gangstas, too – I'm talkin real gangstas, not freshmen who haven't even done a Five-Cent in jail. Guess she represents a heap of them. There's that dude from the Four-13 you always see on the news taking cases to court, you know, beefing with the pigshits for the right to get to wear his club's patch around town. I think Shana actually rep'd him on that one. Won the case, too, said they were fuckin' with his human rights.

There's contacts in the Pinoys, the Blues, the Insane White Boys, Devil's Demons, Billionaire Boys, the Monster Energy Mob, you name it. My heart's always raced from smoking too much rock and living off burgers and fries, but my heart's whamming away at its cage door right now worse than ever. I'm about to encounter something major. I totally know it.

I figure if Shana's shit enough at security to leave her Zoom logged in on a computer with no password, she could've left anything else logged in, her Facebook, her Instagram, shit, even her internet banking with the obvious password.

I open her Facebook DMs and there's like a hundred of them. There's this one client so scary that an electric shock goes through my arteries as I glimpse his profile. He doesn't use his Club name on his profile.

Shana's messaged a certain Glenn Hamm. Interesting. Asking him for her sister back, I hope…?

*Im putng myself on th line asking for more than one hund thou*, she's sayin to him.

*I put myself on line everyday woman*, Pork's written back. *Get us a mil if u can.*

Okay, okay, tonnes of surprises here: so Pork has some literacy? Holy shit. And he's comfortable talking to Shana? Holy Sequel.

*I'm not saying you don't*, Shana writes. *I'm just saying I've gt about 3 tricks that work w Mum n Dad and ive used up 2 of them. Not sure I cn get a million.*

*U remembrin to delete ur msgs last thing we needs forensics readin ur computer*, Porky Pig replies.

*I shall delete as soon as we sign off.*

*U better remember. Oi Wots da 3 tricks then woman*

*1st make them believe Barbs is really dead and gone for good*

*2nd, keep them on the hook. Get insider connection 2 say there is a chance Barbsy is still alive and if they hand me the cash Il gt her bk*

*3 – Chuck someone nobody will miss in the harbour. Let the cops worry over it.*

My head's spinning, reading this shit. Shana and Pork sound close…like, real close. Who's next to turn out crooked – that Nancy Drew woman? Richie McMullan?

And – this really makes my stomach lurch up my throat and into brain cavity – it's sounding like there is a smidgen of a tad of a crumb of a fragment of hope that they're keeping Barbie somewhere, meaning she could be – I hate to say it –

Alive.

*Insiders gta be staunch not a pushover if he tels police hes playin everyone the whole thing wil fall thru hand the case back to cops no ransom no 5050 and I gta sell about three art works to get out of debt*

*I can help with a insider know just the bloke. Herd of nomad hes a hard worker.*

It gets hard, reading what comes next. Pork is a huge barrel of a man. I'm amazed there's a working penis in there, but they start sexting. And Shana's gross too. Shana is… Shana basically looks like one of those floppy-haired teen heartthrobs from the 90s. The cartel they've set up is a pretty bad crime, but forcing me to picture them two doing it is a way worserer crime.

*I work with u and u only on this Glenn. Pls remember that babe*

*WOMAN I DINT SAY USE NOMAD FOREVER JUST SAID HED DO FOR NOW GET US SOME CASH MONEY THEN AXE THE NOMAD*

They finish with a whole load of *GTG* and *Luv u xoxo*, leaving me stuck with mental imagery of neat petite wee gallery-owning community law-supporting Shana riding fat biker penis. I want to puke and not just from the silica gel I probably shouldn't've seasoned our dinner with.

I close the laptop lid and light a smoke. Outside, birds start to squawk. The sky's turned cyan. I must've stayed up all night reading Shana's computer.

Not too far from here there's a good girl to try save, plus a certain little sister to ask some hard questions of.

I'm seasick from stayin up all night, but I don't reckon I'll ever sleep again.

Not if there's a chance she's alive.

# 23

# "You got nark written all over you."

A city of tents on the riverbank. Rows of shiny motorcycles. Dudes in leather, long-sleeved t-shirts covered in scary symbols. Chicks on the backs of bikes. Lots of blue paisley, lots of 2Pac t-shirts, lots of bandanas on hoodrats' faces. Classic American cars spilling onto the highway, shiny chrome bumpers and big whitewall tyres, squeezing the highway traffic into a tight trickle. Palm trees and dropped bottles of Johnnie Walker and ciggy butts and face masks like tiny parachutes.

I'm standin outside the Twin Pines Manor and Community Hall in Haruru, located in that sweet spot between the north end of Paihia and the arse-end of Kerikeri. She's an old towering creaking four storey manor-style pub with a balustrade for people to chuck bottles off, and real bullet holes in the weatherboards from when the Bay of Islands was the Hellhole of the South Pacific back in the 1820s (and let's be honest, parts of it still are). The hall's been sectioned into booths and it's joined to the pub with a canopy so the whole thing looks like a boxy circus tent. Out back of the buildings, the lawn marches all the way down to the fat lazy muddy Waitangi River and the famous Haruru Falls, where they say, if you weigh-down a body properly, it'll sink for ya. The pub, the carpark, the benches on the lawn beside the brown river oozing into the Bay, this is where a galaxy of freaks gather round Mos Eisley spaceport or, as it's known on earth, Bay Blue Tattoo Convention 2024.

*Let her be here, man, please,* I'm praying as I thank the driver and hop out of the shuttle. I don't wanna spend the rest of my life rooting skank after skank. There's only one skank I want, and there's a 50/50 chance she's inside.

I farewell the van and tell my European girls I'll see them in Valhalla. Sounds like the kinda thing you're sposda say to Scandinavian-type people. Bruni reaches her hand out, strokes my fingers, pulls her door shut. We're not gonna do long-distance. We're not swapping phone numbers. I'm not telling them they should stay at my mum's pad if they're passing through my fuckin' birthplace.

Just you on your own. Now we're doin things Karlito's Way.

I'm squinting through the summer haze, tryina decide how to shut down the whole tattoo fest to get Barbs back. There's a banner stretched between palm trees. The font is Gothic, 90s gangsta. Also from the 90s, gangstas in blue paisley. Plenty of them blue/black motherfuckers here. Like those nasty bluebottle jellyfish on the beach, but y'know... hard instead of squishy.

To get some proper air into my lungs, I suck spicy happytime smoke and go over everything that I can remember saying to Shana. I don't know what that woman is up to, man. If she's pointed me to the princess I'm here to rescue, okay, fine, I'll grab her snatch and run, er, I mean snatch and grab her and run. But I'm thinking there's an extremely high chance Shana has sent me into a pit of snakes so that "unpredictable events" will finish me off and so that I'm not available in jail to become a supergrass informant, like one of those elite crims that investigators are desperate to get information from, like that Blowfella from James Bond.

At this whole Bay Blue thing, the Smurf-blue boys are in charge, meaning the implication is that if you're trying to wear yellow or red 'n white, you have to be prepared to staunch it up. Me, I'm not feelin especially staunch – I shat my pants in the back of the van on the way here, actually. Well a turd came out then I used my butt-muscle and pulled it back from the brink, tucked it back up where it belongs, but the point is it touched my undies and it made me think Karl, bruz, wear the blue scarf that you borrowed from Dötti, keep your head down and get the target away from danger.

If the target's here, that is. And if she's alive.

I approach the entrance of the hall. Guarding the door is a watermelon-shaped motherfucker with a rusty chain for a belt and a padlock holding his pants up to his jacket. His colleague's a lanky Lurch-type in a XXXL hoodie that looks like Snoop Dogg, wide shoulders, with a big jaw and cheekbones. I give them a chin-up and a flash of my eyebrows.

'Wanna buy some police shit?' I blurt.

Everyone loves police shit. Get enough items together and you can impersonate a officer for a whole month. I sling my backpack off my shoulders and rummage till my fingers settle on a stack of palm-sized cardboard pieces.

'Business cards. You can say you're Senior Constable Richard McMullan.'

'Nah, G,' the fat watermelon bouncer with the padlock pants goes, 'Already tried it.' He pats his belly. 'Jokers don't really buy me as a cop, so... .'

So that's Padlock Pants not buying.

I have a go with the tall lanky Snoop-Lurch dude instead, who's gazing out across the heads of all the lowlifes here.

'You keen, G? You can go into stores and take whatever you want, y'know. Slap down your card, tell em it's official police business. Help yourself to free Subway cookies'n shit, the good ones with M&Ms.'

Snoop-Lurch leans down to my level. There's a tat on the side of his face. Big-ass black fist.

'I'll take a taser. Gemme a taser.'

'No tasers today, G.'

The big units shake their heads. I'm wasting their time and they want to shoo me in, which is good news.

'Get the fuck on in. Hit me up when you get that taser, G.'

The light shrivels up behind me as I walk into darkness. The hall can't be that big, but they've turned it into a maze. Those dividers they use to separate offices into cubicles split the building up into 60 or 80 little booths.

I grab me a beer from a little stall. I doubt they've got a licence to sell beers here, but they're being sold for $4 each anyway. Normal amount's $9 for a beer in Northland, so the price is all good. Blues are a cheap people, they'll smash you with planks broken off pallets, they'll throw bricks at your car, they'll pummel you while wearing oven gloves, but they know how to avoid poshness. I respect that.

First section of the show is these brown girls giving things away. The brown girls wear tight black shirts but there's no skin showing, unlike what you get with white chicks. These honeys, they're re-selling slices of $5 pizza from Domino's, approximate value: one dollar a slice. Sell eight slices, make three bucks profit. Genius.

Moving on from the promo girls, munching my dollar pizza slice, sucking beer, trying to be in Special Forces mode, strutting like I'm not nervous, I get into the guts of the show, the core, where the real tattooing takes place. The floor of this hall probably held some local chief's 70th birthday party last weekend. The floorboards are pitted with dents from ladies' heels, there are electrical cords duct-taped all over the place, and there are Rolls of Honour naming all the local old timers that died in the World Wars up on the walls, with carved flags and scripture saying 'We shall remember them' and all that whiny shit. I wonder what the old patriots would think of a thousand scumbags running this dirty convention. There's a booth printing fake vaccine passes, a booth selling scary biker skull-masks and bulletproof helmets, hell, there's even a booth with some old fat aunty selling pre-filled WINZ applications so you can get all sortsa interesting benefits. I toss my pizza crust in the bin, put my beer bottle in a recycling bin, check out some of the new ink colours you can get. The guy selling ink's got a small A4 poster of some beach afterparty in Paihia stapled to his shirt.

'What happened?' I go to the bony rasta hawker. 'How come you're wearin a poster?'

'Had my red threads on. Blues made me cover up my colours, bro. Dress code 'n shit.' He's got friendly bloodshot eyes, meaning he's blazed, plus a bit of a belly and no muscle in his shoulders. He wears a leather vest, track pants and red sneakers that someone's wrapped blue duct tape around, Jesus.

'That's harsh they stapled that shit to your shirt, bro. Ouch.'

'Better'n gettin a hiding.'

'True true. Listen bro, uh, I'm thinkina getting me some new ink. What colours you got? Don't tell me the Black 'n Blues told you you couldn't sell red ink here?'

'Nah, nah, my brother, I've got me this, oi, check it: Thas a cherry red, all the way from Laos.'

People are frickin eccentric here, yo. I walk deeper into the convention, grab the bro a beer, come back, slide the beer over to him, and we clink bottles. He's got no idea that a deep undercover bounty huntin' predator just clinked him. 'I actually wanted to arks you something,' I go to Bony Rasta. 'My ex is here and I gots ta get her to sign some paperwork 'n shit or they'll cut off my dole, know what I'm sayin? White chick, tall, tiny nose, bony, tonnes of tats and piercings and stretchers 'n shit, looks a bit like a Barbie doll if you'd left it in the garden all summer and a dog'd chewed it a little?'

My man stretches his arms wide. 'My bro, you see any ladies fittin that description round here?'

'Not really.'

'I think you can get head in one of the booths, but apart from that, you might be outta luck.'

*Concentrate, Special Forces Karl. Less talk about sucking dicks. More snatchy grab.*

A couple of 18-year-old boys stumble my way, drunk and cheeky, aggro violent aura. The way they swing their arms it's as if they want to bump into someone and start a fight over it. I squeeze past them side-on, adjusting my blue scarf, creeping past a booth selling tattoo mags, past a cartoonist drawing pictures of people with his Sharpie, past a booth full of weed wallets, vapes and Zippos. The violent boys mutter something, burst out laughing, and I hear them follow not far behind. Possibly planning to roll me.

I get another beer and another slice of dollar pizza and find a fresh set of promo girls. These ones are giving away samples of hair extensions.

I wait until these big, loud, fat people with afros and thick fluffy blue hoodies have walked past, sucking on chicken drumsticks, then talk to the promo babes.

'Hey, uh, girls. You know where I can score?'

'Score what?' the girls go in unison, and giggle and check their cellphones.

'Look, it's not so much about the sweets. It's about this chick, name's Barb, or Barbara she sometimes goes by. She said she'd meet me buuut I'm not gettin any reception on my phone and I can't spot her, think she's dyed her hair... .'

'You should, like, ask at Lost and Found,' a girl goes.

'Oh really? Yous have Lost and Found here?'

'I'm pulling your leg, you dumb cracker. Fuck off. You got nark written all over you.'

When someone says the N word to you, you get the hell away as fast as you can before they say it louder. There are two types of N word in the world, and nark's the worserer one.

I turn a corner, check out the new booths in front of me. Booth selling baseball bats, sledgehammers and axes. Lots of three-walled makeshift tattoo parlours with a padded tattoo chair, buckets of ink, extension cords and battery chargers for the needles. Rolls of paper towels to wipe up ink and blood, industrial tubs of Dettol, boxes of rubber gloves. Hand-drawn designs of dragons and swords and Scarface and Notorious B.I.G. and script of bible verses. I must pass fifteen or twenty different tattooists, working on about ten people getting ink done. The buzzing of the tattoo needles make the place frickin' noisy, plus there's reggae music on boomboxes everywhere. Black t-shirts, blue trackpants, white singlets. Shirts with stuff printed on it threatening the cops. Stickers, decals, Bob Marley flags – and weapons. Legal weapons. There's sets of steak knives and butterfly knives, dive knives and hunting knives and filleting knives in metal cases, and it's obvious the fat woman in the wheelchair, wearing sunglasses indoors, a woman with gang patches on her ain't selling the knives for chopping up onions. She's wrapped stickers of skulls and tombstones around the handle of each knife.

'Yo, whiteboy,' she goes to me, 'Lookin to stick someone, or... ?'

I wanna ask her if there's a Caucasian Corner where all the whites are penned up, but I can't afford to get called a nark again. If those 18-year-old fighty cunts herd me into a corner where there's no big fellas to break up a rumble, I could die here.

Fuck it. 'Need the smoking section, there one here?'

'Smokin what, ciggies?'

'Nope.'

The woman tilts her head towards a set of toilets. There's a guard outside, meaning it ain't no ordinary toilet. It's the end of the hall, a quiet area most people won't bother to come to. The show ended a coupla booths back. This here's backstage. This is the afterparty. Well, apart from the actual full moon beach/bikes DMC supporters afterparty, which is on the beach at Paihia, tonight, according to the posters and flyers stapled to every damn wall.

I go up to the guard-guy and I actually have to pinch my nose, there's so much smoke leaking out from under the men's room door. 'Need a place to smoke,' I go.

'Depends what you're smokin,' he goes. 'There's a fee. Twenty bucks.' These people are entrepreneurs, yo. Sellin tickets to a hotbox? Genius.

'How long do I get in there?'

'Gotta be out in 30 mins. I'll give you a stamp on ya wrist.'

I hand over twenty bucks and the flick of his head tells me to go in. The rusty door hinges scream as I push it open. Poor-ass Northland gangstas oughta splurge on some WD40 sometime. There's one bend and then I'm in this parlour of losers occupying the toilet stalls. Whole mess of people on the floor. Like a shooting gallery, except no one's shooting up. It's all smoke.

Don't get me wrong -- I'll pash a glass barbecue most days of the week. But when you're straight and you see other people fucked-up, telling themselves they're 'partying' when they're actually just hugging a public toilet, holding the seat so they don't fall off, you think to yourself, Maybe drugs make you kinda act like a douche sometimes.

Trouble is, I'm a bounty hunter and I'm undercover. I have to pull out all stops to succeed right here, so I light up a Marlboro with a little special sauce in it and I take a goooooood suck. My eyes get tiny fireworks in front of them and I descend deeper undercover.

The bathroom is long, over ten stalls deep, maybe fifteen, with endless washbasins and old mirrors and bad wall colour and it's stuffed with smoke at head-level, so most people are crouched or doing the floor thing. No windows are open. This here's a hot box. We're sealed in. Every breath will fill our lungs with happy gas. The lights are off. Everyone's got their cellphones out and they've got Tinder going, half of them, that's where all the light's comin from. Tinder's one of the main ways people hook up to swap drugs, 'cause of the type of app it is – it doesn't leave any details on your phone. The pigs can't monitor it. There's hardly any record of transactions. I slide my phone out, open Tinder casually, searching again for women aged 27 to 31. I narrow the search settings. It would be nice if Tinder told me there's just one person in that age range, location one room away, but that's not quite how it goes.

Tinder tells me there's 2034 women within my range in the Bay. I do the maths on my phone's calculator. At the rate of 1-2 seconds swiping per profile, 2034 chicks will take something like 2500 seconds to scroll through, which iiiiis...

41 minutes.

Fuckin fuckburgers, that's a shitload of swiping. *Please be here, Barb*, I tell God. *Hey Lord, dog? If you're listening, let my crazy Tinder lead be a good one. And in your infinite mercy, let me get my smoke on. I haven't smoked in three days and I need it.*

Alongside me in the smokehouse-bathroom we have skinny girls sitting on the benches, their arses a little bit wet from water coming out of a dribbling tap that could seriously use a plumber. They're stroking each other's hair and giggling. They're not holding anything dodgy – that means I've missed the dodginess by about five minutes. Just along from them, about four little Indian dudes are having a push-up contest and rolling on their backs and giggling. They have white foamy sticky shit around their lips. Each toilet stall has a couple of people in it. Some tanned hippies with sticky dreadlocks, coloured like sand and oil and treacle, are sitting cross-legged, having little discussions.

'Any of yous wanna buy some police shit?' I sling my bag off my back, take out my merchandise, waggle it. Halfa this police junk I've been draggin round for years; the other half, I stole off Rich just last week. 'I got business cards, I got police bumper stickers... I got police undies, if anyone's interested. They've got the logo over the crotch pocket.'

Yep. Been carrying Richie's boxer shorts in my bag for a while, now. Stole them while I was at his house, playing GTA.

'What kinda *protection* you got?' asks a sifty white guy in a suitjacket with smashed-up hair that used to be gelled. He looks like he sells real estate, except his eyes are both green and purple with bruises and he's got two smokes in his mouth.

'No guns, brother. Sorry. More boxer shorts, sorta thing. Oi, these could be your size, actually. I'd give 'em a wash, though.'

He waves me on. I descend deeper into the smoky hotbox'd bathroom. Gorilla in the mist, yo.

While everyone's distracted with their smoked-out conversations, I drift from group to group, opening all the stalls subtly, searching in case Barbs is buried in here. If any of these cats get a shiver down their spine saying something's not right about the way I'm creepin round, I could knock 'em out, sure, I could stomp or choke every person in the room, but if they slip the N word to the guards and thugs outside, I'm a dead man. Any excuse to stomp a white boy cruisin on his lonesome.

I take a seat on the bathroom floor, right down the back, twelve stalls down. I fold my legs, not offending nobody, shuffle against the wall. I find half a dipper on the ground that somebody's dropped, light it up and sip it thirstily, num-num-num. What I wanna do whenever I smoke is get behind lots of creative projects, pledge to make documentaries or write stand-up material or new songs for this metal band I'm planning to call Glaring Ömission that just needs four more members, hell, cause one time I even planned a whole concept album-slash-musical while I was under the influence – but I tell myself *Karl, concentrate.*

A bounty hunter's gotta stay focused.

Some Ethiopian-lookin motherfucker's got a stall to himself. It's just by my left arm, and he seems like he could use a friend. His eyes tell me he's been smokin what they call Coloured Glass, which is basically the sweepings, the dregs you get when you clean out the trays they grow meth crystals on. He'll've felt like a worthless piece of shit as he tiptoed through hippies and found a empty stall by himself, reached inside his breast pocket, took out his happiness kit, sprinkled crystals into his pipe, felt like a loser until the yellow smoke hit his lungs, and then felt like a champion when he'd smoked the whole bowl. Instant elation.

I offer my Ethio-Bro the stub of a dipper I've been sucking on. 'You want a little of this?'

I wanna smoke this guy out and see what he can tell me. He says, 'Yep' and I light it up for him. Only one dipper left in my Marlboro ciggy box after this. I try and enjoy my buzz while I strategise about how this motherfucker can help me with my Spastical Forces… no, Spacial? Space Force?

Fuck. Delirious. Get a grip, Karl. Don't get too relaxed. I know the toilet floor is comfortable and your blood feels like warm milky coffee waking up your muscles, but don't chill too much. Every lungful of air I take in tastes like chocolate on the way down. The names of the women and men across Northland who dissed me, who told me I was a worthless piece of shit who drops every vase he's asked to hold, those names, those leering faces dissolve and swirl away.

As I'm swirling, I open my phone, log into Tinder under my man-hunting profile, narrow down the search parameters, hope some miracle occurs on my phone…

'So, um, you been to this thing before?' I ask my Ethiopian bruz.

'This ees my first time.'

'Live close, or… ?

'I work de hotel.'

'Righto. Good job?'

'It is not de good job,' he goes, then starts chuckling. His voice is deep and warm. Druggies can be real welcoming sometimes. 'De Defiant Motorcycle Boys come into this hotel. They assault the manager, even. They have an evil man. He give the manager cash money so he not complain. Devious cursed man, the dreadlock, you know? Next morning, they are gone. Police do not care.'

'Typical pigshits, eh.' I suck my smoke. Mr Ethiopia hands me a glass bottle. Whatever two drinks are in it should never've been mixed. It tastes like wine with spirits poured in. 'This evil dude with the dreads, he wasn't called Kenny D'Souza by any chance was he? Real scuzzy creep? Calls himself a DJ?'

'It is heem.'

We suck smoke silently for a while, sitting on the tiles of the bathroom floor.

Need to get ahold of motherfuckin Kenny.

'So he's still about. Who'd they chuck in the ocean, then? Any woman with him?'

From out of nowhere, Ethiopia goes, 'I carry a great sadness. My family, they are being keeled, you know? In my country we have had terrible dictator.'

'I know, bro, I know. My best bro, he was a fuckin dictator. Probably worse than your one.'

'You have had personal tragedy?' Ethiopia asks. 'You have suffered de sadness?'

'Depends… I got the bash in jail this week. Didn't make me that sad, to be honest, more frustrated… My best bruz won't talk to me anymore. That hurt way badder than any stomping. And, like, I lost the love of my life. I'm thinking she's here, actually. Was actually hoping you mighta seen her?'

I open my phone again, scroll to Barbie's Facebook page and show Ethiopia a pic of her.

He nods long and deep, not to say, Yes definitely, more like letting me know he's thinking.

Ethiopia pulls out a bag of weed, packs a little pipe covered in sticky resin, offers me the first hoon. It's smooth shit – probably that 8 Foot Sativa.

After the smoke, Ethiopia stands up, brushes his knees. 'Thees apprentice woman she tattooing me at one o'clock, she is bearing the resemblance.'

Resemblance... Fuck's that word mean again... Resemblance? Re-zem-blance?!

'You've seen her here? She's tattooing peeps?'

He steps over me, thinks I don't see him pulling his roll out of his pocket and checking how much cash he's got. 'I see you later, my friend,' he goes, 'Barbara I am thinking ees name of this woman.'

I grab his ankle. 'You've gotta take me to her.'

We exit the smokehouse, give the door-guard a chin-up to say cheers. Time slows down. It takes a million years to crawl through the hall, turning around bends and booths, my heart seizuring every time a person lurches out of a booth towards me.

We turn down some corridors which have been stuck on the back of the pub. All of a sudden there's springy soft trampoline-y grass under our feet. It's the back lawn. There's as many hoes as there are bros out here. Every woman with her arm gripped by a tattooist, every promo girl carrying a tray of liquor shots. Leaning against the booth, a DJ plays doof-doof music, every honey rolling a cigarette on her thigh. Any of them could be Barbie. For example that wobbling bony thing over there with inky gloves, or  the one with the headful of light-coloured hair dyed blue, pinned up into a beehive as if she wants to change how she looks so no one'll take her away from her drugged-out adventure. She could be this girl laughing and cackling and chewing gum, wearing fuck-me pumps and a black miniskirt who appears to be learning how to tattoo, leaning closely over the jiggly stomach of a fat guy, etching a big-ass black fist while black blood speckles her, solid massive thick strokes with a super-wide neeeeeeeeeeeedlllleohhhhhhhmyfuckinGod, it's her. Definitely – cause her skanky tank top doesn't cover up her shoulder and I can see two scars with ink in them that look like letters. A K and a B.

I'm staring at a zombie. A living corpse. The woman I'd given up for dead. Karl, man, you could grab her right now, except she's got people around her supervising every move. No escaping from the tent. Not that she looks like she wants to escape. Plus she's someone else's property, and if I grab her too rough, well, that's like shoplifting.

Minders, guardians, thugs, pillars, blocking the view of her. Four massive motherfuckers out there on the lawn with her, plus one sleazy greasy dreadlocked skinny little rat-looking man in the DJ booth. The big bastards are all Defiant bikers, all covered in spikes and hard leather and chains.

One of them sees me standing there. Starts grinning like a hyena.

I see his jaw and lips mouth the word 'Nark.' He opens his leather vest a little, reaches into his chest pocket, pulls out half a sawn-off shotty. Just the handle, mostly. Couple inches of dark barrel.

Piss trickles down my leg. When a tide of people come through the corridor behind me, laughing and drinking beer and chomping pizza, their necks gleaming with fresh ink, I fall into the tide. Follow them out, past the DJ booth, past the pizza girls, past the four-buck beers, past the booths and benches and beer kegs, past the poster for that beach party tonight in Paihia. Find myself blinking on the carpark gravel.

There is a gun between me and my baby. I cannot get past a gun. There's a warrant out on me for not showing up to court. I cannot call the cops for help. I've got nothing but a few dole dollars to pay any of these TruBlues with, and nobody here likes me.

I give myself a mental pat-on-the-back, Good on you bro for really fucking this up good and proper.

I pick up my nuts and retreat back to my hostel, my base. Pull the curtains. Watch the Barbie movie with my hippies and think *How the hell am I gonna get Barbs outta there?*

# 24

# "Find out if that fish-eaten corpse is your sissie or not."

My YHA hostel is a couple kays' hitchhike down the road from where they're having the tat show. The noise of the tat show travels all through town, doof doof doof, ts-ts-blaaaarp, doof-doof-doof. Tat Convention afterparty, down on the Paihia foreshore. By 8pm the sound is intense. Somethin on Facebook about a noise control officer being stabbed. Cops monitoring the sitch.

I let the long December evening stretch out and the sky turn black at 10 o'clock and try to enjoy a final night at the hostel, though the music from the beach party is rumbling the whole town, interfering with my thoughts, making plates and glasses rattle in the dish rack. Sounds like the drums are right outside, and they must have one mother of a bonfire goin on. Either that or they've set a palm tree on fire. The sky glows orange. It's like seeing city lights from a distance. Bass guitar, drums, electronica, speakers strung from the palm leaves, people clapping and shouting cuss words at each other. There are fights and fuckings going on without me. There are motorcycles. I wish I was back among the tattoo people, tapping them for information, but I can't have a sawnoff pointed at me again. Maybe one last little bit of expionage before Karly goes kaput.

I coax the door of my dorm shut, ease back onto the creaking bed, draw the curtains and flip the laptop lid open and search Shana's Zoom conversations in case there's anything I've overlooked. Set to automatically record, these things. While I'm on the Zoom, I nosy through her Facebook Messenger and her emails too. Why the fuck not. Maybe my fresh eyes can spot a helpful clue for old Shaney. Just as I'm getting distracted reading hot-slash-gross messages between Shana and Pork, a video call pops up. For a second, I'm sure someone knows I'm on Shana's laptop and they can see me. Then the video opens up all by itself. It's invited me in automatically and I've joined a video conference Shana's set up from –wherever she is.

Holy smokes, this is tense. It's a good thing Zoom doesn't lock you out if you've got open two accounts from the username. Good thing I've got the webcam turned off.

It's Nomad. He's talking to the cops. From his pad in Raumanga. Over Zoom. Why though? Karl's on the kase.

I'm laxing back on the top bunk bed, settling in for a good old fashioned eavesdrop on their group video chat when the back of my skull donks the cinderblock wall and I grunt, '*Fugginshitballs.*'

Oh God. My cover's blown. Quiet, Karl, quiet, mutemutemute–

'Fuck was that?' goes Nomad's voice. All they get from my corner of the screen is audio, so I say next to nothing. Nomad's voice, Shana's voice, and the country's anal-est straighto-est Perfect Square police officer, Senior Constable Snitchie Richie. Plus his dominatrix.

'Zoom's notorious for interruptions to its signal,' goes Integrity Inspector Nantakarn. 'Let's discuss progress to date.'

'Integrity Inspector's right, we need an update,' Richie's grumpy voice goes.

*Nice to see ya, ya snitchy prick.*

'I'm here too, hi everyone,' Shana goes. She's using her phone for this one.

'Patience, you lot, patience.' I hear the click of a Zippo opening, a Zippo closing, and the world's staunchest 60 year old inhaling smoke. Then Nomad's screen shakes like we're in Jurassic Park and a t-rex is coming.

A hefty old beast waddles up onto the Raumanga driveway, alright. Leather and chains rattling. Pink skin steaming.

'Got a representative of the Four-Thirteens with me. Just so you all know.'

Nomad's let Pork into his flat. Fuck me. You'll work with anyone for a buck, won't ya, Nomes.

"So the reason we're all here, might as well broach this first,' goes Nantakarn through a mouthful of stones. 'We have some funds with which to discretely – and I must emphasise that word – *discretely* purchase some leads from your motorcycle, shall I say, "club," Mr Hamm.'

'Tell 'em there's operating costs need payin first,' we all hear Pork go. The fat cunt's basically standing behind Nomad, working him like a venturelocust dummy, telling him what to say.

'There's operating costs,' Nomad repeats. 'Defiant've got an invoice here for two hundred and fifty grand. For helpin, uh, facilitate the search for Barbs. They need that up front before they lease out their private bounty hunting services. They also need an official Police letter that they've been cleared of suspicion for the disappearance of Ms Konstantinou.'

'Bounty?!' Nantakarn scoffs, ignoring Pork's wind-up. '250,000 dollars? Mr Hamm, you will shake your tree of contacts, and you will tell me before the DNA tests return from Environmental and Scientific Testing whether the remains we pulled up earlier this month are those of Barbara. *Then* you might have something to negotiate with'

Nomad smashes his smoke out in an ashtray. 'Pork says after people give him orders, usually they never say a word again. I'd take it easy on that shit if I were you, ma'am.'

'Can't believe we're having this conversation.'

'Yeah, bitch?' Pork thumps Nomad's desk, wobbling the webcam. 'Well I can't believe you jokers tried to break into my pad. Y'ever seen *Home Alone,* Macauley Culkin 'n shit? That's exactly what it was like. Burglars try to come in, we send 'em away hurting.'

Silent heavy shame for everyone. Then Shana, my favourite two-faced player trickster pipes up. 'I have to speak to reporters tomorrrow. Can we hurry up and agree on the payment of a retainer, an advance – whatever it's called. I'm sorry, Integrity Inspector, but it's my parents who've authorised me to represent the family. This means I'm going to be spending the money on what the money's for: leads.'

'Who's the other Shana?'

'Pardon?'

'You're logged in twice. Into this meeting. Is that a glitch?

Shana's eyes squint. 'I'm not sure where my usual computer is. I've misplaced it. I'm on my cellphone.'

'Lady, you got the Club's bank account number,' Nomad interrupts, saving my life. I'm surprised they can't hear me breathing a sigh of relief. 'Wire the club the cash we need to get the intel. Chances are they'll find your sister's alive and well, they'll lift her up out of there, maybe black a few eyes, get her back home, Bob's your uncle. Just put the money through, Pork says.'

Richie opens his mouth. Nantakarn immediately speaks over him. God damn – she's the one wearing the strap-on.

'We are going around in circles. You will tell us if you are aware if Barbara Konstantinou is dead or not. Also her partner, Kenny D'Souza.'

'Lemme see you hold up your smartphone and shift some fuckin' digits.'

'Okay, okay, let's decompress a little,' Shana goes. 'Hypothetically, if we freed up a tad more cash, what would we get in return?'

'Find out if that fish-eaten corpse is your sissie or not.'

'I'm supposed to tell the Commissioner of Police that The Best Administration responds to extortion, am I? Is that what I'm supposed to feed back?'

Damn, man. For a squeaky little school girl, Nantakarn can really sound scary when she gets sand in her undies. 'Bulletins first thing tomorrow are going to say the best administration in the country's allowed a family to be robbed under *my* watch? That's your proposal?'

Booft. She even thumps the desk.

Shana dabs her eyes with the triangle corner of her blouse. 'We cannot pay a cent more than 250,000.' Either she misses her sister or she oughta get a friggin Oscar.

My hands are wrapped over my mouth. If they hear me breathe, I'm fucked. It's epically frustrating being left out of this negotiation. Five faces on screen, none of them my own.

'So that concludes that,' Richie goes. 'Bedtime for everyone then?'

'It's night-night forever for some of us,' Nomad goes. 'Pork's sayin if you don't pay, there's gonna be consequences.'

'No consequences if she's already dead.'

No one says anything for a couple seconds after this.

'What exactly is "night-night forever" supposed to mean?' Nantakarn says in a slow, creeping voice. She knows something dark's just been said. I'm moving my mouse pointer round, trying as fast as I can to find the button that'll open my webcam back up, bring "Shana Konstantinou" into the conversation from my end, so I can see what's about to happen, 'cause I got me a suspicion about what 'Night-Night Forever' means.

'Just put the quarter mil through and we'll get the girl back,' Pork goes.

Nantakarn throws up her hands. Richie doesn't stop Shana as she holds her phone up.

'Ooookayyyy?' Shana's ready to give fuckin Pork ten times my annual salary. 'I'm authorised to transfer, soooo?' She presses some buttons on her phone.

'It's underway,' she goes. Everyone swallows, looks away.

'Transfer completed.'

'Shot for the cash. Laters.'

The call ends. Everybody drops off within a couple seconds, their boxes shrinking. Just me left, in my little black box, and I don't wanna be trapped in some icky call with Pork.

I'm reaching for the Leave Call button when Pork pulls a fat black handgun from inside his jacket. Sticks the snout into Nomad's silver mullet. 'Nomes, mate, you can be excused.'

POP.

Splat.

A gunshot blasts through the speakers so loud my laptop freezes. The robotic-Godzilla noise makes backpackers rush down the hall desperate to see if I've blown my brains out.

Sound is stuck in the speakers, reverberating.

Nomad is not on his seat.

Nomad is gone – but there is gunsmoke and there are white bits of melted skull on the desk. One droplet of blood against the eye of the webcam trickling down slow and gooey.

# 25

# "Nigga got caught snitchin."

My ears ring. I cry little boogers of sorrow. Try to block out the terror with smoke. Wondering if I should tell the Feds what happened the second they logged off the computer.

Get high, feel low, and somewhere in the haze, I find my balls.

By around 11.30, I have a plan. When the plan finalises itself in my brain, I swallow some proverblial concrete pills, swallow some *actual* pills, jump down from my bunk bed, plant my feet on the ground and point my arse in the direction of the party and just go for it.

As stones and cubes of car window glass are jabbing my feet, making me wince, making me want to weep, I'm noticing I've run out without my shoes, and I can feel sand splashing on my knees as I tread over a dune and a breeze is tickling my nipple rings.

It would appear I've left the hostel in nothing but my boxer shorts.

This is not a good look. I'm just lucky my undies have Cookie Monster on 'em. I hope the TruBlues and little 14-year-old homicidal Crips notice the indigo hues of Cookie Monster and give me a pass on account of incorporating blue into my threads. If not... God man, these cunts are rough enough when it's daylight. Rowdy party at night on the beach? Gonna be aggro as fuck.

I scamper to the end of Kings Road then cross Marsden, the main road, walk through the palms and hit the beach, feeling the eyes of a family strolling in the opposite direction of the beach party, holding late-night gelato cones. Probly staring at my Sesame Street cock-bulge. Probly jealous of my Big Bird.

Pausing in the sand under a tinselly Christmas tree, panting, I pat my naked ribs, hoping a dipper has stuck itself to my sweaty body somehow. No luck. I creep down the dune towards a couple of flags stuck in the sand and some drums with bonfires flickering in them. There are nasty looking just-got-outta-jail-lookin toothless fat chicks in heavy black t-shirts, hair held up in blue Crip bandanas, standing around holding 12-packs of premix bourbon 'n cola. One of them bumps me as I go past like she wants a scrap.

Karly Kockroach is losing his touch with the ladies. Ah well. Can't win 'em all. Better just focus on one crucial lady.

I see the party doesn't have a centre, just two halves – well, not even halves, it's a 90/10 split. The 90 percent of folks are boogying in clusters around burning steel drums, and music's coming from giant speakers with miles of extension cord. There's a DJ on mix deck and there's three places where drumming's coming from, and ten dudes on guitars trying to synchronise their strumming as they sit on logs and beer kegs.

There are ten fat yellow Triumphs you just can't look away from, meaning the Defiants are here. Reflected flames dance on the motorcycles' chrome. Men caked in leather lean against their bikes. They've all either got their helmets on their heads, or they're holding their helmets under their arms. Plastic wraparound shades, even in the dark. Yellow bandanas, yellow towels round hard dudes' necks.

'Oi,' I go, elbowing some person in the ribs. We're in the shadow of a palm tree with about four road cones stuck in its branches. 'Where's the party at?'

'You blind, G?'

'Nah I mean where's the *party*-party, know what I'm sayin? Where can I get some smoke?'

The person looks at my belly button, the goose bumps on my strawberry thighs, the Cookie Monster covering up my cock.

'Thataway.' The person points at the motorcycles. 'Get in quick though. They're makin an example of some poor cat in a second. Used to DJ 'n pimp for the club but then, pssssh. Turned traitor.'

I know a traitorous snaky DJ-n-pimp. One that looked a whooole lot like–

'Not called Kenny, is he?'

'Mm-hmm. Word is the DMC found messages on Kenny's phone hidden on Tinder or something. Coded messages n shit. He was talkin to the poh-leese. Nigga got caught snitchin.'

'What're they gonna do, like, give him the bash?'

The man giggles and sucks a joint which smells like beautiful rotting leaves in a rainforest. 'Gonna give him what everyone gets when they're kicked outta the DMC.'

'So he's not dead yet?'

'Want proof, G? Club's got no more use for him. He ain't bringing in money like he used to anyway, cause he lost his best ho, so *pssht*. Laters. Old news.'

The guy looks at me like I'm on crack, which I should be.

'Nigga's standin right over there. Check it.'

Those big tall bouncer bastards who were guarding the front doors of the tat-fest are shoving this little dreadlocked guy in a trenchcoat through the crowd. The dreadlocked guy's got his turntables under one arm and I see one of the cords he's forgotten to unplug jerk and pull two powerboards into the sand. The big guys slap Kenny's turntables out of his hand and shove him another metre closer to the bikers, who unfold their arms and crick their fingers.

I fantasise for a moment about marching up and goin "I'll take it from here" to the Defiant and chucking Kenny over my shoulder and using him as bait to pick up Barbie before my dick retreats all the way up inside my stomach. My ears are being smashed by drums but I can hear Richie's words nip at my brain. *You, Karl, you will never be a hero*. Right now, in front of me, six black and yellow hornets are tightening the straps of their helmets, reaching into their saddlebags and taking out chains (the hell? How come chains?) and I'm doing sweet fuck-all to stop it.

Guess I'm sorta-kinda glad to see Kenny back from the dead, though he's only got a minute to live and we haven't answered the question of whose bodies were dumped under the Whangārei bridge.

I'm about to wade in and tell them to hold up a sec when they drop Kenny with a hard punch to the skull. The sound is softened by sticky, fluffy hair like dirty backyard sheep-wool. Ken's knees hit the sand. Just as they're shaking out the chains to strap Kenny to their bikes, a woman in a dirty white tank top with a pile of hair behind her headband steps forward to protect her man.

'Pleeeease,' the woman moans, grasping the zippers on a biker's chest, clawing at his patches, 'Pleeaselemmestay, I neeeeeeed you.' Her voice is raw and guttural and full of snot, as if she's been moaning for hours and her tonsils are swollen up. The biker kicks the woman forward and she stumbles into the arms of a big blue bouncer, who unzips his towel-sized hoodie and wraps it around her.

'Yo,' shouts the biker to the bouncer, 'Tat gears. Bonus.' He lobs a backpack at the TruBlue, who catches it. Bottles of ink spill out of it. The big bouncer helper with a Kaitaia Kripz patch picks up the bottles. The stumbling lady-tattooist in the singlet dissolves into the the crowd, and the men resume beating kegs so there's a jungle-tribal rhythm going.

That desperate moaning woman, yo. Hard to make out her face in the dark, but the tats, the hungry neck-bones, her hips, the shoulderblades jutting out from the singlet, the pointy elbows, the way she dangles her fingers. I think it might be her. Only problem is there's a wall of hard cunts between me and her.

Oh no, nonononono fuckin–

'Wish-bone! Wish-bone! Wish-bone!,' the people begin chanting. A channel opens up in the party and the Defiants gun their engines and Ken is yanked through a few metres of sand. He coughs and gasps as they get him in place. One chain is wrapped around Ken's right leg, one chain around his left. The chains are wrapped around the seats of two motorbikes.

'Wish-bone! Wish-bone! Wish-bone!'

A bike with two kids on the back of it. Daddy taking his kids to work.

That bike belongs to Glenn Fuckin Hamm.

Pork. The bastard who shot Nomad. Who sent his boys to pull the head off that SWAT dude. Who laughs in the face of cops and seems to get paid for it.

Four bikes rumble over the sand and stones towards the whispering ocean. The last two bikes follow, dragging Ken through the dunes. He splutters and begs and weeps and I think I even hear the cheap prick asking for one last ciggy.

'Wish-bone! Wish-bone!'

I hope Kenny suffocates from sand in his lungs instantly, not because I despise the cunt, just because no one deserves this thing that's coming.

My trembling hand reaches for my cellphone and finds only my hip. Isn't anyone recording this?

'The fuck you lookin at, Cookie Monster?' Some tattoo skank, it looks like – Jesus Tittyfucking Christ – it's *Barbie*. Right in front of me. And she doesn't even recognise her knight in shining armour. Her hair looks silver or pink or purple-streaked with regrowth and she has scratches on her neck. Our reunion lasts about a second before she's pulled back into the crowd by a Four-18, and the last I see of her is her opened backpack wiggling, dropping small bottles of ink onto the sand.

'Hey – hey! Barbara! Barbs!'

Boom.

Two hands on my shoulders. Some huge cunt shoving me back into the sand. I'm looking up as some Māoris bring down a big crayfish cage and open it up.

I know exactly what it's for. It's for cleaning up, cause there's about to be a epic mess.

'Go. The fuck. *Home.*'

They manhandle Kookie Monster Karl out of the crowd, shoulders and elbows and shoves and chest-bumps. Not sure if the wishbone thing I hear behind me with the revving and rumbling and begging-for-his-life and shrieking-like-a-child and the wet crunchy squirt and the upturned-buckety sound of people getting splattered with guts is a stunt or a party game or the real deal.

Real deal, I'm betting. Cause I hear the squeak of the crayfish cage opening. Cleanup time.

I know they're shoving chunks of Kenny inside the cage. Pretty sure them Māori fishermen'll be puttering the cage of man-meat out to Urupukapuka Island shortly to drop it in the ocean so the crayfish can gobble up any trace of poor Kenny.

Damn, G.

Someone musta spat under my eyebrows cause by the time I find a log to sit down on, my eyes are wet. Almost like I can't take this heavy shit anymore. Almost like I'm crying.

Holding my phone, I bring up Richie's number in the contacts.

Weigh it up. Tell myself I'm not a snitch... .

Then I message him anyway.

I know he'll probably delete it. He's probly got me blocked.

But Barbie's in that tattoo show, and I can't get her back by myself.

Guess you're supposed to make a wish when a wishbone gets snapped – and right now I'm wishing I had my best bruz back.

# 26

# "Just escape with me, a'ight?"

Y'know how that saying goes, 'Today is a gift - that's why they call it the present?'

Well, today's the kind of present I wish I'd got the receipt for, 'cause I wanna take it to The Warehouse and give it right the fuck back.

It's the last day of Bay Blue Tattoo and I've strutted on up full of nightmares and Codral, working on two hours' sleep, my skin all crusty-pink cause I stayed up all night scratching, convinced some of Kenny's blood spattered on me.

Today is the last chance for a last attempt for the last woman on Earth that might tolerate Komplicated Karl. Bruni and Dötti were just lusties, but Barb? She could be true love.

At the entrance to the pub-hall, the goons are blockin the door. Extra large gangsta Snoop-Lurch and the XXXL watermelon-round gangsta with a chain for a belt *(a chain, oh God, not a chain, I never wanna see a chain again)* wanna know what brings me back to the tats for a second day.

'Ceez up,' Lurch goes, throwing up a C-shaped set with his fingers. The C's thing means Crips, but that's about as much of the lingo Non-Crip Karl speaks.

'Uh, C's get degrees?' I offer, hoping I don't get smacked.

'Back for some ink, G?' Chains goes. It's hard to guess how much he knows.

'I's hopin to sweet-talk one of them tattoo apprentice chickypies,' I go. I roll up my shirt and show them my tummy, all abs and ribs, my body constantly tense for the last ten years. 'You're right, though. Too much bare skin. Need me some work done, brother.'

*Please be here, Barb. Please don't have wised-up. Please have stayed for the crack.*

Inside I grab two beers, stand against a wall, chug 'em back. I haven't slept for 30 hours. Stress inside Karl's Kranium. First the bridge bodies, then Nomad painting his ceiling red, then Kenny getting ripped into bits like a Gingerbread man... The fuck have I got myself into?

I go past the seafood stand where people trade crack for crayfish, spot a random tattooist and start talking about maybe getting some ink done, even though I've only got fifty bucks in my pocket. The tattooist is a witchy-looking Indian chick with dyed-orange hair and green arms covered in playing cards and skulls, she's got that skinniness that comes with smokin' heaps. Lots of cheekbones, wild eyes and she's in a singlet. People that party hard don't feel the cold. She says her name's Nadia, asks who I am. I don't have time to make some shit up and she's pretty hot, so I try a little seduction.

'Karl Copley,' I go, then before I can stop myself, 'Pussy inspector... ?'

*Stupid, stupid, stupid.* Sometimes I think I've got Tourette's syndrome, honest.

Her eyes go flat and hard and she fold her arms. 'So you're half cop, half pussy. Look, just pick a design. C'mon, y'see those two, the Tribesmen behind you? They're lining up. I'll do them first if you don't pick something.'

I sit up, pull my shirt down. Deep undercover now. 'You're right. You're right. Listen, I was gettin high with this chickypie yesterday. She's a apprentice, learning how to do tats, chick with yellow hair, sorta platinum, goes by the name of Barb, dunno if you can help me find her again... There still a party on down back, d'you reckon she'll be there?'

Nadia-The-Hot-Witch goes over and fiddles with her tat supplies, squeezing ink into a machine.

'Got something for me in exchange?'

She says to the customers waiting behind me, 'I'll be back. As for you, Pussy Cop, come.'

I nod like a little bitch and follow.

She takes her little lock-box full of cash as if it's a lunch pail. She high-fives and fist-bumps some big units in hoodies so huge the hoodies reach from their necks to their knees. Everyone seems to know Nadia. This is a family place, if you do something degenerate for a job, or you're an addict, or you're on the run from the feds.

We stroll past the t-shirt sales, the bumper sticker sales, several tattoo booths, the food booth with cans of soft drink and buckets of fried chicken, and by the smoking toilets, running a tattoo stall, disposable gloves on and a ciggy in her lips, there's a purple-haired version of Barbara God Damn Konstantinou.

Whoawhoawhoa – Barbs? Barbs. Holeee...

I'm just in time to pull up my Monster Energy hoodie, whip my shades on and stick an unlit smoke in my mouth as we reach her. *Breathe, Karl, breathe. Be chill, follow the plan, get her out of here somehow.* She's about as classy as I remember her. I steal a glance into ...whatever you call them coloury bits in your eyes, ibises or whatever. They're dark brown. She's wearing coloured contact lenses. She's a completely different person, now. She went deep. God, man. What's left of the woman I loved?

I take a breath, feeling the arteries and veins in my thighs tingle as they fill with cold, stiff metal. The tingling sensation floods my guts and I have to piss. Barb has no idea what it's like to see her after so much worry and paranoia, yo.

'What's goin down?' Barb goes to Nadia.

'Customer's payin' for some smoke,' Nadia Witch giggles, and rubs against me like a slutty stray cat. 'Aren't you, big boy?'

'Uh, I guess.'

To Barbs: 'You wanna come?'

Barbie is lucky to have ducked out of the circle of big thugs surrounding her watching her tattoo some schmuck on her bench. There's something different about these goons. Yesterday they were, like, *whiter* – Sandpapery beards, a couple of gingers. Lots of whiteboys. Defiants, Four-13s.

Today's goons surrounding her seem to be TruBlues. Māori boys and Islanders covered in indigo and cyan and navy blue stickers and patches and paisley. I can sense the elephant in the room, yo: Everyone's been told there's a nark walkin round who's been seen workin with cops to try take Barbs away and mess up the DMC's revenue, and that nark looks like Yours Truly.

*Fuck. Gonna be impossible to get her outta here.*

Barbie chews her lip ring. She sways as if she's asleep on her feet. I cannot believe she's within touching-distance. The girl I've been dreaming about for ages.

'How you settling in, darl?' Nadia rubs Barb's shoulder then turns to me and explains, 'She got sold to the Blues last night, poor little thing. Gotta work off a few debts, eh girl.'

'Sold? That's like – '

'Pretty shit, but whatevs. Girl's gotta work.'

'You should just go by yourself, Nadia,' I go, handing her a dipper I've bought this morning from a backpacker. 'Here: get this thing lit up for us.'

She doesn't quite run, but her feet make her scamper in a beeline for the hotbox bathrooms. Drooling like Pavalova Dog for them drugs man.

'So, stranger, if you choose a design, I'll ink ya for fifty,' Barbie goes, moving backwards, parting the blue gangsters and hopping up on a bench in a booth where she apparently does her slave-work.

*Stranger? Please don't call me that, Barbs. I'm your knight in shining armour, I'm like, I dunno, who's someone that saves you when you're in trouble, Jesus or Gandhi or one of them gods. And she needs rescuing, woo whee. She's fallen. The purple dye isn't evenly distributed through her hair. She's got two rings in her lips now, and one looks infected. There's acne on her chin, and her eyes have dark blue rings around them. Her clothes: black t-shirt, black track pants.*

That old Tiffany Spears song plays in the Spotify in my skull. *I think we're alone now, there doesn't seem to be anyone arou-ound.*

'I – I can't believe...'

She spits into a bottle. 'Can't believe you're getting inked? I got two kindsa needles here, if ya catch my drift. What typa needle you after?'

*Now's the time, Karly. Operation GrabSnatch. I can see the rear of the hall is open to the beer garden, sloping down to Haruru Falls. Just roll her out like an old-timey lumberjack rolling logs into the river, Karl.*

'Barbara. Don't you recognise me?'

She squiggles her face.

'I'm here to *rescue* you,' I whisper. 'It's me.'

She chuckles. 'Who?'

'Me! Karl!'

'Right...' She blinks. 'I'm sposda know you?'

'You have to leave right now with me.' I duck my head and gesture for her to do the same. 'We'll make a plan. I have to get you home.'

'Fuck's that sposda mean? This *here's* my home."

'Means I think you're not here of your own free will. Means I think the Four-Thirteen sold your ass to the TruBlues who are now basically your slavemasters, and you've gotta be a slave to about a thousand people to earn your freedom and do all kinds of gross stuff and while you're– '

'You shut your mouth right fuckin now, dude.'

' –while you're workin off your debt for the blueberries, Defiants're makin about a gazillion dollars sayin they're helping bring your arse back home, lady, fuck! Just escape with me, a'ight?'

Instead of crouching with me and working out a plan to save herself, she spins, puts her hands on the tattoo bench, touches her forehead, does the sign of the cross, laughs, pats her cheeks, which have turned bright red, showing how zombie-white her skin is. She could easily activate some kind of alarm right now, the nark alarm, and big boys would surround me and take me inside the girls' toilets forever.

She chews the Hubba-Bubba to the side of her mouth, parking it. 'Last chance to pay for your needles, baby. Only reason you fixin' to be here.'

The nark alarm hasn't yet gone off. I'm lucky I have this corner to formulate a plan in.

What I do next changes her life, my life, everything.

I grab her wrist and squeeze. I pull as hard as I can, making her move two steps. We make it to the edge of her booth. Beyond the booth, onto the back lawn, down to the river and swim to freedom. Just gotta make it over the floor then past the door-goons. We're ten metres from escape, but I've forgotten to bring masking tape to paste over Barbie's mouth, and it's a huge fuckin' mouth indeed and – panicked – the mouth begins to bleat, going,

'NaaaAAAARRRRK!'

No one grabs me, at first – they stand around with folded arms. Nadia the tattooist. She's amongst 'em. So's my friend from the toilet, the Ethiopian. I'm backing away from them, feet on the floor of the hall now, and I can sense the convention stopping around me, everyone tense that there could be cops here, and the back of my hoodie's pressing against something hard, and I fall backwards through a portal to another dimensh–

Huh. A dimension with some cheap Odour Toilette bottles on the handbasins. Musta fallen backwards onto my arse through a swinging door and ended up in the girl-toilets. There's a tiny skylight letting some basic blue light in. Neat rolls of toilet paper with zero piss on them. Unbelievably clean. Nicer than many of the flats I've stayed in, truth be told.

I get up off my butt for a moment and lock the main door, then return to the ground in Cockroach Mode, like I'm crouched to do push-ups, moving backward, watching the door. I figure it'll be about a hundred seconds till they smash it down. There's about 60 centimetres of clear space under the hand basins. I crawl under there and gasp some air into my lungs, swallowing jaggedly.

Posse outside, waiting to get me.

'I think this nigga's poe-leese,' Barb calls through the door. Working for the enemy.

'Come wit us.' It's the voice of the guy from out front, the XXXL Lurch-Snoop Dogg unit. 'I fuck up po-lice fo a livin,' XXXL goes. 'Get outside now. Bare knuckles, motherfuckles.'

My ears detect other voices. The bathroom door is like a magnet attracting bullies one by one. Biiiig big bullies who think they've got a free pass to murk cops and narks and bounty hunters. They could probly wishbone me with their bare hands. Stick me under their armpits and walk in two different directions like giants till I rip apart. Feed my scraps to the crayfish after, like poor old Ken.

'You gotta, you guys, you gotta give me ten minutes to get prepped,' I call towards the door. I stick my head out of my under-basin hidey hole, look toward the ceiling. The skylight's four metres above. The windows are three metres up. They're small, but achievable. Shirt off, pants off, shoes off – I can do this.'

'Come ouuuuut, poh-leeeeses… .'

A hand dryer vooms. I squawk and duck. There's no more retreating to be done in here. Thank fuck they haven't sent the posse in. 'I'm a buh, a bub, b-b-bounty hunter, I'm not a cop, I'm a bou- '

'Get out here already, little bitch. No lady toilets today for you.'

'You gotta let me take her with me, that girl, Barb, 'sall I'm here for, for reals,' I pant. It's forever between lungfuls of air. 'Bounty hunter, honest. Jus' takin her home to her family.'

'Uh uh,' continues Snoop-Lurch. 'You gonna one-out me or not?'

I peel a square of toilet paper off my palm. 'You're massive-as. How the fuck am I gonna fight ya?'

'Pussy-arse chicken,' he goes, thick heavy voice like an iron beam that's been dropped. 'Know somethin, Wicked Wing? You asked a lotta questions yesterday. Got a lotta people real rattled. You're a informant, obvious.'

'I *have* to take her, you don't understand.'

'You honestly think you're gonna take a man's bitch?'

'She's *my* bitch.' Gulp. 'I mean, she's mine.'

Deep panting breaths. The eye of the storm. Calmness.

'D'you promise to let me go if I fight you?'

He tells me if I lose, I'm a dead motherfucker – but it's a yes.


The crowd want their fight, Jiminy Fuckin Christmas do they what. They whoop and catcall and mix swearing and threats, calling me Snitch and Nark and telling me to die with 'Good luck' and 'Fuck 'im up' and 'Go for the nuts.'

The fight's been organised to take place under the pointy canopy tents where the lawn slopes down to the river. I'm so nervous I hallucinate that I can see, like, junior commandoes lying flat on the river on some kind of stealth-boards. Like the typa army men I used to put in the garden, lying on their bellies in sniper positions.

I'm retreating into a shell of fear, my brain withdrawing into my skull as fast as my cock is shrivellin up into my belly.  Snoop-Lurch points to a position where he wants me to stand. It's towards the end of the lawn behind the pub, sloping down to the brown river. I could sprint into the liquid and paddle away, but that wouldn't get me any closer to rescuing Barbs. Gotta get through this, take my hiding and maybe there'll be a smidgen left of me to take her to safety.

I'm boxed in by tough guys anyway, everybody with spikes on their leather and tough jaws and shiny skulls and tattoos on their cheeks. Everyone looking wild and desperate and angry and wanting a spectacle to distract 'em from their shitty lives.

The crowd locks us in. Fifty underworld crims, and two palm trees that the canopy-tents have been tethered to.

I pull my top off slowly, sobbing like the Dargaville Kumara Queen when she takes her trophy.

*Geddim!* The crowd are going. Buncha dogs who can't wait to get fed. *Smash that snitch! Fuck that nigga up!*

I curl my fingers into my palms. Two pathetic fists. As I get into a boxing stance, I see Snoop-Lurch discarding the crap from his pockets, cause the crowd's demanding a fair fight. He tosses away his car keys, his smokes, his cellphone, his knuckle dusters, a short length of chain, a grenade which I reeeeally hope is just a keyring.

Me, I toss out a piece of pizza from yesterday I'd forgotten about, a Band-Aid I was planning on reusing and – struggliest of all – I put my drugs aside. The underworld equivalent of a ball boy scuttles over and collects these things from me.

*Cheers, kid. This your holiday programme or what?*

In my right pocket – the final thing I discard – is something hard and tubeliar. It's cylinder-shaped and full of juicy liquid but it can't be my dick, because this thing is wayyyy too long, four inches at least. I'm about to chuck it to the ball boy when some referee, the bouncer from the door with the chains, yells 'Fight's onnn' and dooft, I'm tackled in the midsection by a walking giraffe with shoulders wide as a door.

I splat on my back on the lawn and the crowd goes, 'Ooooooh' and some joker yells 'World star' and Snoop-Lurch picks me up immediately and tosses me to one side.

I can't believe I get up off my knees. It's the adrenaline of fighting for Barbs, wherever she is. Pretty sure I saw a flash of purple hair and a nose-ring in the audience.

 I feel something dripping around my cock area.

'He's wet himself! Oh my god, you guys!'

I look down and yup, there's a black stain spreading over my lap. I can feel warm liquid fingers reaching down my arse crack, too. It's as if I've somehow cummed my pants and had diarhea, which doesn't make a lot of sense, cause I had a masty and took a shit minutes before I came here.

*Hang on*, I think, standing swaying and bruised on the lawn, seconds from getting crushed. Your shorts only get that black if you've been drinking Guinness – and I didn't drink any damn Guinness.

I quickly yank my shorts down over my knees and kick them into Snoop-Lurch's face. He pulls them off and they leave a stain on his face that's wayyyy too black, like paint or Marmite. I follow up with my boxer shorts, dragging them down over my ankles and flicking them into Lurch's eyes. He's blinded for a second. I'm not worried about the crowd seeing my junk because of the blackness which disguises my junk and, if they actually glimpse it, maybe it'll have become bigger in size from being black.

Black, Karl. Like ink, yo. Think, G, think.

That's what's happened, ahhhh– it's black tattoo ink, and unless I'm a fuckin squid, I reckon the tube of stolen tattoo ink popped in my pocket when Snoop-Lurch crushed me a moment ago.

Here the big bastard comes now, charging up like he's about to kick a rugby ball over some World Cup goal posts. He launches another tackle, wraps his arms around my hips, gets a faceful of slippery dick and slides down my legs. I step out like I'm taking off a hula hoop and I jump to the right, feeling the wind on my nutsack. Wouldn't you know it, my feet land on top of a pair of metre-high kegs. I wobble and sway and claw at the air and the kegs are close to tipping because I'm so inky and slippery, but the kegs don't collapse, so here's me, a metre above the ground. A higher perch would've been nice, God, if that's not too much to ask.

Snoop-Lurch lunges at me as the crowd makes messy howling noises. I step backwards, onto the DJ table, crunching knobs, slipping on screens, and the crowd yells at me to get back in the fighting pit. I can't stay on top of these kegs for long cause I'm about to spill outside the edge of the ring, and in fight code that means you get disqualified, and obviously murked.

I turn to step onto the next thing, grab any kind of support – and lo and behold, I'm hugging a palm tree with my dick pressed against it. It's a thick piece of wood – the tree, I mean. I'm squeezing it and shinning up it, scraping my knees raw. A few inches, a few inches, holy smokes. Snoop-Lurch is dumbfounded that I'm doing this koala shit to avoid fighting him, but here we are. I'm nearly at the top of the trunk, scratching the head of my dick as I scrabble up and leaving a black snail trail where my junk brushes ink against the tree.

I'm high up against the ceiling of the tent-canopy and below me Snoop-Lurch is reaching with one hand, nipping at my toes, but the huge lanky NBA seven-footer cannot get hold of me.

I hug that tree like a stripper who won't let go of her pole.

The crowd can hiss and boo and call me all sorts of mean names, but sticks and stones, yo. These people can't hurt me.

Until the ink trickling out from my fingers and undies makes this whole tree-hugging thing too slippery, of course.

Or Snoop-Lurch's blowtorch gets me.

Yep, he's asked Ball Boy for his lighter and he's picked up a can of flyspray and he's doing a test-flamethrow over the lawn. *Phwooooar* goes the dragon-tongue of fire from the can.

The flames lick my feet and I screech like a guinea pig. Runny black droplets trickle down my legs and fly off my ankles into the breeze. Piss mixed with ink.

I see her, as I press my face against prickly palm leaves and prepare to slide down to death. My love. My angel. The purple fake hair, the I-don't-give-a-fuck-because-life's-treated-me-shit eyes. The bony neck, the starving shoulders, rainbow tats. Teeth like windows on an abandoned building.

My inky, slippery grip loosens.

Koala Karl slides half a metre down the palm tree. Lurch's flamethrower can definitely reach me from here.

Just before I die, I finally see Barbie's nips. Just a glimpse, cause from up here, I can look directly down her singlet.

Amen. I will now go into the afterlife a happy man.

Clomp-clomp-clomp.

What the hell?

A column of... ironing boards? – coffin lids? Nah – surfboards – are marching in under me.

Like bulldozer-barricades, restraining gangsters and girls and onlookers, cause behind every surfboard is a pair of–

I don't fuckin believe it.

It's a dozen of the youth group, dripping juice as if they've come out of the river. They're actually pushing the gangsters back with their boards, they've, they've-they've created some kind of safe drop zone for me to land in, bruz! On the topic of bruz, I'm wondering where Richie is as I slip another metre down, grinding my junk into black sawdust-sludge.

As I hit the ground, relieved that this Karla Koala phase is over, he walks into the middle of the fight. All the Group Awesome surfboard wieners look over their shoulders as their master speaks to the gang mob.

'Gentlemen, ladies,' Richie announces, 'If you'll kindly stay calm. Just here to speak with a couple of people.'

'Fuck outta here,' goes Watermelon Padlock Belt Man, trying to speak over the surfboard pressing him back against a pole.

Snoop-Lurch appears behind Richie, throws a massive punch. One of the Golden Christians calls out 'Rich!' and he ducks, whips out a vial of something and squirts Snoop-Lurch's eyes. A big squirt, confident, like when you've got a fly cornered and you take out all your aggression on it and really mace it into the ground.

Snoop-Lurch sinks to his knees, pulling his fingers down from his eyebrows. Finally, as Richie stands over, Snoop-Lurch collapses on his side, puking onto the grass and rolling in it, colouring his face yellow.

The baying crowd don't really bay that much, now. They look a little scared. Almost ready to cooperate. Or waiting for someone to lead the revolt.

I take a final hand off the tree, enjoy the sweet feeling of the ground holding me. I wobble to my feet.

If I put my undies back on, they'll probly stick forever. Looks like I've been having sex with a jar of Marmite.

Barbie's being manhandled by two Group Awesome boys, presenting her like a swordfish they've just landed.

'Show's over, everyone,' Richie tells the crowd, heading back into the hall to take us out of there. 'Karl: put your pants on. You're coming with me. And Barbara, I know you don't wanna come.'

'Obviously. Fuck you, pigs.'

'I thought you might say that. Boys, cuff her.'

The Christian Cop Cadets slap cuffs on her hands and feet. She wriggles and screams.

She's ready to take away.

Just gotta get through the mob.

# 27

## "Drive, man, drive."

Like Buzz Lightyear and the Toy Story team tryina bust out of Andy's bedroom, our tight little unit battles to get out. The only difference is we have hardly any dudes and we've cuffed and carried away something from the enemy that they really want back, Barb Konstantinou. She was supposed to make the gangs some scrilla. Now someone's gotta pay.

Richie's boys fight hard-out. I'm impressed. They bat away broken bottles and tattoo needles and pizza boxes. They kick out legs and use their Marshall Arts to collapse bigger men like folding chairs, all while urging Barbie forward like a rugby team moving the ball through a scrum.

We can't get Barb out through the lawn/river/backend of the convention, so we're battling through the main hall. We've arrived at the Bob Marley booth where yesterday my friend got made to cover up his colours by taping a poster to his chest. The barricade gets worse – people come over, shoulder to shoulder, a total lynch mob, an army of trashy zombies covered in patches and blue hoodies, jandals and caps. I hear something growling out front, brarrrr, brar-brar-brar-brar, like a T-rex with a chainsaw in its throat.

That's a bike with an engine as big as a car, and a man just as big getting off it. Coming in to give orders.

Even with our surfboards, we don't have a way to break down the human wall in front of us. The wall is fronted by the two ink-splattered bouncers, Snoop-Lurch and the fat one with the padlock pants... plus the Defiants. Four of them. They don't have weapons, but there's no way through them. They'll come up with an excuse to bash us.

'Giz the girl already,' says a thick heavy voice I've heard in my nightmares.

A gap appears in the human wall. Through the gap waddles Pork, pink-faced, wiping his brow, adjusting his big scary colourful patch, rattling and clanking, his thick boots making the ground shake.

My crew looks at Richie. Even Barbs – cuffed and chained like King Kong – gawps at Richie with a *Fuck do we do now?* look on her face.

But Rich isn't an action hero. He's a methodical prick – and he simply solves the problem in front of him.

'Gentlemen: cover your noses.'

Rich raises his hand as if he's snapping a photo. The air fills with biting chili sauce, boiling-hot curry, sandflies and cactus needles in everyone's eyes. In his hand I see the word *Cum Spray 50ml Aim Away From Face.* Everyone crumples and complains and falls to the sides and a big waft of stinging fire hits me. My snot is made of broken glass, suddenly, and there's bleach on my tongue.

As he tucks his spray back into his hip I get an eyeful of the letters I didn't see before, C-A-P-S-I. Capsi-cum, ahh. Makes more sense. Cause people get cum in their face all the time and it's usually sweet and salty, like pineapple, but not if you've been eating capsicums and chilis. The cum spray or capsicum or whatever it is seems to be crumpling the gangstas, though. Y'ever seen someone trying to shove their own face into their lap and rip it off? That's what it looks like's happening to Pork and Lurch and all the big bullies. They're tearing at their cheeks, howling. The noise erupting from their lungs is the boooom of a drum as high as a building.

I jam my arms inside Barbie's armpits and order one of the Christian soldiers to carry her legs out with me and Rich, like we're moving furniture in a hurry.

'Boost,  bruz, boost, I got her!'

While Richie points his cum spray at the enemy, shooting people down like weeds, we carry out our trussed-up woman. Group Awesome form a phallus around us, I think Phallus is what you call it, one of them Trojan tactical formations where the shields make a box that protects you on all sides? Their shields are surfboards and the phallus of Trojans begins pushing forward. The legions of gangstas and crooks make only just enough room to barely let us through. They spit. They swear. They snort ropes of snot out their noses. They claw at their eyes and roar death threats, and Senior

Constable Richie McMullan keeps his chin high.

Daylight, finally. The entrance/exit, the carpark. Palm trees and pigeons.

I slow down. Can barely comprehend that we're actually taking Barb outta here.

Richie feels me slowing, feels Barb wriggle and shudder under his arm. He stops entirely. There's a TruBlue fingering a stainless steel bollard with a huge base plate, trying to remove the velvet rope from it.

I know what he's about to do. He's gonna whirl it at us and splatter our skulls.

Cool carpark pebbles on my feet. The soothing fresh air of highway exhaust-gas up ahead.

I'm pausing, trying to recover.

'Stopping for a beer are ya, Karl?' Richie goes in a flat voice, shifting his half-a-Barbie from one arm to the other while she scratches.

I'm eyeing up the brewskis they've got at the little shack-booth beside the door.

'Not a bad idea, after all that shit back– behind you, G!'

Richie turns. Standing in front of a bunch of dying bluebottles writhing in the hot sticky melted tar of the parking lot, clutching their eyes, is big ol Pork, sweating in his black leathers under the sun, waving two pink oven-mitts which must be his fat hands.

'Think we better have us a chinwag,' he goes. Booming voice turns my blood to jelly. 'You can just hand ol' Barbara back to Porky. Attaboy.'

Still holding Barbie – dragging me along, actually – Richie strides up, pops the cap off a fresh can of poison spray, and squirts Pork's eyes hard enough to wipe them off his face, leaving the fat fuck scratching in a puddle of puke.

As we thud into the car park, Barbs starts squirming. Rest of the angry gangstas are coming through the building, round the corner, chucking bottles off the balcony upstairs. I hope the Christian wieners have waxed their surfboards so our attackers slide off.

'I'm gonna drop her!'

Barb's kicking, now, raising her tummy, twisting her spine. We make it onto some grass beneath a thick huge Norfolk pine.

'Now you can drop her,' Richie goes. We dump her on the grass. She kneels, pushes herself onto her feet, gets a wide stance. I can see each joint in her fingers. They're bent like they're Lego Technic.

'Don't you put me anywhere near my goddamn mum 'n dad,' she growls.

The fuck? That needs explaning.

She's about to claw us and run.

Richie's youth group squat all around us, surfboard-shields positioned to deflect bullets.

'We gettin outta here, boss?'

'Thanks for your work, boys. Ready to hit the water?'

The Christian commando-kids scamper back around the side of the pub, scurry down the muddy river-edge, pour themselves like otters into the milky coffee river and board away.

A cop car arrives in the carpark, white with orange and blue chequers, and it squirts gravel as it skids to a stop in front of the three of us left – the cop, the crim, and the captive with vomit on her chest. The driver reaches behind. A rear passenger door opens.

Oh God. Five-oh. What is it now? They're gonna lock my arse –

'In the back, move it,' shouts the driver. A woman. Little, but in charge. Richie grabs Barb's fingers, twists her forearm and her whole body crumples. Folded up like a tent, she fits nicely into the back of the car. Richie slams the door shut. I rush around the far side of the cop car.

Inside is a difficult little woman with a lesbian haircut and a satisfied smirk on her lips.

'It's you,' I go.

'And it's you,' she replies from the driver seat. The unreadable Shana Konstantinou. Hard to know where to stand with her, though I'm pretty sure, once we get back home, there's gonna be some revelations.

Cause Shana's been playing both sides. Now ain't the time to discuss, though.

She makes the engine roar, bangs the car on a speed hump, gets to the driveway pouring into Highway 10 before Richie yanks the handbrake up.

'The heck are you doing?' Shana yells.

Something smacks the rear window of the car – a beer bottle. It foams as it rolls down.

Richie opens the passenger door, steps out, walks around the front of the car, taps Shana's window with his knuckles.

Another bottle smashes on the back windscreen, and then a brick adds a hash of cracks, and I hear a clang as those metal bollards are lobbed at us, denting our car.

They're gonna break in soon. We have about five seconds before the zombies blink the last of the cum spray out of their eyes and get their hands on us.

'We may be in a hurry, my dear,' Richie goes, 'But you're unauthorised to drive a police car, so if you'd kindly… .'

'They're gonna kill us, get in the fucking car, Richie!'

More and more bottles smash on the back. Then a tomatoey triangle of dollar-pizza splats on my window, trickles down, leaving chunks of pineapple-tomato. The rear windscreen has lines and circles and dents in it now. It reeks of beer. Men are closing in. Richie uncaps his spray and squirts a few metres. The wind carries the cum spray into the attackers' eyes. They spit and cough.

Shana's out of the driver seat, and she's about to go around to the passenger seat, when I get up, get out, feel a beer bottle smack my shoulder, smell stinking beer-foam. Shana lands in the backseat beside her sister. I smell burning rubber, Tabasco. I hear shouts, chants, abuse. I see the last good window of the cop car take a beer bottle and lighting fork across the glass as it cracks. I see Barbara Konstantinou, cuffed and crammed, put her head on the lap of Shana, close her eyes.

Shana strokes her sister's hair.

It's beautiful, man. Really heart-warming. It's the most joyous, rewarding hot lesbo action I've seen since *Hot Tub Twincest 2*.

Rich flips a switch, we hear the doors lock – and the car moves one foot then stops.

'Drive, man, drive, what the fuck are you doing?'

Richie frowns. 'I don't see why we can't spare a minute to put on our safety belts. Karl?'

I put my stupid lame seatbelt on, to shut him up. I know he's about to gimme a lecture for having no pants on and my ink-soaked junk staining the seat of his car but for now, we boost.

# 28

# "Money's how he thanks people."

The *outhouse* I'm staying in at the Konstantinou place has gold walls and flowers and – hang on. Is outhouse even the right word? It's a *house* that's *out*-side... more of a cottage guest house, I guess. Anyway, the wallpaper's got bumpy flower patterns in it. I dunno what you call wallpaper like that. Places I'm used to usually have unpainted walls with holes punched in 'em that leak plaster dust all over the floor. Here, the toilet's got no shit-stains, and there's a little thingy that smells like lemons every time you flush, and the basin's got gold taps and no pubes in the sink-trap. The theme's yellow and gold, everywhere you look. Even the garden, bro. I'd never seen me real legit lily pads till this week. I mean it's part of how they made their fortune with them fuckin' Greek Gardens landscaping franchises you see on the infomercials when you're going to bed at 4am, like the Konstantinou parents don't even have to get dirt under their fingernails these days. They just sell this, like, ribbon with their name on it to small franchise owners. Like if Pizza Hut did your lawns.

Anyway, I think the family business is a bunch of bullshit, but I'm grateful to be here on this posh estate up Three Mile Bush Road, Karanui Estate, the northwest part of Whangaz with mansions hidden behind hedges and stone walls. Kind of place people stick poles waving the Kiwi flag cause they're so grateful the country made them rich.

Me, I'm grateful for the money Barbs can tap, woo whee – although she regularly busts out these weird things like "I don't come from money" and "You have no idea the cutthroat shit my old man did to get us rich."

Whatever. Livin it up in Barbie's dreamhouse, know what I'm sayin? Native birds, native bush.

I think about what's happened over the past coupla weeks as I stroll around the Konstantinous' estate, amongst the avocados and olives. I discover new angles and views everyday, there's just so much shit to look at. This place is even more skuxer than those motels WINZ puts you in. The grass is freshly cut and it bleeds scent into the air. Out in the endless back section there's these things called obelix, like big giant sculpted rocks, I explore those, I explore pathways and steps and tiny bridges over streams, oak trees, silk trees, banana trees, orchards. A goldfish pond full of perfect lily pads, a shed with a fleet of giant ride-on mowers and the shiniest John Deere gardening tools, tiled paths and signs and benches, plus one of those fancy little shacks for proposing to girls in the movies. I think you call it a retarda or rotunda or something.

I walk and I smoke my Marlboros, bought for me by the Konstantinou parents out of gratitude for my heroism. They've been taking care of all my needs since I got to their estate – fancy bottles of Pommy Granite juice, top shelf ciggies, those little steak jerky bars, Nurofen for my crack-withdrawal headaches. My Marlbs don't have any crack in them, these days. Might be the start of a crack-free life for this guy. I guess life's trippy enough without suckin on the synthetic teat.

I walk. I smoke. I look at the clay tennis court out back of the estate. I think about money and wonder if any's comin my way. I get hard-out breakfasts and whatever I want from the Konstantinous' bar, there's a runaround car if I want, a Tesla, and I don't even have to hotwire it and I've got me a new iPhone and a earring with a diamond in it.

Know who gave me those prezzies, bro?

Barbie. My dream girl, come true.

Interestingly, there's no cash in the hand – *yet*. I've been trying to find a time to broach the subject. What is in my hand, though, is something worth more than money, Barbie's fingers. Cause she's here with me, dawg – get it? When I walk around the place, through the glasshouse, over the mini golf course, past the cottages, Barbie'll come up and walk alongside me. She'll grab my hand without realising, like as if deep-down she's dependent on me now. She'll squeeze my hand like a baby squeezes its dad's hand, tip her head onto my shoulder. I dunno if she realises she's doing it or not. She'll stroke my callouses and cold sores and drop little comments about how I can take a beating and how hard I am for a little guy. I knew once you got her off the substance she'd be the best version of herself. Good to see her writing in a journal most days, too. I think she's been inspired by dusting off a box of her old possessions, including her old journals and notebooks and Dinky Diary she used to pour all her private thoughts into when her teenage years were stressing her out.

If my language is sounding a bit flowery, it's cause the Konstantinous've got decorative books everywhere and some of them are teaching me hard-out vocab. There's a hardcover dictionary in the toilet that's gotta weigh two KGs. At first I was doing weights sets with it, then I thought about gluing the pages together and hollowing it out and putting a pipe and some money in it and sending it to myself next time I go to jail but then I was like, "Karl, bruz, you oughta open it and learn some crap." I've been thinking about doing a course possibly, getting my brain fit. Maybe even read that arrogant hardback business advice memoir-book-thingy the Konstantinou dad wrote, *The Konstantinou Gardener.* Learn about small business, I reckon. Get licenced as a bounty hunter, advertise, get some clients, find some fugitives and that's me, set for life, missus by my side – if we get together, that is. Cause Barb doesn't exactly know what I've got planned for her, and if you're fixing to marry someone, I guess it's polite to tell 'em. Manners 'n shit.

I mention my business plan to Barb when we are in the golf cart, speeding down the long driveway to collect the mail. She reckons I'd make a good small business owner but I shouldn't write my advertising myself. Damn good point. That girl's advice is always solid.

I start to need her around all the time. I need Barb at the breakfast island in the main house, I need her at dinner at the huge wooden table. I need her in the car with me. Even when she's taking a stroll by herself across the estate, I need her. I need to joke with her about how wine tastes like the piss you gotta drink out of a gumboot if you wanna join the Mongrel Mob. I need her opinions on what vape flavours to check out. I need Barbs to open a bank account for us so I can start saving for our future. And I need her to interpret the fucked-up phrases her mother uses when she's in the room with us, cause it feels like I'm close to getting pulled into this family. The parents, they're sizing up Ol' Karly Cockroach. La Cucaracha. Seein if I'm really a knight in shining armour or a night with a shiny arsehole. All we can know for certain is I don't have anywhere else in the world to go. No other purpose. I'm here for your daughter, guys. The mental one, to be specific.

In the huge carpeted lounge with the fireplace and Moroccan rug, I watch the evening news with Barbs on the couch, the mum on the right, the dad on the left. I'm not sure how many days pass. My sleep gets all messed up, nightmares about getting chained and torn apart by giant wasps 'n shit. Woken by the maids, I start getting up at lunchtime, which is pretty early for me, and develop these plans about how I'm gonna buy one of them degrees online, like a Masters in Business Ministeration, then open up my own bounty huntin' firm.

I desire and plan and vision and almost taste these things until I need to go back to my guest house and take one last dump with four-ply toilet paper with fancy patterns, or have one last smoke on the deck while I watch peacocks strut, or take a golf cart for one more race, or fry up one more koi carp I've caught from the pond. I think these things until Integrity Inspector Nantakarn crunches slowly up the oak-lined driveway for yet another "one last" conversation. Urgh, Nantakarn is a reminder of being told off. Even her personalised licence plate reads BSTCOP. Just being within a single kilometre of her makes me feel I'm back in that interview room, with her writing a report about me on her iPad and smirking.

Nantakarn is greeted at the door by decrepit wobbly antique-looking Georgios, by shaky old Anna, by a valet who parks Nantakarn's car for her. The parents have had interviews so far with two women's magazines, ten newspapers, a few Zooms with news shows in fuckin Auckland and Sydney and Athens 'n shit. The pigs have had a challenging time working out how to charge the Defiant or the TruBlues. Barbie hasn't made it easy. Basically, Barbs won't put her name to any kind of narking. She won't say she was kidnapped, won't testify she was made to tattoo men for free, won't admit she saw Kenny being chained to two motorcycles and ripped apart like a gingerbread man, won't sign nothing that'll get people into trouble. As we've been lying in bed in our guest house, she's said to me quietly a couple times how she felt enslaved by the needles and pipes, the threats, the bashings, the money, all these carrots and sticks – but Barbie's no snitch and neither am I, so no one's getting prosecuted for Barb-related stuff. That SWAT guy Rohit who got his head pulled off like a Lego minifig? I don't think they can pin that on anyone. The person – probly a hangaround – who got chopped up and chucked in Whangārei Harbour to throw investigators off Barbie's scent? Investigation's ongoing. No justice yet.

The murder of Nomad though, shooting his brains out all across the camera? That shoulda got justice, man. Cause Nomes was like a father to me (a stinky father that beat me up and sweared at me and staunched me out, true.) Yo – the underworld don't care, the public don't care, and deep down, cops don't care. What's the total, three frickin murders at least? That's why I'm stoked me and Barbs got out, man.

The papers and news shows find some angles to cover. Since the three dead men are all ugly, they focus on Barbie (well, old high school photos of Barbie, back when she didn't look like a prozzie.) There's the angle of the parents seeking their daughter, and there's the angle of the little sister fighting to get her big sis back and falling in love with the courageous cop. There's the reality TV documentary series called *The Best* about Nantakarn's goody-good Best Administration team that coordinated it all and never gave up hope they'd get Barbara back. The producers have filmed three episodes, basically a fly on the wall watching Nantakarn organise softball games for at-risk rangatahi at that do-gooder church.

Shana talks, the parents talk and The Best Administration won't stop talking, but Barb still won't talk, even two weeks after things have cooled down. She hangs up on the police prosecutor, deletes Nantakarn's texts and emails and tells reporters to go fuck themselves. She doesn't want her story to belong to anyone but her.

When Barbie sits beside me on a giant leather couch with one warm half of her body touching mine, and folds her tired head into my shoulder, or reaches for my fingers to warmly crush her hand, I know what she's saying. She's saying even though she's spent half her life armoured with piercings and tats and bad boyfriends she doesn't want to be part of these wild arguments anymore, everyone telling everyone off, all prosecutions and trouble and threats and coroners. Barbie wants someone to hold her while she lets scar tissue grow over her wounds. While she heals.

One day when we're in the heated indoor pool playing volleyball as a family, little slimy black-chest-haired Georgios, standing dripping in the water with his hairy brown nipples, tells me he'd like to discuss "career opportunities." The phrase sounds funny to me. Usually, from my experience, 'career opportunities' means doing gay porn. I say Yup immediately but I don't reckon that's what he's getting at.

I wipe water out of my eyes. Georgios is standing in front of me, holding still my can of bourbon as it floats on its kickboard.

'What kinda work?' I go, lookin at him side-on, and then I think – hang on a sec, considerin' I carried his daughter out of the pit of crims and turned full time professional bounty hunter, this guy could be my first client.

'I'd like to interview you, Karlos, in more formal circumstances this afternoon. Does 2.30 work for you?'

'The fuck else would I have on? I spend half the day feeding the chooks.'

'We don't have any chooks…' he goes, slowly.

While he struggles to compute, I go, 'Nah, I mean, 'course 2.30's good. Meet in the bar?'

'I was thinking the conservatory,' he goes, frowning. 'We can have coffee.'

'Irish coffee?'

Dude looks like he's just sucked a lemon. I shut up, meet with him, and say Yep when he offers me a job.

Within a week I'm Greek Gardens' new Franchise Auditor: that's what the big meeting was all about. I'd promised myself I'd take his offer and I went in there and fuckin took it. As for the bounty huntin thing, well. Dreams have to go on hold sometimes.

So yeah, being franchise auditor gets me use of the old man's Mercedes for any trips that are more than two hours by road. Life sounds sweet, the only extra detail being that I'm told if I break the law while on the job, Nantakarn's gonna press charges.

Know what for?

Theft of the Police Association magazine, *Heat on the Beat.* Y'know, the most basic-est ignorantiest crime out of the long list of shit I've done over the past month.

'Didn't Richie drop that frickin' charge?' I go to Nantakarn on the phone.

'Senior Constable McMullan hasn't had a chance to look at your charges. He's been flat-out with standard work since he got back from rescuing Barbara, not to mention pre-enlistment training with his cadets. It takes a lot out of people when they put themselves on the line for you, Karl, you know. Or perhaps you don't know.'

It's comments like this that throb in my head when I'm out on business. I'm not a statue, man. Gangstas cry sometimes.

Mattera fact, I have a bit of a sob with Barb as we're sitting on a giant ride-on lawnmower, in a shed that's even larger than our whole guest house.

'If your olds would just set aside, like, ten seconds to thank me for bringin you back, that'd be nice,' I sigh.

Feels good to be beside her body, feel the intensity of her tats and rings and wild eyes. The good feeling's poisoned with worry, though.

Barbs mashes her cigarette out on the side of a mammoth tractor. 'What's the job he gave you, Franchise Auditor? Whatever B.S. he invented, that's your thanks.' I'm still getting used to her voice. Flat and crusty. Skanky and rough and cigarette-y. A bone-thin woman who always has to have something in her fingers, a smoke or a jay or prayer beads.

'That job's just a paycheque, though. I barely even do anything.'

'Money's how he thanks people. Money's worth more than love, to my old man.'

'Shit, what'd you get on your birthday when you was growin up?'

Damn, I'm thinkin. Maybe this family don't know where to put love.

She pulls a baggie out of her cleavage, opens it up and tries to pack sticky green buds into a copper pipe. She sucks and hisses and gasps.

'Pipe's all dirty,' she goes, 'Usually Kennyboy does the pipework for us.'

'Sorry he's not here,' I go, thinking *There's someone who'd do anything for you sitting right here. I'll clean your pipe with my tongue if you want.*

'Mostly I used to always get money for my birthday,' she continues, lighting up. 'Vouchers, debit cards, credit cards. I'd ask for, you know, like the American Express Zero? That one was just a black card, y'know like zero colour 'cause it's got zero percent interest? Gawd, the holograms on those cards were soooo pretty. Cept a little affection would've been tonnes better, you know? Cause without affection at home, you go and find it, right?'

*Barbie on her back. Barbie on her knees.*

'You go and find affection,' I agree.

I have a toke of excellent vineyard weed and put my veiny arms around her and exhale into her mouth and kiss her crusty lips, including her ring, which has got bits of dried scab on it.

I stroke her hair and my fingers brush her shoulder. 'Sorry I stabbed you with that carving fork in cooking class, Barbara.'

'Don't call me Barbara,' she goes, pulling my belt out from its buckle and reaching down to see if I've got any undies on, 'Doesn't sound right.'

She shows me affection, then. I get off, don't get me wrong, this girl can suck a rugby ball through a garden hose, but it's not the type of affection I want.

I'm not sure if I should've taken Barbs out of the wild. It's like by taking her away from her old drugged-up helium'd floatin-above-the-ground fantasy life we've actually made shit worse for her. And this family, man. Barbie's hair kinda represents what they're all about. Bright colours but underneath, you can't stop the blackness growing through.

# 29

# "Why you keeping me prisoner here?"

I wake up and my buzz is gone. Not just the buzz from my session last night – like, a bigger wider unhappy buzzlessness. I reach for my smokes and they feel heavy in my fingers. I sit up in a posh guest house on a leafy three million dollar estate so big you can't see one end from the other. But I ain't blissed, I ain't fulfilled.

I need Richie. Them Taiwanese twins that doctors separate? One of them usually dies if he's not cajoined to his bruz, right?

I swallow my pride and phone my pet pig. The dude doesn't seem to mind taking my call, but I can tell there's a distance in his voice. A'iit, I know he's been distant-as-fuck this whole adventure, but this is even distant-er.

He's on his way over here already, he reckons.

'Methinks you may be psychic,' he goes.

'The hell does 'methinks' mean? Oi – you still on probation?'

'I am no longer a SCUR, I'm pleased to say. I may actually get another pip. My sergeant's chuffed.'

'So are you coming out here or not?'

'Criminy, Karl, I just said, I'm 37 minutes away. I'm ending this call. Mobile phone calls are one of the top three leading causes of auto crashes.'

'You're positive you're coming out?'

'Yes I'm coming out.'

'Coming out of the closet, ya fuckin arse-rapist. See ya soon.'
When Richie arrives, he doesn't beeline for his bruz. Instead of brotherly love, Richie seems to want to be an old man's son. The way Georgios puts his arm around Richie, I'm glad I've never bothered trying to impress the wrinkly rich old mummy. Snitchie Richie looks up to him, though. The bruz has always thought weak pussy eggheads were, like, role models. Snitch Rich and Old Rich go out on these feminate little errands around the estate, they ride around in the golf cart of the future father-in-law, stopping and hovering and swinging and playing with each other's balls. They drink orange juice that Anna's prepared herself, 'cause she refuses to let maids touch the food. Some days I jog after the golf cart, stopping to shadowbox and kick and punch and practice throat-slitting, trying to be in good ninja condition in case ninja-ing comes up in my job. The smell of herb gardens and manure and compost and pine resin and rose bushes gets to me, though. I'm close to wanting to bail on this place. I don't care how easy life is here. I scream at a pair of magpies, one day, and borrow one of the crossbows from the sports shed and shoot at both the birds till I've wasted like six platinum crossbow bolts and the birds are just up in the trees laughing at me. These things are worth 80 bucks a bolt. I can't take the strain of being Georgios's least-favourite son any more. I'm cracking up.

Barbie's been having these meetings to figure out a new deal with her olds, like as if she's going out on bail and I'm supervising. As for her deal with me, well, I'm not sure where me and Barb are heading. She's promised me she won't put herself on the block for bags of crack any more. I guess that's the equivalent of going steady.

I love her. I've gotta say it. I love her Courtney Love lips. I love how scrawny her torso is. I love digging my fingers into her ribs. I love biting her neck. I love it when she sticks her pipe in her pussy and makes it do little puffs that I suck up and spit back into her mouth.

Don't think she's fully accepted me as her lover in the straight world, nah. More like she lets us fool around when she's blitzed, which is kind of like a softening of her stance.

We haven't actually had, y'know.... Third base... we just get wasted and cuddle pretty intimate – maybe base 2.1, 2.2. Not quite full rooting. Barb went straight into fourth gear in terms of sex after she was 17 – something made her not give a fuck – and she hasn't had any decent guys she can make sensual love with. It's like she's been on this planet running around but she's never learned to crawl.

We meet one day in the conference room. The meeting's a intervention, basically. A whole roundtable of people who think they own her. Time to sort out who gets to decide Barbie's fate. There's the sister who thinks she's setting the best example. There's the parents who try to pay Barb to behave. There's the police who address all comments to her parents and pity Barb like she's a retard without an ego –

And then there's me.

Am I such a knight to her? Does she *want* to be thought of as a damsel in distress? If someone took me away from my partytime friends, God, man… you can't make a fish live on land, can ya.

Lo and behold, the Poo-Lice make themselves an important part of the meeting. Richie rocks up wearing his full-on uniform, boots, belt, shoulder pads, pants pulled up halfway to his nipples – plus a new medal he got for bravery, for the whole rescue shebang, y'know, squirting his cum spray at the angry mob. The medal even has a girly ribbon dangling off it. It dangles and sways when he bends to take off his boots. I can't stop staring at it.

*Bruz: there's another hero in this room, y'know. Wouldn't hurt if you chucked us a bone.*

The Family Group Conference, aka Intervention, warms up with some joke by Georgios. I've never heard him laugh before, and I don't appreciate Richie laughing along with him, the armrests of their big thick leather chairs touching like penises.

Georgios begins the family conference by clearing his throat. 'How's everyone?'

'Everyone's shit,' Barbie goes, perched on an arm of the couch, stroking the leaves of a potted palm tree, crushing her can of Monster Energy, fingering the little bag of gear in her bra, 'Gawd, I need a smoke already. Can we get this shit over with?'

'Don't swear at my parents,' Shana goes, her hand on Richie's thigh.

'They're *my* parents too.'

Richie smells like a car air freshener and he's shaved so recently his throat's pink. Mister Clean 'n Calm gently raises his hands and lowers them. Shush, everybody. Peace. Musta been a technique he learned at the counselling they've made him attend.

'Anna and I would like to announce a donation,' Georgios goes in a soft voice. 'We're privileged to announce our support for The Best Administration Community Trust.'

'Why you gotta give *them* money?' Barbie squawks, 'Don't they get, like, millions from the president?'

'This country doesn't have a president,' Shana goes, clutching her temples. She crosses the room, plops her uppity little bum in beside Richie.

I see you, Shana. And I ain't sure I trust you.

'There was the incident with Mr Sabharwal from the, you know, the Armed Offenders Squad blokes, and that poor fixer who was killed, Darryl, we'd like to make a donation to– '

Fixer? I'm thinking. Darryl? Darryl. *Darryl?!* I've never known Nomad's court name.

'Stop, everyone! Just stop, alright?' Barbie's shrieking. 'What's this got to do with me? Why you keeping me prisoner here?'

'I think it's right, for your family to, *ahem*, help us balance the books,' Richie goes. 'Considering what your escapade cost the country. And you're hardly a prisoner.'

'I'm locked under these dicks' insurance policy. They were deep-down hopin I'd die so they'd get two mil.' She's sniffling now. 'That's all I am to anybody, a fucking dollar sign.'

Two million bucks, G. Sounds sick, when you hear it the first time. I watch the information hit one side of Richie's head and travel through his brain. He keeps a poker face though. Refusin to let a crim ruffle a family of law-abiding peeps.

'Your family cares very much for you, Barbara, and you're free to –'

'Free shit. I'm still stuck a fucking Konstantinou, aren't I. I went to the opposite end of the fucking country and I couldn't get free from this sucky-arse family.'

Anna, the quiet deadly cold mum, continues without looking at her ranting daughter, as if Barbie's howls are just construction noise. 'Would you like to see what we're intending to donate for cadet scholarships to attend the Royal New Zealand Police College? We're rather proud of it, if we don't say so ourselves.'

Barbie is fully roaring now. Venting years of pissed off-ness. 'Would I *like* to see it? Like?! I haven't fucking liked a single thing since I was thirteen.

D'you have any idea how miserable yous make me? The only thing I "like" is this retard Karl here.'

Barbie kicks a lamp off a coffee table. Score, I'm thinkin, She likes me. Points.

She gets up from her seat, opens the ranchslider and hugs me as she shunts us out onto the porch in a stumbling waltz. Guess she never had a reliable man to cling to.

She smears tears from her eyes with the back of her hand. She's tried putting on foundation and mascara today. It's spattered and splashed all over her nose now.

'Everyone's mean to meeee,' she sobs into my ear as I hold her. I peek over her shoulder. Anna and Georgios stare at their laps, shamed. Richie's fiddling with his car keys, eager to get on with work.

Shana's looking at something on her phone, cold.

I cuddle my baby, my soulmate, my fellow fuckup.

Her trembling lips are fat. I lick salt from her cheek. I press her into me. The sunny dye half-drained out of her hair with regrowth.

Dark coming back through.

# 30

# "His own fat arse took him out."

Healing. Repair. Bart Simpson Band-Aids. Everyone forcing themselves to be okay.

We venture out into downtown Whangārei. Summery couples holding hands. Bros wearing their best jandals. Hot chicks in dresses.

We rock up to Lone Star, this pub-restaurant I've thought about going into heaps, but never gone in because I once saw a dude at the door with his shirt tucked in and I thought, Forget that shit. Tuck me into a grave before you tuck my shirt in, bro.

Anyway, we're here for a double date. Meal, drinks, Quiz Nite. Barbs and me plus the couple-I-saw-coming-but-still-shocks-me-and-makes-me-want-to-puke-a-little, Richie and Shana.

Yep, that's where we're at. Total Hallmark sell-outs. Bunch of lame-os falling in love.

Lone Star's got a cactus and bucking bronco and ten gallon hats and horseshoes and cow skulls with tinsel and stocking hanging off them and it does all these foods I've never heard of that Barbs translates for me, explaining she used to root this dude that owned a building company who ate real fancy. Feta's the first thing I haven't heard of. Feta is a cheese people pull out of goats, I'm told. They get the goat to squirt it directly on ya pizza, I guess. Linguine, that's something else I try. Linguine is fancy-arse spaghetti that doesn't even come out of a can. Chablis is another thing. It's some typa wine that Richie and Shana get a bottle of.

To counteract the poncy-ness and keep it real, me and Barbs order Jäger

Bombs: we take a pint of high-strength cider, take a shotglass of Jäger, drop the shot like a depth charger, scull the whole thing back. Our throats catch fire; our ciggies deepen our voices. We light each other's smokes off the heat lamps. We kiss jokingly, celebrating as we waste the other teams in the pub quiz. There's a question about famous criminals and Barbs stands up on her seat and goes, 'Hellll-OOOO-ooo! Ten years field research right here,' which, I realise, would mean she got into crime about age 17, which makes me wonder once again what the heck happened to her.

Richie tugs her back down into her seat. She calls him a pig, hoiks some spit in her mouth and pretends to launch it into Richie's face. I pull her away and pash her, sucking the spit out of her lips. I won't have her spitting in the face of my bruz. I wish they'd get along, but then again, I don't like my bruz's missus that much. That whole thing with Shana driving me up north to the convention and releasing me out the door like a brainless golden retriever? I reckon deep-down that wasn't about getting Barbie back. I reckon it was more about getting me off, hoping I'd get murked, so no one would ever find out what I knew. And not getting me off in a good way, neither.

We try to have a good night at Lone Star anyway, completing the maze and the Word Find on the place mat with a little pencil, joking about quiz questions, sipping beers near a toasty heat lamp – that is until Barbs fucks it all up. I've taken a chip from her bowl of fries and she pushes them at me, says 'Here's all the chips in the world, ya fat fuck. Take everything. That's what it's all about, oi, take my food, my money, my car, use me up like all the other users.' She tugs down her skirt, and Richie spreads his arms to try stop other people in the pub from seeing her wave her private parts around. 'Take this rich ass and tell your fucking snitch cop friends.'

'I only wanted a chip,' I go, and laugh nervously. She shakes her head like, "I'm done with this shit," lights a smoke, and Richie turns away, cause you haven't been allowed to smoke in pubs for ten years. Then – classic temper-mental Barbie – she changes her tune, goes 'I was only joking, c'mon, gimme a kiss.'

I'ma take her to a shrink, I swear to God – after the good times are over.

Problem is, with Barbie Konstantinou, the good times are like pulling toilet paper. They just keep comin and comin till you find yourself buried under poo tickets with no way out.

About five drinks in, 'Achy Breaky Heart' starts up on the speakers and line dancing breaks out, these old couples wearing blue jeans moving onto the wooden dance floor.

'You promised you'd tell us what the hell "Limp Biscuit" is, by the way' Shana says, fighting to be heard over the line dancing guitars, 'C'moooooon. You've been holding out on me for aaaages. Richie said you two used to play it, right?'

My vision's swimming, we've used up all our placemat activities and the night's in fourth gear.

Truths are about to pour out of us, now that we're drunk (and obviously me and Barbs had a little smoke in the toilets). The other Shana in front of me, the Shana that's not across the table, the Shana I saw plain as day on Zoom conspiring to play both sides. I don't fixate on Shana keeping her sister disappeared to loosen cash from her parents. I don't ask Shana where she's stashed her part of the cash that got paid to Pork. I just let myself have a good time with the nice face of the two-faced–

'Limp biscuit!' she screeches. 'That's what you wrote, don't you remember, on Richie's rugby shirt? You had that white fabric pen and you wrote *limp biscuit* and it was like soooooo funny but I totally don't get it!'

'I was partial to the band's, um, music,' Richie grunts, knowing he's about to get humiliated.

'Fuck off you were, that band was horrible,' I go. 'Fess up, bruz: you ate the biscuit.'

'I never ate the biscuit.'

'Biscuit what?' Barbs says around her cigarette.

'Listen up,' I go. 'When you get old enough to cum, right, you gotta prove it by cumming in fronta other people, eh. We'd have these sleepovers when we were, what, 13? 15? Anyway, what ya do is ya get a groupa dudes, and you sit in a circle, 'cept you're all facing away from each other 'cause it's gay if a groupa dudes are starin at each other jerkin off. Anyway, there's just one biscuit –a Gingernut, if possible, 'cause Gingernuts can handle some serious abuse, they're like manhole covers, eh– anyway each dude masties on the Gingernut, right? And by the time it gets to the final cummer, the biscuit's softened up. Now, if ya can't cum on the biscuit, guess what?'

Richie is drumming on the table with his fingers. Barbs is guffawing into her hands. Shana's hands are flat on the table. She's transfixed. For now, while she's an appreciative audience, I'll forget she's dangerous.

'What?' she goes. 'Do you guys, like, beat him up?'

'Nah, if you're the last one to cum on the biscuit, *you've gotta eat it.*'

They crack the hell up and even clap a little and I tilt the bottom of my glass and drink the applause and celebration. It ain't often people react happily to shit that comes out of my mouth. I should give my stand-up comedy another crack, I think, bathing in the celebrity glow. I should stop feeling sorry for myself all the time.

Except Shana the Lawyer wants facts. 'So there's a whole circle of you little miscreants doing this?'

'Well, when I say circle, if it's just three dudes, it's a triangle, innit.'

'And if it was just you and Richie?'

'Let's just say Richie ate so many bikkies, the dude got diabetes.'

Shana and Barbs's eyes crease up and they thump the table, laughing so hard they beg for forgiveness.

I chomp chips and buffalo wings and jalapeño bites, I light illegal smokes and suck them discretely under the table, I chink beers with my crew and I look up every hour at the TV and see someone kick a few points in some pre-Christmas All Blacks test and scream my head off, "Go go go!" and I don't know who I'm rootin for, and I forget the hurt and the problems and the unsteady road ahead.

Barbs, tonight, is filling out in front of my eyes. I figure the less skinny she gets, the less druggy and hopefully the more happy, though it's hard to tell. The girl's bipolar and she swings from emotional branch to emotional branch, if ya ask me. Her wrinkles and glare-lines are filling in, and her chest is getting particularly noticeable – I mean, the other day she fully lost her baggie of weed down her cleavage. Couldn't find it all. The fat from all the sipping milkshakes in bed and scoffing Twix bars and bingeing Netflix has been making her face warm and bringing her eyes forward so she doesn't look like a cruel skeleton no more. Warmer, you could say. More loving, more loveable.

It's all amazing. It's all half-real. Just a couple of days to go til Christmas and this is like a present from Santa. This strange new drunken dimension I wade through gives me love, it gives me pride, but it's a confusing dimension too. I mean, here I am heading towards the toilet for a piss twenty seconds after Shana and I notice her slipping a quick bro-shake to some tough guys she bumps into on their way out of the gaming lounge. Dodgy cunts, they look like, with gold chains round their necks and evil letters on their long-sleeved tees. Weird that she would still need to be friendly with bad boys, if she's dating a cop.

Why doesn't Richie see the same picture? I wanna pull the dude aside and tell him, Bruz – there's something dodgy going on with your girl. Like she's playing two sides.

I try to forget it and stagger back to my booth.

'Tell ya one thing,' Barbs is goin, waving her beer handle. 'Wish I could get my hands on a yearbook.'

'I know, right?' Shana's goin, sittin her ass back down, giving Richie a peck on the cheek, the poor cunt unaware she saves her best kisses for underworld gangsters, apparently. 'You can buy anything. I mean, you can buy a Porsche if you want, but you can't buy being 17 back.'

'Bet you could buy a Porsche with your recent income, couldn't ya Shana,' I go, and before she can go 'What's that supposed to mean?' I'm up standing on my seat. I may've gone down on a girl with six figures in her trust fund, but I'm still a commoner, bro. I haul up my backpack, unzip it, I reach inside it, I pull the yearbook out, still sealed perfectly in its Glad Bag. I've carried the yearbook around for ages. Been waiting for a nice moment to share it with decent peeps. This is as close as we'll get. I don't entirely trust three of the people at the table.

Shana is trying to scream something at me, but she's drowned out by Barbs's screams. 'Gimmegimmegimme!' Barbs's going, and she's throwing pages around, settling on a Year 11 photo of her getting her Princess of the Prom trophy and flashing these big, perfect teeth.

Today, those prom-princess teeth are yellow and there's a couple missing, but Barbs has travelled back in time to her happy place.

'Sis, sis, omigawd, it's you and Richie, omigawd, Shana, look!'

True enough, in the yearbook photos, Shana's awkwardly reaching out and planting a certificate in Richie's hands recognising the amount of money he raised for old fogies by selling firewood in little bags.

Now Richie's staring at Shana in a funny way.

'You were a total paedo!' I yell across the table. Richie rolls his eyes, slugs back a little bit of cider, burps politely into his hand and scatters the burp under the table. Probly only the second or third time Reverend Richie's ever tasted booze. 'Look, in the photo, I can feel the sexual bloody tension. She was 13, bruz. 13. You should arrest yourself.'

Richie speaks for the first time in an hour, doing his twenty-five percent of melting-the-tension. 'I was a teenage diiiiirtbag, baby.'

'Come to my creepy van, don't say maybe.'

Barbs giggles and slaps my shoulder. I wink at her, and our voices all link and chant in perfect unison.

'Oh yeeeah, dirtbaaaag, no, she doesn't know what she's missing, oh yeeeeah, dirtbaaag.'

Barbs, 'I've got two tickets to Iron Maiden, Karly.'

Shana, 'Come with me Friday, Richie is gnarly.'

Richie, 'I think I'm a bounty hunter, Karl, like you.'

Me, 'OooooOOOOOOOOh yeah! Dirtbaaaag! Barbie does-n't know what she's missing.'

'I do know, honey,' Barbs goes, ending the song, snuffling in my ear, resting her lips on my shoulder, letting her excited face collapse in a pile of relaxing wrinkles. 'I know what I was missing, now. Being with you is buzzy as fuck.'

I do the translation in my head. What she's said is Druginese-language for "I love you."

She wraps her arms around me, puts her hands in the pockets of my Monster Energy hoodie, squeezes me. And that's our whole night spent having belly laughs - until the end, that is.

The bar manager's seen Richie on TV, knows that at least one of us is a hero, so he doesn't push us out at closing time, but the couples line dancing finish up and the cleaner starts mopping and the restaurant goes steadily quiet and dim until it's 1.15am and the last glassie who could've removed the beer glasses, cocktail glasses, wine glasses, shot glasses and bourbon glasses, the lemons, the ashtrays, the olives, the little sticks, the tiny umbrellas, the melting ice cubes – that person went home an hour ago.

There's a couple boys with bikes outside sharing one heat lamp that's almost burned out but I'm energised by loving Barbs. I don't have time to get into beefs with bikers any more.

Dawdling near the door before we wrap up the night, we see the TV's still on. Somethin kinda mind-blowing on the screen.

Reporter, outside a compound with big fuck-off numbers and letters and a ten-foot-high detail painted on the fence reading 1%.

It's the Defiant pad. Reporter's up north. Something big's breaking.

There's footage of all these mopey, weary looking bikers, like deflated balloons, and there's an ambo, and something with a sheet being wheeled into the ambo, looks like that huge turkey that got stuck on Mr Bean's head in that Christmas special, a hump, a mountain of stomach under the sheet.

I'd recognise that massive-arse bowling ball-belly anywhere.

'Oi, you guys,' I go, 'I think something happened to Pork.'

I tell the bartender to crank it.

We all turn and stare at the screen.

'....taken to Whangarei Hospital in a critical condition,' the reporter is going. 'While Hato Hone St John haven't commented officially on the cause of Mr Hamm's collapse, sources I've spoken to say they understand that Mr Hamm suffered from obesity-related haemorrhoids which may have released a blood clot, triggering a stroke. Sources have also told me Mr Hamm may have been sitting on the toilet as long as six hours before the door was broken down and emergency services were called, by which stage irreversible brain damage is thought to have occurred. We'll keep you updated on this story as it develops.'

I've seen a lot of crazy shit in my time, but this has got me gripping the bar, blinking.

Taken out by a bumhole-balloon? God damn. Life is crazy.

Richie's looking like he's just been slapped, Barbie's sorta sniggering, and Shana's got her head lowered, giving me this intense look like 'I know that you know that I know that you gotta keep that mouth of yours shut.'

The TV carries on chattering. Nobody's speaking.

'So his own fat arse took him out,' I finally go.

'He's not been pronounced dead yet,' Richie goes, reading his phone. One of those private police comms groups where they all gossip. 'But by the sounds of it... .'

He doesn't finish his sentence.

'So, what, that's the end of the club?'

'Wouldn't count on it,' Richie goes. 'They'll name a new president. Nature abhors a vacuum.'

'Yeah, I know, hoovering sucks,' I go, 'Cleaning out that fat fuck's bedroom would be dirty-as.'

'He means a power vacuum,' Shana says, stroking this stuffed bison with a leather saddle, 'There'll be others to fill the void.'

Fill the roid more like, I wanna say, but that's a little insensitive. We're trying have a good night. And what does the bible say? You ain't supposed to speak ill of people dead from exploding anuses. Well, almost dead. Still some life in the fat fuck, it sounds like.

Shana hops up on the bison.

'Anyway, still can't believe you kept the yearbook,' Richie goes. He's asked for a cigarette, but he's just drunkenly studying it, rolling it in his fingers. It's the dodgiest drug he'll ever touch, and touching it is all he'll do. Cunt leads a charmed life.

'I can't believe yous *didn't* keep your yearbooks,' I tell my group. 'I'll admit, right, I'm not that accomplished compared to most folks, but fuck it, growing up's not for everyone. World needs one or two peeps to stay behind and, like, safeguard our childhood shit. Protect the memories.'

Barbs licks my ear. 'Cheers, Karl.'

'You're not, er, completely unappreciated,' Richie goes, zipping up his jacket. 'The ladies sure are grateful.' Wow. Cheers Rich. Biggest-ever compliment. Then he goes, 'I concede I was actually wrong about–'

A tiger emerges from the darkness. It's a medium-height tiger, with a shaved head and tails and the dark eyes and hungry pinched mouth of a rat. Its neck is covered in numbers and letters.

This skinny yellow-black tiger raises one arm, stares at us with tiny rat eyes, squinting in front of the heat lamp.

Amazing, the details you notice before you die.

'*GUN*,' someone yells

He aims his trigger finger at Barbie and squeezes.

# 31

# "Take a good, hard look at your missus."

Richie's driving like his dick's on fire, changing lanes for no reason, putting classical horn music on the stereo, so calm it's scary. He adjusts the air conditioning about ten times. Whangarei pours past, a black torrent with lights floating in it. We can't wait to get to bed. None of us wanna be in a car together after what's just happened. Bubble's burst. The night's become broken as a dropped pie.

Shana's riding the passenger seat, her head placed in the palm of her hand. Me and Barbie are in the back. It's a reminder. The back is where you put troublemakers.

The Defiant yellowboy, the eager-to-please prospect with cheekbones and stubble and jagged teeth, the rat with the scarred scalp shaved down to the skull, he extended his hand, and we froze, and he jerked his thumb upward, and we all *saw* a gun – but there was nothing in his hand. This guy didn't wanna get arrested. He wanted Richie to *want* to arrest him. He wanted Richie to do what Richie did, to react, to attack, to lose control. He wanted to step to the side and dodge Richie's tackle and see Richie scrape his nose in a pothole. He wanted to've waited all night to do what the two Defiants in the corner of the pub had summoned him to do – to spook us to the bone. Let us know the Club can get revenge on us any time they like.

What happened was we'd been laughing and eating fries and slamming Jäger bombs, and they'd been studying us, waiting to make us piss our happiness down the legs of our jeans. The black and yellow rat-faced little skinhead aimed what turned out not to be a gun at us to embarrass us – a flip-top cellphone clutched in his little rat-paw, filming us – then jumped on the back of his mate's dirt bike, wrapped his arms around the driver and bounced over the speed humps and away.

Doin the Defiants' dirty work. Filling the roid-void. Keeping Northland shit-scared.

We pass a truck stop with a 24-hour laundromat attached to it, the lit-up signs humming in the night. Alongside us, a few steps into the blackness, is a strip of mangroves and whispering water.  Richie's silent but he stinks of rage.

To break the tension, I go, 'So that guy before. Friend of yours I take it, Shana?'

'Meaning?' Shana goes, and stares into the rearview mirror. 'Karl. What exactly is that little quip implying?'

I stare back into the rear-view. 'Dirty crook sticks out their hand, maybe a dirty crook should shake back, that's all.'

The woman gets angrier than a shooken-up bag of wasps. 'Who's a crook, exactly?'

Richie glares back at me. 'Explain yourself, Karl, or I'll pull this car over and leave you here.'

'Shayn, c'mon. That little stunt before. Guy's a friend of yours, right? I'da thought you'd be suckin the man's cock, considerin you been helping out the club.'

Richie throws me out of the car in the Richie-est way possible: he flicks on his indicator, slows the car and only unbuckles his belt after he's stopped… *then* he tells me to get the fuck out. Not that he even swears.

The estuary's a mudflat pocked with rubber tyres, beer bottles and plastic bags, shopping trolleys rusting in the mangroves. Unless we swim the filthy Hatea River it'll be at least a forty minute walk to where the houses begin, and there'll be no taxis, no buses, not at 2am in Whangārei. I've gotta hitchhike home till the sun comes up, not that I have a home.

I hesitate, one foot out of the car, on the road. Most of my butt inside, on the seat. Barbie's positioned the same. Her face is screwed up, confused. To her, I'm just some dick who doesn't appreciate the Establishment. She doesn't know how much I know.

'You were warned,' Richie tells me from the car. 'Any final words?'

'Here's ya final words, bruz. Take a good, hard look at your missus. See how many shoes selling out her sister buys.'

'You will apologise. This is your last chance, then you and I are through, Karl.'

*I can't tell you, Rich. It would break you, man, seriously.* 'We've had a few too many drinks, man, look, something shitty's happened, people are upset, can't we jus–'

A cattle truck hoons past. Poo-gas soaks me. I feel droplets in my mouth.

The moment is over.

'Go.'

The car moves when I'm only halfway out. I back away, against the protective railing. Richie drives ten metres, stops, and Barbs gets out, getting her handbag drunkenly caught on the door. There's shouting coming from inside the car. Thank fuck she's siding with me.

We're together, alone, confronting the night. Discarded like dirty clothes dumped outside the Hospice Shop. She drapes an arm on me, pulls me close. I unzip my hoodie, wrap the flaps around her. She leans deeply into me and kisses my neck a couple times. We're freezing together, vulnerable. All the party gone out of her.

We could be minced by the next passing truck if we don't go down into the culvert and trudge through the plastic bags and stagnant mangrove mud.

'I could kill them bikies, every single one of them, y'know, if I put my mind to it.'

'I know you could, baby.'

We trudge through roadside trash and road cones, kicking away bits of torn tyres and McDonald's bags and dead possums.

I keep thinking we'll find Richie waiting for us behind each next curve of the road, but every time we reach our targets, Richie's car ain't there. He's chosen who he wants to be with.

Finally, as the hills start turning purple, we near civilisation. Buses will probly start at 7am – that is, if Barbs wants to bus back out into the countryside and walk a few miles to her family's estate. Something tells me she'd rather sit with me in the mangroves and cook some crystals in a little glass barbecue.

The first bus of the day pulls in and I stick my arm out and yell at the driver to Wait, bro, wait.

I fish in my pocket for some money for the bus driver and come up empty. The bus hisses as it closes its doors then steams away. No dinero for even a rattly Northland bus. I guess rock bottom has a rock bottom, yo.

'This thing before, you havin' a crack at my sister,' she goes, 'What do I need to know?'

We sit on the steel roadside barrier and I take a deep breath and tell her all the suspicious shit I've seen Shana doing. The closeness with Pork, Shana's wide-on for Defiant patchmembers, handling the money and skimming some for herself, dumping me at Bay Blue Tattoo to get murked. By the end, Barbie's face looks like it's been battered by a hurricane. She's sniffing and sucking hard on the pipe.

Finally she claps, gets up. 'A'ight,' she goes. 'Just the latest shitty chapter in the shitty book of my life.'

'Your life's all good, innit?' I go. 'Haven't you, y'know, found true love 'n shit… ?'

She gives a slow, suspect nod, like the kind of nod you'd do to a little four year old who's just said something dumbarse.

Another bus rocks up. She steps in front of the bus stairs and pulls her top down. Trades a slip of the nips for two bus tix.

I decide I won't repeat the Shana thing, and over the next days, weeks, months, Barbie won't mention it. We'll never talk about it again – except there's something massive that comes up. It's like we've been doing a hundred miles an hour with a big stain on the windscreen and it's finally time to pull over and wipe clean.

It all comes out when we limp into the guest house at 9.30 and straight away start scrapping. It's one of them arguments that only happens when you're over-tired.

'Pretty fuckin good night out, eh Karl?' she goes, rummaging in her drawers, starting up again. 'Where the fuck's my Zippo?' She's throwing shit at me as she searches. 'Get me my Zippo. Here. Make yourself useful, Karl. Here's a scented candle, dick. Here's a vase, arsehole. This here? This here's my journal.' She's holding the Dinky Diary, a happy little book of kiddy stationery from the end of the 90s that used to come with stickers, a special pen, a rubber, plus a little secret pop-out drawer to put your deepest darkest secrets in.

Dozing on my feet, knackered, beginning to dream, I'm flashing back to the good old days when it was all erasers and Duraseal and I'd write essays about my favourite book, *The Magic Schoolbus*, when the diary hits me in the skull.

'Read it.'

'Nah, c'mon, we been up all night, babe, we're over-tired.' I'm touching my owie where the corner of the Dinky Diary's hit me. Dent feels deep enough to drink a bourbon shot out of. 'It'll just give you something else to hate me abouuuu.... Aw. You're serious.' I've pawed through the dense girly script and koala stickers and hand-drawn smiley faces for just three, maybe four seconds, and when I look up, Barb's lip is wobbling like it's flapping in the wind. She's about to bawl her eyes out.

She wants me to understand what she's recorded. There's something massive in this diary, things she can't make her mouth say, in these pages that look like she wrote 'em twelve or thirteen years ago.

'You want me to read this thing.'

Her head flops forward once. Half a nod.

'And, what, it's like your big confession or something? It'll tell me why you're so schizo?'

She sits on the edge of the bed, pushes her face through her hands, fondling a cigarette.

I get it. I get it. This is that thing they told me about in the men's help group at ManAlive that time. Sometimes women want you to do something for 'em but they won't say it. You need to listen better for what they're tryina express. And also give head occasionally.

I suck hard on my vape. Rummage up the guts to read this thing.

The answer to the riddle of why Barbie got so bent. Here we go.


November 29

Have u ever been 2 a actual legit biker club?

I was like 'OMG' at first. Like literally excited. Then afterwards...

After, things were different. Everything in my life changed after a night at the boys' clubhouse.

So it was cold outside and the lawn was steaming and I had 2 take my little sissy Shanapants and I was like 'This totally sucks' or like I thought it was gonna semi-suck. She's like epic cringe, with her manly undercut and how she's always totally organised and tries to be profesh and always taking photos for the school paper. She's way too ~~conscious~~ ~~consciene~~ conscientious too, she worries about making sure our olds have enough money which is like who the hell cares??? But yeah last week at the mall she struck up a convo with this random old man in a suit to see if by any slim remote chance he was planning to get some major landscaping done and would he consider Greek Gardens as his supplier?

Jeez it was cringe, it was like Pleeeeease, sister. Your family is not something to buy, sell and trade. And she's so gross to look at! Except, like, no pimples, cause the Pimple Gods obviously decided her skin's too dry and boring. But can you imagine being my age (17.4) and having a 16-year-old following you around? 'Canterbury Plains' the kids call her at school, cause of her flat boy-body which is like lulz. Or @ least the kids who aren't in Yearbook Committee call her that.

> ANYWAYZ <

As we prepared to sneak out to this badass biker party that this bad boy from school invited me to, Shana followed like a little lost toddler, calling my name.

'Baaaarb?'

'Shut up. They'll hear us.'

We arrived at the foot of the driveway where the last of our house's safe light was overtaken by black. While we stood in the crisp night air, rubbing our arms, steaming and shivering, Shana's mind and mouth started leaking worry.

'What if there's people at this party that want to re-do their landscaping? Should I grab a couple prospecti?'

Plural of prospectus >>> Suuuuuch a nerd.

'Shay. Tonight's not a friggin transaction. Let's just, y'know. Blow off all of Baba's depresso work stuff. Party. Just chill.'

Two yellow car-eyes appeared in the night, came close like the cat-bus on Totoro, washed us in light, and disappeared past. I checked my phone to see if there was an update from Mr Bad Boy who'd told us we'd have an epic time at this biker party.

We stood out front for like fifteen minutes in the black fog, rubbing our shoulders. The excitey pre-party buzz was wearing off like one percent per minute.

'What about some of Dad's business cards? He'll hate me if I miss an opportunity.'

'Hell's the matter with you?' I hissed at Shana, 'We're kids. We're partying. Stop stressing. If our pares can't make enough money, that's their problem.'

Baba'd been needing ten grand to buy out our competitor, Northlandscapes. Well, like, I mean when I say "our" competitor, it's not all of us, not me in the slightest lil bit, like I couldn't give a sh*t who's competing with Greek Gardens but my Baba had been quietly steaming, particularly tonight which was half the reason we needed to get out and get our party on. Apart from phone calls to legit banks and dodgy underworld Greek loan sharks down in Auckland- one of which had him muttering 'Sas parakaló, chreiázomai pragmatiká aftá ta chrímata' in desperate, wobbling Greek –(chrímata meant money, I knew that much)- he'd been ultra-silent, like a deep sea squid, drowning in icky stress. Crushed under debt, I guess. It wasn't a secret. Tonight he'd paced the kitchen in our little house with a phone pressed inside his ear, constantly trying to tuck his sky-blue work shirt back inside his pants, as if these people on the phone could even see my hunched, wiry Greek dad with the muscular shoulders and soil-blackened 'crusty fingers' taking these calls from lenders each telling him bad news about trying to get enough of a loan to scale his business, I think 'scale' is the word for it – like grow just enough that instead of twenty landscaping businesses in Northland with ten staff each, there's just one major playa with 200 people. Shana had been filling me in on all this junk from her bottom bunk as we went to sleep each night. Of course we shared a room. My family's house was halfway up a hill, right on the edge of Raumanga, the hood, the ghetto, looking down over Whangārei's stinky swamps decorated with car wrecks. We knew from going to birthday parties at fancy kids' houses that our Mamá and Baba were – I hope I've got this word right – preservative? Conservative maybe? They loved hard work; hated feelings. Hated telling me and Shay anything other than 'An A is not an A-plus.'

Urgh. Vom.

Anyway, Baba's business target of being the playa with enough revenue for 200 staff? He was starting with only six workers. It would've been twelve, but Shana had told me he'd put through a, what d'you call it, tender to work on the Whangārei City Council's berms in its new estate at Marsden Marina and even though Shana formatted the tender on her computer as like an after-school project, Baba had f***ed up. Like, failed to score the work. And the old boys who worked for him, some real veterans who needed $90,000K a year to do professional-enough jobs to charge a decent amount for, he was screwed if he carried on paying their salaries and screwed if he laid their butts off, cause he didn't have enough put aside to pay their redundancy. So my dad needed dough to grow _(ツ)_/

All this grownup cringe drama drilled into me from Shana's top bunk every night for the past ten months, whispering at me through the darkness an hour after Mamá had told us lights out… Shana wasting brain power figurin how Mamá and Baba could get rich, half-desperate to hold the family's rep, half-hoping some of the money might trickle down to her, probably. Me? I didn't give a sh*t. Didn't, don't, will not do. Having a good time with my bitches at school, that's what I care about. When I graduate at the end of the year I'll work shifts in that kumara factory out at Dargaz then jet to the UK and work in pubs and get famous and never come back.

This thing with Baba glued to his phone trying to get that loan, Shana had been updating me on the numbers, not that I wanted to hear them. Apparently Baba just needed a few extra thou to make it look like business was steady this month. He'd tapped out every source in the world and just couldn't come up with a way to make it look like Greek Gardens was growing instead of losing money, speshly when winter was raining all Baba's work off. Just before we'd gone to the end of the driveway, we'd heard Baba saying something along the lines of "Ees not much more, just one few extra shares," in his second-hand English. He was hoping to become the exclusive Readylawn supplier so there'd be no competition and so Greek Gardens could increase its rate of successful tenders and scale up instead of getting swallowed by Northlandscapes.

Least that's what Mum said when she pulled me and my sister into a corner just before we snuck out on the driveway, speaking low enough that Baba and his lenders wouldn't hear. If Baba couldn't find five or ten thou this month, he would have to declare bankruptcy – which meant we'd have to apply for government housing. Like, as in we go and live in Otangarei. The projects. The ghetto. The hood. And I'm not trash. I don't do hood.

Mum actually had the paperwork in her hands as she told us this. I could see her handwriting on the application, see print-outs of Baba's sad bank accounts, see photocopies of my birth certificate. The livin-in-the-hood threat had really spooked my lil sis. Her eyes ate up the whole thing. She tried to bust out her piggy bank and offer all these five dollar notes and coins and shit and it was like Puh-leeeease, bitch, looking round the kitchen at the flyspots on the ceiling, just picturing the future, not giving a fuck. I woulda preferred my family to have zero dollars, tell you the truth. The best kids at my school all have zero bucks in their family. Coz money f*cks families up.

Try telling that to my sister, though. Seems like she'll do anything for money some days. Like as if all she cares about is looking successful to the outside world.

Shayneypants, I thought to myself, there's nothing you can do for Mamá and Baba. If he wants to stay up all night on the phone begging for a loan to inflate his income, let him do it. If we have to be the second-bestest landscapers, the third, even the worst in Northland, who gives a crap?

But my dad, yo. Money was like the Number #1 source of embarrassment for him. Cause he comes from Thessaloniki. They're all hu$tla$ there and in Greek culture it's like mega-shameful if u take on a loan and can't repay.

Last year my dad borrowed this loan to pay this boy with a dangerous goods handling licence so they could stockpile diesel when it came in cheap and save hundreds of bucks each month. Then he borrowed another two hundred Gs for a hard-out tractor with a lawn roller so he wouldn't get screwed on lease costs each month. There'd been loans to pay for marketing in a big way too, like my dad paid for these ten-second adverts on the radio, then also there was print flyers that I had to help shove in people's mailboxes out in the rich new estates around One Tree Point and Marsden Marina where they're building mini-mansions, walking in a sad pack of three women while Baba drove alongside at five kays an hour, tossing bundles of flyers out the passenger window. Baba had borrowed to pay for bark spreaders and barrows, for asphalt and topsoil bulk buys, even just to get the office expanded and signage put up cost him over $120,000, I heard him telling mum in the kitchen one night. All legit loans, all from banks, and at the end of the day it only got him a tiny bit ahead of the competition and left him with tonnes of debt :O(

What it all came down to was my old man needed just five more grand in his account to show enough revenue to qualify for the One Loan To Pay Off The Other Loans.

YAAAAVVN, though. Honestly, for me? I would've been tonnes happier if Baba had just chilled the hell out. I brought my brain back to the present. Chilly, looking hot A.F. in our miniskirts, sharing a smoke, waiting for our ride. Nuff Home/Baba/Stress/Pretending-to-be-successful shit for tonight. I had a cute boy texting me that wanted me to party with him. He was like three months older. One of the naughty kids that starts with a K. I don't want to write his name, it's not important, but sometime over the past three years, he'd gone from breaking into cars to fencing car parts to becoming a hangaround for like THE staunchest biker gang in like all of Northland.

The DMC. Legitimately scary peeps... except, you know what?

Your dad going bankrupt? That's scarier, to me.

That's why we needed to party. Get our minds off.

Strap in with Barbs. Let me take you there. Tell you how everything got fl*#ed up.

We tiptoe down the wet driveway, gravel ripping up our toes. We've taken our shoes off cause we don't want them dusty or scratched or like bust an ankle when we get to this party.

The night is a dewy black frozen desert, reaching into space. The air is made of thrilling guilt. Every time my hip bumps my phone, a little helium balloon of excitement rises up into my tummy. I shiver and pinch my thighs together. Here's another pair of headlights, burrowing through the black. Could be our destiny. The lights slow and there he is, with his rumbly Ford Falcon. We pile into the rear seats, big, empty, open. There's a whole world in this car. The Ford lurches forward before we've even got our seatbelts strapped. The only light inside the car is the stereo on the dashboard. Me, I'm giggling, flirty, nervous, buzzy. Shana has her mind on other things, though, and when I go to high-five her, she leaves me hanging.

C'mon, li'l sis, I think. Quit worrying about tryina be perfect for three frickin hours.

None of us say much on the drive. After like an hour of Highway One, then some bends, and leaving behind the last gas stations and lights and juddering over ten railway crossings, we arrive – God, not sure where – somewhere up north and dip the car into an epic disappearing driveway that's shaking, bouncing. The heavy metal growl, the speakers, the bass, the screaming, you can hear it from half a kay away, bossing the night. Every thud of the heavy metal makes pieces shiver off this big pile of woodchips. There are rusted old machinery husks with chains between them, and big old-fashioned saws with jagged iron teeth. Pretty obvious this place used to be a sawmill. Fairy lights link a chain of beer kegs. The path curves past two stray guys wearing jackets with PROSPECT rockers on, one palm each pressed against a metal shed, having a convo while they piss, then the road ends at this tent and you see a motorcycle here, a motorcycle there, then suddenly there's a row of like twenty, all perfectly lined up, with black helmets with neat yellow numbers on every black bike seat. The bikers have got a tent canopy covering the party, strung from - what do you call those gross ugly skeletony steel beam things? Girders.

Grotty, dusty , ugly, rusty, gross - so how come I feel wired to be here?

Coz I'm getting away from my dad's dramas, that's how come.

I check the time on my phone. We've only been away from home for 49 minutes. I promise myself later on I'm gonna creep into Baba's room and give him a night-time hug and tell him to not stress about the money. Whisper into his dreams that everything's gonna be okay.

First, I've got to be able to say I survived a biker party, though. We cradle our drinks, sip and observe. Boys everywhere giving us the side-eye, plus a few girls wearing tank tops. Ladies with fake hair, too much cleave, grumpy mouths, ladies that look like they got bought for a buck at a second hand shop, eck. Shoot me if I ever end up looking that skanky.

Speedway flags, Bathurst posters. A Nazi sign on a yellow flag. Jackets and hoods and t-shirts nailed to one plywood wall. Colours and logos from the rival clubs. They take each other's patches, these guys. It's serious stuff to them. Plus a police hat and jacket too. The hat's got tyre treadmarks on it and the police jacket's got a dark splotch. I don't think it's tomato sauce.

Me and Shana edge along the walls, trying not to bump people's beer cans and bottles. We skulk in the shadows. Gossip in the corners. We go to the toilet five times in the first hour. Sometimes our eyes accidentally lock onto the black sunglasses of a Defiant boy and we giggle and look away. These bikers are old men, firstly - well, I mean, the full-patch guys are. They have silver in their moustaches and beards, white hairs sprouting out of their ears, old-fashioned jeans and shorts and boots.Their tattoos are blobs of colour, swimming around their necks, long-ago melted. The only thing my driver boy says to us before he skulks away, actually, are the words 'Pork right there, that's the prez.' We look down his finger. At the end of the fingertip is a shouty fat guy having some jokey argument with two way-taller guys who look like they oughta play basketball. Mister Pork President looks like he's wearing a fat suit, round like a big bowling ball with a littler bowling ball balanced on top, plus a whole loaf of luncheon meat under his chin, and he has medals swinging on his chest like he wants to be a general. Me and Shayn are about to sneak to one of the kegs to fill our plastic cups, trotting lightly enough on our feet that we won't get noticed, when the music dries up and twelve faces are staring hard at us and big fat

President Pork's finger is jabbing directly toward me.

'Yous two,' his voice goes, huge and gruff and deep and bossy. Big pink lips like sausages spattering on his fat chin as he talks. A hundred times manlier than my little bunched-up father, freaking out over spreadsheets and loan terms.

I'm counting the minutes til we've had enough adventure to go home and tell peeps on Snapchat all about it. It's just a bunch of old granddads and little prospects standing in a tent sipping cigarettes and Jack Daniel's while they try to hear each other over Slayer songs screaming out of a stack of amplifiers. Now that the music's been paused, there's not even the heavy metal to thrill us, just a cold fear creeping up my skirt like standing in front of the fridge.

'We should head home,' I tell my sister - except when I bend my neck to pass on the comment, she isn't there. Shana is across the room chatting - whuh - *debating* - Oh my God, she can't be seriously - like, negotiating with the nearest biker to President Pork. I cough, spitting half of my drink on the concrete floor. Is my sissie... asking for smokes? Asking for some Jack Daniel's? Something worser? The way they turn and eyeball me, it's like they've just sold a piece of furniture and they're weighing up where to put me. Shana's suddenly become one of the grown-ups, one of the big people running the show. That spooks the crap out of me. Shana's only like 16 and a quarter. She shouldn't get involved in selling me out, or whatever's going on. Not at 16, not now, not tonight. Not never.

A boy tucks something into Shana's hand - cash? It's a wide-shouldered silent boy, tallest in the room, body like a surfboard. Gelled hair, no beard. Rectangle jaw. I see the wad across the room as he hands money to Shana. Big dollars. Notes I hardly ever get to see. A roll thick and fat, rolled tight and hard as a rubber doorstop. God, there have to be thousands in that wad. The hell's my sister selling?

I start striding across the room to the money, to my sissy - -

A hand clamps down on my shoulder.

'Hang about,' goes President Pork. God knows how he's gotten around the room so fast.

Pork tucks a clean pipe into my lips. Shakes powder in.

Flares his lighter. I don't got a choice.

Grunts to Shana, 'Keep bringing me customers. I'll help your old man out.'

This thing the President's given me, I smoke it. I don't wanna look like a snitch. There's about a hundred pairs of eyes watching me, it feels like.

The walls ripple, the ceiling darts and dips like it's trying to headbutt me, but

It feels good, it feels rollercoastery, suddenly the posters on the wall are funny, and that 'Hang In there' poster of a cop being hanged and my legs are bubbling and all the tension from my family falls off me like shower water.

Pork offers to fill the bowl of my pipe and I'm like Hell yes. Fresh bottle, Jack D and Coke this time, I take it. Shots of Pepe Lopez, Absinthe. My belly bubbles. Feeling tingly, from out of nowhere. Buzzy, giddy, feeling, IDK, feeling like happy kinda on the surface, on the level of my skin. Like I'm an iceberg with a bright coat of paint over it.

F**k it. I'm cool now. I'm partying with badass peeps. If partying means I don't have to go home to sad depresso business bullsh♡t, then sweet. I'll smoke my dad's sadness away.

This is on you, Shay. You, standing in the corner. You selling me out. You, racking up debts I'll have to work off every time I smoke my glass pipe down to ashes. I know they need a new chick for this club. And you knew I wanted a story to tell from tonight.

I learn stuff, at the pad. I learn I can get up and howl along to Def Leppard, dancing on a pyramid of haybales while hard boys, boys that'll never be pushed over, chant my name.

I learn women don't stand up for each other, nah, not when evil boys are in charge.

I learn that peeps who said they care for me are prepared to sell me out for a few bucks. And that my family'll take the money.

I learn the hardest gangstas in Northland will keep you alive and safe if you're bringing money and customers to the club – which I start to do, tugging in all my school friends, all my sports friends, getting people smoking as much as poss.

I learn I can get free product if I go on "dates" with the bad boys. Dates that last about an hour and a half.

And I learn that my dad–as I stumble up the driveway at dawn and the Ford Falcon hoons away and my vision melts in tears, and I fall into mum's arms, sobbing at the table, watching Baba walk laps of the kitchen, pinching his nose, asking my sister Exactly how much money did you say they've given you, five? Five?! And it's all tax-free?– I learn my dad is all about numbers.

See, coz he's spreading dirty smelly notes on the table and counting them and grinning at Shana. Because it's just enough cash to feed into the business to make his spreadsheet black instead of red.

I back out of the room. I go to work, I smoke the sadness away, drink it away, snort it away, f**k it away, servicing bikers and dealers and hangarounds and prospects and Defiants and Tribesmen and Head Hunters and Mongrels and BPs and Crips and Hells Angels and Highway 61s and a boy who holds me when I'm miserable called Kenny.

I'll come back to this house occasionally.

But I'll never go home again.


*Thwap.*

Barbie pushes the diary cover closed.

I finish, and breathe out hard, and slither down the wall, pooling on the carpet with my knees up by my cheeks. I find reading difficult even on a good day, what with cormorants and vowels and all them dictionary rules. This Dinky Diary though, man, Jeepers Creepers. It's like I've found myself in a trans-Tasman league test holding the ball for sixty seconds then from out of nowhere I've been tackled by a hundred-tonne Tongan.

Crushed. Blindsided.

Barbie pushes back a couple of morphine pills with a tall glass of Coruba, puts her earpods in and starts rocking out to Cardi B. Me, I crawl under a pile of laundry and try to nap on the floor. Under the bed I spot a copy of *The Konstantinou Gardener*. Pull it out, flick through photos of Georgios as a kid in dusty dry Mediterranean fields. Then Barbie's old man, shirtless and brown as a walnut, with his foot on a spade in Northland. Barbie's dad driving a front-end loader, scooping out a trench for pipes. Barbie's dad beside the mayor cutting the ribbon for the Onerahi park and playground he'd won the tender for.

Dude, I wanna tell the old fuck, your quick-fix to get a five grand loan wasn't quick. Cause crack sticks, G. What's the expression? Once you smoke crack, you never go back. I oughta know.

I tear the pages out one by one with a satisfying *scriiiiiip*.

Nothin in here about taking a dirty underworld loan in exchange for his daughter working for the club. Pimpin her out and pretending he doesn't know. Washing his hands clean.

Nothin in here about the evil sister with the prefect-face pulling money into her family so she could milk it for the rest of her life. Shana deluding herself into thinking her fam deserves the dough they made.

Nothin in here about three of the family letting the fourth one suffer just to balance the books.

There's a page with a picture of Georgios, Anna and Shana planting flax, squatting, smiling up at the camera. Gardening gloves on so they don't get dirty hands, pfft.

Barb is in the picture, too. She looks about age 18.

Round the time her family sold her out.

I'll bet my poor baby never smiled again.

I peel the page out, stuff it with baccy and weed, lick it and smoke it away.

# 32

# "People need a cockroach."

I spend more and more time in front of a computer screen. We both do – it's not as if Barbie needs to go outside to do dope. She smokes and I study bounty hunting videos on YouTube and we watch daytime news bulletins, and what should be kind of a honeymoon starts to rot. Our guest house or cottage or posh prison, whatever you want to call it, it's right on the edge of the parents' massive estate, over by the pond with the delicious giant goldfish. Greek Gardens keeps spare building timber down here, diesel drums and paving stones and firewood. Our cottage is getting a little gross, now, to be honest, since Barbie won't let the cleaners in cause she's becomin paranoid about her stash. Barb never opens a window to let her smoke out. Our ceiling turns yellow, our white curtains brown.

The Northern Advocate paper tells me one morning that Porky Pig President Glenn Hamm's fat stressed arse has finally killed him. He dies after a week on life support. Two days later, there's a epic show-off funeral convoy blocking the main street of Kaitaia. Local leaders pretending to grieve, trotting out all Pork's supposedly great aspects, like how his boxing gym mentored troubled youth and whatnot. Only good thing about his damn funeral is the press coverage tells me Pork's middle name, Leslie, lol, girl's name. Turns out that the little rat-tiger cunt who made us shit ourselves by pretending to pop shots outside Lone Star was Pork's nephew. He's the new prez, now. God damn, man. Dude's just a rugrat. Kids these days...

But yeah, like Shana said. Nature hates vacuuming. The Defiants get a new president. And they carry on hoovering up fear. Keepin' the public spooked.

I set up alter egos on Facebook and TikTok and Instagram so I can monitor Defiants and Blues and all the other gangstas. The old code of keeping your mouth shut is so damn gone, bro. Modern-day gangstas can't stop bragging about their crimes, especially on the supposedly-closed Facebook groups. Constantly yapping and ratting on each other and bragging about people they've kneecapped and having little disputes. They're like a knitting circle of old ladies, babbling non-stop.

The comments my undercover Facebook profile gets to see tell me the Defiant have ordered the Blueys not to get revenge on Rich (and I'll bet Shana pulled strings to sort that one out). Meanwhile the Blueys chatter about how a certain Cash Cow ain't got no more cash. Ain't got no more milk in her titties, they joke, the arseholes. What's that word– erogenous? Misogynous? The names they refer to her with are frickin heinous – Snitch, Informant, Quitter, Sellout, Police Pleaser – and I badly wanna defend my princess. I wanna hunt down these jokers and punch their faces till their cheekbones look like Easter eggs dropped on the pavement... except there's a little bit of truth to what they're saying.

We *did* work with poh-leece, and we *did* quit the dodgy world. That's hard for gangstas to forgive. Gangstas have brains like goldfish, though, it turns out, and after a couple of weeks, the very last references to tying up Barbs or stomping Karl or hitting Rich disappear. The newfangled thing getting these cunts excited is ripping off dead babies' birth certificates and setting up fake companies to get post-Covid business bailout bucks. It's good news for me and my crew because they've deeperoritised revenge against me and my loved ones. That's right – *ones* plural. As in, not just Barbs. Richie too. He's been a rude dude to me, but deep down I love the wanker.

Not in a sexual way, just to be clear.

I'm glued to my computer as soon as I rise at lunchtime till I go to sleep at 2. I tell my baby I'm writing material for my memoir, but a lot of the time I'm actually keeping tabs on enemies – mostly Shana.

You'd think Shana would close down all her profiles, but she doesn't. Funny gap in her defences, actually. I've ripped her passwords so I can check her Zoom and her Facebook and her email all the time to see when she'll slip and we can reveal to the world that she's dangerous.

I've put myself through so much shit Shana could've spared me from.

I've gotten stomped by midgets, told off in church, had pizza throwed at me, been arrested and chucked in Ngawha and stripped naked and splattered with ink and made to hump a palm tree and then, when I thought all that shit was over, I pissed my pants when a gangsta pointed his finger at me.

Being with the-woman-I'm-tryina-respectfully-call-Barbara, it's definitely worth all that garbage though. I look over at her when she's lying on a pile of pillows with a pipe between her boobs and a chestful of smoke and her eyes are blissed out. I pray I can make her as happy as the drugs do.

I don't go too far from the cottage at the bottom of the estate and when I do, I hardly leave Whangārei much. The exception happens one Wednesday night when the Ol' Peeping Tom side of me rises up and takes me over like some kind of Jacqueline Hyde shit, like a evil double. I find myself at the front windows of Richie's neat little home, peering in. Shana's vehicle's in the driveway, a new Tesla with a new vanity plate, JSTICE, cause she's still pretending to be some sort of legal aid angel. The woman's a two-faced schemer, yo. It'd be nice if a asteroid came down and splatted her, justice from the heavens, although if we're talking God sticking his boot in, I've gotta suck it up and admit God's been more than fair, handing me Barbs. My luck's not gonna get any better than what I've got right now and, because of this arrangement with God, I'm not going to fuck everything up by revealing what a player Shana is.

Urgh. Stalking Shana is draining me, man. Can heroes accept that there's always gonna be a baseline of corruption in the world? I'm not sure. All I know is I should get off Facebook and Insta and stop flicking between feeling threatened and feeling blessed. What do I got to complain about anyway? Barbie's right here and she's not going anywhere (partly cause she's smoked herself into a coma.)

As I watch her, my baby drifts off the side of the bed and thuds onto the floor in a whirpool of bedsheets. I roll her into the recovery position, on her side, adjust her face so she doesn't choke on her own puke. I kiss her chapped lips. Stroke her hair. Blackness coming through at the roots.

It's finally time to move out of Konstantinou Castle. Barbs scores us a cheap flat up in a Whangārei apartment building. It's above the shops in the centre of town so we get to hear all the street fights, homeless freaks off their meds, breaking bottles, shouting, the hiss-pop of Subaru blow-off valves. Place has got no paint on the concrete stairs and our back windows look down into the sewage-coloured river and rotting boats. Try to tell myself winning the woman of my dreams is better than winning a decent pad, but Barbs is far from easy to settle down with, truth be told.

The place is pretty bare. Barbs puts a Bob Marley poster against the window to make her feel at home, and we get a couple of cannabis plants growing in pots, a female named Barbara and a male named Karl, that I keep cause, y'know, the useless males without buds might not give you any THC, but they give you TLC, know what I'm sayin?

Not as if my missus waits for buds on any plant. Always buying party products, that girl. Lady's damaged and drug-dependent, she can't be happy without a sesh. Me, I don't wanna be like that so I ease the throttle back to ten sessions a day, then eight. Soon enough I'm only having a smoke with my morning cuppa, then after 30 days, I'm not doing hardly any drugs at all. I start gaining IQ points. Talking less dumbulent.

I "borrow" Barbs's internet banking login deets and hack in while she's out buying smokes. She's fucking up her money – our money. In November, when we got Barbs back home, she had six figures, we're talkin $101,540.33, because her pares were so frickin happy to have her back, they withdrew this fat term deposit they'd had sitting around and gave it to her.

Next time I looked at her bank account around Christmas, there was $99,949.00 in the account. Then every time I blink, more money's been burned through and our place is littered with Uber Eats, My Food Bag, Delivereasy, all this packaging of new phones, tonnes of dirty tinfoil, empty lighters, bottles, blister packs. Even White Owl cigar boxes. Like she wants to bring back her happy times.

She rides the elevator up, comes in the door one Wednesday with a couple of shopping bags that clink so loud I think they're gonna smash as she dumps them on the floor, saving one calorie by not lifting them onto the bench.

'I got drinks and smokes,' she goes.

'I'll bet you did.'

'What's that supposed to mean?'

'Nothin, babe. What are we doin today?'

'That cruise, with the fishing out by the islands, let's get buzzed and do that, eh?' Seems everything we do in our relationship, we've gotta get high before we do it. We smoke weed before we take dumps. We snort X before we fuck. We gulp Smirnoff before we shop for breakfast cereal. Always trying to create space between how we wanna feel and how our lifestyles should really make us feel.

Barb's way worse than me. She does everything shitfaced, blitzed, blissed. Happy on the outside, numb in the core. The Canopy Bridge Markets, boat cruise to Limestone Island, chartered fishing at the Cavalli Islands, Helena Bay five star restaurant, diving, snorkelling. We go to Whangārei's only strip club high, out the back of the Red Eye pub in that dingey lounge with the dark carpet so the puke stains don't show. At the Red Eye, Barbie's demon-side bursts out of her skin. She jumps up on stage and hollers with the strippers and gets her nips out and takes men's money and sings Pussycat Dolls cranked up to eleven till the bouncers pull her down. Money's mostly gone after all that.

I can't keep up with all this. I don't know if it's my thirty-ish body not handling the drugs or if it's a force inside Barbara propellering her to party crazier and crazier every night, but as I watch Princess Barbara Konstantinou grinding with whiskey-sticky strippers as men howl at her, I think she wants someone who parties a little harder. Judging by the way my heart thuds and trembles – that can't be me. Years of smoking crack have done damage, overheated me. A decade running my engine in overdrive with no oil and no antifreeze. Free check-up at the pharmacy tells me I need to live cleaner. That might mean without Barbs.

Between getting high and coming down, Barbie is blue. Money's all that gets her through the day. She digs and digs at her bank account, and all I can do is try shame her into behaving with little snarky comments to make her behave better, but it's like trying to hold water in your hand. When you're down to ninety grand you'll wish you still had a hundred grand; ninety grand's what you wish you had when you're down to fifty grand. And we both badly miss everything we used to have as Barbie smokes our thousands right down to the last five-digit number before all she's got left is $7500.

'We'll have to do a score,' she says when she's real smoked. 'What do you reckon?'

What she means by a score is robbing some wussy dealer for a two gram bag of crack and breaking it down for smaller retail sales... hopefully. If she's thinking of fucking with harder product or harder dealers, it'll get us killed. The old me would've jumped straight in there, but this cockroach don't scuttle that way any more.

Up in our tower, I stare at the tiny bump in her belly. I hope that baby's mine, and I hope it's not drug-mutated.

I'm not used to sharing a home with someone, thinking of others, protecting. Sharing with Barbs means sharing her problems. I'm with Barbs as she gets into a fist fight with a guy at a liquor shop she screams racial shit at before clawing at his face because he didn't give her a five dollar discount on a bottle of Kahlua. I'm with Barbs when she's at the clinic getting her stomach pumped because she drank all the Kahlua by herself – in front of me, standing in the parking lot, and swallowed a whole pack of Nurofen – to punish me. I'm with Barbs at her Narcotics Anonymous meeting, watching her nod and hug and stroke people's wrists and nibble their earlobes and call them by name and then hit them up in the parking lot for some product 'cause she can't get wholesale prices from the One Percenters anymore and she knows her money's running out. If these suppliers knew about the tiny little seedling in her belly, would they still dispense? I eat wholegrains and slurp squirrelina and fruit smoothies and watch our rafts drift in different directions.

We get kicked off sightseeing buses and party cruises and a frigging TV interview. We get asked to leave cosmetics shops, service stations, cinemas, salons. At the fanciest restaurant in Northland, Schnappa Rock over in Tutukaka, Barbs loses a five-hundred-dollar shoe, biffing it at a maitre D's head after he tells her off for smoking.

Bit of a blur, after that. Barbie's stuck in the same cycles.

Know what they call it when the feeling's gone and you can't go on?

Tragedy.

Time for this six-legged scuttler to scuttle on.


January, we head up to the vineyards outside fancy-schmancy Kerikeri for a wedding at this winery. Hot blue sky, sparkling ocean views. Immaculately-mowed hills painted with grapevines, sculpture garden, white people wearing white. We're here to see some Konstantinou cousin get hitched. Barbs spends the day draining champagne flutes, cackling and twerking with an obvious bulge in her tummy and finally Barbs snatches the microphone off the wedding stage and does a speech about seeing her cousin, the bride, go through "like a hundred boys" over the years and Barbs says something wayyy inappropes about the first time her cuzzy got fingered and they pull the microphone cord out of the amplifier and Barbs spits at the reverend who guides her offstage, squawking "Suck my Covid, mutha fuckaaaah."

Barbs gets put back with me, in the naughty kids corner, as if I'm equally as bad as her. Don't really care if she's with me or not, TBH. Barbs seems unfixable.

Where the salty river comes up into the vineyard there's a boat at a little private dock and everyone's sposda catch a shuttle-boat, eight at a time, out to this private island as the afterparty. I'm waiting in line for the shuttle, havin a smoke, and I say loudly enough to start a conversation with the short chickypie in front of me with earrings, 'These Konstantinous man, they're pretty fucked-up people, eh.'

The short chickypie turns around with a frown above her eyes. Ah, shitballs.

A better haircut, more expensive earrings, but there's no mistaking her.

It's Shana.

'Never mind,' I go, and gulp. 'Great to, um. Great to see ya.'

The people at the front of the line have stepped up the short ladder onto the boat. There's no one behind me, no one in front of Shana. We could say anything to each other. Put our cards on the table.

Instead, Shana takes out her phone, sticks a finger in her ear, steps away a metre or two. I get an electric shock in my heart and the muscles in my legs freeze so tense you could shatter them with a hammer as I realise she's calling the cops.

Well – one specific cop.

I stand there like an idiot, afraid to step aboard and get stuck on a boat with this fuckin' snake.

Shana's pet cop arrives, finally. Mister Guardian Angel is wearing a high-visibility vest with police stripes over his tuxedo. I'd noticed him at the gate when I first came into the estate, marshalling traffic in the dusty heat. Volunteering even when he's sposda be chillaxing and sipping bubbles. Who else but Richie McMullan.

'There a problem, honey?' he goes as he takes a position a few inches beneath my nose and chin. The boat is being prepped, ropes untied from its

Maureen. We could go off and party together, if Richie can find it in himself to be nice to me.

'Bruz – it's been aaaaages!' I pull the spliff out of my mouth and hold it towards Richie, who squints and swats at the smoke under his nose. 'Ain't you missed your best bud?'

Shana smirks, hikes her dress, steps into the boat.

Three of Richie's pig-pals crowd me, just in case I didn't get the message. All hi-vis and hats.

'As for you, mate, you'll extinguish that little number you're smoking right now, or you'll be going in the back of my car. Consider it an official caution, my friend.'

'Am I really?' I go, pulling the spliff out of my mouth.

'You're asking if you're really being officially cautioned?'

'Askin if I'm really your friend.'

That stumps the cunt. He strolls away, over to all his supporters helping at the wedding, Group Awesome and Anna and Georgios, who haven't stopped smiling since their company got listed on the sharemarket. Richie drives back to his sentry box. Always square, always straight. Always working. No time for mates.

Only thing that'd make the Konstantinous smile harder than their twenty-million-dollar listing is if Barbara and me sat down with them and said, Listen, we've brought you here 'cause we wanna announce you're gonna be grandparents.

Get 'em all excited about a grandchild, and they'll pay through the roof for it.

Shit, send 'em a bill to bring their daughter and their grandkid back, and I could be a rich man.

Cause no one has paid me yet, and this babysitting-Barb thing, yeesh. Costly in tonnes of ways.

I stand there with my toes on the dock, left in the wake of Richie's public diss, left in the wake of my crackhead dream girl having a psychotic break nearby. I want revenge so damn bad, I want compensation for everything I've done. At the end of the day, I just want my bruz to call me bruz.

I gather my smokes, my drink, my grumpy woman who's – yup, sure enough – got her tongue in the ear of a security guard over by the portaloos.

When we get back to the car, Barbie thuds into the passenger seat. Crosses her arms in a tantrum. Lights a smoke, killing our baby, and I rip it out of her mouth (rip the smoke, I mean, not the baby) and toss it out the window and she lights another one and I give up. We rumble and rattle and clatter and blurp over 40,000 rocks down that stupid farm driveway.

Arrive at the entrance/exit gate in silence. As we drive out, I see Richie's already in the sentry booth. Barb squits tobacco-spit out the window, which is massively rude and aggro – except it gives me a good reason to leave the troublesome bloody partner in the car, get out and check on my *other* partner.

I leave the car running at the gate. The road stretches off for miles both ways.

Say a few last words under the shade of the sentry box.

'You don't have to stare at us like that, Mall Cop, jeez. You've said you don't want to see me so don't see me, brother. Laters, I guess.'

'Like I told you at the start of this whole... *thing*. There are 418 staff serving in this region who I call 'brother.' You, mate, are not my brother.'

*After all we've been through, Rich? Really?*

I'm just about to punch him in the dick when he adds, 'You're my bruz.'


So yeah, nah. That's my story.

I leave Richie with a good old-fashioned homeboy handshake. Two slaps, knuckle-bump, fist-dump, pssht blow it up.

Barbie jitters and complains as we drive away but I don't hear a thing. I'm *bruzzing*.

You think I'm going off to follow Barbs down a dark one-way hole and end up on K Road, Rich, but nah. I'll be atcha service. You need more bounties hunted, I'm your man.

Cause people need a sly slippery breed of creature that can scuttle under doors and crawl up walls and eavesdrop at night. A creature that'll clean up your dirt and eat your garbage and make problems disappear. The people need a hardy, nimble, agile little motherfucker that asks hardly anything from the world but it'll always be there, through smoke and storms and lockdowns and lock-ups and after a nuclear bomb goes off.

The people need a cockroach.